THE DAUGHTER YOU LEFT

RUBY SPEECHLEY

Boldwood

First published in 2020 as *Every Little Secret*. This edition published in Great Britain in 2025 by Boldwood Books Ltd.

Cover Design by Head Design Ltd.

Cover Images: iStock

A CIP catalogue record for this book is available from the British Library.

Paperback ISBN 978-1-80557-862-8

Large Print ISBN 978-1-80557-861-1

Hardback ISBN 978-1-80557-860-4

Trade Paperback ISBN 978-1-80656-123-0

Ebook ISBN 978-1-80557-863-5

Kindle ISBN 978-1-80557-864-2

Audio CD ISBN 978-1-80557-855-0

MP3 CD ISBN 978-1-80557-856-7

Digital audio download ISBN 978-1-80557-857-4

This book is printed on certified sustainable paper. Boldwood Books is dedicated to putting sustainability at the heart of our business. For more information please visit https://www.boldwoodbooks.com/about-us/sustainability/

Boldwood Books Ltd, 23 Bowerdean Street, London, SW6 3TN

www.boldwoodbooks.com

To my parents,
for their endless love and encouragement.

PROLOGUE
LATE SEPTEMBER 2019

Max stood on the bridge looking down into the black, fast-moving river. The boards creaked as he walked further on. The wood was covered in lichen in places, so slippery you could easily fall through the broken slats. He paused. The damp air filled his nostrils. An owl hooted in a tree silhouetted against the inky sky. It was no good. He'd thought it over a thousand times.

He climbed up the wet railings. Somewhere in the darkness, a man called out. Max's hands struggled to maintain their grip. The rucksack slipped off his back, pulling him to one side. He slid his arms out of the straps and let the bag plunge into the water.

1

MADDY: LATE SEPTEMBER 2019

Maddy is in the back garden deadheading roses when a ring of the doorbell splinters the silence. Poppy and Daisy bark and run around her legs.

'Go away,' she says under her breath and twists off another flower, scattering petals on the lawn. Only strangers come to the front. The ring is more insistent now. She kicks off her sandals at the open back door and pads along the hallway.

'Mrs Saunders?' A policeman and policewoman are standing there, blocking the light; the man has his foot up on the porch step, thumbs hooked either side of his padded vest.

Maddy's mouth opens but she doesn't speak. Instead, she grips the door handle a little tighter.

'I'm PC Dolan and this is PC Wright. May we come in?'

Maddy stands aside. Their shoes are caked in cut grass, the fresh smell unlocked by the mower earlier. The dogs sniff at the half-full bin liner in PC Dolan's hand.

'If it's about my car...' She pushes a tendril of hair behind her ear.

He shakes his head as though she's told a bad joke. 'Is your husband Mr Max Saunders?'

Maddy nods. A spike of heat shoots through her head.

'Can you tell us where he is?' PC Wright towers over them. She stamps her feet on the mat, scattering clumps of grass across the parquet floor.

'He works away; he's in Buckinghamshire this week.'

Maddy follows PC Wright's line of vision, where she is taking in the child-size church pew and the row of various sized shoes neatly paired underneath.

'Poppy, Daisy, come away,' she commands, but they continue to push their noses at the bulging bin liner. Maddy invites the visitors in and closes the door behind them.

'Is there somewhere we can sit?' Their faces are almost lost against the flowery wallpaper. They're not smiling. She shows them into the living room and lowers herself into the armchair facing the French windows. Her heart is galloping. PC Dolan's uniform creaks as he perches his substantial weight on the edge of the sofa, his legs astride to keep his balance. PC Wright sits next to him her hands clasped together.

'I'm afraid I have some bad news.' PC Dolan's fingers form a cradle in front of him.

'Let me fetch you a drink.' Maddy springs up. Her throat pulses as if a hand is squeezing her neck.

'This isn't going to be easy for you.' He pushes himself up, so they are facing each other. A missed cluster of spiky hair on his jaw moves when he speaks. She pushes away a nervous smile. He nods, touches her elbow and they sit down again in unison. 'We believe your husband fell from a bridge over Yeading Brook, in Uxbridge, at around 1.55 a.m.' He refers to a notebook from his breast pocket. 'So far we've only recovered a rucksack.'

Maddy frowns, not sure she's heard him correctly. Her fingers lock together into one large fist. She glances at the policewoman.

'We've got underwater police teams and an RAF helicopter searching for him as we speak,' says PC Wright.

Ice trickles through Maddy's veins despite her face

burning up. Her vision is blotchy. She can't seem to construct a decent question to ask.

'Were you expecting him home last night?'

'Not until Thursday.' Her voice is barely audible. 'A bridge you say, here in Uxbridge?' She shakes her head. 'That wouldn't be him. He's not worked here for a while.' She's been desperate to speak to him, try and get him to come home early so she can tell him what's happened, but he's not answered a single one of her calls or texts.

'He was seen by witnesses, admittedly from some distance. They couldn't say for certain if he fell by accident.'

'Then you're not sure it was him.' Maddy sits up straight.

'It's his rucksack, Mrs Saunders, although nothing is conclusive at present.'

A stream of air escapes her lips. She shuts her eyes, deflates into the armchair and tries to breathe normally. Any minute now Max will breeze in, pat them on the shoulder and say it's all been a terrible misunderstanding.

'Mrs Saunders?'

Her eyes blink open. The room has darkened and closed in on her.

'Can you tell me if there was anything bothering

Max? Anything that might have given him thoughts of... harming himself?'

Maddy smooths out imaginary creases in her jeans. Tears roll down her cheeks. She digs in her pocket for a hanky.

'Money problems perhaps?'

'Chloe.' Her hand springs to her mouth as if she's sworn at him. She swallows and wipes the tears away; they've always been so close to the surface these past few weeks. Unable to speak, she fixes on the latest school photo of Chloe and Emily; their toothy smiles, heads tipped together.

They both stare up at the picture on the shelf above the fireplace. PC Dolan's eyebrows rise as he takes in the dozens of sympathy cards and teddies huddled around it.

'Our youngest died of meningitis three weeks ago,' she says, struggling to swallow the lump in her throat.

'Oh goodness, I'm so sorry,' says PC Wright.

'She was only five.' She sniffs and presses her lips together.

'I'm very sorry to hear it.' PC Dolan dips his head. Tiny pearls of sweat line his top lip. 'This is clearly an extremely difficult time for you already. Is there a relative or friend you can call to support you?'

'My neighbour Sarah will be here soon. She's picking up our seven-year-old, Emily, from school.'

'Good, good. A Family Liaison Officer will be over to assist you.' He rubs his palms together. 'I'm sorry, but I need to ask, what has Max's behaviour been like over the last few weeks?' His voice is softer now and his head nods up and down a little.

'He's not been here a great deal; he's a builder and decorator you see, works away a lot.' Her hands find their way to her belly and rest there. She takes in a breath to control her emotions. 'We've not talked much lately.' She covers her eyes. If only he'd answered his phone. 'It's been a terrible time. We've all been so...'

'I understand.' PC Dolan pauses. 'Is it possible to have a recent photo of him?'

She rocks back in her seat as though a bullet has skimmed past her. They think he's dead. She tries to focus on the framed photo of Max on their last holiday only a few weeks ago, his blond hair caught up in a breeze, arm around his surfboard like it's his best buddy. She points to it on the TV cabinet, and PC Wright reaches across and hands it to her, but Maddy's all fingers and thumbs and the frame crashes to the floor, glass cracking across Max's face.

Maddy gasps and covers her eyes. Without saying a

word, PC Wright picks up the frame, unclips the back panel and slips the photo out. Maddy fetches a dustpan and brush, which the policewoman takes from her and sweeps up the glass.

'I brought along everything that's been found.' PC Dolan's hand hovers in mid-air. 'Could you... would you mind?'

They glance at each other before he opens the black bin liner at his feet, unzipping the rucksack inside it. Everything is still wet although it's all been placed in clear bags. He lays a plastic sheet on the glass coffee table and takes out a Mars bar wrapper; a packet of Rothmans cigarettes; a GAP sweatshirt and a pair of jeans, both splattered with paint; and a Lloyds Bank cheque book. He places each item in front of them. Maddy picks up the bag containing the sodden cheque book, which has been peeled open. Max's printed name is blurred around the edges, the stub clumped together. Her trembling fingers trail across the bags of clothes. A cry escapes her lips. She presses her fist to her mouth.

PC Dolan hesitates, holding something else in his hand, poised like he's about to throw a dice. 'We found this.' He unfurls his palm to reveal a Yale key on a fob. 'It was hidden in the lining of the rucksack.'

She examines the dull brass next to the constable's

thick gold band, worn into the fabric of his skin. She exchanges a look with him, then with PC Wright, and takes the front door key. 'Plot 146' is scribbled in biro on a piece of card framed in an oblong of plastic.

She holds it up, dangling it between them. 'It isn't ours,' she says.

2

Maddy stares at the key and her mind clouds over, blocking her thoughts with too many questions.

Sarah arrives with Sophie and Emily moments later, clattering through the back gate, full of chatter and laughter. Emily is the first to spot her through the French windows, sitting with the constable who is tidying Max's things back into the bin liner. All three of them stop dead and stare through the glass. The constable slides the patio door open.

'Everything okay?' Sarah's voice rings a high note of alarm.

'Mummy!' Emily cries and runs into her open arms. Maddy tries to stand up, but her legs wobble and she crumples back down.

'Mummy?' Emily wails like an injured bird, clinging on to her.

'What's happened?' Sarah asks in a quiet voice, arm around her daughter Sophie. Emily stands between Maddy's legs, searching her face. PC Dolan sits near them.

Maddy's mouth makes strange shapes, barely able to say the words. 'Daddy's had an accident.' She sucks in a breath and the tears come fast, uncontrollable. She pulls Emily to her, sobbing into her daughter's hair as she rocks her back and forth, never wanting to let her go.

'He was seen falling into Yeading Brook last night, but I'm afraid, as yet, he's not been found,' PC Dolan says.

Maddy squeezes the key in her fist and stuffs it in her pocket.

'Oh, dear God.' Sarah wraps her arm around Maddy.

'We're doing everything we can to find him.' PC Dolan's voice is a soft blanket, wrapping her up in comforting words.

'Will you be able to stay for a while, until the liaison officer arrives?' he asks Sarah.

She nods.

* * *

Later, when the police and the liaison officer have gone, Sarah sits the girls in front of the TV, tucked up together under a blanket with an ice lolly each. Maddy follows Sarah into the kitchen. She sits at the table and stares into space. The seconds tick by on the wall clock, louder than usual. She's not sure she can summon the energy to do anything, but while Sarah is making tea, she picks up the phone and presses in Max's number. The line is dead. Her stomach tumbles. How can this be?

Sarah takes two mugs from the draining board and switches the kettle on. 'He must have taken losing Chloe so much harder than he let on.'

Maddy nods. If she speaks, she'll start crying again. The last few weeks have been hard enough, and now this.

'Oh honey, come here.' Sarah hugs her. 'Did he say anything at all to make you think he'd do something like this?'

Maddy shakes her head and gently pulls away. When was the last time she and Max really talked about how they felt? Especially lately, since Chloe's death. What was there to say? The truth is, it's been too painful. Nothing was going to bring her back. But they used to be able to talk about anything. He confided in her when they first met, told her how his gran had brought him up in near poverty. A superstitious lady. A good sort, he called her. Read tea leaves and lived her life by the phases of the moon.

'He's been so excited about the new baby.' Sarah pours boiling water into the teapot and gives it a stir.

Maddy looks down at her bump. A miracle conception in many ways considering how little they made love any more.

'Is there something else? You can tell me.' Sarah sits at the breakfast bar opposite her and leans forward to pour the tea, her straight blonde fringe falling across her face. They've been friends since their girls were born only days apart. Sarah's written about bereavement on her parents' blog, emailed Maddy all her top hints and tips on how to cope. But it's not something that can be fixed by advice in neatly set out bullet points. Will this be the subject of her next post? *How to tell your child their parent may have taken their own life.*

'It's nothing,' Maddy says, and the moment is gone. She presses her palm to her forehead to stop the thumping pain.

'They found a front door key in Max's rucksack.'

Maddy takes it out of her pocket and places it on the counter between them.

Sarah picks it up by the fob, turns it over in her hand.

'I've never seen it before,' Maddy says.

'It'll be from one of the new houses he's been doing up, won't it?' Sarah says.

'I thought that too. I've seen him with a ring full of keys before, but never one on its own.'

Sarah rubs her finger over the number on the fob. 'Plot 146.'

'What could be so special about this one?' Maddy takes it from her.

'Could it be for the house he was working on yesterday?'

'But wouldn't he keep it in the front of his rucksack with all his other stuff?'

'Isn't that where it was?'

'No, it was hidden away in the lining.'

'I wonder why.' Sarah collects up their mugs.

'I don't know, but I need to find out. It might explain why he was on that bridge.'

3

MAX: MARCH 2011

Max grabbed a copy of *The Star* and sat at his usual table after a nod from the dark-haired waitress. She was attractive when she bothered to smile. He scratched his spiky chin and rubbed across it with the back of his hand. His armpits stank; time he had a proper shower. But he didn't even own a bar of soap, let alone a razor. He'd been lucky to scrape a few bits together at all: overalls, work boots and a few coins from under the bed. This was his only proper meal of the day.

The waitress came over, her flat shoes peeling off the floor with each step. He preferred heels; didn't all men? An image of red stilettos and the sexy swagger of hips flashed in his mind.

'Back again?' The waitress smiled.

'Can't keep away.' He winked. Fourth time this week. Under the table, he nudged his suitcase as if it were a snoozing dog.

'Is it your usual?' She held a little notepad in the palm of her hand, ready to take down his order.

Today she wore a tight red jumper which showed off her shape to perfection. Her nametag pinned to the left read, 'Madeleine Dunn, Manageress'. The hem of her skirt skimmed the top of her knees showing off her tidy pins. With the right pair of heels, he reckoned she'd look the business. This was a first. He never went for dark and curvy as a rule, but this woman was quite some exception.

'Yep, you got it.' He winked. 'Pot of strong tea, full English, no tomatoes, white toast.'

She scribbled it down. Her nails were chewed with a tiny blob of red in the centre of each. Back behind the counter, she chatted to a skinny blonde who looked over at him and giggled. She was more his usual type, but next to Madeleine she was ordinary and shapeless, with a laugh like a blocked drain.

After his breakfast he took a cigarette paper out of his pocket. He held his hand out in front of him: it had just about stopped shaking. The bruises on his chest, legs and stomach had turned green. He'd been lucky to get away alive. Bastards. He pinched tobacco from a pouch in his bomber jacket, rolled the paper and stuck the cigarette behind his ear.

'Delicious as always,' he said, standing at the till. 'You on holiday?' She pointed at his battered suitcase.

'I wish. Looking for work as a matter of fact. Been staying at a hostel but now I'm at a mate's house in West Drayton.' He stacked a column of fifty pence pieces on the counter.

'It is a good area for work.' She tipped her head to one side, the rich chocolate eyes drawing him in. 'So, what do you do exactly?' She counted the coins, chucked them in the till and pressed the drawer shut.

'Painting, decorating, building, carpentry, you name it.' He leaned on the counter and grinned at her.

'I'll ask around for you.' She smiled.

'What about you? Got any jobs you need doing?'

'I can think of a few.'

He laughed. 'Seriously?'

'Yeah, actually. My mum died recently and the house needs sprucing up; it's badly out of date.'

'Won't your fella do it?'

'I don't have anyone.' Her cheeks flushed pink.

'Oh, right, on your own then?'

She nodded.

'Me too. Near here, is it?'

'About ten minutes' walk. Close to Uxbridge Common.'

'I'll call round and give you a quote if you like? No obligation.'

'All right then.'

'Great, speak to you soon, Madeleine.' This was potential long-term work, just what he needed.

'Call me Maddy. And you are?' She held his eyes with hers, hand on hip.

'Oh right, yeah, I'm... er... Max.' His cheeks flashed with heat. Jesus, look at him getting all flustered. He took down her address on the back of his receipt and smiled to himself. This looked mighty promising in more ways than one. With any luck he'd landed on his feet.

4

MADDY: LATE SEPTEMBER 2019

Maddy wakes in the night and senses Max isn't there. The bedroom door that doesn't shut properly has swung open. He must have gone downstairs for a drink or is he away on business? Sleep fogs her memory. She turns to the space next to her, the duvet pulled up, untouched. A shot of adrenaline surges through her body; she sits bolt upright, eyes wide, chest clenched tight so she cannot breathe – he's not away, he's not downstairs, he is missing.

She forces herself to breathe deeply, in out, in out, in out, focusing on the cool air sweeping the curtains to and fro. She reaches for the grey outline of a glass next to the bed and takes a sip of water. The tinkling sound of rain on the window quickly accelerates into a downpour. The white noise is welcome, filling the silent room.

She hears Max's voice, distant, apologetic: '*Sorry darling, I couldn't go on.*' Sarah's right, he's not the sort of person to do something like this. Since Chloe was born, they haven't been as close. It doesn't help that he spends so much time away, much more than before. But Chloe's death has pushed her to the limit, why not him?

Within the music of the rain she can hear a cat wailing, louder and louder. But they don't have a cat.

She stalks along the landing. The noise is coming from Emily's room. For a second, she listens at the door before easing it open. Emily is standing at the open window with her thumb in her mouth, holding her ragged old comforter. Giant tears of rain are splashing on her face. Maddy tries to wrap her arms around her daughter, but with surprising force, Emily pushes her away, burying her head in the blanket, calling for Daddy. Maddy smooths a hand over the mattress. As she guessed, the bed is wet again.

After she's washed Emily, she helps her into clean pyjamas and sits her on a beanbag, covering her with a fleece while she changes the sheets. She tucks her back in bed. Maddy stands at the window, breathing in the damp, earthy air, praying that this is all a nightmare she's going to wake up from, that Max will come home.

* * *

In the morning, Maddy rings Emily's school and tells them what's happened, that she'll be keeping her at home today. She texts Sarah who insists on calling in after school to make them dinner.

The Family Liaison Officer, Susan, arrives early with an update.

'How are you?' Susan follows her into the kitchen.

'We had a bad night, as you'd probably expect, especially Emily. I'm leaving her to sleep in.'

'I'm afraid I don't have good news for you yet, but they are still scouring the area,' Susan says.

'They're not going to give up, are they?'

'Not until they've done everything they can. There will probably be an appeal on your local news station later today and police boards have been put up near the brook appealing for eyewitnesses.'

'What do I tell Emily?'

'Tell her the truth, but I'd keep her away from the TV today if you can. It could be upsetting if she sees it on the news. Have you got people to support you, Maddy?'

'Yes, my neighbour Sarah is coming to cook me dinner, and our book club friends on Facebook are being really kind.'

'Good, it's important to know you've got people there for you. I'll be back as soon as I have more information.'

When Susan has gone, Maddy gently wakes Emily. She'll do as she suggests and make sure the TV and radio are off today. But she will need to tell Emily he's not been found yet. His smiling face in the photo she gave the policeman flits through her mind. Their holiday on the Isle of Wight feels like an age ago. It doesn't seem possible that all four of them were a happy family and now two are gone.

After breakfast, Maddy takes Emily's school project down from the windowsill. 'Let's have a look at your caterpillar,' Maddy says, peering in the clear container. Emily shrugs. They need to keep busy, stay hopeful that Max will still be found alive, but every minute is like wading through wet sand. All she longs to do is go back to bed.

'Do you think it's grown?' Maddy gives her the caterpillar check list and pen.

Emily nods.

'Has she eaten any food, do you think?'

Emily peers closer at the pile of leaves and nods

again. 'Do you think it will turn into a moth or a butterfly?'

'Moth.' Emily purses her lips, pushes them out in her sulky way, meaning she didn't mean to speak.

'It says here that when the caterpillar is ready to change, it will climb to the top of the jar and hang upside down from the paper on the inside of the lid.'

Emily gives a little smile. Maddy hugs her and puts the jar and check list back. Exhaustion tips her off balance, like a ship in a storm. She reaches out for the counter to steady herself.

'How did Daddy get lost?' Emily asks.

'We're not sure, sweetheart. Sometimes things happen that we can't control. They really are doing their best to find him.' She takes the caddy of used teabags she's collected and empties them in the compost bin outside the back door, next to two drums full of cardboard and wine bottles that Max was supposed to take to the recycle centre. Tears prick her eyes. Why is this happening? What was he even doing on that bridge so close to home?

'Please can we help the police?' Emily asks.

'I don't think we'll be much use.' The dogs follow her back inside.

'Why not?' Emily shouts and pulls her hair.

'The police have special equipment. We'll get in

their way.' She kisses the top of Emily's head. She imagines Max sinking in the deep black water, his clothes ballooning.

Maddy pours Emily a glass of water and hands it to her. Emily trails after her outside, face tipped up expectantly. Maddy pats the space next to her on the bench. How is she going to do this? She bows her head. Her eyes and cheeks are so sore and puffy. Surely there are no more tears to shed. But her eyes fill up again as she tries to find the right words. 'Sweetheart, you know Daddy and I love you very much, don't you?' Emily nods. 'I don't really know how to say this.'

Emily stops mid-drink; water puffs out her cheeks. She swallows it in one gulp and coughs, spluttering droplets on her skirt. Maddy reaches over and slaps her on the back.

'Are you okay?'

Emily nods, eyes bulging.

'Please don't do that.' She stares into Emily's eyes and watches her closely. 'They still haven't found Daddy.' No reaction. Her words sound distant; she hardly believes it herself.

Emily lengthens her back until she's sitting upright. Her hands clasp the glass a little tighter; the frosted pattern makes it look shattered.

Did she understand? Maddy strokes Emily's hands. Her head throbs. Can this really be happening?

Emily presses her lips with the back of her hand as if to seal them shut forever.

'I'm so sorry, sweetheart. They're doing all they can.'

Emily's eyelids flicker; her eyes roll back in her head as she tips sideways off the seat. Maddy leaps forward to catch her, just managing to slide between Emily and the ground in time. She cradles her daughter's head in her lap, the breathing is shallow, limbs locked, body juddering. The small stiff frame twists, head thrashing from side to side like she's trapped in a nightmare.

When Emily's body is still again, her eyes flutter open. A silver thread of moisture hangs from the corner of her mouth. Maddy rocks Emily gently, humming a tune, like the time she held her as a baby, wrapped in a towel, face and limbs blue, keeping her warm, holding her tight.

At last the grey, sometimes moss green, eyes look up at Maddy, but there's no expression. They could be the glassy eyes of a doll, with eyelids that open when tipped back.

Gradually Emily recovers, tries to sit up, but Maddy gently says, 'Sssh,' and holds her around the

shoulders like a blanket, kissing her temples, still rocking, still humming, smoothing the glossy hair, noticing
the eyes begin to recognise her as she watches her
daughter come back to life.

* * *

Emily sleeps through the night and is so much better
the next morning and wants to go to school. Maddy
drops her off and drives into town because she can't
bear another day stuck at home, waiting for news. She
stops at the supermarket and collects milk, a loaf of
bread, and a pack of chocolate digestives for Emily.
She eyes up the Jammie Dodgers, Chloe's favourite.
She's been buying them every week for so long it's
hard to stop herself picking them up. She takes the
escalator up to the home department. As she rises to
the top, she sees him. Max's face fills a row of television screens on the back wall – the photo of him she
gave to the police. A reporter from the local news is
standing in front of a bridge. He turns and points. The
TV camera pans in close to the grey, fast-moving water. His words appear as text at the bottom of each
screen.

Could the tragic death of his young daughter

have led Max Saunders to jump from this bridge?

Heat flashes through Maddy's head. Max's duplicated face stares back at her, his unmistakable smile. Putting down the basket, she stumbles out of the shop, back to the car, where she sits gripping the wheel, her hands shaking.

5

Maddy sits at the kitchen table with her coat on, shivering. Does this mean he's dead? They've not told her he is. Not in so many words. It's strange that John's not called her yet. Surely, he must be wondering where Max is by now? She should call him. He might know something. But she can hear him now: *'What are you going on about? Max is right here. Hang on, I'll pass you over.'*

She rummages in a kitchen drawer for her address book and flicks through the pages. She's scribbled it somewhere. There's hardly ever been an occasion when she's needed to call him, except that time Max had food poisoning. There it is. She picks up the phone and dials.

'Can I speak to John Sutton, please?'

'Speaking.'

'It's Mrs Saunders, Max's wife. I don't know if you've heard the terrible news?'

'No, what's happened?' The shrill sound of an electric drill or some other power tool almost drowns out his voice.

'Max is missing.' She's almost shouting so he can hear her over the racket.

'What do you mean?' he shouts back. The drilling stops.

'The police think he's fallen into a river.'

'Fallen? You're kidding, right?'

'Or jumped. They don't know. They've not found him yet. It was in Uxbridge.' John is silent.

'Did he mention where he was going after work last night?'

'Nothing, I'm sorry. He was heading home as far as I knew.'

'But he didn't *come* home.'

John doesn't answer. She can hear someone whispering.

'If you know something, John, please, you have to tell me, I'm going out of my mind here.' Maddy presses her palm to her neck.

'You know he left yesterday, don't you?' he says quietly.

'What are you talking about?'

'I mean he resigned. Told me after lunch. Right out of the blue.'

'How could he do that when you're business partners?'

'We're most certainly not. Is that what he told you?'

'Yes, two years ago. I gave him the money for it.'

'We were talking about it two years ago, until he backed out, said he couldn't get enough cash together.'

'But he showed me the papers; they were all drawn up.'

'Well, I never signed anything. Good job too, because to be honest with you, he's been a bloody nightmare.'

'I don't understand.'

'Never knew if he was going to turn up for a job or not, from one week to the next.'

'This is not making any sense.'

'I'm sorry, love.'

'Would you know anything about a key for Plot 146? It was found in his rucksack.'

'No idea. Sorry, I can't help.'

The line goes dead. Maddy slams the phone down,

her cheeks burning as if John has slapped her hard across the face. She hurls the address book at the wall. Her mind flits through the times Max stayed away longer than planned, to finish a job or work extra shifts. And what about that time he was late for Chloe's school concert? He blamed it on work. If John is right and Max didn't always turn up for work, where was he going?

6

MAX: MARCH 2011

At 9 p.m. Max knocked on the solid oak front door and waited in the open porch. It was an imposing house with ornate brickwork around mock Tudor beams. After a couple of minutes, the door inched open. He could see Maddy in the gap, a chain separating them.

'Oh, hello,' she said.

'Sorry, I know it's a bit late. Did I get you up?' She unchained the door and stood aside.

The light in the hall was dim. A dirty cream pattern like hundreds of faces lined the walls, hanging down in strips in places. There was a smudged outline where a picture had once hung, framing a cleaner patch of wallpaper.

'I'm making a milky coffee, do you want one?' She stifled a yawn.

Without all the slap he could see the beginnings of crease lines around her eyes and mouth; must be pushing thirty at least. The woody bong of an old-fashioned clock chimed far off in another room. He followed her past an iron coat stand, into the kitchen. It looked like nothing had been modernised for years – free-standing cupboards, a Welsh dresser, and a twin-tub in the corner covered in pot plants.

They sat at the huge pine table which showed patchy signs of having been varnished once, long ago. She took a packet of Bourbon biscuits out of the larder and emptied them onto a plate.

'Would you like a splash?' She held up a bottle of malt whiskey.

'Yeah, go on then,' he said.

She poured a generous measure in each mug. The ribbons of steam slowly entwined.

'My plan is to find permanent work and hopefully do a few jobs on the side.'

'You could try around Hayes or Yeading.'

'I've heard they're looking for someone at the builders' yard, off the big roundabout. I'd rather stick to Uxbridge with the town centre and everything.'

'I've never lived anywhere else. Been on my own since Mum died.'

Max raised his eyebrows. The beginnings of a wrinkled skin floated on top of his drink. He pushed it aside with the spoon and drank a mouthful.

'What does that stand for?'

He put the mug down. She was looking at the letter 'A' tattooed on the inside of his wrist.

'Nothing important.' But she was waiting for an answer. He wasn't about to tell her. He pressed his thumb into the skin and rubbed it, as if it were there by mistake and might come off. 'I'm kipping at a friend's place in West Drayton but not much in the way of work over there.' He eyed her up as he took another slug of the warm, milky whiskey. She seemed quite green for someone her age. The way she took delicate little sips of her drink was kind of sweet. What was she thinking about behind those deep dark eyes? Perhaps she was amused by his hair which badly needed a cut, or his old jeans, full of holes he was trying to pass off as fashionable. The first thing he'd do when he made some cash was go up town and splash out on some quality gear. 'When'd you lose your mum?' he asked softly. Their eyes met.

'Three months ago, now.'

'I'm sorry. Must have been a tough time.'

'I was caring for her. She'd been ill for years.'

A glass domed clock on the Welsh dresser built up its rasping click to strike the half hour with the clear tinkle of a bell.

'Dad bought that for Mum when I was born.'

'Is your dad still around?'

'No, he died when I was at school.' She put their empty mugs in the sink and led the way back into the hall. 'Let me show you around. It's in dire need of modernisation as you can see.'

'I can get that sorted.'

'Everywhere will need doing except the study. I'll probably keep that as it is.'

Max followed her into the living room. Even with the light on it was dark, filled with chunky oak furniture. There were overgrown plants on every available surface. One had reached the ceiling, stooping over like an elderly man.

'It would certainly brighten it up in here with a fresh lick of paint,' Max said, calculating in his mind all the prep work that would be needed.

'But I'd like to update it too, perhaps sell some of the furniture. I'm afraid my parents' tastes were very old-fashioned.'

'Everyone likes different styles, don't they?'

'And those old curtains have to go.' She pointed to

the faded, emerald-coloured material. 'I've never liked them.' She tried to open the door to the dining room. 'Sorry, can't get in here at the moment, it's a bit of a dumping ground.'

Max craned his neck round to see in. He'd never seen anything like it, beautiful pieces of old furniture stacked up to the ceiling, probably all priceless antiques. 'I like this dressing table,' he said, running his hand over the polished veneer.

'That old thing? Its legs don't match its body, they were stuck on at least fifty years later, which means it's not worth much at all.'

'You know your stuff then.'

'Picked it up from Dad. He ran his own antique business.'

'Oh, I see.'

'The whole house needs new carpets and curtains, maybe wallpaper on a few accent walls. Is that what they call it? What do you think?'

'Sounds good. Whatever you want.' He saluted her and they laughed.

The worn carpet on the stairs barely held in the tarnished brass poles and in the bathroom the chequered floor tiles clashed with the avocado green suite.

'Not seen one of those for a while. Very seventies. Coming back into fashion though,' Max said.

'You are joking?'

'Yeah!' He laughed, and she smiled, shaking her head.

'Can you do bathrooms?'

'I've done a few.'

'Good. I'd be willing to help, if you needed any.'

Max winked at her. 'I'm always happy with a helping hand.' They laughed and Maddy blushed. She pushed open a bedroom door. 'I'm not in a hurry for the decorating to be finished so it would be perfect to fit around other jobs, if you want to take this on that is. This was my mum's room.' She opened the door keeping hold of the handle. The orange patterned curtains were drawn, giving the room a strange syrupy light. There was a faint smell of urine, but he wasn't about to say so.

'And this is my room. I've tried to keep it looking nice over the years, but like everything else, it's in desperate need of a change.'

The daisy chain wallpaper looked more like something a young girl would choose. Under the window was a solid oak dressing table with three adjustable mirrors. On a matching chest of drawers stood a photo of what he presumed were her parents on their wedding day. A stiff looking couple if ever he saw one. Not even smiling.

'There's quite a bit to do then,' he said as they traipsed back downstairs.

'Please say if it's too much.'

'It's not that. It's just that it will take a while, weeks if I'm honest, months if I do find other work.'

'Like I said, I'm in no hurry, believe me. After all these years, I can wait.'

'When would you want me to start?'

'It's up to you.' Her eyes brightened momentarily before she looked down again, as though she shouldn't have spoken. He guessed she was quite shy at heart, which was cute.

'I can crack on straight away if you want me to.'

'Let's both have a think about it over the weekend, shall we?'

'Fine by me.'

'And if you could put a quote together for me and come back, say, Monday?' She opened the front door.

'Sounds good, thanks.' He held her gaze and made her blush again. There was definitely something special about her, a real sparkle. Gran would have loved her, that was for sure. And regular work, how could he say no to that? This could be the fresh start he needed. There was no going back, he'd got that message loud and bloody clear. He touched his bruised leg. It was about time his luck changed for the better.

7

MADDY: LATE SEPTEMBER 2019

'The liaison officer came today to tell me the police are going to call off the search tomorrow night.' Maddy sits with Sarah at the kitchen table after the school run.

'But it'll only have been four days.'

'They've almost finished dredging the river and searching the surrounding area.' She takes a teaspoon from the draining board and scoops a heap of coffee into each mug.

'Don't give up hope.' Sarah rests her hand on top of Maddy's.

But Maddy can't help fearing the worst. The last time she saw Max keeps flashing into her mind. He was going to work as usual, rucksack over his shoulder. He kissed her goodbye for the first time in ages. He smelt so good it made her smile with longing. But now she thinks about it, as he opened the front door, he turned to glance back at her and there was that same lost look in his eyes as when she first met him. And he'd hesitated. Oh God. He'd stared down at the floor then back at her. He'd wanted to tell her something. Why hadn't she picked up on it? Damn! She should have talked to him while she'd had the chance to, but she hadn't wanted to make him late for work.

'So that's it, if they don't find him, they just give up?' Sarah asked.

'They said there is nothing more they can do. A scarf was found by the riverbank. They think it's his, but I can't say for sure. Black, M&S, how many men have one of those?' Maddy pours boiling water into the mugs and stirs in milk. 'They said...' Maddy's voice breaks, '...his body may never be found.'

'Oh Maddy, that's awful. Is there anything I can do to help?'

'Not really but thank you. You know how much I appreciate everything you've done. Sometimes I wonder how I'd cope without you.' Sarah has helped her contact all their friends to let them know what's happened. She thought it would make the national news, but apparently some bloke falling off a bridge is too ordinary to be newsworthy.

'You're more than welcome. We love having Emily over. She's no trouble.'

'Except for the bed-wetting.' Maddy is grateful for her help, but she wonders if Sarah would be as accommodating if Greg hadn't left her. Sometimes she feels like she is Sarah's project to distract her from meeting a new partner.

'It's not every time. It's fine, really, you know I don't make a fuss.'

Maddy has read Sarah's article on her blog. She knew it could happen in older children when they suffer a trauma like bereavement, especially someone close like a sister, but she didn't know it could carry on for weeks. 'She loves going to yours. You seem to understand her better than I do sometimes. We're not always on the same wavelength.' Maddy places the coffees on the table.

'Don't be so tough on yourself. We've talked about this a million times – you were ill when she was born – you missed a great deal of those crucial first weeks together.'

'She blames me about Max, I know she does.' Maddy sighs.

'I'm sure she doesn't.' Sarah strokes Maddy's arm.

'I know he's never forgiven me for... you know.'

'What happened to Emily wasn't your fault. Max would be the first to say it. You've got to stop blaming yourself.'

Sarah is being far too kind. Max may have forgiven her on the surface, but it has always been there between them. The damage can't be undone.

'And then Chloe dying so suddenly. Perhaps that's why he did it.'

'Max didn't say anything to you about not coping, did he?'

'Nothing at all.'

'Would he really have jumped though? It's hardly the Max we know, is it? Maybe it was an accident.'

Maddy takes a tissue from her pocket and wipes her damp eyes.

'Did you phone his business partner?'

'Yes, but it was really weird. John says Max resigned the day before he went missing.'

'That's odd. Why would he do that without telling you?'

Maddy shakes her head. 'Why would he jump off a bridge? I don't understand any of it. John said he was never in partnership with him either.' She cradles her forehead. The side of her face has started to throb, a sure sign of a migraine coming. 'I mean what on earth did he do with all that money I gave him if he didn't use it to buy into the business?'

Sarah sips her coffee.

'Do you think John could be lying?'

Sarah rests her mug in her hand. 'Why would he?'

'Because he was annoyed at Max being unreliable? What if they had a massive argument and he pushed Max in the river?'

'Did the eyewitness see anyone else?'

'They said someone saw Max fall in. What if that person was someone he knew? Someone who pushed him? If John is lying, how would I be able to prove it?' Maddy stirs her drink, clattering the spoon round and round.

'Max would have his copy of the partnership agreement, bank account details et cetera. We can soon prove that. Where does he keep his important paperwork?'

'In the garage.'

'Right, shall we go and check, clear this up right now?'

The garage door swings open in a wide yawn. The aroma of oil and creosote wafts out. Years of her parents' junk still takes up more than half the space.

'He keeps them all up there.' Maddy points to the highest shelf on the wall.

Sarah helps her move the bikes out of the way and pulls the ladder out. Maddy climbs up. She drags out the first box file, named 'New business 2017'. It's heavier than she expected. She wipes off the dust and opens the lid. Inside is a pile of *Top Gear* magazines. She flicks through them. The papers must be underneath. But she can't find any. She tips the box up to show Sarah and lets the magazines slide out into a heap on the floor.

'Try another one,' Sarah says.

Maddy pulls the next one out: more magazines. She empties every single file onto the floor until the shelf is empty.

'Bloody hell,' Sarah says.

Not one piece of paper to prove that he was in business. Not even the agreement he showed her. Where the hell is it?

Back inside, Maddy sits at the table, her face in her hands.

'Oh God, come here.' Sarah reaches her arms around her.

'Why has he been lying to me and what's he done with my money?'

'Could he have put them somewhere else? Perhaps he moved them and forgot to tell you.'

'I don't know where. Perhaps John's telling the truth.' All she needs to know right now is what is going on. She rubs her bump. How can any of this be happening to their little family? She so desperately needs to speak to Max.

8

When Sarah has gone, Maddy marches into the garden. The dogs are tucking into the newly fallen apples. The gusty weather has died down for now. She yanks open his shed door and goes in. It feels wrong to be intruding, but this is too important. There are no folders or piles of paper on the shelves, only models and books about the phases of the moon and the moon landing. In the summer he recorded every programme on the landing's fiftieth anniversary. He was obsessed with every detail of the old footage. She pulls open the drawer of the small desk tucked in the corner, but it's full of junk, nothing relating to a business.

She wanders outside, picks up the spade that's

leaning against the back gate and starts digging out the weeds. She mustn't neglect the garden, or she'll regret it come spring. After her dad died, she took over all the gardening. Her mother let everything go to seed and wouldn't let Maddy touch it to start with. But she would sneak out and do little jobs so that her mother didn't notice and before long she was oblivious to it anyway.

Maddy stands up and stretches her back. She hears a child laughing in a nearby garden and sees herself at Emily's age running up and down the lawn playing tag with her dad then him bathing his feet in the paddling pool, splashing her with water so she shrieked and giggled. Her mother, cutting roses for the vase in the living room, smiling at the happy commotion. She remembers the summer parties they had with all the neighbours. Her father at the centre, captivating them with tales of his adventures around the world, her glamorous mother looking on.

Her stomach pinches. A bitter taste rises from her throat. She was so young, it's difficult to pinpoint exactly when things started to change – the arguments and her dad staying away took over and all the fun came to an end.

She goes back inside and plods upstairs with a pile

of Chloe's ironed clothes. In the child-size wardrobe she hangs Chloe's favourite party dress and in the bottom drawer she tucks the paint-splattered jeans she wore to help Max paint her room. There's the T-shirt she wouldn't give away, even though it was too small and the jumper Maddy knitted for her. She'll take them out and wash them all again next week.

Sitting on the bed, she folds back the pillow and smooths over the unicorn print pyjamas. She pictures Chloe bouncing into the room, arms open, launching herself at Maddy for a hug.

At the window, her hand brushes away the invisible layer of dust. It leaves a grey shadow on her skin. She opens the window and wipes the specks into the passing air.

As she leaves, a drawing of them on the wall above the bed comes unstuck. *Daddy, Mummy, Emily and Me.* When she presses the corner back, it immediately pops out again. She can hear Chloe's giggle.

Downstairs, she puts a saucepan of hot water on the hob and wanders into the living room. The sleepless nights are catching up with her. Lying on the sofa, she switches on the television, but soon drifts into sleep. She dreams about chasing Max, trying to make him come home. Everywhere she goes a line of blood trails behind her from an umbilical cord. When she catches up with him his face has changed; it isn't Max at all.

An hour later, she wakes to a faint nutty smell of burning. She staggers into the kitchen. The sleepy dogs plod after her. The empty pan hisses on the red cooker plate. The water has evaporated, and the bottom of the pan has burned. She can't remember what she was heating water for. She switches the cooker off and drizzles cold water into the pan; it sizzles and turns cloudy. Max has told her so many times not to leave the kitchen while she's cooking. Once, she gave everyone food poisoning from not cooking frozen chicken pies for long enough. Max was angry that he was too ill to go to work for the rest of the week. She'd joked that it was the longest time he'd spent at home in ages.

Back upstairs, in Emily's room, she struggles to push open the door. Discarded clothes catch underneath, wedging it open. Her collection of teddies is lined up neatly above the bed. Maddy takes a grey school dress from a pile of clothes on the back of a chair. It smells of cakes. She'll give it a quick rinse, freshen it up for tomorrow. She opens the wardrobe and looks inside for Emily's new school shoes. They're not under the clothes that have fallen from their hangers. She reaches in further, feels around for something that resembles a shoe. Instead, her hand lands on a fat bin liner. She finds the handles and tries to pull it out, but it won't budge. Curious, she gives it another tug and out tumbles a pile of Max's jumpers, T-shirts and sweat tops. She kneels on the floor, sniffing back tears. He can't be dead. He's alive and he loves her. He'll need these when he comes back. She folds each garment neatly into the empty basket and carries them back to their bedroom. She'll make sure they get back on track. They've both let things slide too far. She's never liked asking him too many questions, she respects his privacy, but she needs to know what he's done with her money.

Downstairs, she stuffs Emily's dress in the washing machine and switches it on. She takes an apple from the fruit bowl and a sharp knife from the draining board. The blade slides easily under the rosy skin. Her fingers turn the apple, revealing the pale flesh while the skin hangs in an irregular line. Her mother used to do the same with oranges. The peel cut away so perfectly she could put it back together as though untouched.

The peel turns brown while she eats the apple, ready for the compost. She counts out six pips, takes them outside and scatters the seeds in the freshly turned earth. Hopefully one day they'll grow into trees. Hot tears fill her eyes and spill out. Max will arrive at the crack of dawn tomorrow, waking her up with a lovely cup of tea like he always does. He'll make sure he's here to take them to the cemetery. He won't miss Chloe's sixth birthday for the world.

9

MAX: MARCH 2011

When Max returned on Monday afternoon, he gave up ringing the bell and went around the side of the house. He unlatched the rickety gate and called out as he went in. Maddy was in the greenhouse by the back fence, planting seeds in a series of small pots. She wore a floppy hat, T-shirt and shorts. She didn't seem to notice him at first. He touched a wooden wind chime hanging from a pear tree, just enough to make her look up without being startled.

'Oh sorry,' she said as soon as she saw him.

'How are you, Maddy?'

'I'm fine.' She smiled. 'Let me get you a cold beer. We must make the most of this spell of heat.'

He followed her into the kitchen.

'I was sowing lettuces, broad beans and carrots. I grow all my own veg.' She rinsed her hands.

'I used to help my gran. She grew onions, tomatoes and potatoes mostly.'

'So satisfying, isn't it? And so much tastier than shop ones.' She took two French beers out of the fridge.

'We had whopping great tomatoes every year. God knows what she did to them.'

They laughed. She stretched up to the top shelf of the cupboard but couldn't quite reach the glasses.

'Let me do that,' Max said, touching her arm to gently move her aside. She gazed up at him and their eyes met for a second.

'It's all right, I'll get the step.'

'It's no trouble.' He took down two half pint glasses.

'Sorry, can't abide beer being drunk straight from the bottle, has to be in a glass, much more civilised.'

They sat under a parasol at the end of the garden, near a gnarly old apple tree. Maddy poured the beers and handed him one. 'Now then, you have a quote for me?'

He handed her a folded sheet of paper from his pocket. She glanced over the figures for some time. Perhaps she'd changed her mind. He surveyed his surroundings. It was one hell of a garden, mature and substantial. He'd love to get his hands dirty here.

'All looks fine to me. I think we have a deal.' Her smile made her whole face glow, as though she'd just delivered the happiest news of her life.

'That's brilliant. It's a no-brainer for me, to be honest. It'll really help me get on my feet.'

'I'm glad. You can start tomorrow if you want to.' She took her hat off and ruffled her shoulder-length hair. 'I'll get you some cash for materials.'

'That would really help, thanks.' He couldn't believe his luck. A measly £6.74 was all he had left in the world after the bus fare. Maybe it was obvious how skint he was.

'Good.' She raised her glass. 'Here's to a fresh start for both of us.'

They chinked their glasses together. It felt so good to be starting somewhere new, to be someone different earning an honest wage instead of being stuck as someone's lackey.

* * *

He arrived the next day and every day at 6 a.m. Maddy would let him in and go off to the cafe, leaving him a massive fry up and a pot of tea. After the lunchtime rush, she came back to make him a sandwich and see how he was getting on. They spent the afternoons chatting and he'd usually finish about 6 p.m.

'I've finished prepping all the walls in the spare room. Thought I'd better make a start in here as it's the biggest room,' he told her one Saturday. He'd started pulling up the worn-out carpet in the living room.

'This is going to be the hardest so far, I think,' she said.

'I reckon you're right there.' The rubber backing had turned to mounds of black dust. Instead of under-lay, there were sheets of yellowed newspaper which had imprinted blurred lines of words onto the grey tiled floor.

'I'll get changed and give you a hand. Tea?'

'Please.' He rolled the carpet up and vacuumed.

When Maddy came back, she'd changed into cut-off jeans and an old buttonless shirt she'd tied in a knot at her slim waist. She'd wrapped her hair up in a red checked scarf and tied a bow on the top. For God's sake, did she realise how sexy she looked? She left the tray of tea on a chair and knelt on the floor.

'It says here that on 20 March 1983, Prince Charles and Princess Diana began their royal tour of Australia. Must be around the time my parents moved in. I re-member Mum saying there were no carpets.'

'These nasty tiles instead.' Max jabbed a flat-head screwdriver under the corner of one. 'A hell of a job to get these up. See how gluey they are? No wonder your parents carpeted over. You might want to do the same.'

'I don't mind leaving them. What about wooden flooring?'

'Yeah, that could go over the top, would look great. Last longer too.'

'Let's do it then. I want to transform the place.' She sat back on her heels and sighed. 'Living here has always felt like living in the past.'

He nodded, gulping down a mouthful of hot tea. 'Not good to live in the past, is it?' He gazed out of the window at a flock of starlings. This was his chance to move on too, forget about the family of sharks that ruined his life.

'Talking of which, you've not told me much about yourself,' she said interrupting his thoughts.

'Nothing to tell. Parents died in a plane crash when I was ten years old. Gran brought me up. Been living in and out of digs since she died when I was fifteen.' He watched her face crumple in sympathy.

'That's terrible. Don't you have any other close family?'

'Not that I know of. Cousins in Canada, I think. I was fortunate to get on a building and decorating apprenticeship. It set me on my way. I'll build my own house one day.'

'I can see you doing that.' She smiled and pointed a knowing finger at him.

She seemed to believe in him more than he believed in himself. He put his mug back on the tray.

'So, what's next in this room?' she said.

'I'll strip the paper and prep the walls for painting. Have you decided what colour you want?'

'White, I think it'll freshen it up. Dad painted this room dark green once. With all his plants in here, it was like a forest indoors – I loved it, but it was very oppressive. Trouble was the cracks in the walls started to show through, so Mum made him paper it over.'

He pulled at a torn strip of cream paper exposing the green paint. 'That's going to be a bugger to paint over if you have white walls.'

'I wrote my name and the date somewhere,' she said, tearing at the paper with a ferocity that surprised him.

'Here it is,' she said, breathless. She stood back and unveiled the scribble in black pen: 'Maddy Dunn 22 July 1997'. 'I was fourteen.' She stared at it, entranced. 'The following year Dad died and I finished school.'

'Was he ill?'

'No, nothing like that.' She looked away.

He wasn't going to push her if she didn't want to talk about it. He continued stripping the paper around Maddy's name.

'It was probably the last time I was really happy.'

He stopped what he was doing. 'That's a sad thing to say.'

'It's true. Until now, that is,' she turned to him, beaming.

He winked at her and finished his drink. Perhaps he should tell her what really happened to his bastard parents, how they ran off to Canada in the middle of the night, leaving him with Gran in a pokey old flat and the rent overdue. Gran's voice was forever carved in his memory: '*Well I never – gone without so much as a cheerio!*' It did make him smile in a sick sort of way. Married too young, Gran decided. They wrote to him once. Promised to come back for him, but they never did. Joined some sort of cult or commune. Said they'd all be together again once they'd set up their new life. His guts twisted just thinking about how fucking selfish two people could be. As the years went by, he gave up hope of ever seeing them again. It became easier to think of them as dead. Gran always said, '*They weren't the people we thought they were.*' She was the only one who ever cared about him. Nursing her until her last breath was the least he could do. Aged fifteen and all alone. Nice way to start out in life. Thanks for nothing, Mum and Dad. Shame you're not worth a second thought.

They'd almost finished stripping the second wall when chips of plaster began to fall away with each strip, revealing deeper cracks.

'Bugger. I'll have to dig out all the loose pieces and fill the holes before I can do any painting,' he told her. 'It's going to take twice as long as I thought.'

'This house is full of cracks. They're worst at the front. Dad said the old lady who lived here before them told him a bomb fell on the house across the road during the Second World War.'

'This is actually crumbling away, though. I've never seen anything so bad. When was it built, 1930s?'

'Yes, 1933, I think. Dad said something about the glue they used back then wasn't very good.'

'So the plaster wouldn't stick to the brickwork.'

'Something like that.' Maddy picked a chunk out of the wall. 'Mum pretended the cracks weren't there. If we pointed one out to her she'd say, "*There are no cracks in my walls.*"' She gave a half-hearted laugh and followed the jagged line with her finger. 'He papered over them. Do you know she'd really lost it by the end? I think the anger kept her alive.'

Max didn't know what to say. Her parents sounded as fucked up as his.

'I'd better take this chair out. I don't want it getting damaged,' she said.

'I can do that.' He picked it up.

'It's an Arts and Crafts piece,' Maddy said, following him into the sitting room. He carefully placed it against the wall. 'Mum loved it.'

'You're wasted in that cafe. You should have been an antiques dealer.'

'Mmm, maybe. I didn't really have a choice.'

'Why was that?'

'I had to keep an eye on Mum, look after her. I ended up being her carer and taking over the cafe soon after I left school.'

'So the cafe was her business originally?'

'Yes. Both my parents ran businesses, but unfortunately it meant they didn't spend enough time with each other.'

'What do you really want to do? You have a choice now, surely?'

'I have been wondering about selling up.'

'It would set you free. You can do what you like now.'

'I suppose I can. Look, why don't I fix us something for lunch while you carry on here?'

'Yeah, great.'

'I've got Lincolnshire sausages from the butcher and some fresh white rolls. Does that sound good?' She gave him one of her warm smiles that made all his bad thoughts melt to nothing.

'Sounds perfect.' He smiled back, letting his eyes sweep over her. She'd started wearing a bit of make-up, not too much, not tarty, but it really suited her, made her even more gorgeous. Lately, when he got back to his lodgings in the evening, he couldn't stop thinking about her. How crazy was that when he was with her every single day? But it was real; it made his chest ache with longing. He hadn't known anyone apart from Gran who was so straightforward and kind. For a second he fought the urge to pull her to him and kiss her. But he needed to pick his moment, not scare her off.

He covered his nose and mouth with a dust mask and got back to work.

10

MADDY: LATE SEPTEMBER 2019

Maddy wakes early, still paralysed by sleep, mouth slack. Her dress hangs with his suit outside the wardrobe like spectres in the grey light. She listens for the door clicking or Max's footfall on the stairs. Nothing. He'll be back soon. He has to be. There's still time.

She pushes herself up. It took hours last night for her mind to finally stop racing, going over where Max could be and everything they'd last said to one another. She's been so deep in her own grief, it didn't occur to her that he wasn't coping. Out of the window, the birds are pecking at empty feeders in the dim light, fooling themselves with their vainglorious chirping. Peals of laughter from Chloe's previous birthdays rise up from the garden. Why didn't she stop to savour each moment; Chloe pulling silly faces or blowing out her candles?

She crawls back into bed on Max's side, cold as a slab. Her hand goes straight to her bump. Her eyes shut. She conjures up Max's boyish face, always smiling or winking no matter how bad things were. She fights the urge to cry and folds her arms over herself, trying to rub warmth into her skin. She dreamed last night that Max had been standing at the front door, knocking endlessly. The only reason she hadn't seen him all this time was because he'd been standing there, and she hadn't heard him.

Absentmindedly, she picks a hair off her pillow, then another. She drags the pads of her fingers across the cotton, collecting enough hair to twist into a thin rope.

In the shower she stands under the heat for too long, leaving her skin blotchy and scalded. When she peers in the mirror, there are lines she hasn't noticed before. Her skin is pale as though she is fading away. Where her hair is pushed back, a fan of thinning white frames her face. For a split second, it's her mother staring back at her. A wisp of air wafts in from the window. She closes her eyes and breathes in Chloe's sugary scent.

In her dressing gown, she wanders downstairs, into

the garden to refill the bird feeders. The Black Moon pansies are in full bloom around the sundial. Chloe helped her plant the flowers last autumn. They'd had such fun. Chloe squealed every time she came across a worm and was mortified when she found one sliced in half.

It must be an hour before Emily discovers her sitting there. 'Mummy, you need to get ready.' She is wearing one of Max's sweat shirts over her dress. It looks ridiculous but Maddy is too exhausted to complain.

'Have you seen these, darling?' She points to the pansies.

'You said Daddy would be here,' Emily whines and stamps her foot.

A lump rises in Maddy's throat. Her eyes fill up. He can't be dead, he can't be! Not her Max. But why isn't he here? She covers her face with her hands and grief chugs out of her like a steam train, in deep shattering gasps. She doesn't think she will ever be able to stop.

* * *

The taxi pulls up outside the house at eleven. Maddy stumbles outside and leans against the car door. Somewhere between getting up this morning and walking to the car, she has lost her balance. She can't do this. Not without Max. But she must. She climbs into the back. Emily sits next to her, looking paler than ever. Has she even eaten? Maddy locks her hands together, flexing her fingers. She gazes at the world through dark tinted glass and when she's certain she has no more tears to shed, her swollen eyes brim again. This must mean it's real, it did happen. Chloe's gone. And now him.

The car pulls through the cemetery gates and up the narrow pathway. Tall oak and sycamore trees around the perimeter block out the sun, creating a pool of light in its centre. Maddy stares up at a weeping stone angel as they pass by.

They stop alongside Chloe's grave. Maddy opens the door and takes a moment to breathe in the fresh air. Emily leans over and hugs her. When Maddy steps out, she feels like she's arriving from a life-long journey. Her knees almost give way. She links arms with Emily, and together they shuffle towards the graveside.

She imagines Max's strong arm holding her up as he did at the funeral. He shook people's hands and exchanged whispered words. But she couldn't speak. There were no words for this. The reverend strode towards them, long swathes of dark material swishing behind him like beating wings. He took their hands between his smooth cold palms and asked if they were ready. Max's nod was so slight, his eyes creased into tiny chips of black jet. She remembered thinking *how will I ever be ready?* And now they have to come to terms with Max not coming home either.

Maddy kneels and places the wreath on the small mound of earth and blows a kiss. 'Happy birthday, my darling angel.' Her fingers lightly touch the ceramic teddy bear. Head bowed, arm around her bump, her sobs roll through her body. Emily clings to her coat arm, hiding her face.

Just then a dark cloud of cackling jackdaws swoops across the sky, blistering the silence. They land on the branches of the tallest sycamore, weighing them down, squabbling for position. Maddy and Emily hold hands tightly, heads bowed. A distant gunshot scatters the birds into a splash of black across the sky. Maddy watches them circling the church spire, their mocking chatter grinding through her head.

* * *

After Emily has gone to bed, Maddy runs out to the garden and picks up the scythe propped against the greenhouse. Her arms swoop as one in a wide curve, beheading her beloved China roses. This renewed strength surprises her. She clenches her teeth to temper the force pushing her on, groaning with the effort into the eerie silence. Her mind fills with Max's blackened face floating in water. She tries to shake the image away. She hacks at the rows of delphiniums and hydrangeas, scattering them across the grass. She holds up the blade and turns it so it glints in the light. She wields the scythe again chopping at sunflowers and gladioli, slicing through dahlias and chrysanthemums, watching them topple before she moves on. The compulsion doesn't end until she has massacred the whole garden. With a last burst of energy, she throws off her shoes and stamps on the fallen flowers, crushing their heads, staining the soles of her feet.

All around her are the remains of the plants and flowers she's nurtured over a lifetime, like children to her.

* * *

The following day, dressed in black and wearing sunglasses, Maddy takes Emily to the nearest garden centre and selects pots of towering black millet, Oriental black bamboo, Black Knight irises, Can-Can Black Moon pansies, Queen of the Night bulbs, black dahlias and Black Baccara roses. She loads them into the car, cramming every space with their fresh pungent smells. The foliage covers all the windows, even part of the windscreen so it's almost impossible to see out.

Back home, Emily silently helps her unload the various sized pots, lining them up against the wall like a gathering of monks. Maddy digs up any remaining roots, twisting them out of the earth with her fork while Emily sweeps away remnants of the coloured flowers.

They plant deep rows of the millet, bamboo and irises, creating a shroud of darkness in front of the fences. They fill the rest of the borders with roses and, finally, nearest the lawn's edge and around the island of bushes enclosing the sundial in the middle. By the time they finish planting, daylight is fading.

Later, Maddy stands alone in the garden with a glass of white wine, watching the moon's silver sheen highlight the outline of dark leaves and flowers. She lets out a deep sigh. At last, a sense of peace and calm descends on her. No more pink or blue or yellow flowers, only shades of black.

11

After spending the next day in bed, Maddy drags herself up in the afternoon. Emily is staying the night at Sophie's. She wraps her dressing gown around her. Sarah said she ought to close his accounts or freeze them at least, sort out all his paperwork, but where is it if it's not in the garage? She needs to find out what's happened to her money. Did he buy into another business? She sits back on the bed. But if he did, why not tell her? She groans and throws her head back on the pillow, shutting her eyes. When she opens them, her vision rests on Max's suitcase on top of the wardrobe. The one covered in scuff marks that he was carrying the first day he walked into the cafe.

She jumps up and drags a chair over to stand on so

she can reach up and pull the suitcase down. Thankfully, it isn't heavy. She wipes the dust off the surface with her hand. Under the light she can see it is real leather by the feathered lines of the skin. She lays it down on the carpet and kneels in front of it. When Max asked her not to open this case, she respected that. Her dad had been a very private man: she'd never have dreamed of looking through his things... until the day she had no choice. She sits back on her heels. There are speckles of rust on the metal buckles and a cut in the leather, a flap of skin. On an intake of breath, she unclips the case and opens it a few inches. A musty smell of paint and dust wafts in her face. Without looking in she lets it drop shut. The leather balloons for a moment, as if it's taken a breath for the first time in years. Then she flips it open in one swift move.

Both halves are lined with dark material. Stacked inside is a pile of roughly folded clothes: overalls, T-shirts, bleached jeans, all splattered with paint. There's a book about the night sky, the moon and eclipses. Maps of various towns: Manchester, Sheffield, Norwich, Uxbridge and Huntingdon. In one corner she spots something shiny. She picks up a brass lion-crested button and turns it in the light. As she puts it in her pocket, she notices a length of thread where the lining is coming away from the leather. Slipping her fingers inside, she feels a sharp edge and takes out two envelopes. One contains a parking fine addressed to Max – she remembers now, the one issued in Huntingdon that she asked him about. The other envelope is faded, the plastic window disintegrating. Inside is a photo of a blonde girl with angular features. She's kicking up water in a rock pool on a stony beach, jeans rolled up under her knees, her top not quite reaching her navel.

She's about to close the lid when she notices the lining is sagging at the bottom. Drawing her hand across the bulge, she feels the weight of paper. She delves into the lining deeper until her fingers reach the slicing edges. Out come blank Inland Revenue expenses and benefits forms, a list of vaccination dates typed on an old typewriter and a bundle of vehicle licence stamp cards, almost full and all from Huntingdon Post Office. There are bank statements and a few paying-in receipts. She finds one for the twenty-thousand-pound cheque she gave him. She scans through the statement to find the same date. The money went in then came out again only a few days later. But who was it transferred to? The letters and numbers don't mean anything to her. She rakes through several more papers and comes to a bundle clipped together at the back. But these are not Max's. They belong to someone called Adam Hawkins of Lawn End, Huntingdon. Her mind goes into a spin. Why would he have these? She's never heard him mention an Adam Hawkins before. She sits on the edge of the bed and deals out each sheet one by one, like it's a pack of cards. There it is. The sum of twenty thousand pounds leaps out at her – transferred from Max's bank account to this one on Friday, 24 November 2017. She swallows hard but her throat catches, her mouth is so dry. Who on earth is Adam Hawkins and why did Max give him the money without telling her? Then her eyes are drawn to a letter addressed to Mr Hawkins. The subject of the letter is underlined: <u>Plot 146, 29 Lawn End</u>. Why does Max have this man's house key? What else has he been keeping from her? She knows only too well how secrets can destroy a person.

12

MAX: MARCH 2011

It turned out that all the living room was riddled with cracks. By Friday afternoon, Max had started the prep work on the last wall. He didn't want to stop until he'd finished, but even with Maddy's help, he hadn't banked on it taking till almost midnight.

'I meant to tell you I found some work with a local firm, fitting kitchens.' He'd been dreading telling her all day.

'Oh.' Her face fell. 'When do you start?'

He couldn't help feeling pleased that it bothered her. He'd been seriously tempted to turn it down. The thought of not spending every day with Maddy hit him hard, like trying to cling onto the edge of a cliff.

'Monday.'

'That's good, isn't it?'

'I s'pose. But I like being here though.' He searched her face for signs that she might miss him too. She blinked up at him with her dark innocent eyes.

'Do you have any plasters? I didn't realise I'd caught my thumb. It's not bleeding, just sore.' He showed her the split in a patch of dry skin.

'There's some in here.'

He trailed after her to the kitchen, where she dug out a first aid kit from a drawer in the dresser.

'Here, let me do it for you.' She turned his hand on the side.

He watched her carefully peel back the plastic strips and place the plaster gently across his thumb. As she pressed the sticky tabs to his skin, she gazed into his eyes. With his fingertips he lightly touched the back of her hand and, when she didn't protest, he caressed her smooth skin.

'Thank you,' he said.

Her warm smile widened, eyes still fixed on his.

'Would it be okay if I have a shower?' He'd been sweating buckets all day and she was too polite to complain.

'Of course. I'll get a clean towel for you.'

Upstairs, he stood close behind her at the airing cupboard. She spun round, towel in hand.

'I really appreciate everything, you know,' he said. She didn't move away. Her breathing quickened and her hand brushed his as he took the towel.

After his shower, he wandered downstairs wearing it around his waist. Maddy's face flushed at the sight of him.

'Can I get you a drink or something to eat?' Her red face deepened.

'A glass of water, thanks.'

He was amused at her stealing a glance of his toned chest. As she handed him the glass, he let the towel fall to the ground. She gave a little gasp. He leaned down and kissed her on the mouth. She was more eager than he'd expected and didn't resist when he led her up to her bedroom and started to undress her.

* * *

That night he lay awake in the dark with the curtains open, Maddy fast asleep. Such a stunning girl, bit old-fashioned in her ways, but that wasn't her fault. She was incredibly kind and eager to please.

He got up and stood at the window in the silver light of the waxing moon. Gran had sworn by the lunar rhythms and told him it was foolhardy for anyone to ignore them. Below him, a network of gardens was fronted by large houses like this one.

He'd have a go at building his own one day. He lit a cigarette and inhaled deeply, tapping the end out of the window. The ash fluttered away like a mini flurry of snow. His mind drifted back to the heavy fall in February. A brother holding each of her arms, pulling her back with every attempt she'd made to lurch forward, face criss-crossed with tears, voice brittle. The shadowy outline of her father in the background. There he went again, as if he didn't have a future, only a magnet to the past.

* * *

When he woke in the morning, Maddy was already up. He washed and joined her downstairs.

'Morning.' She laid a knife and fork on the table.

'You all right then?' He pressed himself against her and fingered her hair.

She pecked his unshaven face. 'I don't usually...'

He shrugged. 'Don't worry about it.'

'I've never...'

'There's a spark between us, end of.'

'You could say that.' She smiled, her face pink.

'Those bruises on your back... your legs...' Her nose wrinkled.

'A nasty fall.' He half smiled, remembering the sharp kicks as he'd curled himself into a ball.

She poured him a mug of tea and laid his breakfast on the table.

'Perfect. Now, is there anything you need doing before I start the serious business of painting walls?'

'Actually, there are a couple of things.'

He scoffed down his breakfast and wiped the plate with toast. 'Do you mind?' He pushed his plate away and waggled a packet of Rothmans.

She shook her head.

He lit one and tipped his head back, blowing smoke up to the ceiling which was already tar-stained.

'Mum's furniture needs dumping – bed, mattress, armchair. I'm sorry, I don't really have anyone close by to ask.'

'I offered, didn't I?' He hooked his arm round the back of his chair. She had no clue how naturally beautiful and damn sexy she was. He liked that.

Her face reddened again as though she'd read his mind. He winked at her and couldn't help but smile; he was falling completely under her spell, and he liked it a lot.

13

MADDY: EARLY OCTOBER 2019

On Saturday morning, Emily falls asleep as they approach Huntingdon. It's been a clear run of an hour and a half from Uxbridge. Maddy couldn't sleep all night, thinking over what she should do. She thought about writing a letter, but it would be too easy for him to ignore it or she could be waiting for weeks. She needs to know now. She drinks a mouthful of coffee from a flask. In a folder tucked in the footwell are Adam Hawkins's bank statements. What if he won't answer her questions? She'll have to come right out and ask him what dealings he's had with Max. She decides it's best to watch the house for a while and gauge the situation before she makes a move.

Maddy pulls into the quiet village. Number twenty-nine, Lawn End. Ivy hangs over an upstairs window like a patch covering a lazy eye. The front door is at the side, with the driveway running the whole length of the house to the garage. A blue Nissan is parked outside. She spots the number plate. That's Max's old car he sold two years ago. *Who is this man?*

She sits watching the house, sipping the last of her coffee. After thirty minutes, a woman with blonde hair scraped back into a ponytail comes out with a boy of about eight. A springer spaniel runs out and cocks its leg up against a lilac tree in the front garden. The grass is as tall as the top of its legs and the kitchen window could do with a clean. In contrast, the woman is immaculate, wearing large sunglasses, high heels and a mid-length A-line coat. Could she be the same woman in the photo, about ten years older? Perhaps she's Adam Hawkins's wife, or is it possible Max had a sister he never told her about? The dog runs back inside. The woman locks the front door, helps the boy into the back seat, jumps in her car and drives off.

Maddy is shaking, but she has to speak to Adam even though it's possible he could have pushed Max off that bridge. What if Max owed him money? He's always coming to her when he's run out. He used to know some unsavoury people, loan sharks that broke people's hands if they didn't pay up on time. Is Adam Hawkins one of them? She needs to be careful.

Maddy checks in the mirror; Emily is still asleep. She grabs the bag of papers and climbs out of the car as quietly as she can. There's only the hum of a lawn mower in the distance. She dashes up the drive and taps on the door before she loses her nerve. The dog starts barking. She looks around, not wanting to draw attention to herself, but there's no one there. She remembers Max selling the car because he was so pleased to get rid of it. They'd been after a people carrier for ages, so it made sense to sell the Nissan. She hadn't minded paying for it because she was going to be the one using it the most. He used his work van all the time unless they were going out as a family. Five thousand pounds he said he got for it. But she hadn't noticed any deposit for that amount on his bank statement.

She knocks again, louder this time. The dog goes crazy. Adam Hawkins is clearly not in. He's probably at work. Perhaps it would be better to try earlier in the day.

Maddy climbs back in her car. There's no doubt he must know Max. He transferred all that money to him, bought his old car. Emily begins to stir in the back seat.

'Where are we, Mum?'

'Cambridgeshire.' She starts the car and drives away. 'Do you fancy a quick trip to the beach?'

'In October?' Emily giggles.

'It'll be fun.'

'Can I have an ice cream?'

* * *

They last went to Hunstanton when Chloe was a baby. There are photos of her sitting on the sand in a cream frilly dress and matching sun hat with Emily surrounding her in sandcastles. Max drifted out so far in his inflatable dinghy, she lost sight of him and had to call the coastguard. He isn't a strong swimmer, which makes her fear for him falling off that bridge.

They park in Old Hunstanton at lunchtime and carry their packed lunch in a wicker bag, holding a handle either side. On the beach, the droning whirr of a kite circles above. A man further up is pulling at two strings, making a colourful dragon dip and curve through the salt and pepper sky. She breathes in the salty air. They find a sheltered spot in front of a row of colourful beach huts and grassy sand dunes. Lunch consists of ham and pickle sandwiches and ready salted crisps followed by homemade fairy cakes and small bottles of sparkling water. After, Maddy lets Emily buy an ice cream from a shop along the front. The aroma of fresh fish and chips follows them as they stroll.

A weak sun begins to break through a cloud, illuminating the ghostly white posts of the wind farm out at sea. Emily sits under a blanket, her head in Maddy's lap. There's a brush in her holdall somewhere, one of those fold out types. Once she's found it, Emily sits up in front of her and she brushes her hair while telling her the story of *The Little Mermaid*. Maddy stops and looks at the brush. It's choked with a surprising amount of dark wavy hair. Surely, she can't be losing this much? Could it be stress? Her own hair loss probably is. She hides the brush away and passes Emily her wellies, bucket and spade. She runs down to the water while Maddy follows at a slower pace, through shadowed dips in dry sand, of people who have come and gone. Further on it's wet and the sand is crusted with millions of broken shells, giving a satisfying crunch under her feet. The tide is so far out, the water reflects a silver edge next to the black streak of mudflats.

Emily joins a boy of about ten who is digging a moat for his sandcastle. Bleached twigs and razor shells decorate the turrets. Emily digs down and soon reaches the bed of gluey mud underneath. Maddy leaves them to it and strolls on until she reaches a small pool of water. She crouches down and dips her fingers in. It's warmer than she expected. Warm like blood. So much blood. She doubles over and tips onto her side, landing in a puddle. I need you here, Max, I can't do this on my own. Emily calls to her, but she doesn't respond. She doesn't want to move. She wants to stay here and lose herself in the vast sky.

14

On Monday morning, Maddy drives back to Lawn End. The roads are busy but she arrives at 8.30 a.m. The woman with blonde hair leaves with the boy at 8.35 a.m. At 8.45 a.m. a woman with chestnut-coloured hair and an empty laundry basket walks from her house across the cul-de-sac and lets herself in. Five minutes later she comes back out. The basket is so full, the woman can just about see over the top of it.

At 11.30 a.m., the neighbour brings the clothes back on hangers and a neatly ironed pile. There is no sign of Adam Hawkins, or any man come to that. Maddy checks her watch. The longest she dares stay today is midday because of getting back for the school run.

She's about to leave when the Nissan whizzes past

her and parks on the drive. The blonde woman gets out, slams the car door and goes in the house. Is she Adam's wife or girlfriend or maybe sister? Maddy's been toying with the idea of putting a note through the door, explaining her situation. But now she may as well go and speak to her in person.

She stands on the doorstep for a moment thinking through what she'll say. She taps lightly, but no one comes. She knocks louder. The dog starts barking and the door swings open causing another out the back to slam. The blonde woman is still wearing her coat. Maddy's eye is drawn away from her to the flowery wallpaper, so similar to theirs at home. How odd. Her mind goes blank.

'Yes?' The woman scowls in a husky voice. She's younger than her, fierce red lipstick perfectly fills her pouty lips. Maddy's eyes are drawn away from the woman's made-up elfin face, towards the carpet on the stairs and its crimson border running all the way up. Identical to the carpet in their house.

'Erm... could I speak to Adam Hawkins, please?' she manages to ask.

'What do you want him for?' The woman taps her long, painted nails on the door frame.

'I think he knows my husband.' Maddy focuses back on the woman. 'He's gone missing.'

'What's his name?' The woman is squinting, looking her up and down. The petrol blue smear of a badly drawn tattoo peeps out of her cleavage.

'Max Saunders.' Her eyes wander back to the wallpaper. She blinks at the large burgundy flowers which merge into the beige background.

'Never heard of him, sorry love.' The woman starts to close the door.

'When will Mr Hawkins be back, please?'

'God knows.' She continues to close the door.

'Thank you, anyway.' But Maddy doesn't think she heard her. She stands there in a trance for several moments.

As she wanders back to her car, the woman comes out, bundles a bulging black bin liner into the Nissan and drives off.

Maddy curls up on the back seat, staring at the folder of bank statements in the footwell. Nausea settles in her throat. The car, the wallpaper, the carpet, the money, all swirl around in her head like litter on a blustery day. What does it all mean? What if that woman does know Max and is something to do with his disappearance?

15

MAX: MARCH 2011

On Saturday morning, Max hired a van to dispose of all the old furniture. The bed frame was falling apart, and the mattress had compacted with years of human debris.

'I'm off to the dump,' he called. Maddy was at the bottom of the garden, where she seemed to spend most of her time when she wasn't working at the cafe. He couldn't see her face under the floppy hat and sunglasses, but he waved at her all the same. On the way back, he drove along Uxbridge High Street, pulling up at a pelican crossing to let a group of students cross. He spotted a petite blonde woman strolling past The Crown and Sceptre. Her outline, the sway of her hips looked just like Ali's. He honked his horn and the woman turned, but her features were all wrong: the lips thinner, the hairline higher. He banged his fist on the horn at a group of kids pushing and shoving each other in the road. No point dwelling on what could have been. Maddy was good for him, and everything felt different and exciting with her. She was crazy about him, too, he was certain of that.

When he got back, Maddy answered the door wearing a satin dressing gown. A warm, sweet aroma filled the hallway.

'I thought I'd have a nice bath while you were out,' she said, beaming at him.

Her features seemed to have softened in the steam. Her hair was arranged high on her head, clipped back so it looked sexy, with a couple of tresses framing her face.

'I've got something for you,' she said.

He followed her into a room at the back of the house. It was the only room he'd not been in.

'This was Dad's study. I love this desk,' she said, stroking the highly polished black surface. 'It's ebonised wood – mahogany lacquered black to make it look Japanese. It was all the rage two hundred years ago. Isn't it beautiful?'

Max nodded. He'd never heard of such a thing, but it looked quality. Worth a few grand. He could taste dust in the air. Heavy velvet curtains, which had long since faded at the edges, were half pulled across the tall window. One wall was full of pristine leather-bound books and opposite the desk towered a grandfather clock which had stopped at five minutes past six. Maddy opened the top drawer of the desk and took out a key. The sun flashed on its silver fob.

'For you,' she said, letting it fall into his palm. 'You asked about renting a room.'

'You sure?'

Their eyes fixed on each other for several moments.

'I'm more than sure. I've been thinking about it a lot and I'd like you to move in.'

'I'd love to.' He slowly pulled the belt on her dressing gown, and she allowed it to slip to the ground. As she stood naked in front of him, he smelt the warmth from her skin mixed with an intoxicating, but delicate, scent of roses. Her body was full and curvy. He'd always gone for skinny girls like Ali, preferring a clothes-hanger frame, but while they might look better in clothes, a voluptuous figure like Maddy's was more pleasing to the eye when naked; no hip or rib bones in sight.

He took her hands in his and kissed her lips. He'd never had such a full body surge while kissing a woman before. What was it about her? He held her in his arms, smoothing his hands up and down her silky skin. He couldn't get enough of her. He shut his eyes and nuzzled in her rose-scented hair. He'd never felt so happy and secure. No complications, no games, no threats. Would he be able to hang on to her without fucking it all up? God, he hoped so.

16

MADDY: EARLY OCTOBER 2019

In the morning, Maddy takes Poppy and Daisy for a walk after dropping Emily at school. All the way round the park she goes over the woman's responses to her questions. Can she have really have never heard of Max? Seems so unlikely when she's driving around in his old car. And why did she rush off like that? Shouldn't she tell the police in case they are involved with Max's disappearance? Her thoughts twist and turn each time they skip back to the wallpaper and carpet. Her mind refuses to contemplate what it could mean.

Back home, she unclips the dogs' leads. A beam of low autumn sun illuminates the room. She can't settle. She needs answers. She cancels her midday hair appointment and drives back to Huntingdon. Thankfully, it's a clear run.

She's there by 10.45 a.m. She parks in the adjacent road, tucked far enough out of sight so as not to arouse suspicion, but still giving her a clear view of number twenty-nine. Her silver-grey VW people carrier is sufficiently ordinary looking so as not to attract attention.

Max's old car isn't on the drive. The woman must have gone out. Still, she'll wait, watch the house. This is crazy; is she going to sit here all day until she comes back? And what's she going to say to her this time that's different from before? They could be dangerous. She should leave, call the police, tell them this couple might know something about Max's disappearance. But an overwhelming urge to find out what's going on is eating at her. There has to be a reason why they have the same patterned wallpaper and carpet. Something is going on and she wants to find out what it is right now. She digs around in her handbag and takes out the key for Plot 146 then drops it into her coat pocket.

Easing herself out of the car she sidles over to the front door. There are pots of lavender either side of the mat, except one plant is dead and the other is wilting. The dog starts barking; a relentless one-note bark that confirms no one is in. Without thinking, her fingers dip into her pocket. She draws out the key and stares at it in her palm. The truth is painful, but so is ignorance, her mother told her many times. Would she rather not find out?

The key slides into the lock and turns. Her heart drumming, blood pumps loudly in her ears. One more bark rings out as she opens the door. Taking a quick glance behind her, she slips inside.

The springer spaniel jumps out of its basket in the living room and runs towards her leaping up, a string of saliva swinging from its mouth. She stares at the wallpaper, the carpet and rocks backwards. It's not just like their wallpaper at home, it's exactly the same. She stares agape at the flower pattern duplicated up and down the hall and stairs. Dizzy, she blinks hard trying to take it in. The dog jumps up at her again. The nametag under her chin reads *Poppy* and a phone number. The same name as one of theirs – but this dog is male. She gently pushes him away. What is all this, a sick joke? He barks again before sitting back down, tail wagging. A moment later, he picks up a ball in his mouth and snakes around her legs, thumping his tail against her. A clatter of envelopes shoots through the letterbox, startling her. A pain sears through her head and down the side of her face: the start of a migraine. She picks up the mail addressed to Adam Hawkins and Alison Wood.

Turning left into the living room, she stops dead. French windows overlook a corner garden, so similar to theirs, except this lawn is more like scrubland. The sofa and chairs are the same dark chocolate leather, even the layout of the room is identical. Bright coloured Lego is scattered on a rose-patterned rug, the pattern she chose for their house. She runs a finger along the display cabinet central to the room: dust. Her eyes are drawn to a photo above the mock fireplace. She peers closer, but her eyes blur. It can't be, but it is. Max is grinning back at her, his arm around the blonde woman, and a boy sitting at their feet. She sways backwards and has to grab onto the sofa to stop herself collapsing. How can this be? This is *her* husband. It must be a mistake. Are they related? Does Max have a brother, an identical twin? But there, on his upturned wrist, is the unmistakable tattoo of the letter 'A'.

Stupid, stupid, stupid! She yanks open one of the cabinet doors and a top-heavy pile of board games slides out. The adjacent cupboard is stuffed with colouring books, car magazines, and photo albums. She plucks one out. Bile rises in her throat. Pain pulses through her skull as if her head is about to crack open. She flips open the cover. No, please no. Max's face is in picture after picture, his unmistakable smile. In one photo, his arm is wrapped around this Alison woman, captured in profile; her small, upturned nose close to his cheek, her eyes shut, as if she is inhaling him. On every page Max is with her and the boy, at so many of the same places they've visited with the girls: Legoland, London Zoo, The Science Museum. And on holidays where they go: Hunstanton and the Isle of Wight. A memory of her father slides into her head. She is standing in front of the stove, pouring Ready Brek into a bowl. Bright sunshine darts through the kitchen window. Her dad and Lisa are out on the lawn, standing close, laughing. He pats Lisa's shoulder and gives her the kind of smile he usually saved for her mother. And even when they stop smiling, his hand is still touching Lisa and they're gazing into each other's eyes. Then he leans closer still until their lips are touching. The milk on the hob boiled over the top of the saucepan. She tried to move it off the heat but ended up slopping it down her bare legs. She screamed so loudly her father came running in, Lisa close behind him, pretending to care. Pretending to be her friend. *No. No. No!* She's tried so hard to block out these memories.

The album drops from Maddy's shaking hands, its spine bent back as if contorted in pain. Years of not knowing this was going on. Nauseous, she stands and leans against a chair. Sparks fly in front of her eyes. She shuts them for a second. When they open, she focuses on a child's handprint pressed against the television screen, shown up in the layer of dust.

Around the downstairs of the house, she pushes open door after door and stops at the kitchen. On one side is orange patterned wallpaper, peeling at the corner like a dried leaf. On the bench, letters flop out of an upright basket. She runs her fingers through. Some are unopened. Ms Alison Wood repeated over and over. A bitter taste coats her mouth. Nothing for Max Saunders. Instead, Mr Adam Hawkins. She tears an envelope open, slicing her finger. A line of blood bursts from the cut. She licks it clean, shaking open the folded letter. Joint Account Bank Statement: food shopping, garage, mortgage, car insurance, food, hairdresser and clothes. She looks at her watch. Five more minutes and she'd better go. She opens the double-fronted fridge with ice maker. On the middle shelf is a four pack of draught Guinness. Max's favourite.

The spaniel gives a solitary bark, making her jump. She peers through a rectangle of glass in the front door. Nobody there. She stands at the bottom of the stairs, straining to hear, her heart pounding in time with the dog's tail thudding against the under-stairs cupboard.

She creeps up the stairs, past all the piles of papers and toys on each step, and hesitates at the top, outside the master bedroom. The door is wide open, the bed unmade. The boy's room is to the right, dinosaur and Pokémon pictures pinned to the door. Bathroom to the left, a shell mobile rattles in the breeze from an open window. She leans into their room and imagines Max stretched out on the bed. Did he ever think about her when he was here? Stacks of DIY books on the right-hand bedside table, same as at home. On top is a half-empty bottle of Lacoste Eau de Toilette. The only fragrance he ever wears. She steps over the threshold, through a sickly smell of deodorant hanging in the air. A pair of trainers are tucked under the bed, size nines, and his dressing gown is across the back of a chair. She picks it up and breathes in his familiar smell. In the dressing table mirror, she sees her face buried in the towelling material, muffling the sound of her crying, soaking up her tears.

In front of her is a photo of them taken up close, slightly out of focus; they're laughing, sharing a double ice cream; the tattoo of the letter 'A' again, not only on his upturned wrist, but on hers too.

Maddy puts the dressing gown back, stirs a finger through the pile of make-up scattered across the dressing table. A familiar silver-coloured canister standing at the back amongst expensive bottles of foundation, serums and face creams catches her eye. She picks it up and presses, but all it can manage is a splutter of perfume: SHE by Armani. It's almost empty. Max buys her the same perfume religiously every Christmas. Is he buying it for this slut to make sure he doesn't come home smelling of another woman? She wrenches open drawer after drawer, full of make-up and fake tan creams and lotions, false eyelashes, hair pieces and nail varnish. Another fucking tart, just like Lisa. In the top drawer of the chest of drawers, she pinches out a pair of white lacy knickers, drops them on the floor and squashes them into the carpet with her shoe. She smiles to think of the time she pushed dirty underwear through Lisa's letterbox and hung muck-splattered bras and knickers in the leafless tree of her front garden. Four years she'd been having an affair with her dad. Four years of lying to her mother and to her. How long has this been going on?

She stomps back downstairs and shoves the album back in the cupboard. The door springs shut. Something shifts inside.

As she turns to leave, she spots a woollen jacket hanging on a coat rack behind the front door. Running her fingers down the line of brass lion-crested buttons, one of them is missing.

17

It's mid-afternoon by the time Maddy arrives home. She opens her front door to their springers bounding towards her, jumping up and sniffing her coat. Her head is pounding. She reels at the identical wallpaper again and runs to the downstairs toilet, retching so hard she thinks she might choke. This can't be happening. She washes her face, hardly recognising her pale reflection in the mirror. She takes a couple of migraine tablets and texts Sarah to see if she can pick Emily up from school.

Upstairs, she throws back the covers and lies on her half of the bed. Her whole body is agitated, as though electricity is surging through her veins. She burrows inside the duvet, cupping her bump and sobs until she sinks into sleep.

The dogs' barking wakes her from a shallow nap. It feels like she's not slept for days. She sits up with a gasp as though she's been holding her breath under water. Max. She blinks. It wasn't a dream.

Noise from the TV vibrates through the floor and the smell of toast wafts in the air. Sarah has collected Emily from school. For a few minutes, she lies there, reluctant to leave the warmth. She likes the dim light, the certainty of a heavy downpour at any minute. Reaching over to Max's side, she fans out her fingers. Eyes closed for a moment, she imagines feeling his bare skin, his face turning to her, smiling.

Sitting up, she is drawn to the photo on her dressing table of her mum and dad on their wedding day. She picks it up and looks closer at her mother's loose curls framing her serious, nervous face. Perhaps it's the moment before a smile or is she about to speak? There's a light tap on the door and Sarah looks in.

'Are you okay?'

Maddy nods and stands the photo back up. Sarah comes over and touches her shoulder.

'Goodness, Maddy, you really look like your mum there.' Maddy holds the photo next to herself in the mirror.

Although Maddy is several years older than her mother was then, they do look similar, the pale, flawless complexion and dark hair, before the pain and anguish of being cheated on stole her away.

Downstairs, Sarah, Sophie and Emily are in the kitchen eating cheese on toast. Emily leaves a wall of crusts on her plate. Maddy leans down and Emily wraps her arms around her neck.

'How was school?' Maddy kisses the top of her head. 'Good,' says Emily, 'I got a merit point for reading.'

'Well done.' Maddy tries to muster a smile. She gives Emily another hug.

'You don't look well at all. Do you want me to make you a drink or something to eat?' Sarah switches the kettle on.

'Just tea.' Maddy stands at the kitchen door and stares down the hall. She has a sudden urge to rip the wallpaper off in shreds. It feels like her home, her life and her family have been violated. She strokes her bump.

'Did they say you're both doing well?' Sarah asks.

Maddy wonders if she could find a decorator by the end of the week.

'At the hospital...?' Sarah comes over and touches her arm.

'Er yes, all well. Sorry, I'm so tired. I need to eat more but the thought of it makes me feel ill.'

'Are they worried it's a bit on the small side?'

Maddy stares at her.

'Do try and eat a little something, maybe mashed banana on toast?'

Maddy knows she means well, but she really doesn't need any of Sarah's advice right now.

'Any luck finding out why Max resigned?' Sarah clears away the girls' plates.

Maddy gazes into space. 'Maddy?'

'Nothing so far.'

* * *

After Sarah and Sophie have gone home, Maddy opens the ironing board in the sitting room. She sorts the basket of clothes into piles. Max's polo shirts and jeans go straight into a black bag, except one T-shirt and a pair of jeans. She irons the T-shirt and hangs it with the jeans on the back of the door. Next, she irons and folds Emily's clothes into a neat stack and takes them upstairs to put away.

In their bedroom, she hurls open Max's wardrobe doors and yanks his shirt sleeves one by one, as though she's tugging at his arms. The naked wire hangers jangle and swing. She pulls jumpers and T-shirts off shelves and slings them behind her, like sloughed-off remnants of him.

'Daddy's clothes!' Emily screams, running into the room.

Maddy glances over her shoulder, but the jumper she's thrown across the room is still airborne. It lands half on the bed. Emily scoops up a bundle and pushes them back in the wardrobe and tries to shut the door.

'You don't understand!' Maddy's shout is more like a growl, pulling Emily away, teeth clenched, dragging the clothes out in a heap on the carpet, strewn in different shapes like they're a pile of bodies. Emily tries to push the clothes back again and Maddy grabs her arms to steady her, but they collapse together onto their knees, sobbing.

18

MAX: LATE AUGUST 2011

By the end of the summer, Max had been living with Maddy for five months. She seemed eager to please him, both in bed and when they were working on her house together at weekends.

'I was never allowed to bring boyfriends home,' Maddy said one Saturday evening.

'What, even as an adult?'

He took his T-shirt off to have a wash in the corner basin.

When he turned back, she was staring at his chest. 'I'll have to start charging for that.'

She laughed, her face glowing. She held out a towel. He took it and rubbed under his arms.

'Mum didn't like it at any age. I always had to sneak around. Relationships never lasted more than a few months.'

'Wouldn't it have been better to put her in a home?'

'Not in the state she was in.'

'What do you mean?'

'She turned to drink after Dad died. It was a slow decline; I tried to stop her, hiding her bottles, but she was worse without it, vicious and bitter.'

'So you cared for her since when you were at school?'

'I'd come home, and she'd be on the sofa, passed out drunk. Once she'd left the cooker on. It was lucky I came home when I did. I ended up staying off school more and more to look after her. I missed part of the last year.'

'And they let you do that?' He hung the towel up.

'They sent work home, but I don't think they really understood that I was caring for her alone.' She opened the wardrobe door. 'Mum wasn't able to cope on her own. She couldn't get over what Dad did to her, all his lies.'

'What do you mean?'

'I'd rather not talk about it right now.'

'We couldn't have done things like this then.' He pulled her towards him.

'God no, never.' Maddy laughed and shut the wardrobe door. 'She would've been banging on the ceiling with her broom, calling me for something, anything.'

She held up a navy suit.

'Hey, what's this? I don't do suits,' he said, 'except weddings and funerals. Gotta be a good reason.'

'It's one of Dad's. He never wore it.' She looked hurt.

'I don't change the rules for just anyone you know,' he said softly, lifting her chin. He kissed her lips.

'I thought we could maybe go out for dinner, that's all.'

Perhaps he should have come up with the idea himself. He watched her substantial backside as she left the room. It sounded like she meant business.

* * *

They arrived at The Swan and Bottle by the canal in Uxbridge at 8 p.m. and were shown straight to their table. A single candle flickered between them in the semi-darkness. Maddy ordered champagne.

'Special occasion?' asked the waiter, his moustache expanding with his grin.

Maddy smiled at Max.

Max reached across the table and took her hand. 'You look beautiful,' he said, admiring her red dress and softly curled hair.

'You look pretty good yourself.'

'Yeah, the suit fits all right, doesn't it?'

The waiter poured two glasses and placed the bottle in a silver bucket by the side of the table.

'Here's to us.' Max raised his glass and tapped it against Maddy's.

'And here's to you, Max, for making me so bloody happy.'

He took her hand again and leaned across to kiss her. Who'd have thought a few months ago that he'd be drinking bubbly and wearing a suit?

The waiter served wild salmon for Maddy and steak and ale pie for Max before topping up their glasses.

'Have you thought any more about selling the cafe?' Max asked.

'Not really. I might sell Dad's shop first and go from there.'

'When did he buy it?' He tucked straight into the pie.

'My granddad bought the freehold in the 1960s. Dad left half to me and half to Mum but with the stipulation that the sale of the antiques, then the rent, went to her during her lifetime.'

'So you've had no income from it?'

'Not until recently. All I've had is what I've earned from the cafe.'

'That seems a bit mean,' Max said. Maddy was hardly touching her food.

'Not really. Mum paid the bills and I did everything else for her. I suppose he didn't plan for things to work out the way they did.' She gave a wry smile.

'It sounds like she never really let you grow up.'

'I think part of her was worried I'd end up like her one day.'

'So was she punishing you?'

'In a way. She thought I'd betrayed her.'

'Did you?' He finished his food, scraping the plate clean.

'Let's say I tried to shelter her from the truth.'

'Are you going to eat that?' Max asked. The waiter was standing at the table.

'I think I've had enough thanks, sorry.' The waiter took their plates.

They shared a raspberry pavlova and finished with coffees. 'You must miss your parents a lot,' Maddy said.

'Not any more.' He looked down at the empty

plate. 'They didn't actually die in a plane crash. I only tell people that because it's easier. It means I don't have to explain what they really did.'

'It must have been something bad for you to lie about it.'

'It was.' He told her the whole story about how they upped and left one night leaving him and Gran a goodbye note promising to call for him to join them. But they never did, and the disappointment grew deep in the core of him like rings in a tree with each year that passed.

'That's so sad. I'm sorry they did that to you. It sounds like we've both had a tough time.'

He nodded. There weren't many people he'd been able to trust like this.

Maddy held up her glass. 'These last few months have been wonderful, Max.'

'Yeah, it has been for me too.' He smiled and clinked his glass with hers. This was the life he'd craved. A good job, money in his pocket and a beautiful, kind woman by his side. The waiter brought over the bill. For once he could pay without hesitation. He placed his credit card onto the silver tray, not even looking at the total. When he'd paid, he took out a crisp tenner and left it under the candle. Maddy smiled and nodded her approval. He gave a little tug of the suit cuffs. He could get used to this. For the first time in his life, he felt good about himself.

* * *

On the way home, he asked the taxi to stop at the north side of Uxbridge Common, so they could stroll back in the moonlight. Another couple were by the pond and a man passed with his dog along the pavement.

They sat on the grass. Max laid his hand over Maddy's and edged closer to her. Paint and plaster rimmed his nails, dirt etched into the lines of rough skin.

'See the full moon?' he said, gazing at the sky. 'My gran used to say that it represents a full belly, a full purse, a full womb and a full life.'

Maddy cocked her head at him. 'I like that.'

'And it's supposed to be lucky for romance,' he added.

'Do you believe it is?' She smiled.

'I'd like to think it's true.'

'We get on really well, don't we?' She squeezed his hand. 'We do,' he said, pressing her hand back.

'Tell me more about when you lived with your gran.'

'We rented a barge for a while, when things got

worse money-wise. Her brother owned it and didn't charge us for the first three months, but it was damp and cold most of the time. I went to school in all the wrong clothes and shoes. That's when I learned to fight my corner against the bullies. I had to survive somehow after she died, so beating people up for a loan shark was how I got by. I'm not proud of it.'

'I wish I'd known you then. I might have been able to help you take a different path.'

'I did okay. I went to college eventually and got into the building trade. Anyway, about two years before Gran died, she took me on holiday to Cornwall. It was the only proper holiday we ever had. She'd always wanted to see a Moon Garden, so that's where we went. I'll never forget it. It was a warm night and there was a lemony sherbet smell in the air. Gran said it was from the flowers that only bloomed in the dark. The eerie light of the full moon illuminated all the silvery-leafed plants and a massive circle of glowing white angel's trumpets and moonflowers. Right in the centre was this fairy, sculpted from wire, blowing dandelion seeds and tinkling bells hung up across branches laden with white cherry blossom. It was an unbelievable sight, so magical.'

'Sounds beautiful. It must have looked quite ghostly too. I've heard of a few plants used in night gardens, like evening primrose, night phlox and silver sage. But moonflowers are really special because they stay tightly shut during the day and only start to open their massive white flowers at dusk.'

'It was a pilgrimage for Gran. She'd saved up for years to go there.'

'She sounds like a very special lady.'

He nodded. 'You'd have loved her.' He stroked her face with his fingers. 'I've never told anyone all this stuff before.'

'Then I'm very privileged. I feel like we've known each other for years.'

'Yeah, me too.' They really clicked. She made him feel comfortable in his own skin. For once he didn't have to pretend to be a hard nut. He could show his softer side and be himself with her more than anyone he'd ever known.

'You're one of the only people I know who understands how rewarding and soothing for the soul gardening is, getting your hands dirty, digging into the earth, planting and watching things grow. We may not realise it, but we all draw comfort from the cycle of the seasons.'

'And the moon.'

'Exactly. We all need those certainties in life. Gardening is about the only thing that's kept me sane over the past few years.' She gave a nervous laugh.

He gently pulled her closer to him. She'd been through a shit time the same as he had. No wonder they understood each other. They both gazed up at the sky. How amazing to meet someone who was interested in the same things as him. You'd have loved her, Gran. No doubt at all.

'There is something I've been wanting to ask you,' he said, shifting round so he was kneeling in front of her, looking right into her eyes. He wondered what she saw in his, how much she could read him. 'You can say no to this, if it makes you uncomfortable. And we don't have to straight away.' He pushed a fallen curl behind her ear.

'Let me decide that.' She touched his chin and ran her fingers along the newly shaven skin.

'I want us to be together always – I don't want to lose what we have.' He took her hands between his. A flood of adrenaline pulsed through him. Maybe it was a little bit crazy. You're moonstruck, Gran would say. But it was time to start laying down roots, stop wondering what might have been. A ripple of clouds surrounded the bright moon. Beautiful things like this didn't happen to someone like him. But here he was, and it was happening all right and it made his whole body light up like never before.

He took her hand and kissed it. 'Maddy, will you marry me?'

An instant smile brightened her face and eyes, fingertips pressed to her lips as he watched his words sink in.

'Oh God, Max, I'd love to.' They reached out at the same time, clasping each other tightly in their arms.

19

MADDY: OCTOBER 2019

It's been almost two weeks since Max disappeared, although it feels like an age. He's still not been found. In an interview for the local newspaper, she was asked if she thought he was still alive. She said she couldn't bring herself to think of him as dead, although she realises it's a possibility. It's also possible that he's alive and well and living with that woman, but she didn't tell them that. Either way it's a lot to come to terms with. But it doesn't stop her expecting him to call her or turn up. She thought she saw him at the supermarket, but on closer inspection, the man was much older with a chubby face. She imagines him doubling over with laughter at all the fuss being made. He'll tell her it hadn't been him on that bridge. But the day after the interview, Max's van was found abandoned in a street, less than a mile from the river.

When Alison drives away in the Nissan, Maddy follows, being careful to keep plenty of distance. Alison is a careless driver, she concludes, driving way over the speed limit. The drive is shorter than she expected. Less than five minutes and they are pulling into the car park at Tesco. She hoped she might be meeting Max but nevertheless she follows her into the store, pushing a clunky trolley.

Alison stops to pick out three red apples and two green ones. Maddy sees that she's not always so precise; taking a handful of potatoes she pushes them into a bag. Then she chooses a pineapple, turns it over, sniffs it, and adds it to the shopping. She click clacks away in her kitten heel mules. Her calf muscles are tight. She must work out every day. An unwelcome image of Alison's legs wrapped around Max pushes its way into her head.

She pulls into the meat aisle, but Alison misses it out completely. Bet she's a bloody vegan; can't believe he went along with that. He loves his steak and chips. Is she going to be the one to tell her he's missing, presumed dead? She follows her to the dairy section. He must have enjoyed being two different people, leading two lives. Maybe that was part of the appeal: that, and having sex with two women. Not as often as she wanted though. She should have realised there was someone else. There must have been signs; how could she have missed them?

Maddy drops a bag of stewing beef into her trolley. She imagines the security cameras watching her, knowing that she's not really shopping. Alison comes to the end of the aisle but instead of turning down the next one, she is spinning round, heading back towards Maddy. There's nowhere to hide. She is certain Alison will know who she is. Maddy backs up, crashes into a shelf. Alison stops next to her, peers into the fridge. Maddy freezes holding her breath. Alison moves on and Maddy slowly exhales.

And then she's gone. Vanished. Maddy races down the centre of the shop, scanning up and down each aisle, both sides. Perhaps it dawned on her she was being followed. Maybe she recognised her from when she knocked at her door. What if she knows who she is? She's probably calling security right now. She'll be frogmarched off the premises. How humiliating. She wants to shout, but she's been living with *my* husband!

There she is, standing at the Pharmacy counter, talking to the chemist. She's unbuttoning her coat. Maddy edges closer, gripping the trolley. Alison is rubbing her belly, which should be flat on someone so tiny, but it's not, there's a distinct swelling.

As Alison talks, she wipes her eyes with a tissue. The chemist brings a chair forward, and as she sits down, her hands reach around the now unmistakable bump. Maddy's mouth opens in a silent scream. A pain shoots through the side of her head. She abandons the trolley and presses the heel of her hand to her temple, running haphazardly towards the doors, colliding with people as she tries to escape.

Outside, she steadies herself against a pillar and doubles over, arm around her own bump. A low groan escapes her lips as she straightens up, her nails scraping into the brick.

20

MAX: DECEMBER 2011

'I've found it,' Max called from the loft. He picked up a long box with a picture of a Christmas tree on the front labelled 'Scandinavian Fir', held together with Sellotape, yellowed and crispy at the edges. He'd tried to persuade Maddy to buy a new tree to celebrate their life together as husband and wife, but she said this tree was special, from her childhood.

'I'm passing it down,' he called through the hatch. Maddy reached up and took one end.

'It's not too heavy for you, is it?'

'I'm pregnant, not ill,' she laughed, placing it on the ground.

'There are more boxes here marked "Decorations".'

'I've forgotten what we have. Shall we have a look through them?'

He heard her go down to the kitchen as he wiped the dust off an old rocking chair and sat down for a few minutes. This would be perfect for Maddy nursing the baby. He wondered if she knew it was up here. Seemed sturdy enough. It was taking some getting used to – the idea of having his first baby. But he couldn't wait to be a dad. Maddy was almost six months gone already. When she told him she was expecting, it was like a shooting star ignited his heart. He wished he could share the news with Gran.

Downstairs, he put up the spindly looking tree in front of the window. Maddy was so excited he didn't want to spoil it for her, so he wrapped the bushiest strips of tinsel around the middle to hide how bare it really was. He found a set of multi-coloured lights still in their original Woolworths packaging and wound them around the branches. He switched them on as Maddy was bringing in mulled wine and a plate of hot, sweet-smelling mince pies.

She let out a little whoop of delight. 'That's beautiful.' Maddy gazed at the tree with the wonder of a child.

Max took a swig of the warming drink.

'Mum wouldn't have the tree or tinsel up the first Christmas after Dad died, or any year after that.'

'That must have been tough for you.'

She nodded. 'What were your Christmases like?'

'Usually there was only me and Gran but sometimes her brother and his family invited us over. Gran made it lovely. We'd decorate the tree together and I'd help her make mince pies and a massive Christmas pud. Presents were always jumpers she'd knitted or second-hand toys she'd picked up from the charity shop. I didn't mind though.'

'At least you had someone to care about you. From the moment Dad died, Mum seemed to give up on life. She wouldn't set foot outside the house. She couldn't face any of the neighbours. I wasn't allowed to talk about his death to any of them, but I confided in my closest school friend, Jo.'

'You were lucky to have her.'

'Yeah, I was. She was really supportive.'

Max put his arm across her shoulders and kissed her temple.

'I had to do all the shopping for Mum, cut her hair, and get the doctor to come to the house if she fell ill. Sometimes it felt like I'd have been better off on my own, which was a bit mean because I realise now that she must have been in a deep depression.' She pulled out a bunch of sleigh bells woven onto a thick gilt rope and gave them a gentle ring.

'Our child will know and love Christmas,' he said, 'I promise.'

Maddy nodded. 'I want everything to be right for this baby.' She cupped the curve of her bump. 'Mum used to say it was Dad who spoilt Christmas, not her. But it was her who let the misery go on for all those years.'

'What, she blamed him because he died?' Max wiped away her tears with his fingertips.

'She said everything was his fault.' Maddy picked out a silver fairy. It glinted in the light. Its delicate mesh petticoats were beginning to crumble to dust. 'I don't think she realised how much it affected me too. I wanted to go to college and on to university to study horticulture, but I couldn't leave her alone, especially when her drinking got worse.'

'I'm so sorry.' He squeezed her hand.

'Before everything happened, Christmas was a magical time for us. I remember Dad lifting me up to put this fairy on top of the tree. He bought it in Hamleys when we were in London to see the panto *Mother Goose*. I'd never seen Mum so happy. She wore a glamorous sparkling emerald dress and a honey-coloured coney fur coat, and we all strolled arm in arm down

The Strand, with huge snowflakes blowing about us in the night sky.' For a moment, Maddy's face was animated, lost in the memory. She picked out a felt Father Christmas and slipped her finger through the golden thread.

'They worked so hard, we didn't go out together as a family very much, so it was a really special day. I shouldn't complain, we were comfortable. I always had new clothes and plenty to eat. We lived here in this beautiful house. Dad's antique shop was thriving by then and Mum had opened the cafe, so she was working long hours too. I'd always hoped for a brother or sister, but Mum didn't want any more children. She wanted to concentrate on building her business. Dad of course wanted loads of children, so it became a real bone of contention between them. After he died, Mum said that when they first got married, he'd expected her to stay at home, but she'd fought hard against it. He thought it made him look impotent only having one child.'

'I hope you don't think I've pushed you into giving up work.'

'Not at all, I needed a change. It was time to sell the cafe and move on. I'm looking forward to being a full-time mum.'

'You're going to be great. And I promise you one or

two children is enough for me.' He laughed. 'I doubt if my parents went on to have any more kids. I'm not even that interested.'

'Maybe you'll want to find out one day.'

He shrugged. 'Possibly when I'm old and grey. Anyway, enough about that. I hereby declare that we're officially reinstating Christmas as of today.'

A smile passed over Maddy's lips, but it was going to take a lot more than that to cheer her up. It was pretty much her whole childhood memories in that box. 'We should do that sometime, go and see a show. It's been too many years since I've done anything like that.' She reached up and threaded the Father Christmas decoration on a branch. 'We will, we'll do everything with our son or daughter: panto, sledging, Father Christmas's grotto, ice-skating, you name it.' He stood behind her and kissed her neck. All the things he'd dreamed of doing as a child too.

'Look at this one!' she said, taking out a wooden snowman. 'This was my favourite.' She kissed it and cradled it in her hands. 'Oh, why did Dad have to ruin everything?' She sighed and dropped the snowman back in its bed of tissue paper.

He gently pulled her round so she was facing him. 'Tell me what you mean, what did he do?' He took her cold hands and warmed them between his.

She looked away for a long moment before her eyes flashed back at him. 'My dad died of a heart attack in bed with another woman – our bitch of a neighbour at number twelve.'

'Oh God, Maddy, I'm so sorry,' he said, shocked by the raw pain in her eyes. He wrapped her in his arms and let her cry silently on his shoulder.

21

MADDY: OCTOBER 2019

All the way home, Maddy's head is a jumble of emotions. She wants to believe that Max is alive and well, but if he is, does that mean he's living with that woman? Is she carrying his child? That's insane. *How dare he!* She smacks the seat next to her. How long has this been going on? The photos suggest a year, maybe longer, but how can that be when he's been with her and their girls? A lump forms in her throat. Her hand goes straight to her bump. She needs to stay strong but her eyes brim with tears.

Pulling onto the drive, she sits there staring at the garage door, not sure what to do next. The dogs won't stop barking, so she forces herself to get up and go inside.

The dogs run into the garden as soon as she opens the back door, almost dragging it out of her hand. Who is this woman, Alison Wood? While the dogs belt up and down the lawn, she takes out her phone and taps the name into Google. There's probably a million people called that. She'll be impossible to find. But no, straight away a link comes up for all Alison Wood Facebook profiles. Without hesitation, Maddy clicks and a list of photos of different people with that name appears. She clicks on the face she recognises and Alison Wood's whole life opens up to her.

She scrolls down her never-ending stream of posts: some are photos of her with friends at glamorous-looking parties, a nail bar having false nails stuck on, at the park with her son, on a merry-go-round, swings and football. She's clearly much younger than Maddy, maybe as much as ten years? Her elfin features, tiny frame and the smallest eyes rimmed with electric blue eyeliner are finished off with ridiculously long false lashes. Down and down Maddy scrolls through this woman's life. Cutsie cat GIFs, affirmation slogans, clips of beauty bloggers, celebrities on the red carpet. So much rubbish. Is this what her life is full of? Is this what Max really wants in a woman?

She opens a folder named 'Isle of Wight holiday, June 22–28, 2019'. Wasn't this the time he told her he was working in Southampton? There's the three of them together, all smiles. Max with this woman and boy at the same bloody cafe on the beach in Sandown where they always go. Instantly, an image of him chatting to the head waitress pops into her mind. She'd not taken much notice at the time but now she wonders if she recognised Max with this other woman and said something? Was he asking her to keep quiet? Come to think of it, she was always over the top with their girls, giving them extra scoops of ice cream and lollies at the end of their meals. Did she feel sorry for her? Maddy kicks Emily's football hard at the fence. Both dogs start barking and howling.

She skims through dozens of photos of them on the beach, the pier, the arcade, bumper cars, even the saucy life-sized postcards where you put your head in the cut-out to have your photo taken. Why would he take this woman and child to the same holiday destination they always go to? Prickles rise on her head, her neck. Memories of her father with Lisa flutter through her mind. His lies, his carefully constructed double life. And now Max too? This is *their* place. There are even photos of the same hotel, the pool and gardens where they've spent year after year because he insisted on it. He told her it was nicer for the girls to feel like they were going to a home away from home. When she suggested they go to France or Spain instead, he said they could do that when they were older and would appreciate it more.

She zooms in on one of the hotel photos. There's a couple of waiters in the background. What if the staff recognised him? Were they laughing at her behind her back?

There are no recent photos of Max but plenty of her with her growing bump. If it is his, wouldn't he be posing next to it, to see if he can hear it or something equally cheesy? She seems that type, wanting to show off every aspect of her life to the world.

She clicks on the Instagram app and searches for her name. It comes up straight away with the same profile picture. Over three thousand followers. Staged photos of the perfect life: cups of creamy coffee or his and hers glasses of wine next to fairy lights in jars or trailing from a parasol. The side of Max's handsome face holding a beer to his lips. Maddy joined Instagram several months ago but hardly uses it, so she doesn't have much on her own page to distinguish her, none of Max or her own face, so she presses Alison's 'follow' button, then closes her phone and shoves it in her pocket.

She kicks off her shoes at the back door and slips on her gardening sandals. There are bulges where over time the leather has compensated for her wide feet. She opens the sliding door of the greenhouse and a cloud of stale air wafts out. Max's gardening gloves are too big, but hers are worn and a mouse has nibbled through where the thumb should go. She decides to cut down the nettles around the back fences where the apple and pear trees line the garden. It's a job Max promised to do. Tears fill her eyes. She imagines him standing on that bridge, the dark water coursing beneath him. *What have you done, Max?* She takes a scythe and hacks at the expanse of tall nettles, until they are only a few inches high. A sharp tug and they snap at the base. With a fork she digs into the ground; there seems no end to the stringy, knotted roots, the earth's veins, buried deep, choking the other plants. If she doesn't get rid of them, they'll be back next year. Max told her it's not until you start on them that you realise what a huge task you're getting into.

Why have you lied to me? She shuts her eyes and lets herself sink down to the soft earth, rubbing her bump in circles.

Her mind slides back to the first day Max walked into the cafe. She remembers giving a huge sigh as if she'd been holding her breath all her life waiting for him. His ruffled sandy-blond hair and unshaven face reminded her of Robert Redford as the Sundance Kid.

He had one of those open faces that was always smiling. But he seemed lost, drifting. For the best part of a week, they chatted and joked like best friends. She'd never felt at ease with anyone like that before. He needed work, so she let him decorate her house. She needed a fresh start after Mum died, so it suited her. They got on so well, but it scared her because she wasn't sure she could trust another man. But equally, she couldn't bear to let Max walk out of her life.

The dogs come sniffing round, panting in the sudden warmth. She pats her bump then pushes herself up and continues digging, eyes squinting until the low autumn sunshine switches off, the coolness returning. Amongst the clumps of earth, the stones and dust, a metal edge catches her eye. She picks it up. The sunshine switches on again like a spotlight. She loosens the disc from the mud. It's a silver pendant. She slips off her gloves, turns the water-butt tap on and rinses it. An engraved letter 'C' emerges. She dries it on her jeans. Chloe lost it last summer. She hunted for it everywhere and cried on and off for days over the loss. They bought one for each of the girls. She stares at it, cupped in her hand. Tears fall easily from her eyes. Every day there is something to remind her that Chloe has gone. She gives it a kiss and tucks it in her pocket. Max promised to buy her a new one, but he never did. A breeze picks up, blowing around in all directions, chilling her arms. She shivers and wipes her eyes and nose with Max's cotton hanky from her pocket. One of many she's borrowed and forgotten to give back. In the shed she finds the largest spade and slices into the earth like a guillotine. Her muscles burn as she digs deeper, shovelling the earth to one side. *I trusted you, Max, how could you betray me?*

When the last of the sunshine has gone, she slumps into a weather-faded chair and sips a glass of water. The velvet darkness of the black flowers draws her eye. Now the colour has been stripped from every bed, there's a strange sense of calm, an acknowledgement that part of her has died too.

Sarah calls to her over the back gate.

'Come in,' Maddy sighs. She'd rather be on her own but doesn't say so.

'I wanted to check how you are, if you need anything?' Sarah hovers beside her. Maddy guesses she can sense her prickly mood.

'I'm coping,' Maddy says, but is she? Grief plays tricks on her, lets her forget for a few moments then it's a physical thump to her gut all over again. Max should be here helping her and Emily through this; they should be helping each other come to terms with losing Chloe.

'When's your next check-up with the midwife?' Sarah reaches out then lets her hand drop down again.

'In about two weeks, I can't remember exactly.' Her phone lights up as it buzzes in her pocket. She takes it out. The message is fixed on the locked screen.

Alison Wood has accepted your friend request.

Maddy holds her thumb down to unlock it. Sarah pretends she isn't having a nosy at the message.

'One of the mums at the clinic,' Maddy tells her before she asks.

'Good you're making friends.'

'Yeah, it is.' She should go to the police, tell them Alison Wood has information about Max. But how can she face the humiliation of not knowing what's been going on? Anyway, she wants to deal with it herself. If Max is alive, she needs to hear the explanation from him. She shuts the phone off and pushes it deep into her pocket. Now she can keep a close eye on Alison and if she knows where Max is, she *will* find out.

22

MAX: FEBRUARY 2012

Max was soap washing the walls of the nursery when Maddy came in wearing dungarees, loosely held up over one shoulder. The other strap dangled to her waist.

'Coffee?' She stood sideways in the doorway, filling the gap with her bump.

'Mmm, please,' he said, squeezing the sponge in the solution and slapping it back on the wall.

'We need to decide on a colour,' she said.

'What's the hurry?'

'I want everything finished in time for this little one.'

'It will be. I'll have the basecoat on by the end of the day.' She stood facing him, the neat bump thrust forward, straining the strap in its buckle. He cupped her chin with his wet hand and looked into her eyes.

'Trust me, okay?' He gave her a kiss on the nose.

She smiled. 'The cot will be delivered on Thursday,' she said, 'and I was thinking of bringing the rocking chair in here for when I'm nursing.'

Her face had a beautiful natural glow. Sometimes, when she wasn't looking, he liked to observe her unselfconscious beauty. She was one of the few women he'd ever seen really bloom when they were pregnant. He'd never felt part of a proper family, but here he was with a wife and a baby on the way. He wiped his hand on his overalls and reached out to touch her belly. He shut his eyes as he felt for movement. Like a puff of smoke, thoughts of Ali clouded his head. What if it was her standing here with him instead? His eyes snapped open, disgusted with himself.

'Shall we stick with off-white?' Maddy asked. 'Then it won't matter if it's a girl or a boy.'

'Off-white it is then.' He couldn't bring himself to look at her.

* * *

They were in Marks & Spencer's looking through a rack of baby clothes when Maddy's waters broke, three weeks before her due date. An hour later, she was in Hillingdon Hospital wired up to a monitor. Despite looking forward to this moment for months, Max wished it was all over. They were told she was only two centimetres dilated, which meant it could be a long night.

As each contraction came, the tightening of her belly became harder to bear and with no quantifiable progress. The contractions were still six minutes apart, but Maddy seemed to perk up, even complaining she was hungry.

It was already getting dark outside when Max crossed the quiet road to the small parade of shops. A breeze picked up, sweeping the rubbish along the pavement. Only the Fish and Chip Bar was open. It was empty except for a woman behind the counter hunched over a crossword. It surprised him that life was still going on outside the labour ward. The woman took his order and emptied a bag of frozen chips into the sizzling hot fat. 'They're for my wife,' he said, sorting through a variety of coins he'd found in his pocket, 'she's in labour.'

'Is it your first?' The woman smiled looking up and shook the metal container submerged in the bubbling gold liquid.

He hesitated for a second. 'Yes, it is,' he said.

'You never forget your first being born,' she said, shaking the metal container again.

He'd quite like a boy, but he hadn't the nerve to say so to Maddy. It wouldn't matter if it was a girl, as long as they could have a boy next time. Next time! Hark at him. He pictured Maddy in pain, calling for him, the skin across her stomach stretched with pink jagged lines.

The woman seemed to sense his urgency. She lifted the metal container out and scooped a generous helping of chips into a paper bag.

'Salt and vinegar?'

'Please.'

The smell made him realise he was hungry too. She wrapped the chips in paper and took his money.

'All the best for your new family,' she said, holding the small package out to him.

The wind carried him back across the road. A waxing crescent moon was lighting up as the sky darkened. His new family. He could hardly believe it. At last he was going to be a dad.

* * *

Emily Alexandra was born the following morning at 4.12 a.m. Max cut the cord but struggled not to keel over with exhaustion. Maddy was barely conscious and didn't respond when they put the baby on her chest. They lifted Emily away, weighed and cleaned her up before handing her to Max.

'She weighs 5lb 6oz,' said the midwife as she wrote it on her sheet of notes.

He'd never held a newborn baby before. She felt so light. He couldn't believe he'd hoped for a boy when nothing was more beautiful than his baby daughter.

'Maddy,' Max whispered, trying to rouse her. He could understand her need for sleep. It had all been going so well until Emily's heart rate began to fluctuate. In a matter of moments Maddy had been surrounded by doctors and nurses and bright lights.

Maddy opened her eyes a fraction.

'They asked if you want to breastfeed,' he said. She hesitated then shook her head.

'Are you sure? You said you really wanted to try.' He knew how disappointed she'd be.

Maddy shut her eyes.

'It's okay,' he said and kissed her forehead. 'What formula milk do you want her to have?'

'You choose.' Her voice was croaky.

Max sat in the corner of the dimly lit room while Maddy went to sleep. The midwife showed him how to feed his daughter with a bottle. After, as Emily slept, he watched the sun rise across the rooftops until the transformation from night into day was complete.

* * *

Max brought them home the following lunchtime and encouraged Maddy to rest while he saw to Emily. He enjoyed feeding her, listening to her faint snuffling sounds and smelling the soft powdered freshness. Maddy hadn't taken much interest in her; all she wanted to do was sleep. The midwife told them Maddy had a touch of baby blues, that she needed time to adjust and how lucky that Max could be around to help.

* * *

On Saturday, Maddy was first out of bed. Max heard the grating noise of her pulling back the garage doors. When he looked out of the landing window, he saw her dragging out an old Chinese rug wrapped in plastic. It was one he'd taken up from her mother's bedroom when he first moved in. It needed a good clean. He banged on the window but she didn't hear him, so he ran downstairs and out the front door.

She wheeled out a Silver Cross pram full of rusty

birdcages and planks of wood. Everything smelled dusty and mouldy.

'What are you doing?' he called, stopping the pram with both hands. 'You should be resting.'

'I'm sick of resting, it feels lazy.' She stomped back into the garage and came out carrying a stringless guitar.

'Let me take that,' he said grabbing it from her. Behind her were oil paintings, an old Belfast sink and stacks of newspapers tied up with rope.

'Go and get some clothes on,' she said, snatching the guitar back. He looked down at his boxers.

'All right, but you need to wait for me.'

By the time he came back out, Maddy had stacked each item on top of the other in a straight line along the driveway. Max stood on the front doorstep, watching her. She stopped to acknowledge him standing there.

'Everything must go,' she said and disappeared into the gloomy depths of the garage.

'What do you want to do with it all?' he said as she emerged again, this time with a brown ceramic bowl that said 'Dog'. 'And why now?'

Out of the bowl she lifted a scruffy leather collar. There were tears in her eyes as she handed them both to him. 'We need to get a dog.'

'Whatever you want, but are you sure about getting rid of all these things?' He didn't know how to stop her building this wall.

'What else should I do with it?' She held out a set of long-handled paintbrushes. 'Do you want these?'

'I might be able to use them.' He took them from her and flicked the hairs. 'Come in and have breakfast.'

'I'm fine,' she said.

He took hold of her wrist as she turned away. 'Maddy, stop...'

'There's Dad's old Morris Minor at the back there. It's a wreck.'

'Please...'

'What's wrong? I'm clearing out some old things; it needs to be done. They kept every little thing.'

'You've not held our daughter for two days.'

'You're managing.' She was facing him now.

'But I need to go back to work on Monday.'

'You can't leave me on my own.'

'You won't be. Sarah is across the way and the midwife is coming over again.'

'Why?'

'Because I've asked her to. You're a bit out of sorts.'

'I'm fine, really. I just don't know how to look after a baby.'

'Hold her in your arms, feed her. She's a good baby, she'll sleep.' He led her indoors. Emily was crying in her crib.

'See, she keeps crying and I don't know what's wrong.' She gripped Max's arms. He gently peeled her fingers off him and guided her to sit on the bed. Then he lifted Emily out of her crib and she stopped crying. He handed her to Maddy and helped her hold the baby in the crook of her arm.

'You stay sitting there and I'll go and make up her milk.'

When Max came back a few minutes later, Maddy was standing by the window, gently rocking Emily in her arms.

'That's the way.' Max put his arms around them both.

'I was showing her the garden, telling her that she'll have lots of fun playing in it when she's older.'

'And I'll build her a playhouse with all that old wood.' Max kissed Maddy's hair. 'See, you're going to be a wonderful mother.'

23

MAX: MAY 2012

Max turned off the road and into their drive. Emily was three months old already. Everyone warned him it would go in a flash. He wondered how Maddy had got on at the health centre, if she'd even gone. She kept making excuses about it not being necessary for Emily to be weighed. But he liked to encourage her to go. She still wasn't completely herself. The health visitor told them she was suffering from mild postnatal depression and any contact and conversation during the day would help her. He wished she'd mix with the other mums a bit more. She'd refused to take antidepressants when the GP offered them to her. Sometimes he didn't know what to say or do. This wasn't how he'd imagined parenthood to be. He tried to call her at least once every day. But today he hadn't been able to. It had been one of those days he'd rather forget. A nightmare house John had sent him to renovate. It would be quicker and less hassle to knock it down and start from scratch.

As he got out of his car, the shriek of an ambulance siren startled him as it roared into the street. Max expected to see it turn into another road, but as it reached their house it slowed down and pulled into the drive.

At that moment, their new neighbour, Sarah, opened their front door to let the paramedics in. 'Thank God you're here. Come quickly, Max, please!'

In the sitting room he tried to take in the scene in front of him. Maddy standing with her hands clamped across her mouth, eyes bulging, and three paramedics leaning over the sofa. Beneath them, a miniature pair of feet, the skin mottled blue and grey. Maddy's denim shirt was dark and patchy with water. He'd never seen her look so pale. When she saw him, she let out a whimper and rushed towards him, arms outstretched, her face crumpled with all the pain and anguish he felt too. He shivered despite it being a warm day. Words he wanted to say were stuck in his throat and came out as a pitiful groan. Everything around him appeared to be floating. He lunged forward but someone pulled him back. He watched their mouths open and make shapes, but he couldn't hear a thing, like being under water.

Then the muffled silence broke with a familiar cry and he saw Emily's tiny feet moving. Thank God she was still breathing. A paramedic crouched by him on the damp carpet and in a quiet voice she explained that Maddy had left Emily in the bath for a second or two to answer the telephone. The suckers on the bottom of the bath seat had come unstuck and Emily had fallen out and slipped under the water by the time she came back. They weren't sure exactly how long for, but they were going to take her to hospital.

Max stood up and took Maddy's hands as they watched a paramedic carry their baby daughter to the ambulance.

24

MADDY: OCTOBER 2019

After Maddy has dropped Emily at school, she checks Facebook and Instagram. Alison has already posted a selfie at the charity shop she works in, showing all the bags of people's stuff she needs to sort through that morning.

Without hesitation, Maddy jumps in the car and heads straight to their house again. She waits in the adjacent road to see if anyone else goes in or comes out. Part of her is willing Max to turn up so she can have it out with him. She can't believe she's here again snooping around, but the urge to know why this bitch is with her husband is overwhelming. There's not a minute of the day when she's not thinking about them together. His lies are gnawing away at her, constricting her chest as though, between the two of them, they're squeezing the life out of her. How could she have been blind to his deceit? She believed they were comfortable and happy together, that they trusted each other. What a fool, thinking any man could be any better than her cheating father.

Once inside, she knows her way around. The layout is similar to hers, so he didn't make too many mistakes no doubt. She closes the front door quietly, empties her pocket of biscuits for Poppy. Such a beautiful dog, but he seems neglected. She carries Max's ironed T-shirt and jeans upstairs and hangs them on the back of the bedroom door. See what little miss perfect makes of that. Hopefully her reaction will tell her where she thinks Max is, if she's expecting him home. Can he really be living here while pretending to be dead to her? It's still so hard to take in the enormity of it. But from all his unopened post in the kitchen, he's not been here for a while either.

She wonders when they bought the house. Must be what he used her money for. She grinds her teeth together and tries to pinpoint when all this might have begun.

Methodically, she goes around the house, opening every drawer and cupboard, searching for paperwork to give her some answers. She cannot rest until she knows how he got into this situation, if he spent the money she gave him on buying this house. It wouldn't have been that difficult for him to get a mortgage as her house was automatically paid for when her father died. She's glad now that she hasn't bothered putting Max's name on the deeds. Maybe that's the only sensible thing she's done.

Next to the bathroom she finds a cupboard with shelves full of bedding and towels haphazardly piled up. On the floor is a short filing cabinet with the key left in. She opens the top drawer and flicks through the files. Mobile phone statements, gas bills, store card statements, water rates. The mortgage statements seem to be the only ones missing. She opens the bottom drawer. Inside is a pile of unopened envelopes hidden behind a few *SkyWatch* magazines. She rips them open and checks each date. The muscle below her eye starts to twitch. The oldest is dated December 2017. The house cost £179,000 with a tidy deposit of £20,000, of her money. The mortgage is in both their names. She clenches her jaw and stuffs the papers back in. In the box room a crib has been set up with blankets and a Disney character mobile clipped to the side. Packs of disposable nappies are stacked under the dressing table, a baby bath propped up in the corner. Maddy thinks of all the things she has ready for her baby: Moses basket, new linen cloths and packets of baby wipes she's collected when they've been on offer. She smacks the mobile making it jangle awkwardly. She should chuck the whole lot of this stuff out of the window. How dare this girl think she can have a baby with her husband? She yanks open a drawer on his side of the bed and finds half a tube of cough sweets, a *Spotter's Guide to The Night Sky*, a handful of screws, coins and a used-up tube of KY Jelly. She smirks, imagining him trying to get it in, her like a dried-up flower. She laughs out loud. Her voice sounds strange in the empty house. The dog shifts positions downstairs. She guesses he's leaning against the understairs cupboard because the door rattles. A few moments later, the house is quiet again.

In Alison's bedside drawer, she picks up a leaflet for a local beauty salon, a nail file, sparkly gold nail varnish and a pair of diamante hoop earrings. She catches sight of herself in the mirror. There's nothing wrong with a natural look, it's one of the things Max said he loved about her. Or was he lying about that too, and a tart is what he really prefers? Underneath, she finds a folder of maternity notes for Alison Jane Wood. She reads through the details of her antenatal appointments, birth plan and the hospital she's booked in with, noting that the baby is due six weeks earlier than hers. She wants to rip them to shreds but she slams them down on the bed. A piece of paper flutters out. A handwritten list of mostly boys' names with numbers ranking them from one to ten. In a blink it's the page torn out of a notebook on her father's desk, beneath a jar of barley twists. She shudders at the memory of their taste.

She'd been looking for a crossword puzzle but came across a sheet of lined paper instead. On the left-hand side was a list of women's names she recognised: Judith, Jayne, Linda, Caroline, Barbara, Lisa and Bunny. Bunny was their babysitter. Linda was her mother's friend. All neighbours in their street. On the right-hand side each was scored from one to ten on their looks and, in another column, their performance in bed. She thought she would be sick right there on his ebony writing desk. Picking it up, she vowed that her mother must never know. She had to burn it. But in that same moment, she felt someone's presence behind her. Spinning round, her father was standing there, looming over her, frowning. He snatched the piece of paper out of her hand, a nasty grin distorted his face as he tapped the side of his nose.

That was the first time she realised she didn't know her daddy at all. She wished he'd dropped dead on the spot to avoid all the heartache to come.

The phone next to the bed rings, making her jump. The dog grumbles and gives a half-hearted bark. The phone rings off. She peers out of the window at a woman approaching from the house across the road. Blood drums in her ears. Moments later she can hear a key slide into the lock and the front door is opening. Maddy freezes.

'It's only me, good boy,' the woman says in a gruff smoker's voice. The dog's nametag jangles. Then silence. A foot on a stair, then another. Maddy glares at the papers strewn over the bed, the drawer hanging out like a tongue. The footsteps stop and go back down in heavy stomps. Maddy tries to swallow, but her mouth is so dry her lips stick like flypaper. She listens to the squeak of the understairs cupboard being opened then closed. After a long minute the front door rattles open then slams shut. Maddy lets out a breath and leans towards the window. The woman is waddling across the road holding a full laundry basket. She disappears around the back of her house. Maddy tidies everything away and, checking there's no one outside, she leaves the house as quickly as she can.

25

MAX: OCTOBER 2014

Max lay the baby in Emily's lap and Maddy took a photo. Another daughter. His heart could burst with joy. They'd both liked the name Chloe straight away. They didn't disagree about much at all, and he was all for an easy life.

Maddy passed the camera to him and picked Chloe up. Time to feed her again already. He'd forgotten how relentless it was at the beginning. He'd enjoyed bottle feeding Emily and wished he could help more with Chloe. Maddy was breastfeeding this time. She promised to express some milk so that he could do the next feed. Wonderful how she'd taken to it so easily. Shame she hadn't been well enough when Emily was born. It had taken several weeks for them all to get over the accident. Once Maddy was receiving treatment for postnatal depression, she slowly got better. Thankfully she wasn't showing any signs of it this time. Now he'd finished renovating the house he'd found a big contract doing up new houses in nearby Hillingdon. There were estates popping up everywhere. Even the old RAF camp in Uxbridge was going to be developed. As long as there was plenty of local work for him so he could be near his family, he was happy.

He took Emily's hand and led her into her newly painted bedroom. She'd only just started walking. They'd been worried about her slow development because of the accident, but the doctors didn't think there was anything to worry about. He sat with Emily in her play tent and they took turns dropping the brightly coloured balls down the slides. Her laugh and the surprise on her face every time the ball appeared at the bottom, was a picture.

This was the life he'd dreamed of. He'd proved to himself he could be a better person and stay out of trouble. The blokes at work ribbed him all the time for sticking at home with what they called his pipe and slippers, and yeah maybe he did miss going out and having fun sometimes, but those carefree days were over. He'd grown up and was a responsible family man now. He was sensible and straight like Maddy, nothing like his useless father. He had a lot to thank her for.

When he thought back to the flat he'd shared with Gran, he pictured damp walls and curtains that were falling down, no double glazing, draughty windows and stick-on carpet tiles. The fridge was never packed with food like it was here. Now he earned a good wage and someone to share the bills with. They were lucky not to have a mortgage; by the time Maddy inherited the house the insurance had paid it.

'Are you ready to go?' Maddy called out.

'We're coming.' He scooped Emily up and carried her down the stairs. It was almost lunchtime and a few of the mums that met at the library for story-time and crafting were meeting at the park for a teddy bears' picnic.

He strapped Emily in the car and grabbed the hamper of food and drinks. Maddy brought Chloe out in her pram car seat and strapped it in the front facing backwards. Emily had chosen the blue fluffy teddy bear they'd bought her for her first birthday. She called him Beau although she meant 'Bow' because of the large bow around his neck. It was the source of endless jokes between them.

'Can you drive today, Max, I'm feeling tired.'

'Of course. We don't have to stay too long if you don't want to.'

'I'll see how I feel. It's such a beautiful autumn day and I didn't want to let Diane down. She's been organising this for weeks.'

'You wouldn't be letting her down, she'd understand. It's only been three weeks since Chloe was born.'

'A few of us are going to talk about starting a book group. We've sort of been doing it while we were pregnant, but we don't want to let it drift away, so we thought if we made it more official, maybe invite a few other readers in and organise how often we meet et cetera, it'll give us all something more interesting to share other than weaning recipes and feeding times.'

'That sounds perfect for you.' He climbed in the driver's seat.

Maddy got in next to him.

'It is. My friend Jo and I used to spend hours discussing the books we'd read.'

'The one from school? Are you still in touch with her?' He started the car.

'No, she died in her early twenties.'

'Oh, I'm sorry.'

'Cervical cancer.'

'Shit, that's young. So this new book group could be in her honour?'

'Yeah, I like that idea. I'll see what the others think.'

'Do they realise you've practically got your own library?'

Maddy laughed. 'Those old books of Dad's? I don't think they'd be interested. They're more into the latest crime series or contemporary romances.'

He only read DIY books or newspapers, but as long as she was happy, so was he.

The other mums and dads were already there when they arrived. Diane jumped up to greet them, kissing them on both cheeks. She always managed to look like she'd stepped off a French catwalk. After lots of hugging and cooing at Chloe, they joined the rest of the group on the picnic blanket. An array of home-made food was already spread out. Max held Chloe while Maddy offered round the quiche and lemon sponge they'd made that morning.

After they'd eaten, Max fed Chloe her bottle while Maddy chatted about the new book club. Diane made notes on an A4 pad. They decided after a lot of discussion to meet once a month and take turns choosing a book. Once a year they would select the book they all enjoyed the most and give it the 'Jo Sawyer Best Read

Award' in memory of Maddy's school friend. He was pleased to see Maddy back to her old self, making plans with her friends. He wanted to support her as much as he could.

When they returned home, he insisted that Maddy go and get some sleep while he put the girls to bed. Although she was doing well, he was aware that if she became overtired, she could slip into depression again and he wanted to do everything he could to avoid it.

It was the best part of the day for him, reading them bedtime stories, making up silly voices then watching them drift off to sleep. He hoped Gran was looking down on him, happy to see how lucky he was and that he'd not turned out so bad after all.

26

ALISON: OCTOBER 2019

Alison unlocks the front door and cracks open the silence. Jamie runs in and switches on the television. She's not keen on the amount he watches but is grateful he's not asked for a phone yet, even though some of his friends have them already. She doesn't need another expense. Eight seems far too young anyway. Poppy is asleep on the sofa. He gives one bark as an afterthought.

'Great flipping guard dog you are,' she says. There's a strange, sweet aroma in the air. Sandra must have been round for the ironing, wearing some god-awful hairspray. She guesses Adam's not home, but she stands at the bottom of the stairs and calls out to him anyway. Still with her coat on, she wanders into the kitchen. The post is in a neat pile on the edge of the worktop. Adam's post has been opened. The washing up has been done and the clothes from the dryer are folded in a basket. The kettle is still warm. Must have just missed him. She lets the dog out of the back door and slams it shut. Thinks it's all right to breeze in when she's not here and not bother to leave her a note, does he? Not one reply to her texts to see if they're okay. Jamie comes in pestering for a drink. She pours him a beaker of orange juice.

Upstairs, a pair of Adam's jeans and a T-shirt are hanging on the back of their bedroom door. He'll be back later full of excuses. She changes out of her work clothes and sits on the bed, throwing herself back on the mountain of cushions. She'll tell him she doesn't mind if they don't get married, even though she's found the perfect dress. She clicks her phone and it's there, glistening on the screen. It's gorgeous and it would so suit her. Obviously not right now, but one day. After the baby is born, he might change his mind. But as long as they're all together as a family, that's the most important thing. This is the longest he's been away without calling. He's more than pissed off with her. A creeping chill runs up her spine. What if he doesn't come back?

Downstairs, she shouts at Jamie that he's standing

too close to the television. He's holding his football under his arm and the patio door is open. In the kitchen, she rummages in the back of a drawer to find a pack of cigarettes tucked under a magazine. There's one left. She can't believe she wants to smoke, but she needs it. She can stop again. Secretly, she hopes Adam's started again too.

She stands outside the patio door and is about to light up when the baby kicks her. Shit, what is she doing? She stuffs the cigarette back in the packet, breaking it in the process. Serves her right.

'Where's Dad?' Jamie whines. It's hard to know what to say to him. He gives her a blank face every time she says his dad's at work. The scrubby grass that died in the summer has turned to mud, churned over by the dog running in circles. There's a square of lawn left and a tangle of plants they don't know the names of. Adam isn't much of a gardener after all and neither is she. Somewhere for Jamie to play, that's what they decided when they moved in. If he's not coming back, she'll have it cemented over. She steps back inside and slides the door closed. Most evenings, lately, after Jamie is tucked up in bed, she browses fashion websites and buys a few bits and bobs to cheer herself up. They can't really afford it, but a few more pounds here and there isn't going to make much difference. If Adam were here, they would watch television after dinner or listen to music, usually his choice, Snow Patrol or Coldplay. She knows she should check up to see what bills have been paid and how much is left in the joint account, but Adam normally deals with the money side of things. Her shifts at the charity shop only cover a quarter of the mortgage and a few bills at a stretch, so there's not much she can do about it until she talks to him. She daren't even look at her credit card statement.

Once she's confirmed her order for slipper socks and a new scarf and gloves, she makes herself a hot chocolate and sits on the sofa to sketch last night's dream, still vivid and disturbing in her mind. That bloody apple tree. She's convinced it's haunted, or there's some bad karma about it. Adam said it was so old the developers decided to keep it, especially as it fell within their boundaries for a garden. But it gives her the creeps.

In the dream, she could make out a face etched in the bark: a wide, twisted smile as the tree came to life. It bowed down and picked up little children, placed them on its branches, but the tree turned nasty, dropping them to the ground, breaking their bones. It's been months since Jamie's accident, but that day still haunts her.

Her AI sketch book is almost full. She's done most of it while Adam's been away. He'd be impressed. Rob thinks she should see if they'll include her work in the local artists' exhibition at the library. She's not that good though.

As she draws, she listens out for the front door, hoping to hear Adam's key turn in the lock. She glances up from her sketch pad at the French windows. It's almost dark outside. The parasol Adam never bothered to put away is flapping in the wind. A duplicate of the room is reflected in the black glass; the sofa, TV, houseplants and lights look like they are out in the garden, overlapping images of reality.

From where she is sitting, the tree isn't visible and even standing at the window, her ghostly face looking back at her, she imagines its branches reaching out towards her. If someone were standing out there, looking in, she wouldn't be able to see them.

The room is quiet except for the sound of Poppy snuffling then licking the floor. What if someone was watching her? She's all alone in the house with a child; it would only take someone to note her movements to know that. She wants curtains. He's always said no because of the extra expense but three panels of voiles would surely be better than nothing?

She sits back at her drawing pad and sketches the

features in the bark. She believes that if she can get this down, she'll stop dreaming about it. Her hand moves quickly across the paper, smudging here, pressing more heavily there. She draws the children sitting under the tree, not wounded as in the dream, but smiling and laughing. If they had an axe in the shed, she'd like to go outside and chop the bloody thing down. Adam would go mental, but she must keep Jamie safe. Adam said he understands her fears, but that boys need to climb trees. She often wonders how they would have coped had things turned out worse that day. The thought of it makes her shiver. She stares at the front door, willing him to walk in.

27

MADDY: OCTOBER 2019

Maddy takes her mum's Liberty print scarf out of her dressing table drawer and wraps it around her neck and shoulders. She's started wearing the garnet necklace Mum wore every day too. It's in the shape of a heart and outlined with tiny diamonds. Feeling close to Mum will give her the strength she needs to get through this nightmare.

She's promised to take Emily to a soft play centre after school. Not her usual one, she tells her in the car on the way, but a new one she's heard about in Huntingdon. According to Alison's kitchen calendar, Jamie will be there for a birthday party, so Maddy thought it would be the perfect opportunity to meet him. While she was last having a good look around their house, she made a note of Alison's phone number from the top of her credit card statement because she never knows when she might need it.

They pull into the industrial estate and park in front of Wacky Warehouse. Emily bounces out of the car with excitement. Inside it's packed with screaming children and loud pulsing pop music. She takes Emily's shoes and coat and lets her run off into the ball pit, while she keeps an eye on her as she navigates through mesh tunnels with hordes of children.

It's not long before she spots the boy, pulling himself up a slide. A child is sitting at the top waiting. Jamie's distinctive golden hair is stuck to his forehead with sweat. He turns around and slides down. The younger boy launches himself after him, his socked feet thudding into Jamie's back. There's no sign of Alison.

'Hello Jamie.' Maddy smiles and holds out a hand to him. He's turned to shout at the boy behind but thinks better of it and frowns at her. She moves her hand closer to him. 'Grab hold.'

He takes her hand, and she pulls him to his feet. When they are facing each other, she stops and blinks at him. Seeing him this close up is a shock. He's so like Max.

'Are you all right? He gave you quite a kick,' she stumbles over the words.

'Do I know you?' Jamie mumbles.

'I know your dad. You probably don't remember me. Is he here?'

'No, Mum brought me. She's gone shopping. I'm with Ethan for his party.' He points at some children, but there are so many, he could mean anyone.

'How do you know my dad again?' His cheeks flush.

'Oh, from years ago, we err... worked together. You'll tell him you bumped into me, won't you?'

'I don't know when he'll be home.' He says it in a sullen accusing way.

'So, where is he?' She rubs her hands together then twists them round, trying hard to suppress her impatience and irritation. She wonders if she grabs his shoulders and shakes him, he'll answer her questions more quickly.

'Working again, but I want him to come home. He doesn't tell Mum when that will be and she moans at me all the time.' He whinges like a teenager but he's not even ten. How easy it would be to say she knows where Daddy is and why doesn't he come with her to see him.

Behind him, Emily is coming down a slide. Maddy

waves at her, but by the time she reaches the bottom, Jamie has run off into a crowd of children and she's lost sight of him. She berates herself. How could she think of doing such a terrible thing?

'Where were you, Mum, I couldn't see you?' Emily says.

'Sorry, I didn't see where you went.' They buy muffins and drinks at the cafe and sit at a table near the area reserved for parties, where Jamie is eating nuggets and chips. A woman comes out with a huge cake and the children sing 'Happy Birthday'. Some of the parents arrive but there's no sign of Alison. The birthday boy hands out party bags to the children leaving. Jamie is still sitting down drinking and eating his slice of cake. Perhaps Alison has been held up in rush-hour traffic?

Before long there are only three children left waiting for their parents. The birthday boy is already opening his presents from the enormous stack on the table, while his last guests look on. One of the teenagers who works there is going around the tables with a black bag, clearing away all the paper plates of uneaten food and drink. The mum is holding a list while speaking on her mobile. Maddy hears her say to a ginger-haired boy that his dad is on his way. 'It's your mum picking you up, isn't it?' she then says to Jamie.

He nods but doesn't seem worried, as though he's used to being abandoned.

'Come with me,' Maddy says to Emily when she's finished her juice. She takes her hand and practically drags her over to the sectioned-off area. Jamie is sitting on his own now. 'He can come with me.' She touches his shoulder with her fingertips.

The mum looks up at her, then at Emily.

'I know where he lives. Alison is probably stuck in traffic and can't answer her phone.'

'She didn't mention anyone else picking him up, I can't just...'

'She knows my dad.' Jamie shrugs.

'And you are?' The woman is staring at Maddy as though she's a serial killer.

'Family friend. Don't worry, though, if it's a problem.' Maddy casually flicks her hand. She gives Jamie a sorry look and turns to leave. What on earth is she doing? Where would she have taken him? She squeezes Emily's hand and tries to blink away dark blotches in front of her eyes.

Alison is marching towards her. Maddy turns away just in time. 'So sorry I'm late,' Alison says loudly, waving as she pushes past Maddy, thankfully not noticing her, and Maddy doesn't stop to look back.

28

MAX: MARCH 2017

Max could hear Maddy upstairs reading to the girls when he came in.

'Daddy!' Chloe ran along the landing to greet him. He picked her up and gave her a hug.

'Mummy's reading *Alice*,' Chloe told him.

'*Alice in Wonderland?*'

'Wonderful land.' She giggled.

He put her down and she took his hand, pulling him into Emily's bedroom, where Maddy was sitting at the end of the bed holding the illustrated hardback from her own childhood. 'You're early,' she said. He bent down and kissed her cheek. 'Hello, Daddy,' Emily said, standing on the bed, arms wide for a cuddle. He kissed her forehead and hugged her.

'We finished the job up in Ely, so I came straight home.' He winked.

Chloe got in bed next to Emily and picked up her comfort blanket, a sure sign she was ready for sleep. Maddy continued reading the part where Alice opens the little door and sees the beautiful garden.

Max crept out. In their bedroom, he changed his clothes. He'd been working such long hours since Chloe was born. They were a happy little trio, sometimes he felt left out, like he was intruding.

'Your dinner is in the oven,' Maddy called out to him from the landing.

He came and took Chloe from her, but she was already asleep, so he carried her to bed.

Downstairs, Maddy took his dinner out and put it on a tray. The Cumberland sausage, sweet potato and peas looked dry, but he didn't say anything. It had probably been cooked hours before.

'Shall I make you gravy?' she said, reading his mind. 'Please.' He took a Guinness out of the fridge and popped the can open. The kitchen table was full of crafting stuff, as usual; two painted animal masks cut from old cereal packets were drying on newspaper on one side and on the other stood a plastic tub full of old milk cartons cut in half and filled with earth.

'What's in those?' he asked, pouring his drink into a glass.

'We thought we'd grow our own sweet peppers on the windowsill,' Maddy said. 'I'll have a glass of wine if you're offering.'

Later, they sat in front of the television. Maddy turned over to *Endeavour*. He'd have preferred *Top Gear*.

Maddy picked up her knitting. She was always making or mending something and teaching the girls how to do it too. It was the sort of thing his gran used to do. Saving money and saving the earth, Maddy always said.

The clicking needles weaving a symmetrical pattern distracted him. Maddy worked at such a rapid rate. Her mud-stained nails showed up against the cream-coloured wool. It had been a long time since they'd been out together, just the two of them, but Maddy didn't seem bothered. He often suggested going to a restaurant, but she was always too tired or would rather cook something at home and watch a film on TV. She didn't care about her appearance like she used to. She wore the same pair of jeans most days and it must have been months since she last went to a hairdresser's or wore make-up. It didn't matter that much to him, but sometimes he wondered if she was still a bit depressed. She'd never been quite the same since Emily's accident. He wished they could talk more, or even watch the same crap on TV, but they didn't agree on much of anything these days. All he seemed to do was work and sleep. But he didn't like to complain. He was grateful for this new contract in Cambridgeshire, to be able to bring home a good wage. He wanted to give his children everything he never had and then some.

'Have the dogs been for a walk?' he asked, when her programme finished.

'Yes,' she said. 'I'm off to bed.'

Long gone were the days when they went up together. He moved from the chair to the sofa and lay down, flicking through channels until he fell asleep.

* * *

On Friday, Max finished a long day on a job in Brampton and agreed to join Tom and Bob in one of his old haunts, The White Hart, in nearby Huntingdon. Work with John around Uxbridge had slowed down over the last couple of weeks but luckily, he'd landed this new contract with his old mates.

It was already busy with early evening drinkers. Fortunately, he didn't recognise anyone. He didn't fancy bumping into any of the Wood family, except Ali of course. Now that would make his day. Shit. What a bastard he was thinking that.

All week he'd been working late to get a new home finished and a swift pint with the boys wasn't going to hurt anyone. Bob and Tom followed him to a table near the open fire. The low-beamed ceiling looked like it had been given a recent lick of paint. Shelves of antique gardening tools lined the walls. Must be under new management. Maddy would be in her element. 'Cheers Adam,' Tom said, lifting his pint of bitter. Max chinked glasses with him, then Bob.

'Yeah, cheers.' Bob downed half his drink in one go. 'God, I needed that,' he said, and wiped his mouth on his sleeve. 'Hey, is that Kath over there?' He nudged Tom's elbow. Plaster dust puffed out of his overalls.

'Looks like it. Do you want me to call her over?'

'Yeah, go on, see if she's got that blonde mate with her.'

Tom gave a wolf whistle. The woman glanced round smiling. She put her hand on her hip and held a pose in her leatherette minidress and knee-high patent boots.

'Looking good, girl,' Bob said, slapping his knee that was jogging up and down like a piston. She slid herself onto his leg, but it didn't stop moving. Bob's face flushed under his dark skin.

'Where's your mate today, Kath?' he asked.

'And I thought you wanted to see me,' she said, standing up.

'Don't go.' Bob pulled her back.

'Here she is,' she said and released herself from his grip.

Max watched a blonde saunter towards them. She seemed familiar but he couldn't place her.

'Hiya guys,' she said in an imitation Texan drawl.

'I should be getting off.' Max stood up.

'Going so soon?' said the blonde, easing herself into his chair.

She crossed her tanned legs.

'You're no fun, mate,' Tom said. 'I reckon he's going home to his pipe and slippers.' They all laughed.

He imagined Maddy in the garden with the girls helping her water the flowers. She wouldn't mind if he had another drink. She'd tell him he deserved it for working so hard.

He drained his glass and worked his way over to the bar, squeezing past a group of bikers. A short, squat man with a ring through his nose shoved into Max, winding him.

'Better watch yourself, mate,' the man said. Max was about to reply, but the man had gone.

He cradled his stomach and held out a ten pound note to attract the barman. His sleeve inched back showing the small tattoo on the inside of his wrist. It had been months since he'd thought about Ali. He tried to picture what she would look like now. If she was married too. It was natural to be curious, wasn't it? Especially considering their relationship ended so abruptly. Why couldn't she be in here tonight?

'Don't let them get to you,' said a voice at his side. The blonde leaned on the bar next to him. 'I'm Jaz, Jasmine.'

'Adam. What can I get you?' He pointed in the direction of the colourful line of bottles.

'It's okay, I can get my own. I don't do rounds.'

'This isn't a round. I don't expect one back.'

'What do you expect then?' She smiled pouting. Out of her lacy fingerless gloves sprouted slender hands and long black-red nails.

'I expect you to drink it and be grateful,' he said with a smile.

She laughed. 'I don't accept charity, but I'll make an exception. Whiskey. Neat.'

'I've not seen you down here before.'

'You've not had your eyes open then.'

She was what you'd call confident. He openly looked her up and down. Tight denim minidress and stilettos. He caught a glimpse of her cleavage and looked away. No bra. She knocked the whiskey back in one go, slamming the glass on the table.

'You married?' she asked.

'What do you think?' He fingered his wedding ring in his pocket. He always took it off for work.

'I don't think you're the type,' she said.

* * *

He wasn't quite sure how he got there, but he ended up at Jaz's flat sometime after midnight. When he woke, he found his legs were threaded through hers. At least it wasn't morning yet. He scanned the room. In the darkness he could make out a heap of clothes on a chair.

He eased himself out of bed. What the fuck was he going to say to Maddy?

'Going so soon?' said a croaky voice from under the duvet. He glanced behind him as he pulled his T-shirt from the chair, causing the whole pile to fall.

'I'm meant to be somewhere,' he said, untangling his overalls. 'I should never have dozed off.'

'That's a good sign, isn't it?' she said, pulling back the sheets.

'Maybe. Look...' He stood over the bed, trying not to look at the inviting creaminess of her skin.

'I know. It's a one-off; you're with someone. Happens to me all the time.'

'Sorry.' He squinted, trying not to sound so grateful.

'Still, fulfilled a schoolgirl's dream.'

He frowned and pulled up his trousers.

She laughed. 'You don't remember me, do you? I wouldn't expect you to. I had fuzzy red hair and buck teeth.'

'Do we know each other?'

'Everyone knew who you were. Dated Ali Wood on and off for years, broke all our hearts.'

He laughed nervously. He still couldn't think who she was.

'Wait until I tell Ali I bumped into you.'

'You... you see her?' He switched the bedside light on and leaned over her.

'Yeah, although she doesn't live here any more. Moved away, cut herself off from her crackpot family completely. Don't blame her. She was well out of it. Their cab fleet business got raided and the loan shark side was uncovered, whole lot of them were banged up.'

'Really, what even her dad?'

'Yeah, amazing, isn't it. About time too, I say, like the bloody mafia they were.'

'Yeah, tell me about it. So, when do you see her?' He was close enough to see a pierced hole above her lip.

'She visits sometimes, lives near Peterborough, so not a million miles away.'

'What's her number?' He took out his phone. It wasn't a question – he had no intention of leaving until she'd given it to him.

'I don't think she'll want to see you, to be honest.'

'Shall we let her decide that?' Crafty cow, not telling him about Ali earlier. He remembered her now, always flirting with him. Jealous as hell of Ali and her petite figure.

'Why'd you leave her anyway?' She reached down to the floor for her handbag.

'She didn't tell you?'

'Always thought you two would tie the knot.'

'You said I wasn't the marrying kind.'

Jaz gave a smirk. 'She disappeared, then you disappeared. So what really happened?'

'Nothing for you to worry about.'

'You'll have to tell me if you want her number.'

They stared each other out, but he couldn't help himself, he caved in and told her.

She scribbled on a pad of paper by the bed. 'Here.' She held it out to him and yawned.

Max looked at the numbers as if they were the winning combination for the lottery.

'Don't tell her' – he waved a finger between them – 'you know.'

'That you slept with her friend? I'll be sure not to mention it.'

'Don't say it like that. I'd just rather keep this our little secret.'

* * *

When Max reached home, he slipped into bed next to Maddy without disturbing her. He lay wide awake, heart pounding. Had he got away with it? He wasn't bothered if he never saw Jaz again, but Ali... Ali.

The bed creaked as Maddy turned towards him, her face chubby with curved lines of sleep. He listened to her rhythmic breathing. Her eyes were shut, but he felt she was watching him. He tried to sleep, but scenes from the past played out in his mind over and over. He couldn't block them out. It wasn't until the first bird-song when, at last, sleep claimed him.

A few hours later, Max woke up. He could hear the girls playing in the garden. Ali had appeared in his dream, but not as he remembered her. She'd looked much older, and he was standing by a river, but she walked straight past him as though she didn't know who he was. Did he look so different? He climbed out of bed and gazed in the mirror, drawing his hand down his mouth and stubbly chin. One or two brilliant white hairs, a few lines around his eyes. He didn't look so bad, did he? He went over every moment of meeting Jaz and everything he could remember afterwards. What an idiot, going back to her place. A sick feeling lodged deep in his stomach that wouldn't shift.

* * *

When he surfaced, he expected to get an earful from Maddy, but she didn't ask what time he'd come home. Sometimes it seemed like she was happier with it being just her and the girls and didn't really care if he was around or not.

After lunch, he told her he was going to sort out his painting gear ready for his next job. He often went in his shed these days for a quiet moment to himself.

He'd spent one summer insulating and painting the walls, laminating the floor. He'd even built in a skylight window and wired up electricity for a heater and kettle. Often at night, he'd sit there gazing at the sky through his telescope. He'd decked it out with a small desk and chair where he kept his binoculars and books. The walls were covered in night sky posters and moon calendars going back the last twenty years. One poster was dedicated to the total eclipse in 1999. His gran would have loved all this, especially the moon clock Maddy had bought him, which was made of recycled paper packaging. As well as showing each lunar phase, it predicted tidal heights, peak gardening times and even mood swings, which they used to joke about.

He sat down at the small desk under the window and pulled a photo of Ali out of his pocket. He'd found a couple hidden inside his old suitcase. She was wearing shorts, a T-shirt and red stilettos, smiling and posing with her hand on the bonnet of his old Ford Fiesta. Her hair hung around her shoulders like molten gold. He held the picture up as if he had the camera in his hands and she was looking right at him through the lens. That was one of their happiest times. The summer of 2008. She'd turned eighteen and had agreed to go out with him properly at long last. Everyone said she could have had the pick of her year at school. He was already working for her dad, Ron, by then. Roughing up the late payers. Ali was a no-go, he'd made that clear. But he couldn't help himself.

Chloe came running in, giving him a start. She was holding a painting, babbling something about a rainbow and a pony.

'Not now, darling, I'm in the middle of clearing up,' he said and turned away.

'What's that, Daddy?' She pointed to the photo he was holding against his leg.

'It's nothing for you.'

'Can I see?'

'It's just an old photo.'

'Please,' she whined.

'Why don't you show me your painting?'

'I want to see.' She grabbed it, but he was still holding one corner and it tore in half.

'Look what you've done!' he shouted, incredulous.

Chloe dropped the piece on the ground and ran off crying. He hadn't meant to snap but he couldn't believe she'd done that. He called her but she'd gone inside. He could hear Maddy stomping down the path. He held the two pieces together and covered them with a box of brushes.

'Max, why is Chloe so upset?' Maddy stood at the shed door, hands on hips.

'I'm sorry I was busy and she...'

'She only wanted you to look at her painting.'

'I know, I'm sorry.'

'She said you wouldn't show her some photo?'

'I told her it wasn't important.'

'Go and speak to her, Max, she's really upset.'

* * *

Chloe was in her bedroom when he went upstairs. She'd stuck a picture of the rainbow to her door and drawn big black lines of rain all over it.

'Is this your painting?' he asked.

She was sitting at her desk, drawing something else. She nodded in an exaggerated way.

'But why is it raining?'

'Because you didn't want to look at my beautiful rainbow.'

'I'm so sorry, darling.' He knelt next to her desk. 'Who is this?' He pointed to what she was drawing.

'It's me.'

'But you don't look very happy.'

'I'm not.'

'Could you draw me another picture? You're so good at rainbows and I really would like to see one after it's stopped raining.'

She took out a new sheet of paper and smiled. Max kissed the top of her head. He was so lucky to have a beautiful family. He'd moved on. He needed to leave the past well alone. Trouble was, Ali had a way of worming into his head, which was difficult to control.

29

MADDY: OCTOBER 2019

Maddy stands by the shower curtain holding a towel ready for Emily to wipe shampoo lather from her eyes. The sweet berry aroma fills the air. It's hard to believe Emily will be eight next year. It won't be long before she's self-conscious about her body and doesn't want her mother in the bathroom with her.

She doesn't let Emily have baths any more, which may be selfish, but the anxiety dreams she has about her drowning have never gone away. Max installed hand grips on either side of the bath, and they bought a long rubber mat to make sure she doesn't slip, but it doesn't stop her worrying that if she leaves the room something bad will happen.

She reaches for the garnet pendant around her

neck and rubs its cool smooth surface. In the steamed-up mirror above the sink, she can make out the outline of her mother's face. She's always been there these last few days, keeping a watchful eye over her. Only she understands what she's going through.

After Emily's accident, Maddy found out she was suffering with postnatal depression. Now and then she wonders if it made her want to harm her baby; after all, she knew not to leave the bathroom, yet she did. Emily could have died. The memories of what happened that day are fixed solid in her mind. If only Mum had been around to help her, none of these terrible things would have happened. Chloe might still be alive, too, because Mum would have noticed the early signs of meningitis. Why didn't *she* pick up on them? What kind of mother is she that she couldn't protect her children when they needed her most? Why didn't she know her husband had another family? What is *wrong* with her? She sits on the toilet seat with the towel across her lap and presses her fingers into her forehead.

She'd laid everything out ready for Emily's bath that day. Emily was three months old and loved sitting in the plastic seat she'd picked up at a baby sale. She'd just finished washing Emily and had the towel ready on her lap when her mobile rang. She remembers glancing at the bathroom door, which she'd left ajar. Her phone was out on the newel post at the top of the stairs. It could wait, she told herself. But the moment after it rang off it started ringing again. It would be Max, stuck in heavy traffic letting her know he was going to be home late. He could leave a message then she would call him back a bit later. Emily was happily splashing around with her squirty toy fish. Maddy drizzled water over Emily's shoulders making her giggle. The phone rang a third time making her jump. The tone seemed louder and much more insistent. She became convinced Max had been in a car crash and someone was calling from the hospital. Without thinking, Maddy ran out of the bathroom and grabbed the phone. In her head she'd convinced herself it would only take a second and Emily was secure in her seat. But it wasn't Max calling, it was someone churning out their sales pitch to her, *when was the last time you had your gutters cleared, madam? Would you be interested in 25 per cent off our usual price?* Their stupid questions distracted her.

'What the hell?' she shouted and hung up. She'd suddenly lost all sense of time and couldn't think how many seconds she'd been away from Emily. She could hear splashing and dashed back to the bathroom, chucking the phone on the towel. But Emily wasn't sitting up in the seat any more; the suckers had come unstuck and the whole seat had tipped forwards. Emily was lying face down in the water, arms flailing around with the seat on top of her.

Maddy swooped down and grabbed Emily's now floppy body out in a heartbeat. She screamed for help, out of the open window as she gently tipped Emily upside down, carefully supporting her body along her arm, then she smacked her back. With wet and shaking fingers Maddy managed to press 999 on her mobile and speak to the emergency services on speaker phone. A minute later, Sarah had burst in saying she'd heard Maddy's screams from the garden and let herself in through the back door. The paramedics had arrived moments later, followed by Max.

Every day she's reminded of what she did. Emily's fits are becoming more frequent. Sometimes she's a bit slower than other children. The brain damage was slight, but it should never have happened at all. She'll never forgive herself.

After Emily has gone to bed, Maddy retreats to her own bedroom and shuts the door. She pulls open her wardrobe doors. One by one, she picks out every garment and lays them on the bed in two piles. One for keeping, the other for charity. She holds up the red dress she wore when she first went out with Max and the blue shift dress with short sleeves from the evening they celebrated their engagement. Everything she's hung on to because it was precious is going. There's no longer a place for sentimentality in her life or for seeing the best in people. Not when she's been hoodwinked and humiliated. Now she knows what her mother went through and why her voice is as clear as a bell in her head. *I'm the only one who you can trust.*

She stuffs the clothes in a bin liner and when the wardrobe is almost empty, she shifts the few remaining clothes from the furthest end to the centre. Right at the back she spots her wedding dress in a clear plastic cover. She reaches for it, sliding it along and stuffs it straight into the black bag. Behind it is her mother's coney fur coat. She's clean forgotten she'd kept this. How can she let it go? If there is one garment that embodies the glamorous mother she remembers from her childhood, it is this. It's soft and luxurious between her fingers and slips easily off the hanger into her hands, releasing a faint waft of Chanel N°19, unlocking the bolt on a whole chapter of her life.

Instantly it sends her back to the theatre, her mother standing next to her, shimmying the coat from her shoulders. The three of them sitting in a stall: mother, father and her. How beautiful both her parents were. They seemed so content and happy that night. She looked up to them, wanted a marriage like theirs one day. But was it already a lie by then, had they dressed up and pretended for her benefit?

It's natural to want to try the coat on, to know how it feels. The weight of it is surprising. She rummages in a drawer for her mother's bottle of perfume and squirts it behind her ears, breathing it in. In the mirror she sways this way and that and her hands dip into the pockets. An edge of something digs under her thumbnail. She pulls out a square of paper, folded at least a dozen times. Scribbled on the outside, in her mother's perfect handwriting:

Don't trust anyone!

Maddy's body jolts. Slowly, she unfolds the paper and with a gasp lets it flutter to the ground. 'You knew all along,' she says aloud to the mirror. It's her mother looking back at her. She can hear her mother's voice saying the words: *Don't trust anyone*. Maddy slowly shakes her head. They're the words Mum kept repeating in her final days. Dementia had stolen the person she knew, but was she saying this in more lucid moments? When did she find his list? How long did she know? All that time Maddy kept his secret to protect Mother, but she already knew he was seeing these women, their own friends and neighbours. Every one of them pretending to her, arranging play dates and dinner parties. And Father, the biggest charlatan of them all. The late-night meetings and overnight stays in Bristol, Manchester and London, when all the time he was across the road in someone else's bed. Is this what Max has been doing to her? Are there other women and he's with one of them now? Or is he really dead? She picks up the piece of paper and rips through it, shredding the names into tiny pieces; all the while she is being watched in the mirror.

30

ALISON: OCTOBER 2019

When she arrives back from work on Saturday, Alison hopes to see Adam's van on the drive, but again there's no sign of it. Her heart thuds like a stone on wood. None of her friends have seen him lately. Where can he have gone? Why isn't he answering her calls and texts? The thought of calling the police crosses her mind, but if something had happened to him, they'd have contacted her, wouldn't they?

Once inside, she calls up the stairs out of habit, and for a moment she thinks she hears a muffled reply. Jamie drops his coat on the floor.

'Pick that up!' she yells at him. She unloads the shopping on the kitchen counter.

'I'm hungry,' he whines, making a half-hearted attempt to hang his coat on a peg. 'I thought you said Dad would be back.'

'If you listened, I said he might be.'

He trails after her into the kitchen and she pacifies him with a bag of crisps and sends him off to the living room. A blast of cartoon laughter roars from the TV.

The post has been sorted and Adam's opened again. So he must have been here. What is he playing at? Three parcels for her, too large for the letterbox, have been brought in and left on the side.

Again, the kettle is warm. She tops it up with cold water and switches it on. One washed mug is still damp on the drainer. Is he just not talking to her? She sends him a text for the millionth time asking what time he's back. That's odd, the spider plant on the windowsill above the sink is dead; brown shrivelled leaves hang over the edge of the pot as if they'd been gasping for water. But she can't understand it. There is water in the tray. She's made a point of checking on it every morning. It's not as if she even likes plants, but Adam keeps going on about how healthy they are for the home environment or something. The last thing she wants is for him to find them dead, she'd never hear the end of it. Maybe that's why he's mad at her? He's popped in and seen it. Usually, he'd leave her a scrawled message on the back of an envelope. Isn't she even worth that? She moves it onto the draining board. The compost is saturated. She must have overwatered it.

After a cup of tea, she starts dinner. Still no reply to her text. If he's not back any minute with a bottle of sparkling wine, there'll be trouble. She smiles imagining him coming up behind her, kissing her neck and she'll inhale the musky eau de toilette she adores.

As soon as the ready meals and chips are in the oven, she checks on Jamie in the living room. He's lying upside down on the sofa watching cartoons, his feet stretched out up the back. Her friends are coming over later to throw her a baby shower. She ought to tidy up a bit.

'Don't you have any homework?'

'Nah.'

She takes out his school journal. 'What about maths?'

'Oh yeah.'

'Five minutes, then switch that off, do you hear?' As she turns, she notices the flowering plant behind the door. The pot is surrounded by shrivelled leaves with marks like burns. She reaches down and picks up the giant pot. The rotten smell makes her turn her head. Perhaps it was too near the radiator. But to die that quickly... How odd. She never liked it though. If plants would only stop growing and trying to take over the house. When one has died in the past it's been more of a gradual process, except the plant which grew so big she decided she couldn't be bothered with it any more. Every time she had to squeeze past it in the hall it left pollen on her clothes. In the end she left it outside in the frost to die. Adam's never forgiven her.

'Dinner,' she calls. It's not until she's dishing up that the tears come. She hurls her plate across the kitchen, the steaming food flying up the wall, lumps of tomato like clots of blood, pieces of spaghetti hanging like tassels. He must hate her to stay away this long and not even bother to call her. She needs to know they're okay and can carry on as normal. She won't mention weddings or rings or honeymoons, if that's what it's about. She'll promise to be happy with the way things are.

31

Julie arrives at Alison's early with a handful of helium balloons. She arranges them around the sitting room ceiling with their alternating pink and blue ribbons curling down. Alison is not in the mood for a party, but Julie has gone to loads of trouble. She helps out by emptying bags of nuts, crisps and Bombay mix into bowls.

'You're not supposed to be doing anything. Go and get yourself ready.' Julie checks her watch.

Upstairs, Alison looks in the mirror: blue-black circles under her eyes from lack of sleep and her face is fuller with this pregnancy, almost bloated. She looks a mess. As she pulls her T-shirt off, a strong twinge tightens around her bump. She grips the back of the chair. Adam will be back in time, Julie keeps telling her. Perhaps he's waiting to give her a surprise. But she's fed up with his bloody games. Does he think she's stupid or what? If he doesn't turn up by the time she has the baby, she's not sure she'll want him at all. She needs to be with someone who worships her, that's what Dad always told her.

Once the pain has subsided, she opens the wardrobe. A stack of unopened mail order bags falls out. Shit, Adam must have been in here. He'll be mad with her for spending more money on the credit card. No wonder he's not getting back to her. She could say they're Christmas presents, that's why she's not opened them. But the truth is, she's gone on another mad spending spree trying to make herself feel better. He's making her unhappy. Strange that he found them though, she'd deliberately hidden them at the back. She pushes them aside and takes out a new white top she's been dying to wear because she loves the slogan across the front in gorgeous white diamante lettering: *the pitter patter of tiny feet*. She curls her hair and reapplies her make-up, finishing by applying berry-coloured lip gloss.

She comes downstairs, to a soft inviting scent. Julie has dimmed the lights and lit special candles in the living room, making it look magical.

'Do you like it?' Julie has changed from jeans into a satin wrap-over dress.

'The house looks and smells gorgeous, thanks honey.' She gives Julie a hug. On the dining room table, pram-shaped confetti is scattered around a stack of wooden bricks which spell 'Baby' and 'Charlie', the name she has chosen without Adam. It'll be perfect, whether it is a boy or a girl.

Jaz is the first to arrive and is already a bit tipsy, followed by Louise, a girl with thick red hair they know from school.

'Where is that lovely man of yours?' Jaz says. She's wearing a leather studded miniskirt and a white see-through blouse.

'Away on business,' Alison says.

'Surely not. When you're about to drop? Hey that rhymes.' She giggles and drops down on the sofa.

'Keep your trap shut,' Julie hisses.

'You look blooming marvellous in any case.' Jaz stands up again and helps herself to a glass of bubbly from the table.

'Why don't I get you a glass of water, Jasmine?' Julie says.

'Good to see you, Jaz.' Alison takes the oddly shaped gift from her. Julie steers Jaz by the elbow into the kitchen.

When everyone has arrived, Julie shows Alison onto a chair which is decorated like a throne. 'Time you put your feet up,' she says. One of the mums brings in a pink fluffy footstool, made specially for her.

'That's lovely, thank you.'

'But before you sit down, you need to put this on.' Julie places a sash saying *Mummy 2 B* over Alison's head and straightens it out across her bump. All the girls clap and cheer.

'Open the presents then.' Jaz claps her hands like an excited five-year-old.

'Ali will open a present before each game.' Julie refers to her list. 'So, which one would you like first?'

'It has to be this one, I suppose.' Alison picks up the odd-shaped present from Jaz, who is busy knocking back a large vodka. Alison unwraps a V-shaped pillow and cover.

'It's good for when you're breast-feeding, apparently,' says Jaz, 'but also great for getting in all those Kama Sutra positions.'

Everyone groans.

'She won't need it for a while then, will she?' Louise says, and everyone laughs.

'I'm sure Adam has a healthy appetite.' Jaz grins and finishes her drink.

Julie glares at her.

'So, the first game is called the Prediction Game.' Julie hands out a card to each guest. 'You need to fill in which date you think baby Charlie will be born, what time, what he or she will weigh, eye colour, hair colour and, of course, sex.'

Everyone starts scribbling on their cards.

'Do you realise, Ali,' says Jaz, waving her card above her head, 'you wouldn't even be pregnant if I hadn't bumped into Adam.'

'I know, you've told me a hundred times.' Alison smiles and rolls her eyes. Everyone tuts.

'Shame he didn't find out about Jamie sooner, isn't it?' Jaz swallows another drink. 'Missed out a whole big chunk of his life.'

'Will you shut up?' Julie hisses.

'Shame Daddy told him you'd had an abortion, then paid him to leave.'

'How do you know that?' Alison moves to the edge of her chair.

'Jaz, I'm warning you…' Julie points at her.

'Do you think that's why he hasn't married you?' Jaz puts her glass on the table and flops backwards.

There's a long silence. Alison turns her card face down on the table and eases herself up. 'What a shame, Jasmine. You used to be such a pretty girl.' She reaches over and plucks a hair extension from Jaz's head.

'Fuck me, that hurt!' Jaz presses her hands above her ear.

'Get out!' Alison shouts and jabs Jaz's head with her elbow.

Jaz shrieks and clutches her ear.

'Call me down when she's gone.' Alison leaves the room, watching as she climbs the stairs.

'You've had more than enough to drink. I'm calling you a cab.' Julie picks up the phone. Jaz rubs her head, looking around at all the faces staring at her.

* * *

It's almost midnight by the time Alison goes to bed. Again, no message or call from Adam. Jaz is right, Dad lied to him and paid him to stay away. But she thought they'd got past that and were committed to each other. He hadn't been pleased about the baby though, had he? But why bother calling in while she's out? Can't he tell her if he wants to end it? She cries herself to sleep but wakes again an hour later with the sound of a car revving. The dog barks, padding up and down the laminate floor, groaning as he lies back down.

She peers out of the window on the landing and

spots a car parked opposite. Someone gets out and stands in the road. She can't tell if it's a man or a woman because it's too dark except for the yellow glow of a streetlight halfway down the road. It can't be Adam, not tall enough and this person is plump. What are they doing here?

A roll of thunder rumbles far off in the night, then a flash of lightning darts through the landing. The rain begins lightly, playing a tune on the dormer roof, tinkling on the pipes. Soon it is heavy, slicing the sky with iron sheets, blurring her vision. But still the person stands there not moving, taking the beating rain on their head like a punishment.

Alison runs to the spare room. Her heart flicks into an uncomfortable rhythm – too fast for her body to contain. She peeks out and the person is looking straight up at her, startling her, so she steps back into the safety of the shadows. Sitting on the bed, she puts a hand on her bump to soothe the kicking baby.

After several minutes, she looks outside again. The person and the car have vanished. Relieved, she presses her chest and the bursting heartbeat begins to subside. The baby settles down when she rubs her bump and whispers that everything will be fine, Daddy will be home soon. She goes back to bed hoping he will be, that whatever she's done, he'll be able to forgive her and start afresh with their new baby. She doesn't want to bring up another one of his children without him. Lying there, she listens to the comforting sounds of a motorbike speeding in the distance and the musical drip, drip, dripping of rain from the gutter.

32

MAX: APRIL 2017

Max sat in his van dialling Ali's number from his mobile. In all the days he'd been trying, he'd got through once, but the line went dead. If he had to, he'd go and see Jaz. She must have given him a dodgy number. He knew she didn't really want to put them back in touch.

With every flash of blonde hair, he imagined Ali. His pulse quickened each time he thought of her. When he closed his eyes, he could smell the soft musky scent she always wore. And that laugh of hers that made his heart fly. He had to stop this. He was with Maddy now. But Ali was unfinished business. They'd had something special. If he could see her once, it would be enough. To know those bastards hadn't messed her up. To know she was all right after the abortion. Six years. She'd be twenty-six now and almost certainly not single. Not someone like Ali. One more try. After two rings, an answerphone kicked in. It was her voice. An elastic band pinged in his chest. She sounded chirpy and professional, as if he'd called some fancy office. 'Ali, it's me,' Max said after the beep. He hesitated, 'Adam.' Tom banged his fist on the van door as he walked past. Eight o'clock.

If he wasn't on time he'd have to forfeit lunch. He repeated his mobile number and finished the call.

The elderly woman made them an endless supply of tea that was so weak it tasted like warm milk. They joked about it when she left the room. Bob said it tasted more like brush water. Max climbed a ladder to steam off the thick wallpaper. His mobile phone buzzed.

'Can you get that?' Max said, jabbing at the crusted paper, trying to loosen it up.

Bob picked the phone up. 'What's her name, lover boy?' he said waving the phone in the air. He undid his overalls and shimmied around with it down to his shoulders, showing the tattoo of a dotted line around his neck and the words, 'Cut Here'. The men wolf whistled.

Max stomped down the ladder. 'Give it here.' He

snatched the phone, but it rang off. There was no message. Max shoved him away and chucked the phone on the mantelpiece. He climbed back up the ladder.

'Everything all right?' the woman said in the doorway.

'No problem, just a bit of friendly banter. Sorry if we disturbed you,' Tom said. The woman gave a weak smile and shut the door.

'Come on, Bob, Adam, let's get this paper off.' Tom waved his steamer at them.

If Ali hadn't called by the end of the day, he'd try again. He picked up the steamer and pressed the button but nothing came out. He pressed again and turned it over. A blast of steam shot into his face.

'Fucking hell,' he screamed and dropped it on the floor, his hands shaking, hovering inches from his face.

'Quick,' shouted Tom. He and Bob dragged Max down the ladder and out of the room. They rushed him to the kitchen. 'Excuse us, accident.'

'Goodness. Can I help?' the woman asked.

'Please call an ambulance, as quick as you can, he's burnt his face.'

Tom turned the tap on full and in seconds Max's face was plunged into cold water.

'Get some ice cubes,' Tom shouted and pulled

Max's head up for a few seconds. 'Breathe,' he said in Max's ear.

Then he was in the water again, ice cubes bobbing against his raw skin. The men's voices muffled, blood pumping loudly in his ears. He didn't recognise the miniature scarlet face in the shiny plug, the swollen slit eyes reflecting back at him. He couldn't breathe. He grabbed at Tom's sleeve and tugged hard. The pressure on the back of his head eased and he lifted his head. He took in a deep breath. The water on his skin burned like acid. Tom pushed him in again.

At last the burning sensation began to subside as his face became numb.

'The ambulance is here,' he heard Bob say.

Tom pulled Max up and shoved a towel into his hands. 'Catch the drips,' he said. 'Don't touch your face with it.'

They sat him back in a chair and he caught a glimpse of the elderly woman staring at him, like a ghost standing in the corner waiting to take him to the next world. His face started burning again. As if answering his prayer, a paramedic appeared in front of him with what looked like a piece of skin. He placed it on Max's face, moulding it gently around his nose and eyes. It soothed the pain while he was led to the ambulance. As the doors closed, all Max could think of was his mobile phone left on the mantelpiece.

33

MADDY: OCTOBER 2019

The day dawned with a widespread frost over much of the British Isles with freezing fog in places. A light sprinkle of snowfall quickly turned to rain as the temperature rose. Snow has been heavy in parts of Wales, Scotland and Northern England.

Maddy switches off the radio.

These trips are becoming a daily occurrence, but she can't help herself. She's constantly on high alert. Her family has been invaded. No wonder it's impossible to sleep. Sitting behind the wheel is getting more uncomfortable as the bump grows bigger. She ought to be at home with her feet up instead, but she needs to find out where Max is and what he's been doing with this woman all these months, why he's been lying to her.

Her drive to Huntingdon is taking much longer than usual because everyone is driving slowly. Today, she can't afford to be late. Everything is arranged. In her head she can hear her mother's voice advising her on what to do to make this bitch suffer.

When she arrives in Lawn End, the Nissan is still on the drive. According to Alison's kitchen calendar, she has the morning off. Good, at least she's not gone out, as she worried she might. Maddy parks at the end of the road, keeping the front door and driveway in view.

While she's waiting, she opens Facebook and checks Alison's page. Checking her page has become automatic. There's still nothing to indicate that she knows where Max is. She doesn't expect him to have a Facebook account under his Adam name, but she checks through Alison's whole list of 573 friends just in case. She must be used to him being away for long periods because about 70 per cent of the time Max was with Maddy.

Alison's posted a message on a colourful background in shouty text:

HAS ANYONE SEEN ADAM? HE'S NOT BEEN IN TOUCH FOR WEEKS, BUT IT LOOKS LIKE HE'S BEEN COMING IN THE HOUSE WHILE I'M OUT!!! WHAT'S GOING ON???

Maddy scrolls down. Alison has posted photos of his jeans and ironed T-shirt and opened pile of post. There's another post that she added that Maddy didn't see before:

A woman offered to take Jamie home from a party this afternoon – said she used to work with Adam and knows where we live. Any ideas who this is? Weird huh? Creepy/not creepy?

She's added the messages to Instagram too. Although she's tempted, Maddy doesn't click 'like' in case she draws attention to herself.

Five minutes later, a van hurtles around the corner and pulls up next to the house. Right on time. One man in overalls climbs out and flings open the rear shutter while the driver knocks loudly on the front door. It's only a few moments before Alison is shouting at them. She stomps outside, arms crossed. The second man has a fridge freezer on his trolley, ready to wheel into the house. Alison shakes her head but the driver points to his paperwork. It will be Alison's name printed there. She'll assume Adam has ordered it.

Somehow, Alison persuades the men to take the fridge freezer back. As they close the van doors, a florist drives up behind, blocking them in. A man carefully takes out a large funeral wreath. The driver of the fridge delivery van unwinds his window and says something. Alison opens the front door, shouts and shoves the man so he stumbles backwards. She slams the door shut. He curses out loud and leaves the wreath propped up against the wall. He has specific instructions to leave it there, no matter what, even if the recipient seems hostile. Grief does funny things to people, Maddy told them.

It is another half an hour before Maddy sees the side gate open and Alison wheel the dustbin out to the pavement. Ducking down, she can just about see her wander out to the road, hands on hips looking in her direction. Any moment, Maddy expects her to march over and bang on her window, demand to know what she's up to. But a woman is calling out to her. Maddy strains to see above the steering wheel. It's an old lady from the house next door. The two neighbours meet in the middle of the cul-de-sac. Alison chats with one hand supporting her back. Twice she points to her house and in the direction of the car. Maddy sinks lower in her seat as far as her bump will allow her. She grips the handle of the door. They look as though they're about to storm over. She'll have to start the car and back out as fast as she can. But one of them spots the wreath. Alison strides over, her hands are over her mouth. She picks it up and chucks it in her garden waste bin.

Maddy takes a deep breath and peeks over the wheel one more time. The old lady waves goodbye. Alison goes back through the gate. Maddy puts a hand to her chest. Her heart won't stop thumping. She starts the car, hands shaking and checks in the mirror to back out of the road. A smile leaks from her lips but when she blinks it's her mum's face beaming back at her.

34

ALISON: OCTOBER 2019

Alison arrives home from the shops with a couple of house plants to replace the dead ones. She doesn't want Adam to think she can't look after them. She hands a couple of bags of shopping to Jamie to take to the door and picks up a couple herself.

A full-length mirror is propped up sideways against next door's skip, a big crack in the glass. Can't be theirs, surely. She stands in front of it, the lower half of her legs and new kitten heel slingbacks are displaced in each broken piece. Jamie pulls at the door handle, whinging that he's missing *Batman*. She lets him in, and he dips under her arm while she's still holding the key in the door. A large parcel addressed to her has been brought inside. Must be her new suede boots. The dog runs past her, onto the drive. She calls him back in and he follows her up to her bedroom. Her mirror, normally against the wall by the window, has gone. 'What the hell?' she says aloud.

She stomps downstairs again and opens the back door. The dog charges past her into the garden. Jamie has parked himself in front of a children's cartoon channel. Outside, part of the hallway is reflected in the mirror, showing all the toys that have ended up along the skirting board covered in balls of dog hair, like tumbleweed mixed with grit and mud. Her mouth opens, letting out a vapour of shame. So this is what her house looks like to other people. She stands closer to the mirror, her hands resting on her hips, elbows out.

She rings next door's bell and waits for an answer. Just when she's going to turn away, Jill answers the door. She's barefoot, her toenails ridged and yellow like claws.

'Are you all right?' Jill raises two badly drawn eyebrows.

'Don't suppose you saw Adam put this here?'

'Sorry, I've been out all day. Don't you want it?'

'I didn't put it there.' Adam must have been back again. Is he clearing out her stuff?

'Sorry love, too busy packing; we'll be out by the

end of the week.' She picks at the flaky skin on her chin; a large piece spins to the ground like a sycamore seed.

'Don't worry,' Alison sighs. She pictures all the skin she, Adam and Jamie must have shed in their house, collected together as a grey shroud of dust on the TV, in between the rungs of the banister, everywhere. Adam must have noticed the stack of magazines tucked behind the front door and the cobwebs on the ceiling. Piles of papers line the stairs like a frill; Lego bricks are still scattered across the living room rug. Is this why he isn't talking to her? He knows she hates cleaning. Doesn't he think she's good enough to be his wife?

She heaves the mirror back inside and drags it up the stairs. Once it's in place she lies down on the un-made bed to get her breath back. Something dark on Adam's pillow catches her eye. Several long dark hairs are caught in the brushed cotton. She sits up and shudders. Sandra has dark hair, but is it this long? Is it her doing these weird things? But why? She needs to speak to her. Between her thumb and forefinger, she pinches the hairs and drops them in the toilet, giving it a full flush.

* * *

When she gets home the next day, a wall of heat hits
Alison as soon as she opens the front door. There's no
way she left the heating on high. Poppy is panting but
the water bowl is full. The new house plants have
wilted. They were fine this morning. The earth is so
dry it has cracked open, separating itself from the edge
of the pots. She collects the crisp brown leaves and
scatters them in the heap of compost out the back.
Adam would be proud of her; he's always nagging her
to recycle.

A pair of trainers she's never seen are behind the
kitchen door. They're his size and there's the smell of
sweat in the air. Why doesn't he wait for her to come
home for God's sake? What's he up to? There's a used
mug in the sink, placed on top of yesterday's plates and
a pan of cooked onions has been left on the hob. She
leans forward and has a sniff. That's where the smell is
coming from, and they're still warm. Has he started
cooking dinner, popped out for wine and will be back
in a minute? Maybe he wants to apologise for his behaviour. He's opened his mail and squashed it into the
letter basket. But no note. She's going to tear into him
for treating her like this.

Thoughts overlap in her head. She's used to him
being secretive and being away, but this is ridiculous.
She needs to know if things are okay between them.

He must realise this is stressing her out. And poor Jamie, it's hardly fair on him wondering where his dad is.

She waits around but after half an hour she chucks the onions in the bin and cooks Jamie a sausage pasta ready meal.

* * *

After he's gone to bed, she sits on the sofa with a mammoth glass of lemonade. The microwave pings. The lasagne is overcooked around the edges, but she cuts it in two and dishes it up. It's too hot to eat.

There's a light tap on the front door. Julie is standing there teetering on high heels and holding a bottle of Rosé.

'Sorry, started drinking without you.'

Alison laughs and goes back to the kitchen. She puts both plates on a tray and carries them in. Julie is pouring herself wine and then tops up Alison's glass with lemonade.

'Cheers Julie, thanks for the baby shower, it was lovely.'

'You're welcome, darling,' she says. 'Sorry about Jaz, I wouldn't have invited her if I knew she was going to be in that state.'

'It's not your fault. Anyway, I wanted her to come. She's been a good mate.'

'Not heard from him yet then?'

'Not even a message. I keep texting and calling, but his phone's always switched off. He's been here though, opened his post, but he makes bloody sure it's when I'm not in.'

'He probably wants to calm down, have some time to himself.'

'But it's been weeks. How long does he bloody need? We have to talk, not hide from each other.'

'You know what men are like, it's a macho thing, they need to feel in charge.' Julie was married and divorced within two years. Single ever since. Never a good thing to say about men.

'Whatever it is, I can't go on like this and I can't keep making excuses to Jamie.'

They chink their glasses.

'I brought our favourite: *Muriel's Wedding*.'

Alison forces a smile. 'I'm not really in the mood for that. What are those ones?' She points to the plastic bag on the floor.

Julie takes all the DVDs out and lays them on the table. 'I don't fancy any of them, do you?'

'It's up to you, you're the one who needs cheering up.'

'Let's put some music on.' Alison puts her glass down and leans over the back of the sofa, 'Something to chill us out.' She switches on an Amy Winehouse album, *Back to Black* and skips straight to song two. It was the first thing Adam bought her after they started going out. He must have saved up for it for weeks because it hadn't been long since his gran died and he needed to pay rent on his room above the fish and chip shop. He was so sweet to her then, worshipped her. She sighs. Shame they never really got those old days back.

They sit with their feet up on the coffee table, both singing the chorus of '*You Know I'm No Good*' at the top of their voices.

'Are you sure this was a good choice?' Julie laughs.

Before Alison can reply, the telephone rings. She slides her legs down and picks up the receiver. 'Hello?' Silence. 'Adam, is that you? I can't hear you. I need to speak to you.' The line goes dead. 'Shit. I couldn't hear a thing.' She lifts a magazine from a pile under the coffee table and pulls out a packet of cigarettes.

'I thought you'd given up.'

'I have, but Adam keeps an emergency supply.' She shows Julie the half-empty packet with a mini lighter tucked inside. 'He hides them in the laundry basket because he knows I'll never get to the bottom of it.' She offers the packet to Julie.

'Just the one.'

'Second thoughts, I better not.' Alison clicks the lighter for Julie. 'I just can't settle. Adam's been away so often before and it's never bothered me. Why do I feel so... on edge?' She opens the patio door and paces around the room.

'You parted on a really bad note. Plus, you're pregnant. Your hormones are all over the place.'

'But why not just text me?'

'He's never been away this long before, has he?'

Alison shakes her head.

'Maybe you should tell the police?'

'But he's *not* away, is he? He's coming home when I'm not here, deliberately avoiding me, giving me the silent treatment, tormenting me.'

'I don't know then. It doesn't make sense. Have you tried leaving him a note?' Julie shakes her head and pours herself another glass. 'I honestly thought he was the sort of person who'd want to clear the air.'

'He lets things stew if something's bothering him. I'll leave him a note but I'm going to try and catch him out when he's here.' Alison raises her glass to Julie.

'Good for you. How are you going to do that?' Julie

blows smoke towards the door and watches it billow out.

'Try coming home at a different time maybe? I need to know what's going on. I keep having this feeling that he's never coming back.'

'Don't be daft. He adores you.' Julie chucks her cigarette stub outside and closes the patio door.

'He disappeared before.'

'That's hardly the same. Your dad paid him to stay away.'

'That's what Adam told me, but now I'm wondering if it's true.'

'Look, the argument can't have been that bad, can it? Anyway, you're having his baby. For all his faults, Adam is not a bastard. I mean, he doesn't knock you about, does he?'

'You didn't hear him. He said we're never getting married, ever, as though there's something really wrong about it. Like he doesn't love me any more.'

'He'll be back when he's ready and you'll make up with him like you always do.'

Alison frowns. 'I'm not sure I should take him back after this.'

'Don't you love him?'

'Does *he* love me? Anyway, look at me, Jules, I'm

bloody huge. It's not much of a turn on, is it?' She leans back and spreads herself out on the sofa.

'You are not, darling, you're gorgeous.'

'Rob keeps coming on to me at work, so maybe I'm not so bad.' She finishes her drink.

'There you go then.'

'Told me I deserve better than Adam. That if he was my boyfriend, he'd do anything for me.'

'Sounds like you're enjoying a bit of attention.'

'Yeah, he's really sweet, but not my type.'

'Now then, what about a comedy, to cheer us up?' Julie switches on the TV to an episode of *Friends*.

The telephone rings again. They glance at each other. Alison picks it up. This time she stays silent, imagining Adam speaking in some far-off place, assuming she can hear him. She waits for a snatch of his voice, but there's nothing. She senses that the silence is occupied. Someone is listening, waiting for her to speak. She can hear faint breathing. Then the muffled sound of the phone being moved. The line is cut, and she's left with the droning sound to confirm it.

'Who was it? You look upset.'

'No one spoke but I'm sure someone was there.' She shakes her head. Was it Adam? What's going on?

Audience laughter fills the pause.

'Maybe there's something wrong with Adam's phone.' Julie flicks her hair behind her shoulders.

'No, I don't think so.'

'How can you tell, if you couldn't hear anyone?'

'I heard someone breathing and I don't think it was Adam.' She dials 1471. 'It's a withheld number.'

'But who else would it be?'

'A crank caller.'

'Maybe someone you know who comes in the shop?'

'But how would they have my home number?' Alison prods at her lasagne with a fork.

'Good point. So, it must be someone who knows you, or Adam.' Julie moves the tray from her knees to the coffee table. 'Or more likely, it's just a dodgy line.'

Alison stares at the screen. She's not so sure. 'Whoever it was, they were listening, waiting for me to react.'

* * *

That night, as soon as her eyes shut, she can hear the faint sound of the clock ticking every long drawn out second. She can't stop thinking about the phone calls, all the possibilities of who it could be. Is Adam trying to frighten her with all these weird things going on around the house? Why would he do that though? He's not a cruel person. Her eyes flick open. There's a scurrying sound above. She sits up, shivering at the thought of stiff long tails and twitching whiskers. Grabbing the duvet, she bundles into the spare room and wraps herself in the puffy material. Only her face is poking out, like a butterfly waiting to emerge. Whoever it was trying to phone, she has a feeling they'll call again.

35

MAX: APRIL 2017

Max spotted Ali as soon as he pushed his way into the cafe. The hum of voices and clang of cups seemed to drain into the background. Her hair was different, straightened with a reddish colour streaked across the crown. Butterflies rose in his stomach. He slipped his wedding ring into his pocket.

She raised her hand as if it was possible for anyone not to have seen her. His grin widened as he went over. All rational thoughts fell away, along with his life as Max Saunders, discarded like a mask.

'Good to see you, Adam.' She stood up from a plump sofa and pecked him on both cheeks. He breathed in her perfume; the same one she always wore. She was older, of course, but well, the same, only more grown up. Dressed casually in a denim skirt, ankle boots, and ruffle blouse. Sexier than ever.

'You too.'

She'd called him a week after his accident but had been undecided about meeting up after all this time. In the end she probably felt sorry for him, especially when he'd told her what had happened to his face.

'Can I get you anything?' He took a handful of coins out of his jeans pocket.

'I'm fine, thanks.' She sat down again while he went to join the queue.

He fingered his wedding ring at the bottom of his pocket. What was he doing? Maddy would be in the garden with the girls and here he was, watching Ali peer at herself in a mirror, touching up her make-up. He'd had to change his whole life because of her and here she was, as if it was nothing. He needed to find out what had really happened but that was it, he couldn't jeopardise the life he had built up with Maddy and the girls.

He carried his coffee to the table.

'So how have you been?' She sipped her drink, leaving red lipstick around the rim.

He leaned across the table and opened his mouth to speak, but she continued.

'Jaz says you're a painter and decorator. That's nice.'

'Yeah, papering over the cracks.' He sat back. 'You look like you're doing all right.'

'I'm manager of a charity shop.'

'How respectable. Didn't join the family business then?' He blew on his coffee before taking a sip.

'It's a job.' She shrugged. 'I like it.'

'Didn't think to contact me at all?' He stretched his arm across the back of the chair next to him.

'How could I?'

'I stuck around for you, why didn't you tell me what you were going to do?' He jabbed a finger at her.

'Dad made me. He sent me away. It would have been too dangerous to come back.'

'Yeah, well they beat the living shit out of me.'

'I didn't know, I'm sorry.' She moved back in her seat.

'Do me a favour.' He rubbed his forehead.

'Honestly. They told me you'd done a runner. I had no choice once he found out we were seeing each other, that I was pregnant.' Her hand spread open on the table. Each of her delicate fingers full of gold rings.

'Ah, dear old Dad lied to both of us, eh?' Max gave a half-laugh. 'To think I looked up to him once, thought he was like a dad to me.'

'I'd never seen him so angry.' Her face was suddenly flushed and shining.

'But how could you... get rid of it... and not tell me?' He smacked his hand flat on the table. The sound silenced the coffee shop for a moment. Max felt all eyes turn to them, but he stayed focused on Ali. He'd wanted to ask her that question for so long.

'He made me. I was really scared.' She looked like she was about to cry.

'We could have sorted it out ourselves,' he said, softer now. He reached for her hand. 'It was *our* baby.' He stroked her palm.

'I didn't know what to do.'

'We could have run away together.'

She moved her hand and sat back. 'Dad wouldn't let me contact you, then he packed me off to my aunt's. Cut me off completely.'

Max sat up straight, his eyes darted around the cafe. 'How do you know he's not here now?'

Ali smiled. 'Because he died of a heart attack two years ago.'

Max spluttered a laugh. 'Wow, I can't say I'm sorry.'

'I know, I know,' she said, lowering her gaze, 'but he was still my dad.'

'Can we go somewhere else?' Maddy, Emily and Chloe seemed distant now, another life entirely.

They stood up. For a moment they stared at each other and the years fell away. Max stroked Ali's arm. She'd been torn away from him when he loved her. Did he still?

At a park a short walk away, they sat on the grass in the shade of a laburnum tree.

'Remember when we used to meet at the coffee shop near my flat?' He grinned at the memory of them sitting in a booth huddled together. A woman stopped at their table one day and said what a gorgeous couple they were.

'Yeah, we used to talk for hours, didn't we?'

'We had so many plans to travel and develop properties and have loads and loads of kids in a massive house.'

'And dogs and chickens and a goat, don't forget.'

'Oh yeah, you were always going on about having a frigging goat.' He shook his head in mock disbelief and they both laughed.

'It ended so suddenly. I was really upset that you didn't come and find me,' she said, kicking off her sandals.

'I had no idea where you'd gone.'

'Dad sent me to my aunt's place in Cornwall.'

'And that's where you got rid of it?'

Ali was silent.

'I should have had a say.' He pressed his knuckles into the grass.

'I didn't have a choice either. You know what Dad was like.' She played with her keys. Her warm perfume wafted towards him churning up memories.

'Well, I'm here now.'

'It's too late, Adam, I'm with someone else.'

Max hung his head. He should tell her about Maddy and the girls, but he couldn't bring himself to. Part of him still didn't want to believe it was over. It felt like unfinished business. They'd been separated against their will. But it was in the past and Maddy made him happy. They were good together. Did he really want to chase a life that was never meant to be? His heart snagged imagining how it would have been, Ali, the baby and him together. But he couldn't imagine life without Maddy and his wonderful daughters.

'Is it serious, you and this bloke?' He looked up at the white puffy cloud above their heads, reminding him of one of Chloe's drawings.

'He looks after me.' The words pinched.

'We were good together, Ali,' he said. 'It was special, you can't deny it.' What was he doing? He mustn't fall under her spell.

She didn't reply. Her keys tumbled onto the grass.

Max picked them up. He turned them over in his hand and gave them back to her.

'I've tried so hard to forget you, to move on.' He pressed his forehead.

'You should have.' She stretched her slim legs out in front of her.

'Have you? Honestly?' He looked for her reaction.

'Is that why you're here? Because you couldn't?'

'I wanted to find out from you what happened back then. I was curious to see how you were. Why you never tried to find me.'

She fiddled with the key fob, sliding the plastic frame back and forth a fraction. 'Where do we go from here?' She dropped the keys back in her bag.

'Wherever you want us to.' He reached for her hands, soft and delicate.

She let him hug her and a lifting sensation filled his chest. 'I don't know, Adam. It's been so long. We're different people now.'

'Just stay in touch. That's all I ask.'

'I need to get back.' She slipped on her sandals.

'Let me see you again.' He knelt in front of her. He must have lost his mind, but he couldn't stop himself.

Ali turned away. 'I don't think my boyfriend would be too pleased.'

'Take my number, here.' He scribbled it on the lid

of his cigarette packet and tore it off. 'If you change your mind. If you need to talk...'

'I already have your number, remember?' She took out a mirror and checked her hair. 'I've managed without you for six years, Adam.'

'Are you saying you feel nothing for me, none of the old spark?'

'Drive me home, Adam, please.'

Outside her maisonette he pushed a hundred quid in rolled-up twenties into her hand. 'Here, treat yourself, buy something nice.'

She took it and went inside without looking back.

36

MAX: APRIL 2017

Max's drive back to Uxbridge took over two hours because of heavy traffic. He arrived home just before 8 p.m. He could hear movement upstairs and the low-pitch sound of Maddy's voice. The television was on in the empty living room, silenced, the screen flickering in the dark. The curtains were drawn and a circle of lamplight showed the sag in the sofa where Maddy had been sitting, her knitting abandoned on the foot-stool. The dogs dragged themselves out of their basket, wagging their tails and sniffing his hands.

In the kitchen, he took the bottle of whiskey down from the shelf, poured a shot and knocked it back, then another. He kicked off his shoes, put on his slippers and plodded upstairs.

Chloe's bedroom door was open, Maddy kneeling by her bed. She glanced up at him. 'She's been having night terrors again,' she whispered, sweeping her hand across Chloe's forehead. 'You reek of whiskey, Max,' she said, drawing back from him.

'Are you all right, my angel?' He crouched down and Chloe snuggled into the crook of his arm. He stroked her damp hair.

'Back to sleep time,' Maddy said.

'I want Daddy.'

Maddy half smiled and kissed Chloe on the forehead. 'Can we read, *My Dad*?' Chloe pulled the book from her shelf.

'Go on then.' He was too tired to argue. They read the book together until the last lines, about how much Dad loves her and always will, which, as usual, he let Chloe recite on her own.

'I certainly will. I love you to the moon and back.' He gave her a cuddle. He couldn't help wishing he'd been a dad to his first child too. He sighed and put the book back on the shelf.

'Dad?'

He glanced over his shoulder.

'Let's tuck you in.'

He pressed the back of his hand to his nose and mouth to halt the threat of tears.

'You look sad, Daddy.'

'I'm okay. Good night, my angel.' He blew her a kiss.

Max crept into Emily's room. She was awake, reading Harry Potter.

'Daddy!' She reached up to hug him.

'How's my big girl today?' He sat on the bed.

'Miss Ryan gave me three cool class tokens for reading and spelling.'

'Three? That's fantastic, aren't you clever?'

'So, as I've been good, can I go on your phone?' He pulled a funny face and Emily laughed. 'Please... Daddy.'

'All right, just for a little while.' He took his phone out of his pocket and unlocked it. She snuggled into his chest and opened Snapchat. They took turns holding the screen up and watching their faces changing, from devil horns and red eyes to cats' ears and whiskers. Emily's favourite was Max becoming Mr Fox but with his own human eyes and teeth. When he spoke and moved his mouth around Emily rolled about laughing.

'Time for sleep now.' He kissed her forehead and switched the phone off. He sat by her side and waited until her eyes shut. He liked to watch her breathing while she slept. Deep steady breaths. He picked up her favourite teddy, the one with a cushioned heart sewn onto its paws, the stuffing bursting out of a seam. Old but loved.

He must be crazy to want to stay in touch with Ali when she still possessed this power over him, like the moon's invisible strings pulling the tide. He stood at the window entranced by the fat silvery ball in the sky, ridiculously bright. Ali was the only girl he'd ever loved before Maddy. He should be over her by now, so why did she make his heart sing just thinking about her? He'd moved on, was happily married and had two wonderful kids. How was it possible to feel this way about someone else? It felt like his own body and heart were betraying him.

In their bathroom, he stripped off and stepped under the shower. He'd call Ali tomorrow, tell her he couldn't see her again.

Back in the bedroom, Maddy slipped into bed naked. A shower late at night usually meant they had sex.

'You look tired.' Maddy stroked his forehead as he climbed in next to her.

'It's been a long day, things on my mind,' he said, wrapping his arms around her ample body. But when he shut his eyes, all he saw was Ali.

Maddy wraps the screwdriver in a plastic bag to take to Alison's house. She's always on the lookout for obstacles such as nosy neighbours. In the last few days she's taken to wearing a professional-looking tabard and carrying a plastic holder full of cleaning products and cloths so that if any were to question her, she can tell them she is Ms Wood's cleaner.

For a moment she stops and stares in disbelief at the bag on the kitchen counter. What is happening to her? Why is she doing this when she longs to stay at home, curl up under the duvet and sob her heart out for her little girl? But her obsession with this woman and compulsion to punish her is too overwhelming. She picks the bag up and grips it so tightly that her hand hurts. Her teeth clench together. The humiliation and betrayal cuts deep. It destroyed her mother but she won't let it destroy her.

Sarah catches her as she is going out the door. She props up her bicycle against the wall after her morning ride. Maddy stops dead and cups her bump with both hands. 'Ooh, the baby's kicking well today.' Sarah smiles and reaches out. 'Can you feel it?'

Sarah moves her hand around over Maddy's coat. 'I think it's stopped, I've missed it.'

'Ah, that's a shame.'

Maddy tells her about her new job.

'Really? Cleaning? You never said.' Sarah sounds incredulous. Thinks she knows everything. Mother was right, don't trust anyone.

Sarah takes a piece of paper with a phone number written on it out of her pocket. 'I thought you might want to enquire about opening up a cafe in the high street?' She carried on. 'Mr and Mrs Blake are retiring at the end of March.'

'But this job is important. It needs to be completed before the baby comes.'

'Completed? What are you cleaning, Woburn Abbey?'

'I can't tell you any more about it.' She'd never understand in any case.

'Why not?'

'Because if it's not done before the baby arrives, it will be a disaster.'

'What do you mean, a disaster?'

'Everything, just everything. This baby is the most important thing.'

'Of course.' Sarah stands there frowning. 'You don't seem yourself. Are you sure you're feeling all right?'

'I'm fine, really fine. Just let me get on with this, please.'

* * *

Maddy doesn't recall the journey to Huntingdon. One moment she was closing her car door outside her own house and the next she is parking in Lawn End. Poppy is there to greet her as usual, and she takes a few moments to stroke him and give him some biscuits. She lets him into the garden and refills the water bowl, which always seems to be empty. When he comes back in, she combs his hair with a brush she found at the back of a drawer. His ears are full of knots and he's clearly not been walked for at least a week because the lead is coiled in exactly the same place in the under-stairs cupboard.

She checks the calendar for any change to routines

and appointments for the coming week. Nails, hair, work, dentist. Sandra is back from a long weekend away next week. Maddy has decided not to come at all on Tuesdays because it clashes with the time she is there. Lately, Sandra has been calling in to pick up the ironing like clockwork at 11 a.m. and drops it back at 3 p.m. The same on Saturdays too. How they can afford it is anyone's guess. Got money for pampering herself and the chores she can't be bothered to do, but leaves the poor dog on his own all day? Self-centred bitch.

She starts on the under-sink cupboard door that has already worked itself loose. She unscrews it so it's barely hanging on its hinges. As she's going upstairs, she hears the squeal of car brakes on the drive. Ice shoots through her veins. She runs up to the main bedroom and peeps through the curtains. Alison is getting out of her car, and she swings the door closed making sure it doesn't slam. Seconds later, the front door opens. Again, it's shut quietly, but still with a clear click. Poppy's nametag jangles. Shit. Did she lock the back door after she let him out? Thank God she brought her tray of cleaning products up with her. But did she leave anything on the kitchen counter? At least she hadn't boiled the kettle yet.

Maddy stands in the en-suite shower room, straining to hear, but there is no sound coming from downstairs. Alison must be creeping around trying to catch 'Adam' out. According to her Facebook page, she's convinced it's him coming back when she's not here. Her mother's plan to break the trust between them is working. She's rather enjoying making her suffer. Any second she expects her to barge in, but she's ready, cloth in hand and a story about Adam employing her as their cleaner in his absence. The sound of Alison's resigned footsteps plodding downstairs tells her that she's checked every room and given up. The front door slams hard and she skids the car out of the drive and up the road.

Maddy creeps downstairs. In the kitchen is a note on the counter:

Adam, why are you doing this to me? I'll be back at 6 p.m. Wait for me this time!! We need to talk!!! A

Maddy fills the kettle and smirks at her mother in the window's reflection.

Back upstairs, she continues with the plan and loosens the screws on the nasty plastic shelf in the shower, packed full of overpriced premium shampoos and scrubs and goodness knows what.

In the living room she has a sip of tea and starts on

the cabinet door. The screws are stiff at first, but she manages to undo them enough and she's able to shut it without showing any sign of it being tampered with.

As she is picking up her mug a large bird crashes into the French window with a deadening thud making her spill tea all down her front. Out on the path, a young crow lies on its back, head on one side, twitching. Maddy opens the patio door and slides her hands underneath it, gently lifting it onto her lap. She sits on a sun-bleached railway sleeper stroking the inky feathers. It blinks its beady black eye at her. The rapid heartbeat soon slows to nothing and the warmth of its body seeps through her fingers like sand. Poppy sniffs it and slopes off into the house. A ghostly imprint of its wings is left on the window.

She takes the bird inside and lays it on a scrap of old newspaper. Poor thing deserves a proper burial, but Max would tell her it is a bad omen, a sign of death or ill fortune. His gran knew all about these things. They shouldn't be ignored. Alison needs to know that she won't get away with what she's done. She leaves her mug in the sink and places the dead bird on Alison's doormat on her way out.

38

ALISON: OCTOBER 2019

Alison arrives back from Jamie's swimming lesson just after 5 p.m. It starts to rain as they get out of the car. Jamie laughs as he's getting wet, turning in circles. Poppy is barking on the other side of the front door.

'Argh, what's that?' Alison jumps back from the dark glistening mound on the mat. Jamie stops laughing and peers closer, poking it with the side of his trainer.

'It's dead,' he says.

'I can see that. What's it doing here?'

'Probably killed by next door's cat.'

'A crow? Isn't it too big for a cat to catch?' She picks up the sides of the mat. 'Open the bin, will you?'

Jamie splashes through the puddles along the

drive and flips open the lid. Alison curls the mat up either end, scoops the whole lot up and drops it in the bin.

'What about the mat?' asks Jamie.

'It might have fleas or something. We can get a new one.'

'When's Dad coming home?'

'Don't start. Hurry up now and get in. I'm soaked to the bloody skin.'

Poppy sniffs them, but Alison pushes him away. She opens Jamie's schoolbag and takes out his reading book and an object wrapped in tissue.

'What's this?'

'We made it in pottery. It's a footballer.'

'Can I have a look then?'

'Yeah.' He runs into the living room and switches on the television.

'You've painted it nicely. Where shall we put it?'

'I don't want to unwrap it yet.'

'Why not?'

'It's for Dad.'

'Oh. I'll leave it on the side then, shall I?' He'd better bloody turn up now. 'Go and have a shower.'

'Do I have to?'

'Yes, you do, you're soaking wet. You'll catch a cold. Go on, get upstairs.' She trudges into the kitchen and unlocks the back door. The rain is now a curtain of steel. Poppy doesn't budge. 'Don't blame you, mate, but you'll have to cross your legs.'

She shivers and slams the door.

Dragging a large pan out of the cupboard, she fills it with cold water. Pasta again. A different sauce. Jamie won't mind. Or rather he won't notice. There's some leftover bacon she could chop up and chuck in. She's never enjoyed cooking. After her mum deserted them for another man, they lived on takeaways and eating out in restaurants, mainly the curry house at the end of their road. Her father would sit at the top of the table like Don Corleone, with his napkin tucked into his collar, and none of them was allowed to speak unless he asked a question. It wasn't until she left that she realised she'd never felt comfortable at home. She misses her mum and wishes she'd kept in touch, but he probably made that impossible too.

The sound of rain begins to lessen. Water starts gushing out of the gutter at the corner of the house. Something else that needs fixing. She opens the carousel door and it comes off in her hand. 'What the hell?' The screws fall to the floor. Poppy sniffs at the packets of pasta and rice. 'Get away,' she shouts and props the door down the side of the fridge. A loud thud sounds above her head. She runs upstairs and bursts into the shower room. Jamie covers himself with his hands. Bottles of shampoo and shower gel have fallen onto the cubicle floor. The shelf has come clean out of the wall.

'How did you manage that?' she asks, passing him a towel.

'I didn't touch it. It just fell and nearly hit me.' He steps past her, onto the mat.

'I'll sort it out later,' she says and stomps back downstairs.

The pan on the hob is fizzing, the water bubbles up and splashes over.

'Jesus Christ! Where the hell are you, Adam?' she shouts.

* * *

While Jamie's eating, Alison goes upstairs. She's not hungry and will grab a snack later. She doesn't see the point in dusting, but she does it now and then to keep Adam happy or when she's agitated. While she is wiping the bookcase at the top of the stairs, she comes across the photo frame edged with ceramic teddy bears. The picture of Jamie as a baby has gone. Shock shoots through her. The back of the frame is neatly secured. It was there yesterday. She doesn't know why but she shivers.

She turns the tiny frame in her hands, thinking there might be a clue, a telltale mark. It was a special photo; Jamie was two days old, weighed only 5lb, too small for any normal-sized clothes, too weak to stay awake and feed from her breast. She sniffs to stop tears rising to the surface. She runs the duster across the top of the book-case. Daft how she still gets tearful over nothing. No wonder her brothers used to call her a cry-baby.

In the bedroom, she slips the frame into a drawer of her bedside table. She opens a window and shakes the duster outside. He'll call soon and come up with a simple reason. And she's prepared to forgive him as long as it's nothing bad.

A series of envelopes drop on the mat as she's coming downstairs. More bills. She collects them up and adds them to the bulging pile in the kitchen, promising herself she'll go through them later.

Jamie has finished his pasta and is curled up on the chair in the sitting room, watching cartoons. She notices a mark on the French window, an imprint of a wing. Opening the door, she scours the area outside for a body, but can't see any. It looks like it had quite a wallop. Could it have flown away? Or is it the same one that was dead on the front doormat? Maybe the cat picked it up from here and dropped it there. Would it do that? She squashes in next to Jamie and gives him a cuddle, kissing the top of his head.

'When's Daddy coming home?' He doesn't give up.

'I don't honestly know.' It's her stock reply but what else can she say when she doesn't know the answer? Perhaps she should never have let Adam back in her life.

She slides the patio doors wider, encouraging Jamie to play outside in the thin evening sunshine now it's stopped raining. The dog bounds past her, racing down the garden, ears flapping. He disappears into the bushes behind the apple tree.

She's wandering back to the kitchen when the telephone rings. There's a moment's hesitation before she picks it up. It's Rob. He wants to know if he can have Monday afternoon off. She passes her finger over the date on the calendar. If he can swap it for Tuesday morning, she tells him, she could wait in for Adam again.

The phone is still in her hand when it rings again.

'What is it, Rob?' There is no answer. Oh, come on, please.

She hurries past Jamie, outside.

'Adam, is that you?' She waits a second. 'Adam?

Adam? Look, whoever this is, stop ringing me or I'll call the police,' she shouts. At that moment an apple falls in front of her, thudding on the roof of Jamie's playhouse. The line goes dead and she's left startled at the falling missile. 'This tree has to come down,' she says aloud. The parasol is flapping round and round in a circle, casting a long shadow on the ground.

* * *

In the morning, Alison walks the dog around the block before the tree surgeon arrives. On the way home, she runs through her argument with Adam on the last day she saw him. Breakfast TV sparked it off. A couple were having a beach wedding in Jamaica. She said that could be them one day. Except she thought she'd said it under her breath, but Adam slammed his mug of tea down, sloshing it over the table.

'I thought I made it clear,' he said, an icy edge to his voice.

She switched the television off. Jamie stopped eating. 'Jamie, eat up.' She followed Adam into the hallway. 'Are you saying you won't ever marry me?' she asked.

'That's right.' He put his jacket on, his back to her.

'But we always said we would. I mean – Jamie and the new baby need security. What's changed?'

Adam lowered his face close to hers, teeth clenched. 'You've sucked every single penny out of me, what security do you think a piece of paper will give you?' He'd slammed the front door behind him, leaving her in a swirling gust of air.

She'd never seen him like that before. It wasn't the Adam she fell for. He sounded more and more like her father. When they were first together, they talked all the time about getting engaged, running away to get hitched so her father didn't find out. He'd been full of it then, told her they could run away to Gretna Green and he'd found a place that sold decent second-hand wedding dresses. He'd been more happy-go-lucky then. Full of big plans about their future. The house he wanted to build. It was his idea for them to get matching tattoos. A and A. They were a team. He made her feel safe. For the first time in her life, she hadn't been scared of her father any more, but that hadn't lasted.

An open-top truck is already parked on her drive. She smiles at the men as she walks past and unlocks the front door. The dog pulls on his lead, barking in a shrill, insistent pitch. She drags him inside by his collar and locks him in the sitting room. It means digging deeper into her overdraft, but she can't put it off any longer, whatever Adam might have to say about it. If it means she'll be able to sleep better again, it'll be worth every penny.

The men unload their equipment and she shows them through the side gate into the garden. The older man is wearing a body harness and safety helmet. The other man, much younger, carries reams of rope.

While the kettle is boiling, she stands at the back door watching the older man climb the tree. He pulls his safety visor over his face. As she pours water into the mugs, she can hear the insistent buzz of the saw. She pictures Jamie climbing up the tree, calling out to her to watch him. She'd looked up from her phone at the moment his foot slipped, and as she ran towards him, she knew she couldn't stop him falling. By the time she looks out again, all the smaller top branches have been chopped down. Adam will go mental. She could shout at him to stop, but as she carries the tea into the garden the satisfying crack of a thicker branch tells her it's already too late.

39

MAX: APRIL 2017

Max tried to call Ali from work the next day, but there was no answer. He rang Jaz but the line was permanently engaged. Three days later, Ali telephoned back and asked him to meet her.

In Hinchingbrooke Park, in Huntingdon, she was waiting for him on a bench. She looked different with her hair tied back in a rough ponytail. It was how he remembered her. A brisk breeze whistled and sighed through the trees. Bruised clouds threatened rain overhead.

'Tony got wind of us meeting up.' She scanned up and down the path.

'Tony?'

'I'm seeing him. He's not pleased.'

'Please don't tell me you mean *that* Tony.'

Her fingers played with the zip on her bag.

'Do you want to kick me in the face while you're at it?' The cigarette in his lips bobbed up and down as he spoke. He took it out.

'Someone clocked you in The White Hart. Why did you go back there?'

'I was working in Brampton. Thought it wouldn't hurt after all this time.' He tried to relight the cigarette, but it fell to the ground.

'You'd best stay away. Mick and Ray know you're back on the scene.'

'Ah, the Brothers Grimm.'

'Mick's still in prison.' She glanced over her shoulder. 'And Ray?'

'Ray's about. I hear things but haven't seen him. We've never talked since, you know.' She twisted her coat belt into a knot.

'Okay, maybe it was a bit stupid, but I wouldn't have got back in touch with you if I hadn't gone in there, would I?' He longed to touch the side of her face, to kiss her lips. But he was here to end it before he got in too deep.

'You should dump that knuckle head.'

'It's not that simple.'

'The guy's a loser.'

'He's done a lot for me, helped me pay my rent, stuff like that.' She pulled at the knitted scarf hanging loose round her neck. 'I can't stay long.'

'We've just got here.' He slipped his fingers around the edge of her scarf and gently pulled it away from her skin. 'What's this?'

'It's nothing.' She tugged his hand away and pulled the scarf up.

'If it's nothing, show me.' He caught hold of her hand and carefully unravelled the scarf. The skin on one side was mottled, red and purple.

'It's a game, a love bite, that's all.' She wouldn't look at him.

'What kind of fucking game?'

'Tony was mucking about.' She slid her hair out of the band and let it fall across her face. 'He likes it a bit rough, you know.'

'Around your neck? Am I meant to believe that?'

Ali stood up. 'I know you're not exactly friends.'

'Err... you could say that. Did you know he helped your brothers kick the hell out of me?'

'I didn't. I'm sorry.' She gathered up her bag.

'What else has he done to you?' He stood up too, pulse racing. The thought of him hurting her, touching her, made him want to spew his guts up. How did she end up with Tony, for God's sake, of all people?

'I have to go,' she said backing away.

'Finish with him, please,' he said softly, taking her hand. 'You deserve better than that.'

'I need to think.'

'Hey, remember that time we got away to London for the day?'

She smiled.

'It was the first time I felt completely free, like I didn't have to check over my shoulder.'

'We had lunch outside in Covent Garden and the statue of the man painted gold made you jump.'

'And you were so scared going up in the London Eye, you clung to me the whole way round.'

She nodded. 'It was a great day.'

'I'm sorry there weren't more days like that.' He took her hand. 'Please don't go back to him, Ali.'

'I have to go. I'm sorry.' She twisted away from him and ran down the path.

'I'm going to call you on Friday,' he shouted after her. But she didn't stop.

Shit. So much for telling her he couldn't see her again. But how could he walk away leaving her in the hands of that psychopath?

40

When he telephoned on Friday, Ali promised she would finish with Tony, but could he believe her?

'I need to be certain you're okay.'

'I'll be fine, Adam, I've got stuff I need to sort out.'

'Let me help you. I could knock off work early.'

But she kept putting him off, and a week later, when he couldn't get any answer from her, he was convinced Tony was still on the scene.

He drove to Ali's maisonette one gusty afternoon and parked nearby. He lit a cigarette and checked his watch. Three hours at the most. He'd told John he had to take one of the girls to the dentist because Maddy was busy. He shouldn't be taking risks like this, but Ali wasn't safe with that nutter.

He texted Ali, but she didn't reply so he switched the radio on low and shut his eyes. The first time he kissed Ali was under Bull's Bridge, in Hayes. She'd passed him a note when her dad wasn't looking, asking him to meet her there. She was so pretty and petite, like a little doll. He couldn't believe she was interested in him. It was the first time someone had properly wanted him.

The roar of a car engine woke him from a light doze. The unmistakable bulk of Tony wrenched himself out of a BMW. He unlocked the front door to Ali's flat and disappeared inside. Max waited ten minutes but there was no sign of him leaving, so he got out of his van, took a deep breath and knocked on the door.

Tony answered.

'I'm here to see Ali,' Max said.

'Well look who it ain't,' Tony roared.

'Ali,' Max called into the house.

'She doesn't wanna see you.'

'She can tell me herself.' Max stuck his boot in the doorway.

Ali appeared at the end of the hallway in a sheer petticoat dress.

'Five minutes.' Tony grinned at Max and retreated into the kitchen.

'I thought you said you'd finished with him,' Max whispered.

He reached out to Ali, but she held onto the door handle.

'I have, I mean, I tried to, but he still comes over. He likes to help out, that's all.'

'You've not answered any of my calls.'

'I'm not sure it's a good idea you being here, Adam. It's... difficult.'

He stepped into the hallway and took her hands. 'Look at me and tell me, is he hurting you?'

Ali stared up at him but didn't answer.

'You still here?' Tony stood in the kitchen doorway holding a can of Foster's.

Max let go of Ali.

'We're talking, that's all,' she said.

'Make it quick, we have to get on the road.'

'You're leaving?' Max asked Ali.

'Only to go shopping, up town.' She reached up and took her coat down from a hook behind the door.

Tony sniggered.

'What's so funny?' Max strode towards him.

'She's leading you on again, matey boy.'

'What do you know?' Max followed Tony into the kitchen.

'Nice little honey trap though, ain't she?'

'Don't talk about her like that.' Max's legs were shaking but he squared up to Tony in front of the sink.

'You know what she did with that cash you gave her?' He snorted a laugh out of his broken nose and moved to the other side of the kitchen with surprising ease.

Max glanced at Ali who stared at the floor.

'Bought me this nice new ring, see?' Tony held out his spade-like hand; a skull tattoo covered his forearm, and he was wearing a huge gold sovereign on his middle finger.

Stolen more like, from one of the poor sods who had borrowed a bit of cash to get by.

'And Ali showed me something you gave her too,' Max said. 'Show him, Ali.'

'Adam, I told you it was just a game.'

'Like roughing up girls, do you?' Max stood one side of the pine table, Tony on the other.

'Yeah and you like knocking them up, don't you?' Tony smirked. He crushed the can in his fists and let it drop to the floor. 'Should have finished you off first time round.'

He shoved the table into Max's groin. Ali shrieked. Before Max could recover, Tony was wrestling with him across the table. Max landed a punch square on the side of Tony's face and for a suspended moment he thought he'd knocked him out, but Tony hit back, and Max banged the back of his head on the table. Ali looked upside down to him as he lay across it, her stricken face as he remembered it all those years ago. She shouted at him to watch out, but he felt dizzy and sick. Tony reached across to the sink and all Max saw was a glint of light followed by a searing pain through his left hand. Ali screamed. Tony grabbed his jacket, before smacking her round the face. Seconds later the front door opened and slammed making the whole house shake. The roar of an engine rumbled away into the distance.

Max screamed in agony and tried to move his left hand, but it looked like it was pinned to the table with a carving knife, blood seeping towards him.

'Call an ambulance,' Ali shouted. She was crying and stroking his arm with trembling fingers.

Max sensed someone approaching behind him. His vision was blurring but he could make out a boy standing with his arms around Ali's waist.

'It's okay, Mum, I've called the police.'

41

'Adam, can you hear me?' The nurse's voice roused him. His eyes gradually opened as she took his temperature.

'They've fixed your hand,' Ali said. She was standing by his bed, her eyes rimmed red. He squinted at the heavy bandaging and swollen fingers.

'They caught him, all thanks to you.' She put her arm around the boy by her side.

'What's your name?' Max asked.

'Jamie,' the boy said.

Max searched Ali's face, but she wouldn't look at him, fussing instead with unpacking a bottle of Lucozade, a bag of grapes and a bar of milk chocolate. He looked at the boy properly now. His thatch of blond hair, a cheeky grin; older than Emily or Chloe. Maddy! He tried to sit up. 'What time is it?'

'Eight-thirty.'

'I have to go!'

'They might let you out tomorrow.'

'No, you don't understand, I have to go right now.' He was supposed to be driving Maddy and the girls to Margate the next morning.

'I don't understand, where do you need to be?' Alison asked.

The nurse beside the next patient came over. 'You're not going anywhere tonight, my love, it'll be lights out shortly. Come on,' she said, pulling the covers up to his neck, 'you've had a general anaesthetic, not to mention painkillers. You're lucky there wasn't more serious damage.'

He pushed his head into the pillow and closed his eyes. He'd have to confess about Maddy and his daughters.

Ali gave the boy some change and told him to get himself a drink from the vending machine.

'He's a good boy,' she said.

'We need to talk.' He pressed his throbbing brow.

'It's been hard finding the right moment.'

'I should have told you sooner...' he began. 'The

thing is...' She sat on the bed close to him. 'We've all done things in the past...'

'I know and I've been meaning to...' She shook her head as she smoothed the sheet.

'What?' He touched her hand, waited for her to speak. She searched his eyes with hers.

'I couldn't go through with it.' He frowned.

'Jamie...'

'What? What are you saying?' His heart fizzed to life like a firework. He made a move to sit up.

'Jamie is your son... our son.' She leaned over and hugged him, but he pushed her away. He tried again to sit up but groaned in agony.

'Shit, Ali! What the fuck are you playing at? Why are you only telling me now?'

'I'm so sorry.' She stood back and dabbed her eyes with her fingers.

'How could you carry on letting me believe he didn't exist?' He screwed his good fist up and slammed it down on the bed, making her flinch.

'I said I'm sorry.' She stepped back.

'When were you going to tell me? Were you going to?'

'I needed to be sure... about us.' She looked tiny standing there, head bowed.

'What, you thought I wouldn't care?'

'You turned up out of the blue after so many years away. What was I supposed to think?'

'I didn't know about Jamie, did I? If I had, well...'

'You'd have come looking for us, would you? Wasn't I enough?'

'Don't twist it around. I can't believe you've had that brick Tony playing dad to my son.'

'He's not all bad.'

'You're kidding, right?' He nodded at his hand.

'I tried to find you.' She opened the Lucozade and offered it to him. He shook his head. 'Turned out my aunt hated Dad, so she helped me hide the pregnancy, thank God.'

'What about your psycho dad?'

'Dad was in prison, until he died. I heard Ray's out. The police raided Dad's cab company and found evidence of loan sharking, money laundering, the whole shebang.'

Max ran his good hand through his hair.

'I named him after you, Adam James, but everyone knows him as Jamie.'

Max repeated the name. 'And you're sure he's mine?'

'Who else?' She put her hand on her hip.

'So what is he, six, seven?'

'He's six, born on 26 June 2011.'

'I can't believe it, Ali.' He squeezed his fingers across his eyes. 'Does he know about me?'

'Not yet.'

'I wish you'd tracked me down.'

'I told you – I tried several times. There was no trace of you; it was as though Adam Hawkins had vanished overnight.'

Max shifted his legs. If he told her about Maddy now, she might stop him seeing his son. *His son.* He shut his eyes and let the thought float in his head untethered.

She perched on the end of the bed, took her keys out of her bag, opened the photo keyring and showed it to him.

'You had this all the time?' He took it from her and examined the miniature photo of Jamie as a baby.

'I told you, I needed to be sure about us.'

'But you're the one who kept putting me off.'

'Tony was very... controlling.' She dipped her head.

'You should have let me help you.'

'Well, you tried and look what happened to you.' She laughed.

'Yeah, all right then.' He handed the keyring back. 'Jamie looks like you.'

'And you, what about that chin?' They laughed.

'Will you tell him now... about me?'

'I promise I'll talk to him tonight.'

'God, if I'd known sooner.' But the thought of not having his girls was unbearable. Gran always said things happen for a reason. But how could he tell Maddy about Jamie and Alison, it would kill her.

'I needed to know you weren't married or serious with anyone,' she said.

Max clenched his teeth and looked away.

Jamie arrived back with a cold drink and a toy tucked under his arm.

'You've been a long time,' Ali said, smiling coyly at Max.

'There's a box of toys in that room down there. They've got Batman and Power Rangers and Poké-mon.' Jamie sat a teddy bear in the space under Max's arm.

'Thank you.' He studied the boy's face, the long lashes and sprinkle of freckles on his nose. The same nose and chin as his.

'We'll see you in the morning. Come on, Jamie, time to go.' Ali kissed Max on the lips.

'Thanks for helping me, Jamie,' Max said.

'That's okay, I didn't mind.' He gave a little shrug. 'Can we come back tomorrow, Mum?'

'We'll see,' Ali said, putting her arm around Jamie's shoulders.

Max stared at the ceiling thinking through every-thing that had happened until long after they'd gone.

* * *

Max didn't reach home until the following evening. He'd managed to speak to Maddy the night before, told her he'd had an accident on site and that the hospital was keeping him longer than he'd expected.

The house was quiet except for the dogs as they slid down from the sofa to greet him. *Jamie. Adam James.* He opened the back door and whispered the name into the night. The ebony sky made the stars shine with intense clarity and the moon's half face seemed to be smiling. The dogs' nametags jangled as they bounded into the darkness. He punched the air and silently mouthed the word 'yes'. He daren't speak aloud in case Maddy heard him. There was no light at their open bedroom window, but it didn't mean she wasn't awake. Oh, Maddy. She'd be devastated if he told her he had a son, born a year before Emily. And what if she didn't believe he hadn't known about him?

He sat on the garden bench and went through the events of the last two days. His hand was in a lighter dressing, his fingers still swollen. He took his wedding ring out of the pocket of his jacket and turned it over in his fingers. Something had shifted. Now he knew he had a son, he needed to provide for him. He'd missed so much of his life he couldn't walk away and pretend he didn't exist. The ring slipped from his fingers into the darkness. 'Shit,' he said to Daisy, who was panting at his side. He crouched down and pressed his good hand into the damp grass until he found it. He pushed it onto his finger. The dogs ran in front of him back to the kitchen.

'There you are. I couldn't sleep.' Maddy was standing at the table, stirring hot chocolate. The smell made him feel hungry. How long had she been there?

'Maddy, I'm so sorry.'

'You want one?'

'Please.'

She lifted his bandaged hand and had a closer look. He flinched.

'No better then?'

'A little,' he said.

She poured hot milk into the mug. 'So, are you going to explain to the girls why we didn't go to the seaside? Emily has been talking about nothing else. They've been looking forward to it for weeks.' She handed him the steaming drink.

'I will, I promise. I'd have come home last night if I could, but they drugged me for the op.'

'You need to tell the girls that.' She glared at him and carried her drink upstairs.

He hadn't meant to let them down, but it wasn't his fault, was it? How could he explain it to them without telling them about Ali and Jamie and Tony? He'd have to try and make it up to them. They were his special girls. And now he had Jamie too. *His son.* He took a large sip of hot chocolate and scalded his mouth.

42

MADDY: OCTOBER 2019

Maddy stands outside the Red Cross charity shop. *Bunty* annuals are displayed on a table in the window. She has some at home, along with a pile of 1970s *Beano* comics and a couple of Matchbox cars Max bought at a boot sale. He was always saying how he couldn't wait to dig them out for the children. He'd hoped for a boy when she was pregnant with Chloe; she guessed that, but he hadn't said. She sweeps her hand across her bump.

There she is, stacking shoes without a care in the world. Sundress skimming her barely-there curves. Except her bump looks twice the size it was before. A ludicrous imbalance, taking into account her twig-like limbs, not even the circumference of her own wrists.

Max lied when he said those skinny girls weren't his type.

She did her usual check of Facebook before leaving the house. Alison posted late last night, asking if a cat would have left the dead crow on her mat. Maddy enjoyed trawling through the answers. Most agreed that a cat would have done it, while other people posted funny GIFs and told her it was a creepy warning.

The bell above the door announces her arrival. Alison looks over her shoulder and smiles. A young man is up a ladder, whistling. Maddy heads for a rack of homemade greetings cards, the only thing in the shop that's new. Her face is burning.

She grips the handles of her shopping bag tighter and keeps her head down. There's a faint musty smell of old clothes, of death. Discarded, unwanted items; a clothes graveyard. People bag them up and bring them here like she did with her mum's things. Maybe some people don't wash the clothes first. She could never bring Chloe's things here. No one is having those. Just the thought of having to let them go, makes her catch her breath. What if she saw another child wearing Chloe's favourite dress? She should bring Max's clothes though. There's no point keeping them. Doesn't look like he's coming back. They'd look strange hanging here on the rail or on a dummy. The thought suspends in the air like an invisible thread.

Gravitating towards a rack marked 'Vintage', she fingers a blue dress, frayed around the seams as a fashion detail. Someone bold must have loved wearing it once. There are whole racks full of people's personalities. She flicks through another and finds a shift dress in a thick woven material with mustard-coloured swirls and tiny pockets above the hem. Similar to one she wore as a child. The sound of funfair music starts playing in her head. Margate beach on a warm sunny day, a bucket and spade and a stick of rock. With the father she loved and thought she knew so well. She looks up to see her mother nod at her from an upright mirror.

Maddy glances over at Alison behind the till. Does she know he might be dead?

'Three fifty, please,' Alison says to the woman she is serving. She holds up each item of clothing and folds them. 'Aren't they lovely?'

'Having a boy next, so I thought, yeah, why not,' the customer says, rubbing her bump, ripe as a melon.

'I'd love a girl,' sighs Alison. 'Always wanted one of each.'

Maddy picks up a candle. The wick is scorched, and the centre is a deep scar of melted wax. She stands in the queue behind the woman and her pushchair. Maddy can feel her baby moving. She puts a hand to her bump and imagines the shape of a little fist or heel kicking out.

When the woman leaves, Alison smiles, sly as a cat. As she takes the candle from her, Maddy's eyes fix on her necklace, a small silver asymmetrical heart. Her hand shoots up to her own neck. It's exactly the same one as Max bought her for her birthday last year, but she's not been wearing it lately. Instead her fingers curl around her mum's garnet pendant.

Alison picks off the label with her child-like fingers and wraps the candle in crumpled tissue paper. 'Thirty-five, please.' She takes the money from Maddy's hand, skimming her palm with her pointed nails. Maddy flinches.

'Sorry, did I catch you?' Her faint blue eyes are surrounded with dark, hollow sockets.

Maddy is silent.

Alison drops the coins in the till.

'When are you due?' Maddy asks, even though she already knows.

'Nine weeks to go, God help me.' Alison smiles and blows air out of her pursed lips. 'What about you?'

'Fourteen weeks.' Maddy looks down at her roundness. 'They say your second is always quicker, don't they?' Alison tips her head to the side, trying to meet her eyes. 'Mine was.'

'So, is this your third?'

'Yes. But my second child died.' Maddy tries not to notice Alison's wide smile suddenly drop.

'I'm so sorry... are you okay, you've gone very pale.'

Maddy's legs start to tremble. Chloe's dead face appears in her mind. She puts a hand to her forehead, it's throbbing and hot. She doesn't want to be here, she wants to be at home with Emily so she can hug her tight.

'Come and sit over here. You don't look right at all.' Alison brings a chair around to the front and Maddy collapses into it. Her back, underarms and neck are drenched with sweat.

'Rob, grab me some water.'

The young man comes down from the ladder and goes through to the kitchen. He returns with a cloudy-looking liquid. Have they guessed who she is? Are they trying to poison her?

'You're not married, are you?' Maddy asks.

For a fleeting moment Alison frowns. 'Doesn't matter these days, does it?' She laughs, turning to Rob next to her.

He shakes his head. 'Unless he's already married, of course.'

Alison's mouth falls open. 'Well no, I'd never do that.'

'Wouldn't you? How do you know?'

'Why would you say that?'

'Because, you can't trust any of them.'

'I think you ought to go.' Rob comes around to the front of the counter.

'Hang on, are you the woman who knocked at my door that time?' Alison says, clutching the carrier bag.

Maddy stands up and slams the glass down on the counter. 'Tell me where my husband is?' She shouts at her.

'I told you before, I don't know him.'

'You're lying, what have you done with him – he's my husband!'

'Get her out of here,' Alison calls to Rob, but before he can do anything Maddy is marching towards the door. She skims past the racks of clothes, knocking a grey dress to the ground. Her mother smiles out from a mirror like the Cheshire cat.

On the drive home, Maddy imagines Max pulling into the drive at Lawn End, wheeling the dustbin back into place, putting his key in the front door. He'll call out hello, give Alison a kiss, ask Jamie what he'd been doing at school that day. When Max was with Alison, Maddy didn't exist.

43

MAX: APRIL 2017

Max stood at the door of Ali's maisonette, his finger hovering over the buzzer. He would offer to pay her a lump sum for back payments of maintenance and come and see the boy as often as he could, but that was where it had to end.

He squinted at the feathery rain. A pair of Spiderman wellies stood outside. He drew on his cigarette, but it was too damp, so he chucked it on the pavement and pressed the buzzer.

Ali looked hot in a tight blue dress and ankle boots. Jamie was lingering in the background. She invited Max in and took his jacket. The smell of roast chicken wafted out of the kitchen. He'd told Maddy he was out with some mates, a few games of pool and lunch at the pub, so he hadn't dressed up, not wanting her to question him, but now he felt scruffy in his old jeans, like he couldn't be bothered.

Ali ushered him into the tiny sitting room. 'Jamie, there you are, come and say hello.'

The boy stood at the sitting room door, his hair glowed golden in the light.

'Hello.' Max had never been so nervous.

'Does your hand hurt?' Jamie asked.

'It's much better, thanks.' Max swallowed hard. Ali put her arm around Jamie's shoulders.

'Remember what I was telling you about me and Adam?' she said. 'Well, he's got something important to tell you.'

Max took a deep breath.

'Your mum and I couldn't be together when you were born, but I'm going to make up for it. I hope you're all right with me being your dad.'

Jamie's lips trembled. Max put his hand out to him, and Jamie touched his fingertips.

'I'd like to be around a lot more, if you want me to?' Jamie nodded and wiped his nose on the back of his sleeve.

'What will happen to Tony?'

'He'll probably go down for what he did to Adam,' Ali said.

'But he promised to buy me a PlayStation.'

'I'm sure we can sort one out for you.' Max winked at Ali.

She nodded and smiled.

'As long as you behave yourself. You can start by helping me with dinner.' She ruffled Jamie's hair and he followed her into the kitchen.

Max wandered around the living room. Framed photos of Jamie as a baby and growing up were on every wall. He wiped his forehead. Emily wasn't his firstborn any more. Did this mean that every first with her didn't count? Were all those special moments tarnished because they'd already happened with his first child? Except he hadn't been there to witness them and that didn't sit right with him. It was a kick in the gut that he'd missed out on so much. Maybe it would be easier to walk away after all. None of this was fair on Maddy let alone Emily and Chloe. He could slip out of the door unnoticed, maybe move abroad with Maddy and the girls. Thanks to Ali's dear old dad, she'd never be able to trace him, not with his new name and the life she knew nothing about. But would he really be able to give up on his own son? *Jamie*. He couldn't deny he was pleased he had a son, and Jamie was a good kid, kind and thoughtful. He'd already had a hard start in life, a bit like his own. How could he walk away now, like his own parents did to him?

'He seems fine,' Ali whispered, standing at the door. 'What did you tell him before?'

'That you had to go away.'

'Poor kid.' But one day he'd tell Jamie the truth, that his grandfather lied to him, told him he'd been aborted because no one was allowed to date the boss's daughter, let alone fall in love with her and get her pregnant. How he wished the old man was still alive so he could smash his face in for making him leave.

'I need to keep an eye on the dinner. Come and have a beer?' He followed her into the kitchen. She opened a bottle and handed it to him. Jamie laid the table, then took his ball out to the small patio garden.

'It's a shock for him to find out you're his dad,' she said taking a lid off a pan, releasing a slinking ribbon of steam like a genie. She was crying and he didn't know what to say. He put his arm around her, and she turned into his chest.

'You will keep coming to see him, won't you?' she said. 'I mean, you will stick to it?'

'Of course I will. It just kills me that I didn't know about him sooner.' He had to make this work somehow without hurting Maddy. There was no way he would do what his own parents did and deliberately bugger off.

She turned to the cooker and stirred the gravy. Max wandered back into the living room with his beer. Jamie smiled broadly at him from the tiny garden.

'Shall we have a kickabout then?' Max finished his beer. The boy's face brightened.

'What team do you support?'

'Peterborough, I guess,' Jamie said. A miniature goal stood at one end of the patio. Hardly enough space for a growing boy to run around.

'I support Arsenal. I could take you to a home game if you like. Do you think your mum will let you?'

Jamie nodded, grinning.

'Let's see how many you can get past me,' Max said.

Jamie concentrated hard before he kicked the ball. It shot straight past Max into the back of the net.

'What? Where did that come from?' Max raised his hands in disbelief. 'You got golden boots or something?'

Jamie's smile spread and lit up his face. He cracked a few more shots at goal and Max only saved one of them. Ali stood watching at the patio door.

'Did you see that?' Max said. 'The boy's got talent, I'm telling you.'

Jamie blushed.

'I always knew it. Wanted to kick a ball about as soon as he could walk.' Ali smiled. 'Couldn't he go to one of those academies?'

'If he wants to and if they think he's good enough.' But he would never become a world class player in a garden the size of a postage stamp.

After dinner, Jamie helped Ali clear the table then he went to his room to play. He was a quiet, gentle child and deserved every privilege his girls had.

'What are your arrangements here, rent-wise?' Max asked, drinking another beer, pacing up and down the room. His brain was spinning into overdrive.

'We've been here about two years, but we need to think about moving soon because the landlord is putting the rent up next year.'

'Will you be able to get anything bigger? I mean you can barely call that a garden out there, it's more like a yard.' He pointed with his bottle.

'I'm only just getting by now. You can see how pokey this is, but I can't stretch to anything more on my wage.'

Max finished his second beer. He wanted his son to have a better life than this.

'Before Tony, there was Ian,' she said. 'He lived with us for the best part of a year. It was easier then with both wages coming in. Jamie was a toddler and got really attached to him, even started to call him Daddy. I thought he was going to stay for good, but Jaz saw him out with another woman, so I ended it. I've been struggling ever since.'

'So, there's no one else on the scene?'

'No, I'd tell you if there was.' She sat on the sofa.

'I promise I'll do what I can to help. I want to be a big part of Jamie's life.'

'You're away a lot with your job though, aren't you?'

'Yeah, but I'll visit as often as I can.'

'Will you though?'

'I said I would, didn't I?' The beer had gone to his head.

'You could do better than that.' She grabbed his hand and playfully pulled him down next to her, kissing him passionately. He couldn't help kissing her back. He'd resisted her for so long. All his senses sprung to life and the years fell away instantly. They were young again, deeply in love. In that moment, no one else existed. The smell of her, the taste, the feel of her soft hair and skin was all he could focus on. And just like before, everything Ali said or did intoxicated him. There was no way he could walk out of her life again, nor Jamie's.

'Why not move in with us?'

'I don't know, Ali, this is all pretty sudden.'

'Is it? But he's your son, the child you always wanted, remember? You said yourself you don't have any other commitments.'

They sat in silence. Max tried to avoid her gaze.

'Unless it's me you're not sure about? I thought you said you felt the old spark still.'

'My God, I do... it's just that...' He moved towards her and pushed a fallen length of golden hair behind her ear. He had to tell her about his family, put an end to this fantasy. 'You wouldn't like me being away all the time, I know you.'

'I'll get used to it.'

'Could Jamie though? I couldn't guarantee exactly when I'd be here. He'd be disappointed all the time.' He pictured her face if he told her about Maddy and the girls. She wouldn't let him see Jamie again, just when he was getting to know him. 'It would drive you insane.'

'Not if I knew you were coming back to us, to our home.' She buried her head in his chest. 'Isn't this what we always talked about? What we dreamt of all those years ago?'

He buried his face in her silky hair, breathing in the warm aroma of perfume. She was right, it had been their dream, but they were kids then and life wasn't straightforward. He moved her hair aside and kissed her neck. He couldn't help himself wanting her. There had to be a way to make this work so he could see all his children and not hurt Maddy or Alison.

'We couldn't stay here, it's too small. We'd have to find somewhere bigger.' Could he really live in two places? What if they moved to one of the newbuilds he'd been working on? Then he could see Jamie whenever he liked, every day, every week, fit it around living with Maddy and the girls. They were used to him being away; it wouldn't need to affect them. He'd be able to take Jamie to football matches, the park, all sorts. But he'd have to find a deposit. Shouldn't be too tricky getting a mortgage as Maddy's house was all paid for when her dad died. Maybe it was possible to make this work without anyone getting hurt.

Alison pulled a photo album out of a cupboard and spread it across both their laps. She flicked through photos of Jamie as a baby. Max thought about the day Emily was born, how he'd felt holding her, the elation at her being his firstborn. But now that was wrong. History had been rewritten.

'And this is Jamie at eleven months...' Ali's voice drifted in and out. He and Maddy had taken an almost identical set of photos of their family. Each a precious and unique moment. Ali pulled on his sleeve.

'Are you okay? You look tired.'

The album was closed. Had he dozed off for a second or two?

'I need some air.' He let himself out onto the patio and leaned over the side of the brick barbeque as the ground swam in front of his eyes.

44

ALISON: NOVEMBER 2019

By the time Alison reaches work, the Saturday ladies are in. One is on the till and the other is tidying up a rack of books. Rob is at the back, dragging in black bags full of clothes and toys people have left by the service door. A plastic sword trails out of one behind him.

In the sorting room, piles of donations spill out of stacked boxes on every surface. Alison steps over a cowboy hat that has slipped off a pile of coats. A mustiness lingers in the air no matter how long they leave the back door open or spray air-fresheners; it never seems to go. They deal with the remnants of people's lives, things no longer wanted, thrown or neatly folded into bin liners, not always washed or wiped. Occasionally she takes home a bundle to wash. Grey water twists and turns the garments in the washing machine, rinsing out people's last remains.

Rob pulls up a chair for her. She sits down, coat touching the floor, her suede handbag curls into her lap like a sleeping cat.

'He's left me, I'm sure of it,' she says, caressing her bump.

'What's brought this on?'

'The row we had the morning he left has been playing on my mind.' She shrugs off her coat and steps through to the kitchen to hang it on the back of the door. 'And that woman that came in here. Do you think she was right?'

'Hey, don't let that crazy bat get to you. You've been doing so well up till now.'

It bothers her to think that her belongings might become muddled with items from the shop. It could easily happen, and she wouldn't necessarily know about it until it was too late. She's always found it difficult to part with things. Their loft is jammed full of boxes from her past. Adam owns almost nothing. When he moved in, he had a small bag full of clothes, a pair of trainers, but not much else.

She fills the kettle. Maybe it was too soon for him to settle down. She's been too demanding. One child should be enough. Some people can't have any. Why did she want more? Greedy, always wants more. Her father's voice booms in her head. She sees her tiny hand scoop up jellybeans from a cut-glass bowl, him crushing her wrist until she dropped them. For days afterwards, her hand was useless, like a grabber machine at the seaside unable to grasp the teddy.

Rob leans across the counter. 'Have you actually spoken to him? I mean he's always staying away without contacting you.'

She hates that he's so pleased. He passes her the milk. She takes the lid off and sniffs. The sourness hits the back of her throat and almost makes her retch. She tips it down the sink, its whiteness swirling, leaving an opaque film over the tea stains. The fridge door sticks as she pulls it open. It's empty except for Rob's lunchtime can of Coke. She is sure they had more milk.

'I'll go and get some,' he says. 'I need to call in at the bookies.'

She tries to smile. 'It's okay, I'll have it without.'

'In that case, I'll go and sort the shoes out before my break.' He checks his watch.

She cuts open one of the bin bags he brought in. It's mostly kids' toys with a faint whiff of vomit. Rob will wash them later. She opens the next bag and it's full of unopened rolls of neon wallpaper. Someone had a change of heart. They can probably go straight out on the shelves. Some arty type will buy them. The third bag is bulging and heavy. Must be full of clothes.

She rips it open and pulls out a neatly folded pile of jeans followed by jumpers. The top one is a cute polar bear Christmas jumper with glitter on white peaks of snow. It's beautiful. She used to have one just like it. It never stops surprising her what people throw out. Underneath is another festive knit, a thinner material, long sleeves, more a tunic. On the front, there's a pattern in silver and gold snowflakes, making up the shape of a wreath. She's recently bought one just like this in the Black Friday sales; in fact, this one still has the tag on it. Shame it's never been worn. The jeans seem familiar. Someone has very similar taste to her. She holds up a pair, then another. Strange. She picks up the oldest pair and sticks her hand in the back pocket. There's a small hole in it, just like in her own pair at home. She tips out the whole bag onto the table. All the clothes are hers. Is this a joke? She's not donated anything from home for ages, so it's definitely not her, she's not going mad. How can this have happened? It has to be Adam, when he's been in the house while she's out. How dare he chuck out her clothes then dump them where she works! He must have known she'd find them.

On the shop floor, she finds Rob crouched in a corner, pairing up shoes. There's a red pair of sandals she's trying to resist.

'Do you know who left those bags at the back door, because I've just found one full of my own clothes.'

'Really?' Rob arches an eyebrow.

'Do you think Adam is trying to get rid of me?'

'Ali, you know what I think about it.' He sits back on his heels.

'Why else would he do something like this?'

'Look at the situation he's left you in – you're about to have his baby. You've got to ask yourself, what kind of bloke would do that?'

She sighs.

'Why don't I pop over tonight, and we can talk?'

She shakes her head and picks up the red sandal, slipping her hand inside it. She mustn't encourage him.

'You deserve better.' His mouth relaxes into a warm smile. She kicks the air with the sandal. 'I wish you wouldn't put up with him.' He touches her arm. A power surge shoots through her. She drops the shoe on the floor and locks her hands together. He turns his back on her, adjusting his crotch.

As he bends down, she examines the back of his neck, the soft springy hairs escaping his Pink Floyd T-shirt, a wing-looking tattoo, just visible. She never knew Rob had tattoos.

His hands work quickly, matching the shoes together, lining them up. She imagines those hands smoothing over her body. No, stop it. Adam's not left her, he's coming home.

45

MADDY: NOVEMBER 2019

It's a gusty day, not the best weather to be playing in the park with Emily, but Maddy won't let it put her off. Squinting at the low, blinding sun, she pushes Emily on the swing, all the time keeping an eye on the path by the hairdressers, which she guesses is the way he will come. A crow squawks angrily in the swaying skeleton tree as the wind rumbles around them. Emily says something, but her voice is snatched away. Maddy checks her phone. It is exactly 5 p.m. Perhaps he can't get away. If Mother's idea works, he won't be able to resist the note she left in his sock drawer, because she signed it 'Dad'.

*COME AND MEET ME AT THE PARK AT 5 PM.
DON'T TELL YOUR MUM. IT'S OUR LITTLE SE-
CRET. DAD X*

There is the possibility that he'll show it to Alison, which is why she's disguised her handwriting by using capital letters. Hopefully it's easy for Jamie to read. She pictures her marching around the corner of the hairdressers and dragging Jamie away by the wrist. By then it won't matter because she'll have turned him against her. Told him things he ought to know about his mother. Maddy will put her hood up, turn away and hope she goes straight back home when she realises Adam is not there and she's just a mum in a park with her daughter.

It's 5.02 p.m. Is he allowed out on his own normally? She's not sure, but he can sneak out of the door, can't he? He'd do anything to see his dad.

At 5.03 p.m., he runs towards them, head down, hood up. Poor boy, probably thinks Daddy won't wait. She keeps one eye on Emily, who is in the climbing frame, while she waves at Jamie. He comes to an abrupt halt in front of her.

'Oh, hi again, have you seen my dad? He said he'd be here.' Jamie is out of breath. He's changed out of his school clothes and is wearing jeans and trainers.

'He's really sad he couldn't make it, Jamie, so he asked me to come for him. I hope that's okay?' She scans his heart-shaped face: the nose and eyes are so like Max, and the long dark eyelashes, Emily has the same ones too.

'But he promised he'd be here,' he whines. 'Where is he?'

'He had to go away for work, but he says he really misses you and he left this for you.' She reaches in her pocket and hands him a present. He rips it open hungrily and takes out a bar of his favourite chocolate; at least, she guesses it's his favourite because she's found enough wrappers in his bin. Inside is another present. He opens it and shouts with delight at the set of rare black star Pokémon cards. Maddy is well aware of his huge collection carefully displayed in special albums, and knows from Emily going to boys' birthday parties that these are the ones they really want.

'You'll probably have to hide them from your mum, otherwise she'll start asking questions and we don't want your dad getting in trouble, do we?'

Jamie shakes his head. 'When's he coming home though?'

'I'm sure it won't be long now. I think he's staying away because he had a bad argument with your mum?' She's searched through Alison's Facebook page and, reading between the lines, that's the main reason she believes he's not come back. But in Maddy's mind there can only be one reason why he's disappeared from Alison's life, too, and she can't accept that, not until a body is found.

'Yeah, they're always shouting at each other because Mum wants to get married and he doesn't. I wish they'd stop, because it doesn't matter, but nobody asks me.'

'Ah, I'm really sorry. That must have been tough for you. She's not very nice to your dad. I think he's had enough.' Why didn't he leave Alison and come home?

He nods and looks like he might cry. Emily is watching them, so she beckons her over. Jamie is looking over his shoulder like he ought to get back.

'There's something else your dad asked me to do. He wants you to meet someone special.'

'Who?'

'This is Emily. She's your half-sister. Emily, meet Jamie.' They look at her then at each other. Jamie frowns and steps back.

'I'd better go home.' His voice is small. It's a shock, of course it is, which is why she's not mentioned the baby.

'Already? You've only just got here. I'm sure your

dad would love you to stay and play with your little sister, so you can get to know each other?'

Emily smiles. Maddy puts her hand out to him. She's always wanted the girls to have a brother.

Jamie shakes his head and bites his lip. Emily stands by his side. She can't take her eyes off him.

'Oh, come on, Jamie, after your dad's gone to all this trouble to bring us together and bought you some lovely presents too?' While she's talking, she slowly manoeuvres herself towards him until she is by his side and her arm can easily reach around his shoulders. Her car is only a short distance away. Emily would love having him around.

'I've got to go.' He turns on his heel and runs off.

46

MAX: NOVEMBER 2017

It was Saturday morning, seven months since he'd first met up with Ali again and here he was, in her maisonette, waking up next to her like they'd been together always, without interruption. He'd hoped that by now he'd have been able to choose between Alison and Maddy, but it was impossible to decide. He loved them both and couldn't bear the thought of hurting either of them or his kids.

He propped himself up on a pillow. Ali opened her eyes. 'Happy birthday,' he said.

She smiled and stretched her arms.

'Penny for your thoughts?' He stroked her hair away from her face.

'I feel like I'm still dreaming.' She turned towards

him. 'This is the best birthday ever. All I wanted was for us to be together as a family.'

He kissed her lips. 'I've been thinking, now we've almost finished the houses on this new estate, how about you and Jamie move into one? Don't want to be renting all your life, do you?'

Ali sat up. 'I told you, I can't afford to move.'

'Don't worry, I'll sort out the deposit.' He'd feel bad asking Maddy for the money, lying to her about becoming John's business partner, but Jamie deserved to have as good a life as the girls with a nice home and a big garden. He wanted to be the best dad to Jamie, so he knew he could always count on him, unlike his own lousy parents.

'Will you move in with us?' she said.

'If you want me to.'

'Do you want to?' She stroked his stubbly face.

''Course, as long as you understand I'll be away for several days at a time.' He turned away and gulped down a glass of water. It would be tricky, but what choice did he have? He'd struggled over it for months. He just couldn't give up Maddy and the girls and he had to do everything possible to protect them from this. Why should they suffer? They hadn't done anything wrong. He'd managed to keep it all on his terms so far, coming here a couple of nights a week and every other weekend. Holidays could be difficult, but he'd work something out. Better than having some judge tell him when he could or couldn't see his kids.

'What are the houses like?'

'Three bedrooms, good size garden, all mod cons, as Gran would say. The one I have in mind has an old apple tree in it.'

She snuggled under his arm.

'It's the best one, corner plot, plenty of space for Jamie to run around.' The truth was, he'd picked it weeks ago because it had a similar layout to home.

'Low maintenance, I hope; you know I hate gardening.'

'I can do all that, it's mainly lawn anyway. Perfect for football.'

'We could patio it.'

'That would be a shame, I was thinking of planting some vegetables.'

'It'd be good for Jamie to ride his bike.'

'Well why don't you come and see it first?'

She sat up. 'Today?'

He thought for a minute. 'Yeah, okay, why not. The decorating is almost finished. I hope you like it – chose it myself.' He'd already put his name down for it so his boss didn't mind him choosing the décor. It was the same wallpaper and carpets he'd used at home so that everything was familiar to him. Less likely to make a stupid mistake.

'It'll be our new start – as a proper family.' She kissed him on the cheek.

Jamie came in holding an Action Man attached to a harness and bungee rope he'd bought him.

'I'm hungry,' he said, climbing into bed between them. 'Hello little man.' Max gave him a hug.

'We'll get up in a minute,' Ali said. 'Shall I make porridge?'

'Yeah.' Jamie rubbed his tummy.

'Then we're going on a secret journey.' Max put his finger to his lips.

He giggled. 'Where are we going?'

Max and Ali laughed. 'It's a secret!' they said together. 'Wait here, I've got something for the birthday girl.' Max went out of the room and a few moments later came back with a large box tied up with a bow. He laid it gently on the carpet.

Ali's eyes shone. The box moved by itself.

'What is it, Jamie?' She threw back the duvet and stood up. Jamie giggled. 'It's a surprise!'

'Take a look inside.' Max grinned at her.

She undid the bow and took off the lid. Looking up at her was a springer spaniel puppy.

'Oh Adam! He's so sweet.'

'Happy birthday!' Jamie and Max shouted together.

'We've never had a dog before, have we, Mum?' Jamie knelt on the floor and touched the dog's velvety face.

'No, but isn't he lovely?'

'I thought he'd be company for you both.'

'Where have you kept him all night?' She picked the puppy up and snuggled her face into the downy fur.

'I collected him first thing this morning, then sneaked back to bed. The breeder lives nearby.' He rubbed his hands together and glanced at his feet. 'I thought we could call him Poppy.'

'But that's a girl's name.' Ali laughed. Jamie pulled a funny face.

'I know, but they didn't have a girl, and I like the name.' He shrugged and pulled one of his persuasive grins.

'All right then,' Ali said.

* * *

Later that morning, they pulled up in Lawn End, part of a new housing estate in a village on the outskirts of Huntingdon. Jamie held Ali's hand.

Max showed them in. 'A few things left to do, and it'll be ready if you like it.' He stood back while Ali felt the wallpaper. 'I love it, Adam! This is just what I would have chosen, very classy.'

From the living room, through the large expanse of patio doors, they viewed the apple tree at the far end of the generous-sized garden. Smaller than Maddy's, but still, a similar arrangement.

'Is this going to be our house?' Jamie pushed his face up to the glass.

'It could be,' Max said. 'Let's go upstairs and you can pick your bedroom.'

'Can I?' Jamie asked Ali. 'Of course you can,' she said.

Upstairs, Jamie ran into all three bedrooms and chose the one at the front of the house.

'Can we see the master bedroom?' Ali asked, pulling on Max's arm like an excited child.

They found the largest room at the back with an en-suite bathroom.

'Do you like it then?' Max asked, draping his arms around her and kissing her neck.

'I love it. I mean, really, really.'

'So do I, so do I.' Jamie spun round and round until he staggered to a dizzy stop.

'We can get you a new bed if you like,' Max said.

'Really?' He looked at Ali who was smiling. 'Can I have a bunk bed with a ladder?'

'I don't see why not.' Max took Ali's hand and kissed it. 'Thank you, Daddy!' Jamie ran over to Max and flung his arms around his legs. Ali's mouth opened. Max's eyes filled with tears. It was the first time he'd called him Daddy.

Max crouched down and Jamie threw his arms around his neck.

'That's it then, it's ours. When do you want to move in?' he said.

47

Maddy and the girls were raking leaves into the middle of the lawn when Max arrived home the next day. Chloe ran up to him and he swung her up in his arms.

'Can we build a bonfire, Daddy?' Emily pleaded. The bobble on her hat tipped from side to side as she jumped up and down.

He glanced at Maddy, whose nose and cheeks were scorched red with cold.

'I told them they could,' she said, a little out of breath. They'd already collected branches and twigs in the wheelbarrow. A wisp of hair hung over her eye. She tried to push it away with her gloved hand, but it fell down again.

'I suppose so,' he said. Chloe's icy nose brushed his cheek as he let her down. She giggled and ran off towards the greenhouse.

'We've been making a Guy to burn.' Emily emphasised the word 'burn' as if she were handing out a death sentence.

'Have you now?'

'They said at school that Guy Fawkes tried to blow up a house. Whose house was it, Daddy?' Emily asked.

'The Houses of Parliament, darling.' Max winked at Maddy.

'He was hung, drawn and quartered. They don't do that any more do they, Daddy?' Emily exaggerated a frown.

'No, darling,' Maddy laughed, 'and thank goodness for that.'

'I think I might go and lie down for a bit.' Max yawned.

'Are you all right?' Maddy's eyes creased with concern.

'Look at my apples, Daddy.' Chloe emerged from behind the greenhouse with a little bucket full of half-rotten apples.

She chucked two across the lawn and both dogs chased after them.

'Tip the rest in the compost, sweetheart.' Maddy

nudged Emily to go and help her. Max trudged indoors and Maddy followed, slipping her wellington
boots off at the door. He turned and kissed her cheek.
She smelled of crisp, woody air.

'Can I get you anything?' She rubbed his arm and
tried to catch his eye, but he avoided the loving look
he knew would be there, in case she spotted his deceit.
These transitions were much harder than he'd expected, and the guilt was a constant thorn digging into
him. He hated saying goodbye to one family while
trying to slip back into the rhythm of the other. But if it
meant they all stayed happy, it was worth it. Plus he
couldn't deny there were many benefits for him.
Having a nap was like cleaning the slate and when
he'd woken up, he'd be ready to be part of this family
again.

'Actually, I've been thinking – John's asked me to go
into partnership with him. Do you think we can stump
up some cash?'

'How much?' She lifted the lid off a pot on the
cooker. The spicy smell of butternut squash soup
wafted towards him.

'Twenty-five.'

She stirred the thick mixture with a wooden spoon
then tested a little on her tongue.

'He'd still be in charge of the building side, and I'd take care of the decorating.'

'Sounds a lot,' she said and took out three bowls from the cupboard.

'It would be so good to be my own boss at last.'

'I'll think about it.'

'I'm sure I can get him down to twenty, no problem.'

'Let's talk about it later.'

'You know it's what I've been after.' He slipped his arm around her waist. 'I'll have more freedom, make more money.'

'And you'll be away more.'

'Everything has its price.' He pulled her closer. 'It'll be worth it, I promise.' He detected the flicker of a smile in her eyes.

He plodded upstairs, lay down on the bed and shut his eyes. What would he do if she said no, especially now he'd promised Ali and Jamie the house? He couldn't help imagining them in it: Ali gliding around barefoot on the new carpets, Jamie still in his pyjamas, lounging on the sofa watching TV. His eyes snapped open. But he would never leave Maddy. She'd given herself to him completely from the start, been open about everything. He scanned their wedding photo on the bedside table, and the miniatures of the girls when each of them was born. The thought of deserting them, abandoning his life here choked him up. He'd never tell Maddy about Ali and Jamie. She'd never forgive him; she'd kick him out, no question. But could he really pull this off? Keep them both happy? He buried his head under the pillow.

* * *

It was dark when he woke. The smell of burning wood filled the room. Shivering, he stepped out of bed and shut the window.

Downstairs, he drifted into the living room. Through the French windows, he watched the bonfire dance and rage. Maddy and the girls held up a gangly-looking Guy. Max banged his fists on the glass, but they couldn't hear him. He rushed outside.

'I'll do that, it's dangerous.' His words hung in a cloud of icy air. He grabbed the Guy by its crudely drawn face and stuffed torso. The frowning eyebrows he imagined resembled his own. The flames crackled and hissed, the heat meltingly hot.

'These are my clothes,' he shouted, trying to take a closer look under the orange glow, pulling at the Guy's jumper and shirt.

'Da-aad,' Emily whined.

'Old ones you don't wear any more,' Maddy shouted back.

'Can't I decide that?' Yes, they had holes in, but they were his favourite T-shirt and jeans from years ago. And the jumper was one his gran had knitted for him.

Chloe started to cry.

'You're being ridiculous, Max,' Maddy shouted.

'You should have asked me. They're my things. They mean a lot to me. Didn't you think to ask?'

'You weren't here, they were in your bottom drawer and I've not seen you wear them for ages.'

'Put him on the fire, Daddy,' Emily growled, hands on hips. Max bared his teeth and swung the cloth body up in the air, his past life landing on the hungry fire. They all stood back, quiet now, watching the Guy being swallowed up by flames.

48

ALISON: NOVEMBER 2019

Alison calls out to Jamie for his dinner. For once he's switched off the TV and gone to his room. He doesn't answer. This is the third time she's called him. She stomps up the stairs. He's probably plugged in to some music or a game and can't hear a bloody thing. She pushes his door open and is about to shout at him but he's not there. He's not in bed because it's been made. She looks behind the door then opens the wardrobe. He'll jump out at her in a second and scare her to death. She searches in their bedroom and the bathroom. Did she hear him creep downstairs or was that Poppy moving?

'Come on, Jamie, no more games, your dinner is getting cold.'

The house is quiet except for the extractor in the bathroom and the wind howling down the road. The back door slams giving her a start. 'Jamie?' she calls over the banister. Still no answer. She marches down the stairs. This isn't funny any more. Jamie is standing in the hallway in his coat. His face is red, tear tracks shining on his cheeks.

'Where've you been? I didn't say you could go out, did I?' She grabs his arm, and he pulls away from her. 'Why did you go out without asking me?'

'It's all your fault Dad hasn't come home,' he sobs and runs past her up the stairs. She shakes her head, unsure of what just happened. She'll leave him to calm down.

* * *

A removals van is parked on next door's drive when Alison and Jamie arrive home the next day. Two men carry a large box marked 'kitchen' through the doorway. A Yorkshire terrier runs out between their legs and stands there barking at her and Jamie. Jamie whimpers and jumps behind her. A middle-aged woman wearing beige cotton trousers, dirtied by dust, steps out and shushes the dog away.

'Sorry about that, he won't bite,' the woman says in

a deep smoker's voice. She steps forward, a large stride for a woman. 'I'm Natty.'

'I'm Ali and this is Jamie.' She manoeuvres him forward, gently tipping his face up by the chin. 'Jamie's dad, Adam, is away on business.' She cringes. She'll kill him for embarrassing her like this.

'He's always away, and it's all your fault.' Jamie stamps his foot and pushes his fist into her side.

Alison gives Natty her best smile, but tears are pricking her eyes. She still hasn't got to the bottom of why Jamie went out yesterday. He's being very secretive. Her fingers slide over his lips. He frowns up at her, but she won't look directly at him. She will not put up with this behaviour.

'George.' Natty catches the arm of a white-bearded man as he appears behind her. 'Come and meet our new neighbours.' George is a short stocky man with surprisingly skinny legs.

He's wearing a big knit sweater, over-the-knee shorts and canvas shoes with no socks. He salutes and tips his sailor's cap then disappears indoors.

'We'll be shipshape by this evening,' Natty chuckles, showing an uneven set of rotten teeth.

'Really?' Alison says. She needs to sit down. This baby feels so heavy today.

'We don't have many things, lived on a boat up till now.'

'Oh.' Alison doesn't mean to be abrupt, but she's put out by people who are more organised than she is.

'Mind you, it'll take a while to find our land legs.' She chuckles. 'When's your husband back?'

Alison doesn't like people assuming she's married, but she also hates not being able to call Adam her husband. She's not about to correct her. 'He probably won't be back today.'

'Busy man, is he? That's a shame.'

Alison thinks she says it like she doesn't mean it.

'He works very hard.' Her voice quivers slightly, making her sound unsure like a child.

Natty smiles widely. It's more of a disbelieving smirk, meaning we both know the truth: he's left you and he's not coming back.

Alison goes to push the key into the lock but misses. She tries again, conscious of being watched. It slides in and she opens the door. Poppy races out barking. The terrier re-appears, growling. Alison pulls Poppy by the collar and shoos him indoors shutting the door behind them.

In the hallway, she detects a fresh lemony smell. The laminate floor looks shiny. She tries to think if it's ever looked that way since they moved in. The pile of magazines on the bench behind the door has vanished. In fact, all the clutter piled there has gone. In the sitting room, everywhere is tidy. Dusty shelves have been wiped down, fingerprints buffed from the windows. There isn't one speck of dust or hair on the rug.

Jamie is holding a photo. Even upside down she knows she's never seen it before. Adam is younger, standing with a dark-haired woman. Their arms are around each other in a garden, but Jamie's thumb is obscuring the woman's face. Without thinking, Alison snatches the photo out of his hand.

'Mum!'

'Where did you get this?' She looks closely at the woman, but the quality is grainy. She seems familiar but she can't place her.

'On there.' He points to the coffee table. The glass is gleaming. Not a single smudge or fingerprint.

'Do you know anything about this?'

He runs upstairs shouting, 'I don't want to talk to you.'

What is going on with him? She catches her reflection. The further time goes on, the more she is convinced that Adam isn't coming back to live with them. But is he trying to torment her to make her leave? Where would she go? She'll have to ring his work again, but last time she did they hadn't seen him for ages. She'll look so stupid asking where he is, like she's lost him. She's thought about going to the police, but it's his house too, and none of what he's doing is a crime they'd recognise. A couple of people on Facebook thought they'd seen him in The Black Bull in Brampton, but nothing came of it when she checked with the landlord.

Upstairs, their bed has been made, smoothed out so there are no creases. All her make-up has been lined up according to size and everything on her dressing table has been placed symmetrically. In the wardrobe, the clothes that are left have been sorted into groups according to colour. But there are big gaps where her clothes have been removed, disposed of, as though bit by bit Adam is trying to erase her from his life. She slumps down on the bed. Why is he doing this to her when they're about to have their second child? His absence feels like history repeating itself. She knows she's not perfect and her messiness drives him mad, but does she really deserve him cleaning up after her and ignoring her? The baby gives a sharp kick. What is she going to do? She's not sure she can face being a single mum again, this time bringing up his two children on her own.

49

MAX: EARLY DECEMBER 2017

The remains of the winter sun splashed in vivid lines across the sky. Emily and Chloe were up ahead on their bikes, side by side. He followed on his, bought by Maddy last Christmas. He'd meant to go out on it more during the year, but he never seemed to find the time.

'Round this last corner then we'll make our way back,' he said, catching up with the girls. The park was almost deserted.

'Do we have to go?' Emily asked.

'It's getting dark. I'll have to take you camping, won't I?'

'Can we? In a big tent?' Emily asked and Chloe repeated it.

'Yeah, why not. When it's warmer though, hey?'

When they got home, Max sent the girls indoors while he wheeled their bikes into the garage. Once he'd locked the door, he did his usual check for messages on his silenced mobile phone. Eight missed calls, all from Ali. What the hell? Was Jamie all right? This was their third week in the new house. He wasn't due to go back there for two days. He hurried inside and put the leads on the dogs.

The girls were already sitting with Maddy, drinking hot chocolate and watching a TV adaptation of *Jane Eyre.*

'I'll just take them for a quick one,' he said to Maddy, pecking her cheek.

'What about your drink?'

'It'll be too hot for me. Can you cover it and I'll have it when I come back?'

He crept out, closing the door quietly behind him. The daylight was fading fast. Perhaps the heating wasn't working, or they'd had a power cut. But would she call him repeatedly for that?

As soon as he reached the field up from Uxbridge Common, he called Ali's number.

'Hello?' Silence.

'Where've you been?' Her voice sounded broken and distant.

'What's wrong?' Max stopped mid-stride. He automatically unclipped the dogs' leads.

'Jamie's fallen out of that bloody apple tree.' Her words came in sobs.

Poppy and Daisy ran around him in circles as flashes of white in the near darkness.

'What's he doing up a tree at this time of year?' Stupid, stupid thing to say. Shit, Jamie!

'Playing, of course. You're the one who said he watches too much TV.'

Max wiped his brow with the back of his hand.

'He's unconscious, Adam. Please hurry up. I have to go in the ambulance now.'

'I can't,' he said, but the line cut off. He stared at the phone, hand trembling. Had she heard him? He couldn't see where the dogs had gone. He called out to them. A flock of birds rose up from a cluster of trees, silhouettes against the clear moonlit sky. He called the dogs again and crouched down as they bounded up to him licking his face and hands while he struggled to fasten their leads.

As soon as he reached home, he told Maddy that John had phoned and asked him to check on a job, ready for the morning. He said he probably wouldn't be back until late.

* * *

An hour into the seventy-mile journey, his legs began to stiffen with shock and, soon, he could hardly feel his feet. At the next lay-by, he pulled over by a truckers' food van. He was trembling all over even though the heating was on full blast. He opened the van door and swung his legs round, but his shoes felt like bricks on his numb feet. He tried stamping the life back into them then walked like a robot towards the aroma of animal fat. A bald trucker leaning against the side of the van eating a burger, nodded to him. Max nodded back. He bought tea and gripped the scalding polystyrene cup with both hands. What if the fall was serious? What if Jamie had brain damage? He pictured Emily's tiny blue feet and the paramedics trying to save her. He put the cup back down and touched his brow. No way could he go through that again. His legs wobbled and gave way.

Someone grabbed his arms as he was falling.

'You all right, mate?' The bald trucker held him up against his wide chest.

'Not feeling great. Bad news about my boy,' Max's voice wavered. His eyes rimmed with tears, grateful for the man's solid arms around his middle, wishing for a split second that his own dad had been there for him.

The man nodded. 'You're in shock. Let's get some sugar in that tea, Barbs.' He took the cup and reached out to the counter and the woman dropped in three cubes and stirred. 'Here you are. You need to take a few minutes, mate.'

'Thanks, it's not far to go now, only a couple of junctions.' Max finished his tea and returned to his car.

Back on the road, he began picturing what he might have to face when he arrived at the hospital. He imagined Ali weeping by Jamie's bedside, blaming him, except it wasn't her stricken face he could see, it was Maddy's. Part of him wished he could turn the van around, drive away and disappear.

He had to pull himself together. Jamie would be fine. He switched on the radio and turned the music up to calm his thoughts, but his hands were trembling again, his legs cold and stiff. He lifted his right hand off the wheel and it hung in mid-air like a dog's wounded paw. When he focused back on the road, the car was swerving across the white dashes into the next lane. The mournful sound of a lorry's horn filled the misty night air. Max's hand snapped back onto the wheel, his heart drumming in his chest.

50

Max parked under a flickering sallow light in the hospital car park. Inside, he followed signs to a desk behind a sliding window. A man with a bandage around his head spoke in a droning voice to the receptionist. A patch of fresh blood marked out the hollow of his eye. The man stepped aside, looking Max up and down.

'I'm Jamie Wood's dad. Head injury.'

The receptionist directed him up a flight of stairs. He peered through the wire-enforced glass. Ali sat alone, hunched in one corner of a dim waiting room. He wanted to walk away; he couldn't face this – he knew the script. As he turned the handle, Ali looked up with her dark smudged eyes, face pale and ragged.

Unsteady on her feet, she flung herself at him, burying her head in his chest.

'He's in surgery for the gash on his head.' She drew back from him and pointed to the same spot on her forehead.

'You never said.' His heart knocked against his chest.

She guessed its size for him with her thumb and forefinger. 'They don't know yet. They don't know if...' She slumped back in the seat.

Max crouched in front of her, cupping her hands in his, gently jogging them up and down. 'He'll be fine, I know he will.' But as he said it, he hoped he hadn't somehow unstitched his son's destiny. It seemed like the right thing to say. He hoped it turned out well. He remembered saying it to Maddy, and her nodding, believing every word. And thankfully Emily had been fine. The brain damage was slight.

It meant she was a bit slower at times and susceptible to fits, but she'd been lucky. A few more seconds under water and it would have been a different story.

Ali wiped her face with a crumpled tissue, rocking back and forth. He slipped into the chair next to her and leaned back, his head touching the wall. Perhaps there was no point in worrying if the outcome of their lives had already been decided. His gran had believed a person had little influence over fate. All he knew for certain was that wishing with every cell in his body was never enough.

The door swung open and a nurse in silent black shoes came towards them. She crouched down and took Ali's hand in hers.

'Jamie's out of surgery and he's responding well.'

'Thank God.' Ali covered her eyes and sobbed.

Max put an arm across her back and kissed her wet cheek.

He swallowed hard and pressed his lips shut.

The nurse turned to Max. 'Are you Jamie's dad? I'm sure you realise, he's a very lucky boy.'

Max squeezed Ali's hand. 'Is he going to have any... lasting effects?' He pictured himself and Maddy asking the same thing about Emily. He could feel Ali's eyes flash at him. He guessed she hadn't wanted to think that far ahead, but they had to know.

'The doctors think not,' said the nurse. 'They're as sure as they can be at this stage, but the next 24 hours are critical in assessing the outcome of a head injury. All his vital signs are normal, so it's looking positive.'

After the nurse had gone, Max leaned back in the chair, his arm covering his eyes.

* * *

Two nurses wheeled a bed-sized cot into the space nearest the door of the Children's Ward. Max and Ali clutched each other's hands, peering at Jamie tucked under the sheets, most of his head covered in a wide bandage. His sleepy eyes fluttered open then shut again. Max sat in a high-backed chair next to him, while Ali folded the small, bloodstained clothes into a neat pile. A nurse wearing transparent gloves pulled the curtains around the bed.

'Is it mum staying tonight?' she asked, pulling a camp bed alongside Jamie's.

Max glanced at Ali and they both nodded. He leaned over the bed and kissed his son's cheek. He lingered, wanting to inhale the sweet warmth of the boy's skin, but all he could smell was iodine and bandages.

Max flicked his wrist. He stared at his watch. How could it be 9.40 p.m. already? He rubbed his stomach. The last thing he'd had was that cup of tea. It felt likes days ago. 'Are you hungry?'

Ali shook her head. The lights dimmed and the ward fell quiet except for their hushed voices.

'You try and get some sleep,' he said and moved round the bed towards her. 'I better be off.' For a few moments their bodies relaxed into each other.

'When will you be back?'

'As soon as I can, I promise.'

Back in his van, Max dragged his hands down his face. It would be easy to fall asleep now, but he wanted to get away from the hospital. He flipped open the glove compartment and pulled out a packet of Rothmans. He knew he should chuck them out of the window; he'd promised Ali he'd kick the habit. He lit one anyway, inhaling long and hard, watching the end pulse and burn as if it was his last. He squashed the remains into the ashtray and lit another. He needed a drink.

The Dog and Duck nearby was packed. A girl elbowed him in the chest as he pushed towards the bar. He knocked back a whiskey and ordered a lager top before last orders. Gripping his glass, he pushed his way outside and sat on a bench, pressing the dull ache in his chest. The waning moon was a mere sliver in the sky. The vast incomprehensible space filled him with awe and reminded him he was an insignificant dot in the whole scheme of things. For a moment, calmness settled on him, but like a sprinkling of unforeseen snow, it soon melted.

Finishing his drink, he checked his phone for messages as he headed to his van. None, good. He climbed into the back and covered himself with his jacket. How long could he keep doing this? It was time to choose between Maddy and Ali. But he loved them both and neither of them deserved to be cheated on. He didn't know what to do. He shut his eyes. A quick nap, then he had to get home. Home. The word expanded in his mind. His eyes opened again, and he stared into the near darkness. Two squares of streetlight glowed through the windows. The musty smell of dogs and paint filled the air in the hollow space. He wasn't even sure where home was any more.

51

MADDY: DECEMBER 2019

From the adjacent road, Maddy watches Alison load a cool bag in the back of the car. It is 8.20 a.m. She goes back in the house and comes out with an open map which she places on the passenger seat. Maddy thinks of Emily getting ready to go to the Science Museum for the day. Sophie and Emily have been pestering for ages. It's Sarah's turn to take them out. Tomorrow, she'll take them to the cinema and for pizza. It's going to be so strange without Chloe and Max. She'll try to be upbeat for Emily's sake, but it's such a struggle when her body feels so weighed down with grief.

Alison straps Jamie in the back seat with a bottle of juice and an overstuffed bag of what she guesses are colouring books and toys. Legoland is at least two hours away. They'll be gone all day for sure because Legoland at Christmas is a special day-long event. Plenty of time. According to Alison's kitchen calendar, Sandra is in the Costa del Sol until Sunday evening.

As soon as they drive off, Maddy sets a timer on her watch for ten minutes. If people forget something, they usually return within the first few minutes after they've left. While she's waiting, she feels a kick. Smiling to herself, she lifts her jumper and presses her hands to her skin. Not long now, little one.

The car doesn't return, so Maddy puts on a baseball cap she's taken to wearing and adjusts it low on her forehead. She snaps on a pair of black latex gloves and picks up her carry tray full of bottles of cleaner and all sorts of tools. The neighbour across the driveway opens her front door as Maddy is about to let herself in to Alison's house.

'Hello there,' the woman shouts, 'you're the cleaner, are you?'

Maddy freezes. The sold sign is lying on the ground in front of their garage door.

'I'm Natty. We moved in yesterday. I wonder if you could give me a quote for a weekly clean?'

Maddy nods.

'Sorry, I won't hold you up. I'm going out shortly, so just pop it through the door when you're ready.' She mimes scribbling on a piece of paper. Hopefully she thinks Maddy is Ukrainian or something and doesn't speak English. Maddy gives her the thumbs up and lets herself in.

Poppy is there to greet her, as usual, and she gives him a cuddle and a biscuit from her pocket. In the kitchen, there is no sign of a water bowl, only an old ice-cream tub with the tiniest drop of water. The bowl is outside, dirty and empty. Maddy has an urge to kick it up in the air. She takes it in, scrubs and rinses it and fills it with clean cold water.

In the living room, there are toys strewn all over the floor and sofa, magazines piled on the coffee table. Does this little slut never clean up? She pulls out their holiday photo albums and unscrews a lid of superglue. Max swimming in the sea, eating out in the evening by candlelight, Jamie waving from a Helter Skelter. All those weeks away when she thought he was working hard, building his business. She squirts glue on each page and squeezes the album shut. She chucks it on the floor and stands on it, stamping her feet.

Upstairs she opens Max's wardrobe and snips several inches off the bottom of each pair of trousers, collecting the cut-off ends in a plastic bag to take away. In Alison's drawer she runs the scissors along each pair of tights. She takes out several of her jumpers and sprinkles itching powder in each. She's tempted to shred the last of Alison's clothes, but doesn't want to be too obvious.

On the dressing table, she notices the jewellery box unlocked. Inside are pieces of gaudy costume jewellery: large hoop earrings and chunky necklaces, fashion watches with glittery faces. On the lowest tier is the asymmetrical heart necklace she saw her wearing, identical to hers. Too refined for this cheap slut. She holds it up to herself in the mirror. Her mother looks back at her, slowly nodding. What would have been the occasion for this? She imagines him buying both at the same time, wrapping them up, writing two cards, thinking he was being so clever deceiving them, all the time with his false heart. Her gut wrenches as she imagines Max stretched out on the king-size bed, Alison beside him, opening the small blue box. Then it's her father lying there with Lisa, while her mum was only a matter of yards away across the road. All those times she dreamed of dropping a match through Lisa's letterbox. She wishes she'd done it the night he died of a heart attack in her bed, so her mum hadn't had to endure the humiliation.

Everyone seeing his body being carried out of another woman's house the next morning.

All it takes is a sharp tug to snap the delicate silver chain in half.

The roar of an engine splits the silence. Out of the bedroom window, she watches Natty drive off in her old estate car. Downstairs, Poppy is waiting for her. She sits on the bottom stair and strokes his tummy. He needs more than a walk: he needs to be loved and properly cared for. She picks up the lead and clips it to his collar. She locks the front door from the inside and takes Poppy out the back, leaving the kitchen door and side gate ajar and walks him across the road. He has no qualms about leaping into her car. Once she's attached his lead to a seatbelt, he settles down with a biscuit. Poor neglected boy. We'll look after you. She goes back to the front garden with a screwdriver and screws a thin piece of wire across the gate, two inches from the ground.

On the drive home, she switches on the radio. Mum's favourite song, 'Baby Come To Me', by Patti Austin and James Ingram is on. She shivers. It's playing just for her. In the rearview mirror she mouths, 'thank you'. She turns it up loud and sings along to the chorus.

This is it. Her stomach fizzes. She knows what she needs to do. It's the definitive sign she's been waiting for.

52

MAX: DECEMBER 2017

On Christmas Eve, Max, Maddy and the girls caught an evening train home after seeing *Dick Whittington* at the London Palladium. Maddy had been planning it for months. She'd been so excited for the girls to go to the theatre and see the Christmas lights, like she did with her parents. They'd chatted all the way home about how funny the show was, until Chloe fell asleep in Max's lap and Emily snuggled under Maddy's arm.

Max stared out of the window at the waning crescent moon in a cloudless sky. Jamie would be tucked up in bed by now, waiting for Santa. Alison had bought him a ridiculous number of gifts for his stocking and on top of that, there was a mountain of presents under the tree. He rubbed his fingers across his forehead. Their credit card bill was going to be crazy. Yes, he was grateful that Jamie had recovered so well, but was it really necessary to spoil him so much? Or was he being a bad father thinking that? He winced, picturing the disappointment on Jamie's face when he'd told him he couldn't be there on Christmas Day. Shit. Why did he ever think it would be easy splitting himself between two families?

When they reached home, the front garden was coated in a crispy layer of frost. Max felt in his pocket for his key. He carried it on a separate fob to Ali's house. He slipped Chloe off his back into Maddy's arms and tried all the pockets of his navy woollen coat. 'Don't you have your key?'

'You always have yours.'

'Why not bring it anyway?' He hadn't meant to snap. 'Let's not argue, I'm tired, the girls are tired, and my feet are killing me.'

He checked each pocket again. 'Are you sure I didn't give them to you?'

'You definitely did not.'

He stood back and looked up at the house. There was a chance they'd left a window open upstairs. He examined the side gate.

'What are you doing?' Maddy sounded irritated.

'Take the kids next door to Sarah's, then come back and give me a hand.'

'You're not going to climb up there, are you?'

'I will if I have to, but I think I can take out the window above the letterbox. I reckon I can get my hand in. Do you have a pair of scissors in your bag?'

She let the bag slip down her arm and into his hands. 'There's a metal nail file in the small inside pocket. I'll be back in a minute.'

He took the bag and she carried Chloe, with Emily at her side. He took out the file and eased the pointed edge into the lead trim. Bit by bit he eased out the small pane of glass. It was a solid oak door, not one of these PVC jobs they put in the new houses. There were still jemmy marks indented in the wood where a burglar had tried to prise the door open years before Maddy moved in.

Max laid the stained-glass pane on the floor of the porch and stuck his hand sideways through the hole not much wider than the letterbox. He pulled back the bulk of his sleeve and wormed his hand further in. As soon as it was halfway up to the elbow, he felt around until his fingers skimmed the latch, but he couldn't quite reach.

'Good thing we weren't any later, Sarah was about

to go to bed,' Maddy said, coming through the open gate.

'Did she mind having the girls?' Max pushed against the door to pull his arm back out of the hole.

'Not at all. I said I hoped we wouldn't be long anyway.' Max stuck his hand in the hole again.

'Emily is worried that Father Christmas won't visit if we don't hurry up.' She pushed the sleeves of her coat together into a hand muff.

'I'm trying my best. Perhaps if we're still here at midnight, Santa will give us a hand.'

'Very funny.' After a silence, she said, 'I remember the night I found out he wasn't real. I was only eight. I couldn't sleep because I was so excited and I was half hoping I might catch sight of him if I stayed awake, but when he came in with the sack of presents, it was my dad.'

'Did you tell him you knew?'

'I remember asking him lots of awkward questions the next morning, like *How did Father Christmas go into every house in every street in all the different countries of the world?* and *What did he do if a house didn't have a chimney?*, and *What really happened if a child had been naughty?* He answered every question, but all I wanted was for him to tell me the truth, that he was Santa.'

'Do you remember the first year we left presents for Emily?' He pushed his arm further into the hole.

'We sat up till midnight in case she woke up.'

'Then I fell asleep, so you had to take the presents in.'

'We were stressing about nothing. She was far too young to even know what it all meant. Maybe that's why we do it, because really, it's more for us than them.'

'So we can relive a fantasy?' At last he could feel the latch with his fingertips. 'Not sure I ever believed in him in the first place. I was lucky if I got a chocolate Freddo and a satsuma.'

'Why do we keep doing it, even if we suspect they've found out?' She pulled her collar up higher round her neck.

'What age do they stop believing?' he asked.

'When they realise the world isn't the magical place we pretend it is.' She tugged his sleeve, an urgency in her voice. 'I don't want their childhoods to end, Max. I want them to go on forever.'

Max hesitated. Did she have an inkling of what he was up to? If they found out about Ali and Jamie, he would be the monster responsible for spoiling their childhoods, wouldn't he? The latch clicked and the door swung open. 'You can't stop them growing up, Maddy. What are you so afraid of?'

'That sometimes the ones who love us the most tell us the biggest lies.'

Max bowed his head. In trying to protect everyone from the truth, was he destroying them instead?

53

ALISON: DECEMBER 2019

In the rearview mirror, Alison glances at Jamie, slumped sideways, fast asleep. The dog will have messed up all over the kitchen floor by now. Good thing she didn't leave too much water. He'll be starving though, poor mutt. It's taken her longer than she thought to drive back from Legoland, but what a great day they've had. Jamie's last treat before the baby comes. He's already asked when can they go back. He's excited about having a brother or sister, someone to play with. When they stopped at the services for something to eat, the sky tipped it down at such a rate they had to wade ankle deep back to the car. She wriggles her damp toes in the soaked trainers. Should have worn boots. It's been a day of getting caught in showers and, to top it all, Jamie wanted to go on Pirate Falls three times, thankfully by himself.

There is a rainbow above their house and the daylight has muted to a pink hue as though she is entering a dream. The side gate to the back garden is wide open. She remembers bolting it. For God's sake, has Adam been again? How is it he seems to know when she's going to be out? She gets out of the car, wades through the long grass and hesitates. A fist of cold presses her chest. It is too quiet. There is no sound of Poppy scrabbling at the back door. She takes a deep breath and strides into the garden, but her foot catches on something and she falls. One hand scuffs along the gravel, the other springs to her bump. A line of scarlet beads bursts out of the ripped skin, edged with tiny stones and mud. Her left hip throbs. She presses the blood on her palm and caresses her hardening bump. Tears sting her eyes. She wills her baby to move. As she shifts to stand up, a silver thread running along the bottom of the gateway from post to post catches her eye. She reaches out, expecting to touch a cobweb, although it's thicker than that and couldn't possibly have stayed intact. Her fingers wrap around a solid thread of steel. She sits back on her heels. The wire has been bolted to the posts two or three inches from the ground. A shiver runs the length of her body. Why would he do this? Does he want her to lose the baby? A pain draws around her middle like a lasso, almost unbalancing her. After it's passed, she carefully pushes herself up. Does this mean the baby's okay? She's had a few Braxton Hicks contractions today, but this is the strongest by far.

The pink light has faded to beige and erased the rainbow. She did not leave the back door wide open. 'Poppy, Poppy!' she calls, but there is no rumble of the dog scampering to greet her. She takes in a sharp breath and calls again. The kitchen is empty. There is water in the dog bowl; it's been washed and brought in. What is going on here? She rushes out to the car and wakes Jamie. His lashes flicker, eyes open.

'Come on, Jamie, please – I can't find Poppy.'

He manoeuvres himself out of the car. 'What do you mean?' he groans, eyes red like he's about to cry.

'I don't know where he is. You didn't leave the gate open, did you?'

He shakes his head.

'But wasn't it you who put the bins out?' She hates her accusing tone, but why has Adam done this? Why is he torturing her? She wants to scream at him and chuck all his stuff out of the bedroom window. Kick him out. Who does he think he is treating her like this?

'That was yesterday.' Jamie is crying now.

She takes his hand and kisses it, leading him into the kitchen. 'Poppy, Poppy! He'll have got himself stuck in a room somewhere.' She takes a tin of dog food and taps a spoon against it. But all the doors are open. Nevertheless, they search every room. There is no sign of him anywhere.

'Who let him out? Where has he gone?' Jamie's nose is running alongside his tears. Darkness has fallen quickly by the time they go back outside.

'I remember bolting it. Someone has opened it.' She stands in the middle of the garden, hands on hips, while Jamie checks behind the shed. What if it's not Adam? He adored that bloody dog. Been a wedge between them from the start; she'd have much preferred a cat, but still. She calls all the local vets and RSPCA, but no one has handed Poppy in.

'Can I make some posters to put up around the village?' Jamie asks.

'If you want to, but let's have a drive around first, we might still find him.'

'Can we?' His eyes brighten.

'After we've changed out of these damp clothes.'

Upstairs, she takes out a clean sweatshirt and jeans. She opens her lingerie drawer and gasps at a pair of tatty grey knickers – size 16 – and a huge black bra with holes in the lace. She swallows a sour taste in her mouth and drops garment after garment on the floor until the drawer is empty – none of them are hers.

She opens the deep drawer underneath and a swarm of moths flies into her face. She screams and tries to cover her eyes and her head, but they keep coming at her as though she is a beacon, fluttering around and crashing into her. Jamie runs in, straight over to the windows and pushes them open.

She drops down on the bed and draws in a breath as another sharp contraction bolts through her. Less than a minute later another comes, then another – even stronger than the last – with barely a pause in between. *Are you okay, little one?* She whimpers, cradling her bump.

'What's happening, Mum?' Jamie rocks from one foot to the other.

'Call a taxi! The baby is on its way.'

54

MAX: MAY 2019

Ali was standing on the doorstep when Max pulled up in his van. She was wearing a pair of mules and a short pinafore dress, flexing her feet up and down on the step. He chucked his cigarette packet in the glove box and went round the back to unload the sacks of bark.

'Do that in a minute,' she called, click clacking towards him on the tiny pair of heels. Her hips swayed in a way most women had to learn. He smiled at her, expecting a hug, but she stood in front of him, clasping and unclasping her hands. She couldn't stand still.

'What is it?' He shut the van door.

'I've got a lovely surprise.' She gave a little clap of her hands. He hated surprises.

She pecked him on the stubble of his cheek and trotted into the house.

Inside, the musky smell of an incense stick wafted towards him. Ali had laid out the dining table for two. In the middle was a bottle of champagne and two glasses.

'Have I forgotten your birthday?' His hands reached for her hips, pulling her towards him.

'No, try again.' She giggled.

'It's our anniversary – do we have an anniversary? Two years, is it?'

'Adam...' She took a deep breath and steepled her fingers, 'we're going to have a baby.'

Max stepped back from her as though she'd thrown ice in his face. 'I thought you were on the pill?'

'I am, well, I was, but when I was ill a few weeks ago, we forgot to take precautions.'

'Are you sure?' He massaged his brow, his thoughts leaping in all directions.

'I've been to see the doctor this morning to book in with the midwife.'

'How far...?'

'I'm ten weeks tomorrow.'

'And you... want to go ahead?'

''Course, why wouldn't I?' She crossed her arms high on her chest.

'Because we didn't plan it.' He followed her into the kitchen and opened the fridge.

'I thought you'd be pleased. I mean, we're a proper couple now, aren't we?'

'It doesn't mean we'll be tying the knot, if that's what you're fishing for.' Max took out a Guinness and cracked it open, but it fizzed into his face. 'Fuck it.' He wiped his arm over his eyes.

'Did I even mention getting married?' She passed him a tea towel and crossed her arms again.

'You didn't plan this, did you?' He wiped his face.

'Is that what you think of me?' She swung round, storming into the hall.

'Okay, so tell me, what are we going to do?' he shouted after her, pouring the rest of the drink into a pint glass.

She came back in. 'Keep it, of course. I can't believe you're even suggesting... Why are you being like this?'

'It's a big thing – something people usually plan together.'

'It hardly ever happens like that,' she shouted.

'What, most kids are mistakes, are they? We should've been more careful.'

'Like the first time? Are you saying you wish I hadn't had Jamie?' She stood at the sink holding her stomach as though she was about to vomit.

'You know I didn't mean that.' Once upon a time he'd have wanted nothing more than a brother or sister for Jamie, but how would they afford another one? Worst of all, it was another level of betrayal. Jesus, he'd never meant to do any of this to Maddy. 'What me and Jamie need, and the new baby come to that, is having you around more.' She stroked her tiny bump. 'I mean things never get done around here. The garden's still a tip and Jamie needs somewhere safe to play.'

'Which I'm doing. Didn't you see I bought bark to tidy up the borders? Anyway, you should trust him to play out the front or go to the park once in a while.'

'I don't think so. Last week, Sharon from number fourteen said some teenagers hanging about the park went up to her Daniel with a flick knife.'

'But a boy needs some freedom. You can't keep him locked up. It's better for him to be a bit streetwise, isn't it?'

'I'm telling you it's not safe out there.'

'I wonder what your dad would make of that.' He laughed.

'Oh, shut up.'

Silence edged between them. Ali took out a pan and started scraping potatoes. She pushed the peelings into the dustbin.

'Why don't you use the compost bin for those?' He scooped the shavings out and opened the back door.

Ali submerged the chopping board in soapy water. 'Because it's easier to put them in the bin.'

'But I've moved the compost nearer the back door for that reason. It doesn't take any more effort.' He lifted the lid and dumped them in. 'Do you have to be so wasteful?'

'If you want to take over the cooking, feel free. I was trying to make us a special meal.'

'I'm not talking about the cooking. I mean everything. Look at this.' He pulled an empty can of baked beans and a folded cereal packet out of the rubbish. 'These can be recycled.' He pictured Maddy digging compost into the flower beds and the girls having fun threading milk bottle-tops around a wire frame to hang in the apple tree. They were always mending and reusing things. He couldn't believe how wasteful Ali was, throwing things away without a thought. Spending money like there was an endless pot.

'Look, we can't have this baby, Ali.' He took a swig of Guinness.

'Give me one decent, unselfish reason why not.' She put her hands on her hips.

'We can't afford it for a start. I've told you to cut down on shopping, stop buying all your silly knickknacks, make-up, clothes, boots, shoes and God knows what else. My credit cards can't take it any more.'

'What, getting my hair and nails done or buying decent shoes and clothes is silly, is it?'

'Can't you do your nails yourself? Do you need so much stuff?'

'Stop turning it around to me being the problem.' She prodded her finger in his arm. 'What about you? Why can't you commit yourself to us a hundred per cent?'

'Why are you arguing again?' Jamie came in with a noisy Batman on a bike.

'We're not. Turn that off,' Ali snapped.

Max pulled a face at him to let him know that she meant business. Jamie laughed.

'What's so funny, laughing behind my back?'

'We're not, don't be so paranoid.' Max turned the toy upside down and switched it off.

'You haven't answered my question.' She pointed the knife at Max.

'Mum, when's dinner? I'm starving?' Jamie asked.

'Give him a biscuit,' Ali said.

'What, before dinner? Here, have an apple, Jamie.' Max grabbed one from the bowl and pretended to drop it.

Jamie giggled. 'Can you cut it up?'

'Please, say please, Jamie,' Max said.

'Please, Daddy.'

'That's better.' Max smiled at him and chopped the apple in quarters. Jamie took it in the living room. 'Why are you letting him eat rubbish? Then you complain he doesn't eat his dinner.'

'One won't hurt. Anyway, you answer my question.'

'You know the answer. We talked about this at the start.'

'Do I, Adam? Do I?' She was pointing the knife at him again. 'Sometimes I don't know you at all. You're away so often, we hardly see you. Perhaps I should have listened to Dad.'

Max stared at her. She may as well have spat in his face. If that's what she really thought, maybe she'd made his decision for him. He finished the Guinness and walked out.

55

MAX: JULY 2019

Max climbed in the front of the minicab while Maddy settled the girls in the back seats. It was going to be a long train journey to London, she told them. He checked round the house one last time. It was strangely quiet without the dogs barking and the children laughing and shouting. He'd dropped the dogs off at the kennels that morning. The only sounds remaining were the fridge and the ticking of the various clocks. He'd grown to love this house, but it wasn't a home without the four of them in it. As the train neared Greenwich station, both girls chatted to him and Maddy. He gazed out of the window at the passing back gardens. Were those people's lives as complicated as his? He'd told Ali and Jamie he was decorating more houses in Manchester for a couple of days. He'd given up trying to think of new ways to persuade her to have an abortion, and now she was too far gone. Would she really have planned it on purpose? These days she only seemed interested in spending his money, which was fast running out. His last credit card bill was higher than he was ever going to be able to pay back. And if she asked him once more if they were going to get married... He clenched his teeth. He would have, once, long ago, if he could have stayed and been accepted as her boyfriend instead of being driven away by her dad. But then he'd never have met Maddy, and that was unthinkable.

Maddy was gazing across at the window too, lost in her own thoughts, he guessed. Good, dependable Maddy. The most caring mother and loving wife. What a shit husband he'd turned out to be. She didn't deserve it. He pressed his fingers to his forehead. Would he ever be able to dig himself out of this mess without hurting everyone?

They got off at Greenwich station and walked to the National Maritime Museum for the special exhibition to mark the fiftieth anniversary of the Apollo 11 moon landing. He wished his gran could have been there with them. She'd told him how she'd watched it on their neighbour's new black and white television –

how thrilling it was to see it and how she'd become fascinated with the moon for the rest of her life.

'Exactly fifty years ago today, the first man walked on the moon,' he told Emily and Chloe as they went in, 'and your great gran watched it on television as it happened. Isn't that amazing? My dad was just a little boy.'

'You've told us a zillion times, Daddy,' Emily said and both girls giggled.

'Well, I'm excited.' He laughed.

'We can tell,' Maddy said, threading her arm through his. The girls sat in front of them on a bench, watching a video of a total eclipse of the moon. Maddy pulled him closer. 'I went to see the doctor yesterday,' she whispered.

'Sorry, I meant to ask how it went.' How could he have forgotten? She'd been complaining of tiredness and nausea recently. What if it was something serious?

'I've been meaning to change my coil for ages, but the doctor says it had become dislodged.'

'Oh, is that painful?' An infection again. He was relieved it was nothing worse.

'It means it wasn't working properly.' She put her hand on his leg and suddenly couldn't stop smiling at him.

'What?' He narrowed his eyes.

'Nothing's wrong. I'm pregnant,' she whispered.

'Seriously?' A pain shot through his head, like he'd been hit by a brick. He stared ahead.

'I know we said two was enough... it's a surprise for me too.' Her eyes were brimming with tears.

'It's great news. It's a shock, that's all.' He hugged her and blew out a little stream of air. Shit.

'Are you sure you're okay with it?' She rubbed his back.

'Of course, of course I am.' He hoped he didn't sound abrupt. His whole body had turned to jelly. What the fuck was he going to do?

'Really?'

'Honestly.' He looked in her eyes. 'As long as you and the baby are healthy, that's all that's important.'

'I don't want to tell the girls straight away,' she whispered. 'How far gone are you?'

'The doctor thinks about thirteen weeks, due in January, about a month after Christmas.'

Weren't those dates close to Ali's? His mind was a scramble, he couldn't think. Whatever it was, this was his worst nightmare.

'You didn't have an inkling before now?' Like that was going to make any difference. He pulled a face, expecting her to be a little bit offended.

'Not for a moment. I suppose it doesn't help that I've put on a bit of weight recently.'

'You are beautiful.' To him she looked as good as she always did. Jesus. He wanted to bang his head on the wall. What an idiot for getting in this mess.

'Come on, Dad.' Emily tugged his coat. They followed them to a luminous photo of the moon. Above it hung the question:

'What Would Happen if the Moon Disappeared?' Answer: 'Disastrous consequences.'

Maddy kissed him on the lips. He loved her so much. But didn't he love Ali too? He couldn't go on living like this. How would he ever decide between them?

56

MADDY: DECEMBER 2019

Maddy pushes the revolving door of the hospital and heads towards the maternity ward. She holds up a small bunch of flowers to obscure her face and slips into Lilac Ward as an elderly couple exit. The woman gives her a lingering stare. Maddy's newly coloured auburn hair is in a bun, and she is wearing her mum's old raincoat and woollen hat. It is after lunch and quietening down, as she expected. She spots Alison's name on the nurses' board. Number 22, bay nine. What if Max is here? Mother hadn't thought of that. Perhaps he'd approve of her behaviour.

The ward is dim along one side, the curtains drawn around two of the first four sets of beds. A light murmur fills the air – quietly spoken men chatting to their wives or girlfriends – not exclusively theirs any more, seeing them in a different light now the transformation to motherhood is complete.

Number 20 is marked above the first bed. Maddy smiles at the woman who looks like she's been in bed all her life. Two along and the curtains are drawn. Maddy stands outside and nods at the bewildered face of a new father opposite, holding his baby in front of him like it's a fresh loaf of bread. Max had been a more confident father right from the start. An image fills her mind of him falling to the bottom of the river, calling out to her. Lately, this detail gives her the tiniest satisfaction.

There don't appear to be any voices coming from behind the floral material, so she scissors her fingertips into the gap. The tightly wrapped baby is in a Perspex crib, and Alison is sprawled on the unmade bed, asleep. Maddy's chest spasms as if she's been punched. She grips herself around the middle. The new father is taken up with trying to change the baby's nappy while it kicks and cries. She slips inside the curtains and stands at the foot of the bed, watching Alison sleeping. Breathing. The young face is haggard, creased like a tissue and there are yellow stains on the shoulder of her shapeless T-shirt. She lays the flowers on the moveable table. At the bottom of the bed is a soft plump pillow. *It would be so easy to hold it over that pretty face.* She hesitates at hearing the voice. The baby kicks in its see-through container, drawing her eye, pulling her towards him.

'There you are. I've been waiting for you.' He's tiny, six pounds, she guesses. A streak of downy blond hair covers the centre of his scalp. Max's nose and chin, no question of it.

Almost as if he knew she'd arrived, the baby's eyes flutter open. He kicks his miniature feet, the skin pink and wrinkled like a newborn bird.

Without another thought, Maddy reaches in. Alison doesn't stir. Newborns are always so much lighter than you remember. She brings him gently to her breast. He curls into her like a snail taken from its shell. Maddy breathes in the soft warmth of the new skin and her heart aches with longing. She could tuck the little mite under her coat and walk away, but he squirms, looking for milk and her sweet baby lets out a mewl. She holds tighter, but he keeps wriggling and one of his arms breaks free from the blanket. 'Baby Boy of Alison Wood', reads the tag around the tiny wrist. A boy. Her heart gives a little skip. She offers her knuckle to his lips, and he tries to suck but his face crumples into a cry. Turning away from the bed she hikes up her top and unclips her maternity bra.

Pressing her fingers around her nipple, she guides his mouth to latch on. His suck is firm and her whole body buzzes at the sensation and sheer wonder of feeding her own baby. His cherry lips move up and down, pulling, pulling on her. Then he lets go and his face reddens as he cries with all his might. Alison stirs. Maddy covers herself up with her coat, jogging him up and down until he stops.

'Who are you?' Alison sits up, bleary-eyed.

'I was passing, he sounded distressed.' Maddy places the baby back in the cot, avoiding eye contact.

'You should have woken me.' She picks the baby up and he starts crying again. Alison looks her up and down, but Maddy is quick to turn away.

'You looked like you needed the rest.' Maddy ties her coat belt.

'Don't I know you?' Alison's eyes narrow.

'He's so beautiful, isn't he?' Maddy steps sideways, blood pulsing in her neck. She'll have to come back for him.

'Aren't you the woman who had a go at me in the shop?' Alison points a finger at her.

Head down, Maddy swishes back the curtain and leaves.

57

MAX: EARLY SEPTEMBER 2019

At six o'clock, Max arrived outside the village hall. Maddy met him in the foyer.

'You're late,' she hissed, 'where have you been?'

'In traffic,' he said, heading for the double doors.

'We're sitting at the back, don't make a noise.'

He followed her in. The audience sat in darkness, the stage lit by one spotlight. Chloe walked on in her red velvet dress. Could she see him? He hurried to the back of the room and sat next to Maddy. Chloe started to sing, 'Over the Rainbow'. Her voice sounded a little shaky at first, but soon Max and the rest of the audience were captivated into silence; everyone seemed to be holding their breath. On the last note they exploded into applause. Maddy was on her feet, Max too, clapping furiously. He'd never heard her sing like that.

'Where did that come from? It was incredible,' Max said.

Maddy nodded, tears coursing down her cheeks. The curtain came down and Maddy grabbed his arm and shuffled out.

'You were brilliant,' Max said as Maddy bent down to hug Chloe backstage.

'You were late, Daddy.'

'I'm sorry, darling.' He crouched next to them.

'Where were you?' Maddy stood up.

'I had a job to finish, took longer than I thought.' He sighed.

He was sick of lying.

'I thought you were going to bring me, you said you would,' Chloe said.

'I'm sorry, I couldn't get away.' It was the truth, of sorts. He'd taken Jamie for his first training session at the local football club. Somehow, he had to try and be there every week. This was not the best start.

Maddy shot him a venomous look and led Chloe into the dressing room, shutting him out.

He wandered off to the crowded bar and bought a pint of beer.

'Are you Chloe's dad?' A petite woman with blonde cropped hair was talking to him.

'That's me.' He knocked back half the pint in one go.

'Do you know, I'm convinced I've seen you somewhere before.'

'I shouldn't think so, but I'm flattered.' He gave her a wink.

Been a while since he'd been chatted up.

Her face flushed but she looked puzzled. 'Wasn't Chloe fantastic? You must be so proud.'

Max nodded and finished his beer.

'I'm Miss Smith, Helen. Chloe's singing teacher.' She held out a small hand, cold and limp.

'Oh I see, I thought you were... you know.'

The woman laughed as if he was joking.

'I didn't know she had a singing teacher.'

'Well, it is my first term here.'

'So you taught Chloe to sing?' He was amused that she was blushing again.

'Not really. I helped her discover her voice.'

'Well, it wasn't there last term.' Max grinned.

Miss Smith's laugh was an embarrassing shriek. He turned away, hoping she'd take the hint. There was still no sign of Maddy and Chloe.

'Can I get you a drink?' He turned back to her now she had quietened down.

'I remember now,' she said, waving a finger at him, 'I saw you at my last school. You were with Jamie Wood, at his school play. He played a very convincing Joseph.'

'That wasn't me. You're thinking of someone else.' He suddenly felt wide awake.

'Oh, really? I suppose I must be. Although you have the kind of face a woman doesn't forget.' Her face turned tomato red.

'What are you drinking?' He steered her towards a table, letting his fingers linger on her arm. She was a good-looking woman but dangerous if she started spouting off in front of Maddy.

'Sparkling water, please.' She gazed up at him longer than necessary. He smiled and winked, let her think he was interested. Hopefully keep her trap shut if she thought she was in with a chance.

'Wait here, I'll bring it over.' He patted her arm.

While he was waiting to be served at the bar, Maddy turned up with Chloe. They were talking to Helen. Shit. They kept looking in his direction, but he couldn't catch Maddy's eye. She didn't look too happy, but then he was already in the doghouse. 'What have you two been gassing about?' He laughed nervously.

'Miss Smith says Chloe has exceptional talent,' Maddy said, taking the drink from him.

He pulled a face at Miss Smith to say sorry. Miss Smith lowered her eyelashes which told him he wasn't to worry.

'The last singing teacher was useless,' Maddy said. 'It's great that you've joined us here. Where were you before?'

'I was just saying to your husband, I've recently moved down from Huntingdon.'

Max glared at Helen, willing her not to say any more. She shot him a seductive glance under her eyelashes. Cheeky mare.

'It's so exciting to come across a voice like Chloe's.' Miss Smith touched Chloe's shoulder.

'We had no idea she could sing so well,' Maddy said. 'She's always been chosen for the choir, but we hadn't heard her sing solo apart from the odd tune in the shower.' They all laughed.

'Let me fetch some more drinks,' Max said. Chloe followed him.

'Why were you late, Dad?'

'I told you, I got held up at work.' He leaned over the bar and ordered another glass of sparkling water and an orange juice. He ground his teeth together. What kind of fucking dad lies to his kids? His own dad, that's who. Well bloody done, he'd become as useless as his own father.

'But you nearly missed it.'

'I know, darling, and I'm as annoyed as you are, believe me, sweetheart.' He kissed the top of her head and squeezed his eyes shut. 'I promise I won't miss anything again.' This was killing him, he had to put a stop to it before he destroyed everyone he loved.

* * *

Back home, Sarah was sitting alone in their living room, watching *Back to the Future*.

'Did Emily and Sophie get to sleep okay?' Maddy asked, taking her coat off. She hung it over the back of a chair.

'Out like a light.' Sarah topped her wine up from a bottle on the table. 'You having a glass of something?'

'Thanks, I'll get myself some lime cordial,' Maddy said. 'Max?'

'I'll have a beer.'

'You'll never guess who has a voice like an angel.' Maddy put her arm around Chloe.

'Has she really?' Sarah sat up.

Chloe nodded. Max smiled as he left the room.

In the kitchen, he took a Guinness out of the fridge. There was a letter for him on the counter. Huntingdon Borough Council was stamped in red on the front. He opened it. Bloody parking fine. He stuffed it into his trouser pocket. Maddy walked in and took a glass out of the cupboard and a box of éclairs out of the fridge.

'Did you get your post?'

Max didn't answer. He poured his Guinness into a pint glass. 'A letter – from Huntingdon Council, wasn't it? I meant to tell you.'

He sipped the head of his beer and, without thinking, put his hand in his pocket. The crackling sound of the plastic window gave him away.

'What is it about?' she asked. 'Looked like something official.' She put the glass and cakes down. He was dumb for being late tonight, dumber for thinking he could live like this and get away with it.

'It's nothing.' He drank a mouthful of beer, hoping she'd move on to something else.

She took a plate out of the cupboard and put the cakes on it.

'Come on, let's see.' She was laughing now, her fingers wriggling in the air towards him.

He stepped back but her hand dipped into his pocket and swiped the letter.

She peered into the envelope. 'A parking fine?' She frowned.

'From a job up there, that's all.' He snatched it out of her hand.

'You didn't tell me.' She wasn't smiling any more.

'Do I have to tell you everything?' He drank down his beer and stomped up the stairs.

In the bathroom he locked the door and took out the letter. Two weeks ago, in High Street, Huntingdon, at 8.05 p.m. He looked again at the date. He'd taken Ali out for a meal at the George Hotel. Some bugger must have swiped it off his windscreen while they were in the restaurant. How could he be so careless? He stuffed it back in the envelope. Chloe was coming up the stairs as he came out.

'You were a superstar tonight, Angel.'

'Thanks, Daddy.'

'Off to bed then.' He kissed her forehead. 'Call me when you're ready and I'll come and read you a story.'

'Not tonight, Daddy, I don't feel very well.'

'What's wrong? Do you want me to get you some medicine?' Chloe shook her head. He put his hand on her forehead.

It felt a bit warm, but they'd known worse, like the time both girls went down with chicken pox.

'You've had a big night. You'll feel much better in the morning.'

Chloe went in her room and didn't answer.

He felt sick too, at being late, at having to lie about everything he did and where he'd been, it was exhausting. He took his old suitcase down from the wardrobe and pushed the letter into a hole in the lining, stop Maddy having a proper nosy. He needed to pay it pronto. He took his boots off and stood at the window. The new moon was so dark in shadow, it wasn't visible. It was known as a black moon, and Gran would tell him it was a bad sign. Hardly needed that, did he? He was getting too careless; he mustn't let this happen again. He'd never forgive himself if Maddy and the girls found out the truth. Did he still want to be with Alison? She was breaking him financially, but what about Jamie? He couldn't bear not to be around for him growing up and he certainly didn't want someone like Tony stepping in. But he'd have to make a decision soon: he had two babies on the way and time was running out.

58

The next morning, Max set off to work earlier than usual. A job near Luton Airport was going to bring in big bucks. He stopped at the services on the way and checked his mobile before getting out of the van. One missed call from Ali. He paid for his coffee and bacon roll then rang her.

'I can't talk for long,' he said straight away.

'The washing machine broke down last night. When will you be home?'

'The plumber's number is on the notice board. Give him a call and mention my name. Tell him it's an emergency and you need him there today.'

'I'm not sure I'll have enough cash.'

'Ask him how much he'll charge first.'

'But I don't get paid until the end of the week.'

Max drummed his fingers on the dashboard. The joint account was already in the red.

'And don't forget,' she continued, 'we're going baby shopping on Saturday.'

'Are we?'

'We need to choose a pram and a car seat.'

'There's plenty of time for all that.'

'Not really, if you think about it. Anyway, I want to catch the sales and I've seen a pram I like.'

'Can't we get one second-hand?' Max's throat was dry. He sipped the coffee through the small hole in the lid and burnt the tip of his tongue.

'You want me to have a used pram, covered in puke and God knows what?'

'Obviously not like that, don't be daft.'

'Is there any cash left in the holiday jar?'

'I had to borrow the last tenner for diesel,' he said.

'So how am I going to pay the plumber?'

'Don't you have any money?' He looked at his roll cooling down; he liked it hot.

'You know I'm overdrawn.'

'Look, get him round to do the job and tell him you've only got a cheque.'

'But it'll bounce.'

'He probably won't pay it in until next Monday.'

'So when will you be home?'

'I don't know yet. I'll call you. Got to go.' He clipped his mobile in the hands-free and started the engine. Moments later, it rang again while he waited at traffic lights on a major roundabout. He clicked the button on his steering wheel to answer it.

'What now?' he snapped. He couldn't hear the voice at first, only sobbing which was faint and interrupted by silent breaks. He glanced at the number. Maddy. The lights were about to change.

'I can't hear you,' he shouted, leaning down to the phone cradle.

'Chloe's dead,' Maddy screamed, her voice almost unrecognisable. The lights turned amber, but Max froze. In slow motion the light dimmed and the green one shone. Chloe, his baby Chloe. She must be mistaken. Maddy was out of her mind. But her voice gabbled repeatedly, *Chloe didn't wake up this morning, she called her and shook her, but Chloe was dead.*

He could hear Emily in the background now, wailing and screaming. The phone cut off.

He lay his head on the steering wheel, sounding the horn's insistent drone until his whole body was vibrating. Someone tapped on the window, but Max didn't respond. A policeman opened the van door and lifted Max off the wheel.

'Sir, are you all right?'

Max couldn't answer. His head lolled backwards as though he'd fallen a hundred feet through a glass floor.

'Sir, can you hear me? Can I ask you to step out of the van, please?'

Max couldn't feel his legs. He tried to move but collapsed at the policeman's feet.

The policeman hauled him up and breathalysed him. The reading was clear.

'Have you taken any drugs in the last 24 hours?'

Max shook his head. Tears fell from his eyes like fat drops of rain.

'Why have you stopped here, sir?'

Max looked at the cars racing past. If he jumped now, he'd catch the front of an articulated lorry.

'Sir? Are you on any medication?'

'You really want to know? Do you?' he sobbed, pulling at his own hair.

'You're blocking the traffic, we need to get you moving.'

'My daughter is dead,' Max whispered. 'My little girl with the voice of an angel.' He cupped his hands as if she were still small enough to fit in them.

The policeman stared at him as he fumbled for his radio. 'Where is she?'

'At home.' Max pointed to his mobile as if Maddy's voice might repeat its mournful message. 'She didn't wake up this morning. She's five years old for Christ's sake.' Max caged his face in his hands, shaking uncontrollably.

'Okay sir, try and take some deep breaths. That's it. Can you tell me where home is?'

'Uxbridge. My home is in Uxbridge.'

'Not far then. I'll take you. We'll get your vehicle moved, don't you worry.'

59

The days after Chloe died felt like they had been sucked into a black hole. Somehow, they got through the post-mortem revealing she had died of meningococcal septicaemia. He was left haunted by the image of her lying in her bed, her beautiful little face unrecognisable, mottled with purple blotches.

And after, the practicalities of ringing friends and arranging the funeral kept him busy in a strange way, but all the time, he longed to escape. He needed to see Ali and Jamie, to touch normality, know that it still existed.

Maddy had stopped cooking and washing herself and lay in bed all day, staring at the ceiling, sleeping or looking through old photos. She barely spoke. At night he could hear her wandering around the house and the garden. Most mornings he found her curled up on the carpet next to Chloe's bed. She didn't change her clothes for days. Thankfully Sarah took Emily under her wing and often came in to cook them meals and tidy up. But Maddy wouldn't eat it. She'd put her hand to her throat as though any food she tried to swallow was stuck there. He had no appetite either, preferring the thought of collapsing into nothingness. Every room reminded him of Chloe. Her rainbow-coloured coat hung by the front door, red sandals kicked under the pew just as she'd left them. In the living room, a pottery squirrel she'd made at nursery for his birthday and her favourite film, *Frozen*, in its box next to the television. The kitchen cupboards were plastered with hers and Emily's artwork. The calendar she made at school last Christmas hung on the back of the door.

He wandered into the garden one morning to have a cigarette. The slide she had pestered them to buy, the climbing frame and swing she'd spent hours playing on, all bitter reminders. When he closed his eyes, he could hear her giggling. Emily wouldn't go near the playground monuments. She wouldn't even speak. He gazed up at the sky, trying to comprehend the enormity of his loss. As if in mourning too, the moon had disappeared.

Behind the playhouse, he found a bucket of pebbles she'd been collecting ready to paint and give away as gifts. He picked one out, licked his finger and wiped over it, bringing the colour to life for a few seconds. He wept silently for all the moments and milestones that would never be. Time frozen for his little girl, while his world kept spinning out of control.

He made a move to go inside as Emily came out of the kitchen. She stood in the centre of the lawn, a solitary figure staring into the distance. He stumbled towards her, sobbing now and tried to hug her but she pushed him away and wouldn't speak.

* * *

After three weeks he decided to drive to Ali's straight from work, explain everything, call things off. It had gone too far. He couldn't keep doing this. His home was here with Maddy and Emily.

On the way, he stopped off at a local garage to fill up. In the shop, he grabbed a sausage roll and a carton of chocolate milk. At the till, he touched his card on the contactless pad.

'It's been declined.' The girl serving smiled at him, chewing gum as she looked him up and down.

Max glared at her.

'Shall I try it for you, sir?'

Max nodded and handed her his card. The young girl swiped it through the machine. He glanced behind him at the growing queue.

The card was declined again. Someone tutted. 'Do you have another card I could try?'

'Can't you see I'm looking,' he hissed, searching through his wallet. He had a current account in his other name, but that would look suspicious, wouldn't it? He handed over another credit card. It was near the limit, but it might just see him through. 'I don't remember the pin number for this one.' It went straight through, thank God.

'Sign here, please.'

His hand was shaking as he took the pen. For a split second he couldn't think which name to sign.

'Come on, mate,' someone called behind him.

The girl handed him a receipt. He snatched it and left, keeping his head down.

A few minutes later he pulled over in a lay-by and tipped the contents of his wallet onto the passenger seat. Two current accounts and four credit cards in both his names, all maxed out and only forty-five pence in cash. He felt too sick to eat. He'd handed his notice in to John that morning because he wasn't getting him any work, and he couldn't ask Tom for another sub: he knew what the answer would be. Three more weeks until payday. He pushed his hands into his face. He couldn't go over to Ali's now. She was bound to have some bill or other that needed paying or want cash for food or yet another pair of shoes. He'd have to go home, cap in hand and ask Maddy to bail him out, but she was in a right state and didn't need more stress, especially from him. He should be supporting her through this. He was a useless, useless idiot, just like his father. Right at this moment, there was only one option left.

He started the engine and roared off into the night, not even knowing where he was heading, but did it even matter? Voices and conversations swirled around in his head. Alison shouting that her dad had been right about him all along and why didn't he want to marry her when she'd picked out the perfect dress? And Maddy explaining how disappointed she was in him. How betrayed she felt that he'd had a child with another woman, used her money to set up home with her. How cocky and confident he'd been, thinking he could keep both lives separate and make everyone happy. Hadn't he just been pleasing himself? His mind flashed back to his father thrashing him with a belt for spilling a glass of orange juice, and his mother's indifference, her coldness turning away, like they were strangers. Had he been a mistake, or just not lived up to their expectations? He'd never found out and Gran never told him, if she even knew herself. More than anything he'd desperately wanted to be a good father to his children. But he'd failed. On top of it all he had two babies on the way. He could barely cope now. What kind of life could he give any of them? If he stayed with Maddy, Jamie wouldn't have him around. And how could he ever leave Maddy and Emily after everything they'd been through? The thought of abandoning any of them was killing him. And now, his beautiful, sweet baby girl was dead. He had to face up to the truth; he'd failed them all.

He parked in a windy street, mostly deserted except for a few late-night drinkers. Skeleton trees were silhouetted against the charcoal sky. Hauling his rucksack on his back, he began to walk, not knowing where he was heading. Somewhere above him, an owl hooted. The waxing crescent moon was a thin silver curved line. The calming rush of water drew him towards a river and a small footbridge. The damp reek of mud and plants and discarded rubbish hit the back of his throat. As he stepped onto the bridge, it creaked as he moved. His foot slipped and his hand shot out to the railing. He climbed up and sat astride. At last, his head had drained of all thoughts and chatter but when he touched his face, it was wet with tears. His grip on the rail slipped sending him towards the edge; the rucksack from his shoulder pulled him to the side. He let the bag drop into the black water with the satisfying sound of a heavy weight plunging into its depths. From across the road, a man shouted something he couldn't hear.

A warm feeling of peace washed over him and he stepped off the edge, arms outstretched.

60

MADDY: DECEMBER 2019

It is a sunny but deceptively cold day. After school, Maddy gives Emily her favourite tea of sausages and mash followed by raspberry ripple ice-cream, then takes her over to Sarah's for a sleepover with Sophie. Sarah is going to call in and feed Poppy and Daisy and their new 'rescue' dog. She told them an old friend of hers couldn't look after him any more and she couldn't say no. Emily became tearful and believes it was meant to be because he has the same name as their dog. She tells them she is meeting an old friend for dinner in London and won't be home until very late.

Instead, she drives through the heavy evening traffic up to Huntingdon. She knows Alison is back home with the baby; she called the hospital earlier to check.

It seems like only moments later that it's approaching 10 p.m. and she's arriving in Lawn End. She watches number twenty-nine for almost an hour until all the usual lights are off and it's safe to stalk up to the door and let herself in. The house is silent. There is the usual lamp on in the landing, which gives her some visibility in the hall. She waits a few moments before putting the door on the latch so she's not fiddling for knobs when she's trying to get out. Any moment, she thinks the baby will cry for her, but there's only the permanent low hum of the air vent in the kitchen.

Looking left, the living room door is wide open. Maddy peers into the gloom and almost gasps aloud when she sees Alison asleep on the sofa. The pram is next to her. She edges closer. It's empty. For a few seconds, she waits to see if Alison moves, then creeps up the stairs, careful to miss the loose floorboard outside their bedroom. Jamie's door is shut. She waits a few moments, listening for any sound. Alison's bedroom door is open. The frilly edged crib is next to the bed. The smell of baby lotion is welcoming and excitement rises in her. She picks up a travel bag from under the bed and slides open a couple of drawers, rummaging through them. She takes nappies and Babygros and stuffs them into the bag.

'There you are, my darling boy,' she whispers, 'come to Mummy.' The baby doesn't murmur as she lifts him into a snow-white blanket. She kisses his nose, and her elbow clips the Disney character mobile. It lets out a couple of heart-stopping notes as it casts its dancing shadow on the wall. She freezes, straining to hear for any movement from Jamie in his bedroom next door or Alison downstairs. With her arms around the precious bundle, she grabs the bag and smiles at her mother in the mirror, then she tiptoes downstairs as quickly as she can. She pulls the front door closed behind her, still on the latch because she is certain that to click it shut would wake even the deepest sleeper.

In the car, she straps the baby into the rear-facing car seat next to her. A thousand fireworks explode in her heart as she turns the wheel and glances in the mirror.

'Look at my beautiful baby, Mum,' she says as she slowly drives away.

61

ALISON: DECEMBER 2019

A cold draught wakes Alison. She shivers and realises she's only covered by her cardigan. The black window tells her it is still night-time. She stretches over and concentrates on the digits on her mobile: 5.10 a.m. Charlie should have woken her an hour ago for a feed, but his bottle of milk is on the floor. She swings her legs off the sofa and picks it up. There's an ounce in it. She frowns, trying to remember. The front door blows open in a clap of wind, as though someone is forcing their way in. She jumps up, her heart racing. In the darkness, branches are creaking and the rustling leaves sound like waves crashing towards her. A glass milk bottle on the doorstep opposite falls over and rattles down the drive. Why is the door on the latch?

She didn't leave it like that, did she? She clicks it shut and climbs the stairs. Her pulse is beating too fast. The house is too quiet. As she nears the top, she shudders involuntarily. There's a musty smell in the air she can't place. A sudden memory of locking the front door comes to her. She hung the key in the kitchen before making up Charlie's last feed. So how could it have opened? For a few moments she stops, one foot on the top stair. Can a newborn sleep so long without food? She takes a deep breath and tiptoes into the room, but in the dim light she can see the crib is empty.

She blinks hard and turns on the bedroom light, staring at the stark white cotton sheet as if he will appear, but shadows of the bulb jump in front of her eyes. The teddy she bought when she first became pregnant is still at the bottom of the crib. The sheets are pulled back, as if she's taken Charlie out. Did she? She is so dazed she can't remember. Traces of his downy hair where he turns his head from side to side are on the flat pillow. The new cotton blanket she bought last week has been dropped on the carpet. Two cupboard drawers are hanging out, empty. Charlie is nowhere to be seen.

She scrabbles around on her knees hoping by some bizarre miracle that he's fallen out. But he's not there. She clutches her throat; it is so dry and barbed she's finding it hard to swallow.

'Jamie!' she croaks and bursts into his bedroom. He bolts up in bed, squinting at her.

'Charlie's not in his crib.' She hears herself scream the words but it's like they are being spoken by someone else. Her face is burning, eyes bulging. 'Is he here? Did I leave him with you?'

'What do you mean? He's not here.' He scratches his head.

'Where is he? Where's he gone!' Back in her bedroom, Alison grabs the house phone and dials 999.

'Which service do you require?' asks the operator.

'Police please, please hurry.'

Jamie is standing in the doorway, his hands lodged in his messy hair, grasping at the roots. 'Where is he, Mum?' Tears fill his eyes.

'I don't know, Jamie, I just don't know.' Her whole body is shaking. She grips the phone with both hands. 'Think, try and think where he could be.'

The operator asks where Alison is calling from and takes her details.

'Please help me, you must help me, I can't find my baby, he's gone, oh my God, he's gone!'

'Okay, I need you to sit down, and take a deep breath. Can you tell me what baby's name is?'

'Charlie, his name is Charlie Wood.'

'And is there anyone else in the house with you?'

'Yes, my eight-year-old son, Jamie,' she reaches out and grasps his hand.

'And where was Charlie before you went to sleep?'

'In his crib, next to my bed, upstairs. But I dozed off downstairs on the sofa. I remember now, I went down to make up another ounce of milk and he was quiet so I thought I'll just lie down for a moment. I must have fallen asleep because I found the bottle on the floor.'

'And he's not there now, or anywhere else in the house?'

'No, he's not in his crib upstairs or in his pram next to me in the sitting room.'

'Where's the baby's dad?'

'I don't know, I've not seen him for months, but I'm sure he's been coming in the house. He makes sure I'm not here.'

'And is there anybody else who might have popped in and taken him out for some reason?'

'Without asking me? When I woke up the front door blew open; it was on the latch, but I swear to God, I locked it.' Alison starts to sob. 'And a load of his nappies and clothes have gone. The drawers have been left open. His blanket was on the floor.'

'Please try and calm down, Alison. Is there anyone else who can be with you?'

'Julie, my friend Julie lives around the corner.'

'An officer is on their way to you straight away. Please don't touch anything in Charlie's bedroom. I strongly suggest you call your friend to come and wait with you.'

As soon as she ends the call, she dials Julie's number and tells her what has happened.

'I'll be there in two minutes,' Julie says.

Alison puts the receiver down. She shakes uncontrollably, clutching Charlie's teddy to her face. Jamie tries to put his arm around her shoulders, but his arm isn't long enough and anyway, she can't sit still. He follows her around the house as she lifts cushions and looks in cupboards. It's ridiculous to search in such places but she has to do something, she has to work out what has happened, what she has done. She stares out of the back door. Perhaps she woke in a dream, took the baby outside and left him there. She heard, once, about a woman who left her baby in his car seat by the side of the road while she loaded her shopping. Something distracted her and she drove off, forgetting the baby on the verge.

Christ, she can't even remember what day of the week it is. The days and nights have merged together.

Was Charlie born two days ago? Or is it three now? She picks up one of his tiny cotton vests and inhales the powdery baby smell.

When Julie arrives, she gives Jamie a hug and he follows her into the living room. Alison is sitting on the sofa staring into space.

'My darling, this is so terrible.' Julie sits down and wraps her arms around her. 'Tell me what happened, sweetheart.' She takes Alison's hands. 'You're freezing. Jamie, can you fetch your mum a blanket, please?'

'I fed him three ounces of milk and laid him in his crib. Then I went downstairs and made up one more ounce because he wouldn't settle. But he'd quietened down, so I lay on the sofa for a minute, thinking he might start crying again, but he didn't. I must have dozed off.'

'Then he has to be in the house, he can't just disappear.'

The thought of Adam flips over in Alison's mind. 'But the front door was open and I definitely locked it. The key is hanging in its usual place.'

'Oh God, Ali, do you think it was Adam?'

The sound of a car door slamming sends Julie to the kitchen to check out of the window. 'The police are here,' she calls.

Alison takes a deep breath, wipes her eyes on the

little vest and meets them in the hall. Inspector Fay Downy introduces herself, followed by PC Blunt. They ask to see the room Charlie went missing from.

'And this is how you found the bedroom?' the inspector asks. Alison nods. Seeing the room in the emerging daylight makes her start shaking again. Julie takes a blanket from Jamie, places it around Alison's shoulders and helps her back downstairs, while the police search the rest of the house.

Afterwards, they all sit at the kitchen table and Alison runs through what happened. Julie quietly makes tea and brings it over.

'You say you locked the front door. Could you have forgotten to do that last night or left it in such a way that it could blow open?' the inspector asks.

Alison shakes her head. 'I always lock it in the evening and so I know I've done it, I hang the key up. If it was unlocked, I'd have left the key in the door.'

'Okay, that makes sense. So, someone with a key must have come in. Can you think who that would be? A relative perhaps who, with all good intentions, has taken Charlie out to give you a break and not clicked the door shut properly? Your mum, perhaps, or the child's father?'

Alison glances at Julie. Would he come in the middle of the night? She presses her hands to her cheeks. For several moments everyone is silent, waiting for her to speak. 'I can only think of Sandra over the road, who does my ironing. And Adam, their dad.'

'Absent father?'

Alison nods. 'He upped and left late September.' Jamie snuggles into her side.

Julie gently squeezes Alison's forearm. 'And he still has a front door key?'

'Yes, he does.'

Jamie twiddles his fingers in the blanket and puts his thumb in his mouth, something he's not done for over three years.

'Would he really take him without telling me?' Alison turns to Julie.

'Perhaps he thought you wouldn't let him see Charlie?'

'Why would he think that?'

'He's probably trying to give you a fright,' says Julie. 'Give him a few dirty nappies and sleepless nights and he'll soon be back.'

The inspector flicks over a page in her notebook. 'And do you have any idea where Adam is?'

'None.'

'Does he go away often?'

'His job takes him all over; he's a builder and decorator, but he's never been gone this long before without saying something. I assume he's left me.'

'I see.' She scoops three teaspoons of sugar into her tea. 'Why would you assume that?'

'He did it before, when I was pregnant with Jamie, although that wasn't entirely his fault.'

The inspector writes something down.

'So, you think it's Adam?' Julie asks.

'Seems the likeliest explanation at the moment,' the inspector says.

'Lately, he's been in the house when I've been out.' Alison sits up and turns to Julie for support. 'He's picked up his clothes and opened his post, for God's sake.'

'Has he now? Have you spoken to him?'

'No. He makes sure I'm never here.'

'Can you think of anyone else?' the inspector asks. Alison shakes her head.

'Hang on. There is someone. It's probably nothing, but there was this woman at the hospital.'

'Someone you know?' says the inspector.

'I think she may have been in the Red Cross shop where I work, but then I see lots of people. Lots of faces are familiar.'

'Tell us about her.'

'She was standing by my bed holding Charlie while I was asleep.'

'Is she a nurse?'

Alison shakes her head. The inspector leans forward.

'The curtains were drawn around the bed. When I woke up, she was standing there, holding him, face close to his like she was talking to him. She said he'd been crying and she tried to comfort him. I was upset. It seemed strange, like she was reluctant to give him to me. You'd think she would have woken me straight away rather than pick up someone else's baby like that. Anyway, she could see I wasn't happy, so she put him back, made her apologies and left.'

'You didn't tell me this,' Julie says.

'I just thought of it.'

'Did you report it?' The inspector is scribbling in her notebook again.

'She wasn't doing any harm. I thought she must have been visiting someone and heard Charlie crying. I didn't want to make a fuss.'

'What did she look like?'

'Medium height, a bit overweight, but well dressed, late thirties, browny-reddish coloured hair.'

'We'll need to do a photofit of this woman. I'll have

the hospital check out their CCTV. And you think she could have your key?'

Alison shivers. 'I can't see how; it was a bit odd that's all, probably nothing.'

Julie puts her arm around her. 'Any grandparents nearby?'

'Dad died four years ago; Mum buggered off with another man when we were kids. Not seen her since; Adam's parents are both living in Canada. They left when he was a child and haven't been in touch since as far as I know.'

'Can we look through your address book? It might jog your memory. Someone with a possible grudge.' Inspector Downy stands up. 'I need a description of Adam so I can radio it through and his contact number so we can search for him straight away. And I think we ought to speak to this Sandra. Is she likely to be at home now?'

'I expect so. She's at number twenty-five. Straight across.'

Julie finds the battered address book the size of a paperback held together with an elastic band. Alison gives her a description of Adam and a photo.

A few minutes later, the policewoman leaves to speak to Sandra.

'Why don't you go and play?' Alison says, kissing Jamie's cheek. He shakes his head.

'Dad won't come home because you're always mean to him,' Jamie shouts.

'Sweetheart, why are you saying that?' Alison tries to take his hand, but he steps away. 'I think it's because he's seen us arguing quite a bit,' she explains to the inspector.

'Can I ask what you've been arguing about?'

'Money, getting married. He's not keen and I am.' She opens the address book. Scraps of paper fall out. It is a multipurpose folder: telephone numbers kept from when she was at school, a list of birthdays, beauty tips she's ripped out of magazines and random sketches she's drawn when she's had an idea for a bigger piece. 'Everyone's addresses are dotted around,' she says, flicking through. She turns a page at a time and then stops at one address scrawled in green ink.

'What is it?'

'My brother, Ray. I've not seen him for years. He wouldn't take my baby.' She shakes her head.

'Don't you get on with him?'

'We've not fallen out as such.' She flicks through some blank pages.

'But he doesn't visit?'

'No.'

'You said it wasn't entirely Adam's choice to leave last time.'

'My dad threatened him. He was angry that he'd got me pregnant. Told him to leave or else.'

'Do you think someone could have forced Adam to leave this time and possibly harmed him?'

'He had a fight with an ex-boyfriend, but he's in prison for stabbing his hand.'

'What's his name?' The inspector purses her lips.

'Tony Willis. Adam only came back into our lives two years ago.'

'I see. And what were his circumstances?'

Alison glances across at the notes but can't read anything. 'He was on his own. Working, renting a place. That's it.' She flicks further through the address book.

'How did he react to you becoming pregnant this time?'

'I'd like to say he was as pleased as I was, but I can't.'

'He expressed doubts?' the inspector asks.

'That's one way of putting it. He didn't want me to keep Charlie. Wanted us to wait. *Wait for what?* I asked him, I've been waiting long enough for us to be together.' Her tea is cold when she sips it. She pushes the cup away. 'He got really angry, said he'd never marry me.'

The tears come from nowhere and choke her up. She can't seem to get a grip. Julie passes her a tissue.

'I'm sorry, I know this is upsetting, but we need to build a picture. Is there anything else you can think of that might help us find your baby?' She closes her notebook. 'Even if you think it might be insignificant.'

'What about the phone calls?' Julie hands her another tissue.

'There's been a few and the person doesn't speak. I know someone's there, but they don't answer me.'

'Have you any idea who it might be?' the inspector asks.

'I thought it was Adam at first, but now I'm not sure.'

'Okay, I think best case scenario is Adam has been coming back to the house quite frequently and the likelihood is that he took Charlie out early this morning because he wanted to let you get some sleep. On the other end of the scale, perhaps his intention is to keep him. It does happen unfortunately. With any luck, he's seen sense and is on his way back right now.'

'But he wouldn't empty drawers and leave the front door open, would he?'

Inspector Downy doesn't answer.

'I mean, what about the day I went into labour? My underwear drawer was full of...' she exhales a breath and tries to hold the tears in, 'disgusting old under-wear, huge bras and grey baggy knickers that aren't mine.'

'And the moths,' says Jamie, 'and Poppy going missing.'

'Yes, there's been a few weird things. The dog van-ished while we were at Legoland. The back door was wide open and there was a wire across the open gate. I tripped on it and soon after I went into labour.'

'It must be Adam playing a sick joke,' Julie says.

'That does all point to something more sinister. We need to check when this ex-boyfriend Tony is due out of prison. But keep an open mind at this early stage. You must try not to worry yourself.'

'How can I not worry?' Alison clutches the tiny vest.

'Most people are found in the first twenty-four hours.'

'But this is a baby.' Tears flood her again. It seems so hopeless.

'I'm sure we're going to find him,' the inspector says.

She wants to believe her, but she has the same sick feeling she had when Jamie fell out of the tree. Her eyes settle on the baby's hospital name tag sitting on the windowsill. She picks it up. There is a long number followed by 'Baby Boy of Alison Wood DOB 02/12/19/09:05'.

'He still had one of his nametags on, round his wrist.' Alison shows the tag to the inspector. 'I meant to cut it off, but we were both so tired.'

'We're already out looking for Adam. The sooner we can establish if Charlie is with him, the better.'

'I feel useless sitting around here, isn't there something I can do to help?' Alison says.

'You need to sit tight. Adam may try to contact you. I'll need a photo of Charlie, please.'

'I don't have any of him. What if he cuts his tag off?'

'Did Charlie have any distinguishing marks?'

'Yes, a small strawberry mark near the bottom of his spine, in a sort of crescent shape.'

'That's going to be very helpful.'

The doorbell rings. Julie answers it. PC Blunt walks in, clearly flustered.

'Sandra, Mrs Walsh, has seen a woman letting herself into this house on more than one occasion,' she says. 'Miss Wood, do you have a cleaning lady?'

'No, I do not. Although someone has been cleaning up. I thought it was Adam. How did they get my key?'

'We don't know and unfortunately Sandra assumed you had a cleaner, and never thought to mention it. But your new neighbour next door, Natty, says she spoke to your cleaner the day you went into labour. Apparently, she was about to let herself in here.'

'But I don't have a cleaner!'

'Sandra's description was very sketchy but Natty's is much clearer. This woman sounds similar to the one you described in the hospital, except she was wearing a baseball cap pulled down her forehead, so it's difficult to get a clear ID. She was holding a carry case full of cleaning products and wearing a blue tabard. She didn't appear to speak English.'

'The woman in the hospital certainly did. How long has this been going on?'

'Sandra first saw her around two weeks ago. Do you have any idea who this woman might be? Could it be someone you know? A customer who has a grudge against you, perhaps?'

'I have no idea.'

'We'll get an artist's impression of her from the neighbours and the CCTV, and we'd like you to do a TV appeal as soon as possible to help find Charlie. PC Blunt will accompany you to that. She'll stay here for now in case Adam contacts you or turns up.'

Julie lets the inspector out. The wind has picked up and the clouds have blackened into a bruise. Alison watches the washing she left out all night flap around like trapped birds: a pair of Jamie's school trousers, her dress with the tiny flower pattern and three Babygros. The first ones Charlie ever wore.

'It's going to heave it down in a minute,' Julie says.

Alison's lips tremble but she isn't going to give in again. She opens the back door to go and collect the washing, but a strong gust pulls it right out of her hand and slams it shut.

At almost 2 p.m., PC Blunt tells her they have no firm leads and want her to go on TV that afternoon. They can't hang around waiting for Adam to be found and a nationwide appeal is the best course of action. All she can do now is hope someone watching will know where Charlie is.

62

MADDY: DECEMBER 2019

'Did you have a nice day?' Maddy asks when Emily comes in from school, followed by Sarah and Sophie.

'Yes, thank you.' Emily shows her a new keyring for her collection. The word 'sister' is in pink capital letters on both sides.

'That's all she wanted from the Science Museum gift shop, I thought I'd lost it, but it was in the bottom of my handbag,' Sarah says with a pained expression.

'I'm still a sister, aren't I, now I have a brother?'

It takes a moment for Maddy to realise that she means Jamie. 'Of course you are, darling.'

Sarah looks puzzled. 'Are you all right? 'You look tired, it must have been a good night.'

'I've never felt better thanks, but I didn't exactly get

to the restaurant though.' She's hardly slept in days but she has endless energy, so a sleepless night with a baby hasn't phased her. He settled well after his last feed. It was a joy watching him fall asleep in her arms. 'There's a surprise for you both in my room.' Maddy takes Emily's coat from her and can't contain her smile. Emily lets out a whoop and thunders up the stairs. 'Thanks for having her today,' Maddy says.

'Are you sure you're all right? You seem... different.'

Maddy nods. Sarah's never seen her so happy, that's why she's worried.

'Mummy!' Emily shrieks down the stairs. 'What is it?' Sarah looks alarmed.

'Shall we go up?' Maddy grins.

In Maddy's bedroom, Emily is peering into the crib and squeals with delight when they come in.

'Is it a girl, Mummy?' Emily asks.

'No, a boy.'

'Oh my God! You mean you've had the baby?' Sarah rushes forward to peek in then gives Maddy a hug.

'I know and it was so quick I wondered if I would make it to the hospital in time.'

'So, what happened? He's so early.'

'My waters broke in the restaurant car park. Took me completely by surprise.'

'Didn't that happen when you had Chloe?'

'Did it? I don't remember.'

'And they let you come home, even though you're what, five weeks early?'

'Thankfully he's a healthy weight, 5lb 9oz.'

'That is quite big for a premature baby, especially as your bump was so small. Look at him though, he's so gorgeous.'

'They said sometimes when people have a small bump, they don't even realise they're pregnant until they're in labour.'

'Well, thank God you knew.'

'They said my dates could have been wrong.' Maddy avoids looking at her directly. *Be careful. She's trying to catch you out.*

'And they didn't notice that before?' Maddy shakes her head. 'Why didn't you call me? I could have picked you up.'

'I wanted to come straight home. Hospitals can be so... unfriendly.' She fusses about, stacking nappies into a drawer.

'Didn't you need a baby seat for the car?'

'I'd already bought one, didn't I tell you?' She wishes Sarah would stop asking questions, it's making her dizzy.

'Look at his tiny fingers, Mummy,' Emily says, pointing at him.

'And everything was all right with the birth?'

'It was so quick. Really. I feel fine.'

'He's so beautiful, Maddy, the absolute image of Max, isn't he?' Sarah stops frowning at last.

'Exactly like him.' Maddy sighs. 'I think he has my eyes.'

'What's his name? What's his name?' Emily jumps up and down on the spot.

'He doesn't have a name yet. You didn't have a name for several weeks.'

Emily squints and taps her lips with a finger. 'How about Sam?' she says. 'I like that name.'

'I think it's lovely too, darling. Hello Sam,' Maddy says, stroking the side of his face.

Emily kisses his cheek. 'Sam won't have to go away like Chloe and Daddy, will he?'

Sarah grimaces.

'Oh, darling,' Maddy kneels and hugs Emily, 'I hope he's going to be with us for a very long time.'

* * *

Maddy is up again through the night, bottle feeding Sam every three or four hours. The lack of sleep bothers her less than she imagined; in fact, she often wakes before he does. She's enjoying having so much more energy. It doesn't seem that long ago since she last had a newborn to look after. Her body glows with warmth each time she looks at him. Sam. Samuel. She likes it. Emily must have remembered they talked about the name when she first became pregnant.

It is Sunday afternoon and an unexpected warmth seeps into the day. Maddy hands Sam over to Emily who places him on the blanket in the pram.

They walk down to the parade of shops in the precinct and are stopped at least three times by neighbours and people they know.

'Five pounds nine ounces when he was born,' Maddy tells Mrs Jordan outside her flower shop. 'Tiny, like my girls.'

'Still, as long as he's healthy.' Mrs Jordan has known Maddy since she was a baby.

'That's what I said to the midwife. They do flap about these days,' Maddy says.

Emily rocks the pram, humming 'Rock-a-bye Baby'.

Mrs Jordan leans closer to Maddy. 'She's taken to him then,' she whispers.

'She adores him,' Maddy says. How happy Emily

looks. Her hair has thinned so much around the crown, but hopefully it'll grow back.

'Good for her, isn't it?'

Maddy nods. 'She loves having a little brother to look after.'

'He's got his dad's chin and hair, bless him.' Mrs Jordan plucks a sprig of gypsophila from a vase in the shop window.

'Yes, he's Max's son all right,' Maddy strokes the downy quiff with her fingertips, 'and Mum thinks he's the most beautiful baby she's ever seen.'

'Does she now? Well, I never.' Mrs Jordan's eyes widen and Maddy smiles at her.

'Don't forget to look after yourself, dear. You look wacked out.' She places the posy of tiny white flowers at the bottom of the pram. 'Baby's breath, for pure of heart. You be good for your mummy, little one.'

Maddy thanks Mrs Jordan for her kindness and heads up George Street. A tunnel of cold wind rattles crisp leaves along the pavement. *Just look at your baby, Madeleine, isn't he perfect?*

'I'm your mummy, and I love you very much,' Maddy leans down and whispers to baby Sam. Every part of her is fit to burst with love.

63

ALISON: DECEMBER 2019

Alison can't sleep. Charlie has been missing for over twenty-four hours. The empty crib and the soft scent of baby powder lingers in the air, making her weep. Her breasts are engorged with milk so she sits on the bed and expresses as much as she can, filling a small bottle. After, she folds all Charlie's clothes into neat piles. She can't believe she doesn't have a photo of him. At least if they find him with Adam, she'll get them both back, although she's not sure she can forgive him. She spent half the night trying to come up with a sensible reason why he would have done this to her. Any alternative leaves her cold.

They're hoping this cleaner might make an appearance so they can rule her out, but there's been no sign of her for the past two days. Natty and Sandra have told them all they can about what she looks like, and the police have released an artist's impression. But it's no one she recognises.

* * *

It's gone 9 a.m. when she answers a knock at the door expecting a policeman to be there with fresh information, but it is Ray.

'Hey, sis.' Ray's voice sounds more gravelly than it used to. His boyish face is now marked with deep lines. She hugs him tight. Ray gently pulls back.

'Hey, they'll find your kid, he'll be fine.' He stamps solid clumps of mud off his boots. She closes the door behind him and they stand in the hallway, suddenly awkward in the thick silence.

'You should have called me,' he says at last.

She can't think why when she hasn't seen him for eight years. She looks past him, at Charlie's all-in-one coat hanging on the coat rack. He'll be freezing without it on a day like this.

He follows her into the living room. 'I'd heard Adam was back on the scene. Knew trouble would follow.'

They sit either end of the three-seater sofa. Ray rubs his rough-skinned palms together.

'The police can't find Adam.' She stares at a stain on the rug.

'Well, they found me all right, so they'll find him.'

Alison shrugs.

'So, his kid's gone missing and he's run away – why am I not surprised?'

Alison covers her mouth with her fist. She knows what's coming. Raking through the past. She's too tired for this.

'Don't tell me – he's left you again?'

'I don't know, do I?' Alison thumps a cushion.

'Adam's got your baby, obvious, isn't it?'

'Is it? The police don't think so.'

He moves over and puts his hand on her arm. 'So why didn't you call me?'

'Because it's been years. I didn't know how things stood between us.'

Ray puts his arm around her shoulders and gives her a squeeze. 'Sorry, I should have got in touch sooner.'

Jamie peeps round the door.

'Hey, is this your boy, how are you doing?' Ray puts his hand up for a high five. Jamie hesitates.

'This is your Uncle Ray.' Alison rubs her eyes.

'Are you okay, Mum?' Jamie gives her a hug.

'I'll be fine. Switch the kettle on for me, there's a good boy. I expect your Uncle Ray could kill a cuppa.'

'Too right,' he says, pulling a pack of cigarettes out of his back pocket. Jamie grins as Ray swoops from side to side pretending to punch his arm.

Alison makes the tea while Ray stands at the back door, smoking. Jamie goes in the living room to watch TV.

'Dad always said Adam was bad news, sis.'

'Yeah, and he knew everything, didn't he?'

'You were barely eighteen.'

'I knew what I was doing. At least I thought I did. Anyway, I've got Jamie, haven't I?'

'I know, but what I'm saying is, you were just a kid.'

'What about you and, what's her name?'

'Now that was different.'

'How?'

'End of story, okay?' He stubs the cigarette out on the outside wall and lights another. Still chain smoking. She remembers when he started, age fourteen, hanging out with a group of older boys down the allotments.

'Why didn't you come to Dad's funeral?' He chucks the dead match in the bushes.

'Why do you think?' She takes the tea bags out of

the cups and chucks them in the sink. The empty baby bottles are little soldiers lined up on the windowsill, waiting. Her hands start to tremble.

'He wasn't always like that. He had your best interests at heart.' Ray speaks out of the corner of his mouth, the cigarette dancing up and down on his lips.

'He sent me away to get rid of my baby. Told me I was a cheap tart like Mum. Never even came to see me.' She stands up straight and faces him.

'He was still hurting after Mum did a midnight flit with the butcher, but you probably wouldn't remember.' He carries the mugs to the table. 'He was trying to protect you.'

'Why didn't you stick up for me? Weren't you on my side?'

'There were no sides, you know that. It was Dad's way or no way.'

'Yeah well, now he's dead.'

'You know Tony's out of prison, right?'

'Is he? You don't think it was him, do you?' Alison can feel the colour drain from her cheeks.

'I doubt it. The police will be checking him out.'

'Do you think he has something to do with Adam disappearing?'

'All I know is that he wants to come and see you.'

'What for?'

'Didn't make the best choice, did you? Should have stuck with him.'

'Are you serious? He was inside for stabbing Adam. He's a bloody control freak.'

'And Adam's any better?'

'He wouldn't do something like that.'

'Seriously?' Ray laughed.

'Adam and I did have a row. He went mental about me getting pregnant again and he's dead against getting married. I don't understand why. I thought it's what we both wanted.'

'Always full of excuses that one. Dad could see right through him. Only used him because he was good at breaking bones, simple as that.'

'That's not the Adam I remember and that's not what he was like when we met up again. He's always been kind and thoughtful until recently.'

'You don't know the half of it. Talk about Jack the Lad.'

'He's always been faithful to me.'

'Know that for sure, do you?'

'Yeah, I trust him.'

'Dad paid him to leave. He gave him a new identity. All the papers, passport, driver's licence, everything, so he could start again, become someone else.'

'Why didn't you tell me before? Have you told the police?'

'There was no point. I don't know what name Dad gave him; he's taken it to his grave. He didn't want anyone to track him down, thought one of us might go soft and tell you.'

'You sure you can't find out? What if Adam's living somewhere under that name, we may never find him.'

'I doubt if there's any record of it. Like I said, Dad didn't want anyone to know; he'd have had any evidence destroyed.'

'I thought he'd been coming in deliberately when I was out, doing all sorts of weird stuff, but the police think it's some cleaner woman he's employed without telling me, probably to snoop on me, the bastard.' She cups her face in her hands for several moments. 'You don't think something bad has happened to him, do you?'

'The police would have told you.' Ray stubs his cigarette out. 'Unless he's living under this other name.'

Jamie comes in with a sketch book under his arm and holds up a picture.

Ray nods his approval. 'Chip off the old block, ain't he, sis?'

'It's a picture of the tree we had chopped down.'

She puts her arm around Jamie's shoulders and rubs his head. 'He fell out of it.'

'Yeah, I thought it looked a bit...' Ray peers at Jamie's head.

'Leave off you.' Alison smacks Ray's arm. They all laugh.

Jamie turns the page.

'I've not seen this one, who's this?' Alison asks. 'My sister.'

'Oh, I thought you wanted a brother.'

'I did, I do, but this is my sister. Her name's Emily.'

'Ah, that's really sweet.' Alison frowns at Ray, but Jamie sees the smirk on her lips.

'You never believe me, do you?' Jamie slams the pad on the floor and runs upstairs.

'This is all a big shock for him. Leave him for a while.' Alison puts the pad on the table.

'I'd better be going anyway; let you get some rest.' Ray finishes his tea. 'I'll be back tomorrow. Call me if you have any updates or if you need anything.'

'I will, thanks.' Alison kisses him goodbye.

Back in the living room, she opens the pad and looks closer at Jamie's drawing. The girl is with Jamie at the park and she's holding a woman's hand. Is this a wild fantasy or is this when he'd been out alone? A shiver runs through her. Who are these people? Could they have anything to do with Charlie's disappearance?

64

MADDY: DECEMBER 2019

It's the windiest day Maddy can remember in a long time. She lifts Sam out of the plastic baby bath and into the towel on her lap. She didn't think she'd be able to do it, but Emily being there has given her the confidence she needs. The leaded window rattles and the wind whistles through a gap in the frame. She lets Emily dab dry his soft cushiony skin. Only once he is dressed and warm is Emily allowed to cradle him.

'Time for a little sleep, Sammy.' Maddy takes him from her and holds him up to the mirror. He definitely has her eyes and ears. She smiles at her mother holding him, reflected back at her. In her bedroom, she and Emily sit for a while and take turns rocking the crib, watching him in contented silence. Emily winds up the mobile and it plays 'Twinkle, Twinkle, Little Star'. 'Shall we make cakes today?' Maddy kisses her cheek and Emily coyly shrugs her off, giggling as she tickles her.

In the kitchen, she rolls up Emily's sleeves and ties up both their aprons. From the cupboard she takes out flour and sugar, and butter from the fridge. Emily picks out two eggs from the wire basket on the counter.

'Are we making Chloe's favourite muffins?' Emily asks.

'That would be lovely, a thank you for sending us baby Sam.' At that moment, a huge gust of wind wallops the house making everything shake. 'Goodness me.' Maddy peers out of the window. The playhouse has blown across the lawn along with toys and broken branches and all sorts of debris. Is their house going to spin into the sky like Dorothy's in *The Wizard of Oz*?

'Can we save some muffins for when Dad comes home?'

Maddy hesitates, contemplating Emily's solid belief that Max will return. They're coping just fine without him.

'Do we have any chocolate chips?' Emily continues, as though she didn't really expect an answer.

'In here somewhere.' Maddy spins the cupboard

carousel full circle but it's going so fast, everything's a blur.

'Slow it down, Mummy.'

She stops it with her hand and tries to concentrate fully.

Emily spots the packet secured with a peg.

'Dad loves chocolate.' Emily spoons an extra helping of chocolate chips into the mixture and buries them with a wooden spoon.

Maddy wonders if Max loves *her* as much as chocolate. Does he love her more than Alison? Does he love her at all? There are so many questions spinning in her head in a mini cyclone. She won't be able to rest until she knows the answers. Emily plops a dollop of the mixture into each paper case, counting them aloud as she goes.

'Two for you, two for me, two for Dad, two for Chloe, two for baby and two for luck.'

Maddy opens the oven door and slides the tray in. 'For luck, eh?' she says, as she straightens up.

'We're allowed one wish each, but don't ask me what it is because it's a secret,' Emily says.

'Because, if you tell...'

'It won't come true.' Emily grins.

Maddy doesn't even have to guess because her own wish is for Max to come home too.

65

ALISON: DECEMBER 2019

It is midday when PC Blunt arrives. 'Can I come in for a few moments?' she asks. 'I have some news.' She's a tall woman with cropped hair and a spotless suit. Her pale, plain face gives nothing away.

Alison isn't dressed and hugs the robe around her tighter. If it was bad news wouldn't there be two of them? She stands aside to let her in, then leads her through to the kitchen.

'We've had a huge response to the TV appeal. Lots of sightings and leads. It's too early to say for sure, but we've taken someone in and we're fairly confident it's Adam.'

'Oh, thank God, and Charlie's with him?' Alison presses her forehead.

'Unfortunately, Charlie wasn't with him, but we can't confirm yet that he didn't take him.'

'What are you saying? He might have taken him and now he's left him somewhere?'

'I'm sorry, Alison, we don't know enough at this stage.' She leans towards her. 'We're checking out his story and all the places he's been living.'

'Living where?' Alison's eyes feel heavy with lack of sleep. They seem no closer to finding Charlie. She leans against the counter and wipes her hand across her eyes.

'We found him in Sheffield, at the YMCA. But he says he's also been living on the streets and in a bedsit.'

'Why?' Alison searches her face. 'It can't be him. His home is here.'

'I don't know any more details. He's being questioned right now. I can assure you we'll verify his identity as soon as we can.'

'Why Sheffield? What the hell took him there?'

'We don't know any more at the moment. He's in a bad way, he had an accident and hurt his leg. He says he's Adam Hawkins. We're sending him to be assessed by a doctor this afternoon.'

'When will I be able to see him, if it is Adam?'

'We're bringing him back to Cambridgeshire tomorrow.'

'But our baby is still missing.' Alison's voice falters. 'If he doesn't have Charlie, then who does?'

66

MADDY: DECEMBER 2019

Maddy drives straight into the mother and baby space at the front of the shop. Sam is asleep in the seat next to her. She's fascinated watching the blanket fibres lifting every time he exhales. She checks the rearview mirror. A smile spreads across her mum's face.

She lifts Sam out of his seat and into the pram. He is due another feed in two hours. The shopping centre is busier than she anticipated for a Friday morning so close to Christmas. After the bank, she walks straight into the baby department at M&S. She doesn't need anything in particular but she loves to be back in this baby world, browsing through tiny clothes, the cute slogans and soft materials. A heavily pregnant woman is choosing a Christmas outfit for a newborn. Her young skin is glowing, just like they say it should in all the magazines.

'It'll soon grow out of that size,' Maddy tells her. 'When are you due?'

The girl hesitates. 'Any day – I'm overdue.' She sighs and puts a snowball Babygro back on the rack.

'Mine was early. Is it your first?'

'Yes.' Her forehead creases. She rubs the huge bump.

'It's such a special time. This is my third, and last, unfortunately.' Suddenly her mother's voice is back, clear as a bell. *Look closer at her bump, you know what sex it is, like you knew you were having a boy.* Maddy blinks and shakes her head, and there it is, she can clearly see the woman's baby curled up inside her. It kicks out its legs and stretches an arm.

The woman gazes into the pram. 'Ooh, it's giving me a right kick about. I wonder if it's a boy.'

Maddy nods. 'You're right – you're having a boy.'

'Really, can you tell?'

'I have a special power to see right into your womb. And do you know, if you want something enough, you can get it. I always hoped for a boy too. I love my girls though, don't get me wrong, but having a boy is special, isn't it?'

'How old are your daughters?' The woman glances over her shoulder and edges backwards.

'Emily is seven and Chloe was only five. She died three months ago.'

Her eyelashes flicker.

'It was so sudden. She had meningitis, you see, except I didn't detect the signs, so really, it's all my fault, but Chloe says she doesn't blame me, but she misses me, misses all of us. But I can't do anything about it except be sorry, which isn't enough, is it? Worst day of my life, what it did to her beautiful face. I couldn't wake her up in the morning and I tried shaking her and calling her and Emily screamed her name and we phoned my husband but he couldn't cope because he jumped off a bridge but they're not sure if he's alive or not and I keep hoping that he is because I can't imagine life without him no matter what he's done because I found out he has been living with this other woman and a boy, who is so sweet and the image of my husband.' Maddy pauses to take a breath.

'Oh my God, I'm so sorry this has happened to you. You don't seem very well though, are you feeling okay?' The woman glances over her shoulders.

'You see, this is why baby Sam is so precious,' Maddy's voice wavers, on the brink of tears again. 'He's my little miracle sent from Chloe, because only she knows how much I've lost and how much I miss her and that I needed to hold my baby more than anything in this world. He's not to replace her, you understand, nothing could replace my darling girl.' She sniffs back tears.

'He is beautiful.' The woman turns to go. 'It's been so nice to meet you. I'm just going to go and get someone for you, see if they can get you the help you need, so if you could stay here a minute?'

'Yes, he is so beautiful and I am very lucky. Very, very lucky,' Maddy says, staring at Sam. When she looks up, the woman has gone, so she turns the pram around and leaves the shop.

Back in the precinct, Maddy marches past the chemist and glimpses a man in profile. Could it be? She's unable to look away. He is talking to an elderly woman who has a terrier on a string. The man's face turns a fraction towards her. The likeness to Max is uncanny. Can it really be him? Two days ago, she's certain she saw him at the petrol station, and the day before that at the supermarket. In fact, he's everywhere she looks. Is he a ghost come back to haunt her? She leans into the pram, pretending to fuss with Sam's blankets, wishing Max away. If he comes any closer, she'll struggle to control herself; although part of her wants to forgive him, she'll want to shake the life out of him for what he's done. When she's sure he's gone, her body relaxes, she straightens up and pushes the pram back to the car.

67

ALISON: DECEMBER 2019

When the police car pulls up outside the house, Alison strains to watch from the bedroom window. Can it really be him? She didn't think they would be here so soon. A man dips his head to get out of the car. He is wearing a short raincoat, despite the mild weather. His hair covers the tops of his ears and there are white threads running through it. She doesn't like the goatee beard. The doorbell rings but she doesn't move. What will she say? Jamie opens the door.

'Daddy!' she hears him cry. Jamie calls out to her. Her chest tightens. She pauses, touches the side of the empty crib. At the top of the stairs, everything is swimming in front of her. She grips the newel post. It's as though she's staring into a pit, with four faces staring up at her. No one speaks. She glances down at her stupid bunny slippers. The man is standing there, studying her with half-moon eyes, his face full of shadows. Jamie with his arm around him, beaming.

'Ali, it's me,' he calls, putting a foot on the bottom stair.

She wipes her face on her sleeve. 'Where have you been?' Her voice is so small and cracked she wonders if he can hear her, he seems so far away. She says it again, and this time her voice is lost completely and her legs buckle. And then she is falling, down, down, down the stairs towards him. Miraculously, he jumps forward and catches her and helps her back on her feet. As soon as she is standing, she struggles with him, thumping him with her fists. 'Where's my baby?' she screams.

Adam backs away.

PC Blunt intervenes, helping her sit on a step. 'Are you okay?' the policewoman asks.

'What have you done with my baby?' Alison sobs.

'Calm down now, that's it, take it slowly,' PC Blunt says.

'I swear on Jamie's life I don't have him,' he says, 'I'm as worried as you are.'

'How can you even say that?' Alison crosses her arms. 'Shall we all sit down?' PC Blunt indicates the sitting room. They follow Alison, who is helped by Jamie.

'Why haven't you answered your phone or called me?' She grinds her teeth.

'I lost my phone.'

'I hear you've been staying all over the place. How lovely for you.'

'Where's Poppy?'

'He's gone,' Jamie says.

'What happened?' His voice is low and calm.

'I can't believe you're worried about the bloody dog when our baby is missing. What is wrong with you?' Every inch of her is shaking.

'Of course I'm worried about the baby, but don't you understand, if Poppy had been here when this person came into the house, he would have barked and woken you up.'

'He ran away.' Jamie wipes his eyes. 'We tried to find him.'

'How did that happen?'

'Someone left the gate open.'

'Christ Ali, he was a lovely boy.'

'Have you been sending a cleaner round?' She feels the heat of tears building behind her eyes, but she won't give him the satisfaction.

'Do I look like I can afford that?' Adam opens the

patio door, stands outside and lights a cigarette. 'Where's the tree?' Smoke trails back into the room.

'I told you I'd have the bloody thing chopped down. You wouldn't listen.'

'Okay, let's all calm down and try not to apportion any more blame.' PC Blunt indicates that he should come and sit down. Adam drags the cigarette stub down the brick wall and comes in.

'Why the hell did you go off in the first place?' Alison takes the glass of water from Jamie and whispers to him to go upstairs. He shakes his head and stands near his dad.

'I couldn't take it any more.' Adam sits at one end of the sofa, nearest the policewoman.

'Take what?' Alison's voice rises.

'You deciding to have a baby without telling me. You spending all my money like it comes out of a tap. Do you want me to go on?' Adam grips his hands together in front of him, turning them over, twisting the broken skin.

'I didn't get pregnant on my own.' Alison moves along the sofa closer to him. His hair is matted, and his skin and beard could do with a good scrub. He smells like he's not washed properly for a while. Even the soles are peeling away from his trainers. She's never seen him in such a state.

'Take your time.' PC Blunt nods to him.

'I had to think...' – he stops and swallows hard – '... about why we were having another child.'

'But I thought you were happy with growing our little family. You said we were good together, remember?'

'It wasn't the right time.' He shakes his head. 'I kept trying to tell you, but you didn't want to hear it.'

'But I was already pregnant by then.'

Adam puts his hand to his forehead. 'I just don't think you and I...'

'It wasn't as if we could change our minds,' Alison says softly. 'Why didn't you come back for the birth?' PC Blunt asks. 'I was going to, but I had an... accident and I needed to be on my own to sort my head out. The thought of coming back got harder and harder. I convinced myself you'd be better off without me.' Adam raises his head and Alison can see streaks of tears on his cheeks. She's never seen him cry.

'Perhaps a phone call or a message to say you were all right would have helped?' PC Blunt says.

'That's the thing, I wasn't all right. I didn't know how to explain that.'

'The doctor confirmed he's had a breakdown,' PC Blunt says.

'He's put me on medication. It'll take a couple of weeks to start working.'

'But you did come back, without telling me,' Alison says, crossing her arms again.

'What are you talking about?' Adam glances at PC Blunt. 'You've been here, opened your post, changed your clothes...' She directs her explanation at the policewoman, 'He even took the photo of Jamie as a baby out of the frame on the landing.'

Adam shakes his head. 'I've not set foot in this house once in all these weeks.'

PC Blunt leans forward. 'Adam, this could be crucial. We need to know the truth for the sake of your baby.'

'I swear on Jamie's life I've not been here.'

Alison lets out a sob.

'Can you think of anyone who may have taken your baby?'

'No.'

'Then we have a serious problem.' PC Blunt gets to her feet. 'Someone has your front door key and has been letting themselves in and out of your house. Possibly the woman your neighbours saw.'

'Before Charlie was taken, nothing went missing apart from the baby photo.'

'Can you confirm that you didn't take this photo?' PC Blunt asks.

'No, I didn't, how many times do I have to say it?'

'And I don't have a photo of Charlie to help them find him.' Alison covers her eyes.

'You're kidding me?' Adam lets out a sigh. 'So how are you going to know it's him if you find a baby?'

'He's got a small strawberry birthmark on his back in the shape of a crescent moon.'

'Right, I'm off to speak to your ex-boyfriend, Tony Willis.' PC Blunt leans on the table. 'Is there anything else I should know?'

'I don't think so.' Alison glances at Adam.

'That bastard stabbed me.'

'He was released from prison three weeks ago. Is there a chance he has a key?' PC Blunt looks from one to the other.

Adam stands up. 'I bloody hope not. If he's laid a finger on our baby...'

'I don't think he would do that,' Alison says.

'Why are you defending him?' Adam walks around the room.

'Because he wouldn't steal a baby. I know him better than you do. He's good with kids.'

'I can't believe I'm hearing this.' He presses his hands over his ears.

'Please answer the question.' PC Blunt sits down again. 'I don't see how he could have a key,' Alison tells her.

'I see, and remind me, when did your relationship with Mr Willis end?'

'About a week before Adam and I got together, two years ago. But I lived somewhere else then.'

'Is it possible he's holding a grudge against either of you?'

'Me definitely.' Adam crosses his arms. 'Stabbing me obviously wasn't enough.' He holds his hand up so they can see the scar.

'I am certain he wouldn't do anything to hurt me, or my baby,' Alison says.

'It doesn't sound like it could be him, unless he's had the opportunity to steal a key from you. I need you to both think hard about who you might have given a key to, or how someone might have stolen a key from you.' PC Blunt stands up. 'I'll be in touch later today.'

When she has gone, Alison and Adam sit in silence.

'I can't believe this is happening.' He pulls Alison and Jamie into his arms.

'Adam, don't...'

'Daddy.'

'Yes, Jamie.'

'Do I have a sister?'

'Who told you that?' He grips his arm and looks right into his eyes.

'You're hurting me.'

'Sorry.' He loosens his grip.

'There was a woman at the park. She let me meet her. Emily her name is.'

'When was this?' Adam asks. 'About two weeks ago.'

Alison takes Jamie's hand and kisses it.

'Darling, I've told you that none of that is real.'

'Will you be all right for a while?' Adam stands up and yanks open the front door.

'Where are you going?' she calls after him.

'I've run out of fags and there's someone I need to see.' He slams the door after him.

68

MADDY: DECEMBER 2019

Sam is napping after a light feed. It won't be long before he sleeps through the night. Maddy switches the kitchen light on. It's dark outside and the gales have passed, but the rain is relentless, like it might never stop. She pours herself a glass of Merlot then rips off a piece of fresh baguette. Lifting the cloth covering the brie, she digs the bread in its creamy ripeness. The taste is tangy and moreish, like nothing she's ever eaten before. She knocks back the wine and pours another. It's so smooth and fruity, the best wine she's ever tasted.

In the living room, she settles in front of the television with the lights off and switches on a recording of the Proms, which starts with Monteverdi's 'Arianna's Lament'. The music lights a touch paper in her body, all her senses on high alert. Standing at the patio door, a rumble of thunder rolls its drums and lightning flashes through the cloudy sky. It's the most incredible sight she's ever seen. Mother's voice is louder and clearer than ever: *This is your special moment, you're in the midst of a miracle.*

After the Proms has finished, she hears a light tap, tap on the front door. At first she doesn't want to answer it, but the tap, tapping grows louder. *Answer it,* Mother tells her. The person has their back to her at first but turns at the sound of the door opening. It is a man with a goatee beard, wearing a raincoat, the hood hanging over his eyes. She slowly shakes her head.

'Maddy, it's me.' The man steps forward into the light of the open porch.

Her eyes blur with tears. His voice unlatches a lock inside her, she is shaking all over.

'I thought you were dead,' she shouts and shoves him in the chest.

He staggers back, loses his balance and lands on the wet path. He pulls himself up and throws back his hood. His blond hair is soaked in seconds. She cups her hand around her mouth, muffling a cry. Neither of them speaks while she studies his face, still unable to believe it's really him. But there's the passing grin Max gives when he's nervous, the tiny mole under his eye, the full Elvis Presley lips. She sways as blackness tries to envelop her. She reaches out to the porch wall, her head swimming. He's alive! In a surge of euphoria, she grabs both his arms and shakes him. But images of him with Alison bleed into her mind. The surge of love drains down the gutter with the rain. She turns back inside, leaving the door wide open.

He follows her into the kitchen. They stand either side of the table.

'Where've you been all this time?'

'Sheffield.'

'Is that it? No explanation? Why did you go there? I thought you were dead. Drowned.' She shivers, pulls a cardigan from the back of the chair and wraps it around her shoulders.

'I had to get away.'

'What for?' The dogs are scratching at the utility door.

'Why don't you let them out?'

'Answer my question.' She opens the back door so she can breathe. The rainfall has softened into a mist and an earthy smell wafts in.

'I couldn't cope after losing Chloe.' Max's shoulders hunch over.

'Was it really you on that bridge?' Sparks fly in front of her eyes.

He looks more through her than at her, and rakes his wet hair, lost in his own thoughts.

'Did you fall?' She needs to know.

He tips his head up, but after a moment, drops his gaze. 'I'm in a lot of debt. I was struggling. The whole partnership with John... it didn't work out.'

'You were never in business together, were you?'

Max's fingers burrow deeper into his hair. He turns his face away and shakes his head slowly.

'So, where's my money?' Her voice sounds like her mother's.

He looks down and rubs his thumb over the letter A on his wrist.

'Gone.'

'Just like that?' She takes two glasses out of the cupboard and pours a slug of whiskey into each.

'You've moved things round,' he says, following her into the living room, 'and your hair looks different.'

'I fancied a change.'

'I thought your bump would be out here by now.' He looks at her as though for the first time.

She hands him the drink and they sit down. The silence curdles. She watches his eyes narrow as he considers the sofa pushed against the back wall instead of across the room, the new plain rug and the pictures on the walls in different positions. Max knocks back his drink in one. He picks up the picture of Chloe and Emily from the shelf.

'How's Emily been?' he asks.

'Don't pretend you care,' she snaps. 'You should have been here for her.'

'I'm sorry.' He puts the picture back, but he stays facing the wall, head down. 'There's something I need to tell you, Maddy. I should have told you a long time ago.'

'Mummy.' Emily appears in the doorway, giving them both a start.

'Darling, what are you doing down here?' Maddy asks.

Emily's eyes brighten. 'Daddy!' She embraces Max with open arms, squeezing him with all her might.

'I've missed you so much.' He kneels in front of her, examining her face, pushing her tears aside with his thumbs. He kisses her forehead and hugs her again.

'Where've you been?' Emily asks.

'Daddy's not been well.' Maddy stands over them, stroking Emily's hair.

Emily links her hand with Max's and swings them back and forth.

'You are staying, aren't you?' Emily says. 'Mummy's been very upset.'

Maddy takes her other hand. 'Back to bed now.'

'Don't leave us again, Daddy.' Emily starts to cry.

'You can see Daddy tomorrow,' Maddy says.

Max nods. 'See you in the morning, darling.' Max clears his throat. 'I'll come and tuck you in.'

Emily's hand slips out of Max's, but she reaches out to him as Maddy leads her towards the stairs.

Once Emily is settled in bed, Maddy lets Max go in to give her a good night kiss. When he comes out, they stand together in the glow of the light from downstairs. His hair is beginning to whiten around his ears. He touches her face, and a thousand lanterns lift her heart. She longs for him to hold her, but when he bends to kiss her, she pulls away.

'You can't snap it back into place just like that,' she says.

'I know, I know.'

'Come and see your son.'

His face is the picture of surprise. 'When was he born?'

'He came early.'

'Oh, was everything okay?' He frowns.

'They said my dates could have been wrong.' For a moment she is pulled back into the murky darkness of another night. 'It all happened so fast.' She can see him thinking it over.

'What have you called him?'

'Samuel, Sam.'

He nods his approval and follows her into their bedroom.

She breathes in the sweet smell of baby wipes and milk. The wooden crib is next to her side of the bed. Sam is asleep.

'He's beautiful.' Max smiles.

'Doesn't he look like you?' She smooths the crochet cover and touches the edge of the crib setting off the gentlest rocking motion.

'That blanket...' Max sits on the corner of the bed.

'It was in the loft with a few other baby bits we'd kept.' She thinks she crocheted it when she was pregnant with Emily, or was it Chloe? She lifts a loose thread from the bottom corner. A flower in the centre of a square has started to unravel. 'Emily's had more fits since you disappeared.'

Max is quiet, pressing his fingers to his temples.

Maddy smiles at her mother keeping a close eye on them in the dressing table mirror.

'I'll make some coffee,' Maddy says. 'You said you had something you wanted to tell me.'

He runs his hand through hers as she walks past. She stops for a moment but turns away and he follows her downstairs.

69

ALISON: DECEMBER 2019

Alison doesn't want to sleep, because if she even dozes off, she wakes up to the knowledge afresh. The shock of it drowns her under a huge wave, like the first time all over again, gasping for breath, not knowing if she'll ever surface or feel solid ground. It takes her all day to learn to cope, to calm her breathing, even to make a cup of tea without spilling it and burning her hands. While she washes Charlie's bottles yet again, she tries not to listen to the television, or contemplate the statistics and theories about how increasingly unlikely it is that her baby will be found alive with each hour that passes. The now familiar sickness is stuck in her throat.

'Adam said he was nipping out for a packet of fags

hours ago,' Alison tells Ray as soon as he comes in, 'and he's still not back.'

He follows her into the kitchen. Breakfast bowls and mugs are stacked in the sink, unwashed. 'I doubt he'd have gone back up to Sheffield,' he says, 'it's only been one night. I suppose he's in shock over it all, to be fair. The police will have told him to stick around until they find Charlie.'

'But why would he go off again?' She takes two Foster's out of the fridge and hands him one. 'What if he does have Charlie hidden somewhere?'

'Then they'll find him.' He pulls the ring off the can and has a swig. 'What's the latest?'

'They don't seem to have a clue who's taken him, and they can't trace any flipping cleaning lady,' she ends with a sob.

'Come on, sit down, you need to calm yourself.' In the sitting room he pats the seat next to him.

'I can't eat, I can't sleep.' She tips the can up and drinks. 'What about the TV appeal?'

'Several leads and a bunch of crackpot callers. The police aren't saying much.' She takes in a long breath. 'Why would he go off again when I need him here?'

Ray opens the patio door and lights a fag. 'I didn't want to tell you this but, well, he was mucking about with someone, before he went to Sheffield I mean.'

'Really, who?'

'That tarty friend of yours, Jaz, is it?'

'What? The little slut.' She gulps her drink down until it is finished and takes the can out to the kitchen. She chucks it in the swing bin. She can hear Adam's voice saying, *Aren't you going to recycle that?* Fuck off. Ray is shutting the patio door when she comes back in.

'Ever since baby Charlie went missing, I've had some of the lads out looking for Adam. Jaz reckons he only stayed with her for one night and swears it was before he got back with you.'

'Bastard! I didn't know they'd slept together. Could Jaz have something to do with Charlie being taken?'

'I doubt it. Don't think they're exactly on speaking terms.'

'How could he do any of this to me?' She takes one of Ray's cigarettes and lights it.

'Darlin', like I said, we warned you about him years ago. Dad did try his best after Mum went, whatever you think.'

'Adam says Dad threatened to kill him.' She slides the patio door open again.

Ray laughs. 'Do you remember Lorna, who ran the cake shop?'

Alison nods and blows smoke out of the door.

'Adam was living with her when he first started seeing you.'

'No, he can't have been, he said there wasn't anyone else. We loved each other.'

'But you were barely out of school.'

'Don't make him out to be one of those sort.' She flicks the ash on the damp flagstones.

'I'm just saying he can't stick to one woman, no matter what he says. He was shacked up with her, a widow, sponging off her an' all, no doubt, and at the same time declaring his undying love to you, sweetheart.'

'Why should I believe you? That's not the Adam I know.' She chucks her stub out of the back door and fetches two more cans from the fridge.

'There's always someone else. Every single time. You need to get shot of him.' He opens a can and takes down a long mouthful of beer. 'How's Jamie taking it all, sis?'

'He's quiet; doesn't like me to be out of his sight. I kept him off school yesterday but he's back today. It's difficult for him, you know, with all the other kids digging at him.' She presses her hands to her face. 'I just want my baby back.'

'I know it's hard, but you've got to try and keep things as normal as possible for Jamie.'

'That story he came up with, about him having a sister that he met at the local park. Now I'm wondering if he wasn't making it up after all.'

'The truth will come out, Ali. You've just got to try and reassure him that everything will be fine, that whatever happens, he'll always have you.'

Alison wipes her face on her sleeve. She can't believe this is happening to her. It's supposed to be the happiest moment of her life, being with Adam, completing their little family with another boy, it's what they'd hoped for all those years ago. How could it have all fallen apart?

'But Ray, what am I going to do if they don't find Charlie?'

70

MADDY: DECEMBER 2019

When Maddy brings the coffee into the living room, Max is standing on the lawn in the moonlight. She leaves the drinks on the table and joins him.

'Remember the moon landing exhibition?' he says without looking at her.

She nods.

'Amazing, wasn't it? We're lucky to have been alive for the fiftieth anniversary. I like what you've done with the garden, by the way, although having only black flowers is quite eerie at night. I'd have preferred a Moon Garden.'

Their eyes meet.

'It's as though all the colour has drained out of your world.' He touches her arm but she twists away.

'I thought you were dead. I've been a widow in mourning.'

'I'm sorry.' He looks away. 'You've kept the tree,' he stumbles over his words.

'Why wouldn't I?' He's full of tricks. Mother warned her. Max doesn't answer.

'Do you know they found your rucksack, then your van? It was on the local news.'

He dips his head.

'Why didn't you call to let me know you were okay?'

'I wasn't well, I couldn't think straight.'

'They told us to expect the worst.' She pulls her cardigan round her tighter and folds her arms. 'Can you imagine what that did to Emily?'

'I'm really sorry. I stood on that bridge and my mind went blank. I felt at peace, like it was the solution to everything.'

'Solution to what?'

'And the next moment I'd jumped.'

'But you got out.'

'I nearly drowned.'

'Wasn't that the idea?'

'I don't know. I damaged my leg.' He bends down to rub his shin. Two bats fly in concentric circles above their heads. 'I suppose I thought you'd be better off without me, that you could claim the life insurance, I don't know.'

Maddy faces him full on. 'On a missing body?' She follows him to the foot of the tree. 'You wanted us to believe you were dead?' The words fester above them like a cloud of midges. She studies Max's profile. The beautiful outline of his jaw is smudged by the new beard. A hint of loose skin has formed beneath his chin.

He looks deep into her eyes in that intense James Dean way he has, this strong power he has over her, and sure enough, the familiar flutter rises in her chest, catching her by surprise. She moves away from him, determined not to be drawn in.

He reaches forward and touches the bark. 'In that minute I wanted to be dead, and for... for Chloe to be alive.' He clenches his fist and thumps the tree, letting out a sob.

'And you don't think I felt like that too?' Her mind flashes back to the summers they've spent in the garden, a jumble of images of Max sitting under the tree reading *The Times*, her planting flowers, mowing the lawn, the girls running around in their swimming costumes, spraying each other with water. The time he helped her put up the archway into the girls' play den, holding the metal posts while he banged them into the ground. Planting clematis up one side and honey-suckle up the other; the memory speeds up and suddenly she can see the plants growing in front of her eyes until they've merged as one at the top of the gothic spike.

There is a rustle in the bushes bringing her back. A neighbour's black cat darts out and disappears across the lawn into the darkness. A shiver runs through her body. Her mother's voice in her head, clear as anything, telling her it's another ominous sign. The dogs start scratching again at the utility room door, so loudly it echoes around the garden.

'Let's go in.' She hurries Max inside and closes the patio doors. They sit on the sofa, closer this time. She can smell him, his stale sweat and whiskey on his breath. She remembers what her mother told her about men like him, how sly and tricksy they are. She pours large shots of whiskey into a couple of glasses.

'The police searched for your body for four days. They'll want to know you're alive.'

'I promise I'll tell them.'

'So where did you go?' She brings the amber liquid to her lips and knocks it back. Like fire through a tunnel, she can visualise it burning its way down to her stomach.

'I've been staying in a bedsit mostly.'

She stares at him until he looks away. She refills the empty glasses. The dogs are whining and one of them barks.

'Shall I go and let them out?' he says.

'I thought you had something to tell me.' She hears her mother's voice, not her own. She pours the whiskey into her mouth, letting it pool there, numbing the skin, before she swallows it down.

'I know I should have told you this straight away... but I didn't know how you'd take it, and I don't want to lose you.'

She slams the glass down on the table. Her body is a furnace, ready to blow. Max fumbles in his pocket and draws out a half-flattened box of cigarettes. The dogs start up a chorus of barking and howling.

'Still not given up?' Maddy shakes her head. 'Find it hard giving things up, don't you?' She grabs the packet and tosses it on the floor.

Max sighs. 'I was with someone years before you and she got pregnant, but her family told me she'd had an abortion. They forced me to move away, change my name. But it turns out she had the baby. I only found out by accident.'

They hear a loud clunk. The dogs have pushed the door handle down and broken out. They scamper and skid down the hall into the living room, jumping up at him, licking his face and hands.

'Three dogs?' He tries to fend them off, but they continue to jump all over him unable to contain their excitement.

'I know all about your other family... Adam,' she hisses.

'It was you.' Max grabs her wrist.

She shakes her hand free. 'I quite like the way you've done your house out. Funny that everything's so similar to ours.'

'Do you know what's happened to the baby?'

'What baby?'

'Alison's baby. Don't you watch the news?'

Maddy crosses her arms. 'You mean your baby.'

'I was coming to that, I'm so sorry.'

'Sorry you slept with her or sorry you've been found out?'

'Please tell me if you know where the baby is.'

'You got two women pregnant and you decided to jump off a bridge. What kind of a father are you?' She flicks her hand at him.

'She got pregnant without telling me.'

'Do you think I'm stupid?' She laughs hysterically. 'You've been sleeping with another woman – living with her, playing happy families.'

'She tried to trap me.'

'Ahh, trouble in paradise. Am I meant to feel sorry for you? Were you ever going to tell me?'

'Yes, I wanted to...' – Max covers his face with his hands – '...so many times.' He leans back in his seat and shuts his eyes. She pours more whiskey for herself, drinking it in one before refilling both glasses. She holds one out to Max, nudging him until he opens his eyes. He takes it from her, staring ahead, unblinking, and drinks it down.

'But it was easier for you if we thought you were dead?'

'I wanted to come back here to be with you and Emily.'

'Why didn't you leave her then?' she shouts.

'I wanted to, but she must have sensed I wanted out. Next thing I knew, she was expecting.'

'And so was I.' Maddy growls in his face. 'What about me and our baby?'

'I didn't know what to do.' His hands twist together. 'You could have come home at any time.'

'It was complicated.' He drags his hands down his face. She sits back and waits.

'Because like I said, she had a baby eight years ago, a son I thought had been aborted.'

'Ah yes, young Jamie; a fine boy.'

Max looks up. 'He knows about Emily. Was it you, coming to the house?'

'So, you never thought to mention you had a son before we got married?'

'I didn't know she'd had him, honestly.' He moves to the edge of the sofa. His hands across his eyes, kneading his skin.

'And you expect me to believe that after all your lies?' She springs up and stands in the middle of the room, hands on hips.

'It's the truth, Maddy.'

'So, when did you find out this delightful piece of news?'

'When I met Alison again,' he hesitates, 'two years ago.'

'Behind my back. Lying to me for two whole years.'

'I'm so sorry.' His hands sweep over his face.

'Are you really, Max? I don't believe you. You had every opportunity to tell me.'

'I'm honestly truly sorry.'

'So come on, help me out here – Max Saunders doesn't actually exist, does he?'

'He does, I mean I do. It's still me, your husband who loves you.' He holds out his hands to her, but her arms stay crossed. He sinks back into the sofa. For several moments they don't speak. The clock in the hall chimes midnight.

'I stupidly convinced myself you were the one person I could trust.' She starts to cry.

'Maddy... please...'

'Now I know how my mother felt when she found out my dad had been cheating with half the neighbourhood. Is that what you've been doing too?'

'No Maddy, no.' He reaches out and tries to touch her arm. 'Why should I believe a word you say? I finally understand the pain my father put her through.'

'I wanted to be a proper father to my son, to the child I didn't know existed until he was six years old.'

She finishes her drink. *Don't let him get away with it.*

'Let's start afresh, move away, if you can just help me clear my debts.'

Maddy stares at the photo of Chloe and Emily. 'I don't think so.'

'We can work it out, I know we can. It's you I love, not her.' Her head is pulsing. Does this even mean anything to her? 'It's you I want. I know I've been an idiot.'

'I can't think right now.' She pours another finger of whiskey and drinks it down.

'Just say you'll give me another chance.' He slides off the sofa onto his knees. There are tears in his eyes.

'I don't think I can.'

'Do you want me to go?'

'You promised Emily you'd be here in the morning.' Her voice stumbles. The thought of him leaving again paralyses her. She tries to block out her mother's voice, but it's getting louder, more insistent. 'Haven't you missed your bed?' The words escape before she can stop them. They stare at each other and he rests his hand on her leg. She lets him gently push her back on the sofa and her mind floats in a cloud of his intoxicating odour of whiskey, cigarettes and sweat. He leans over, pushes up her jumper and kisses the warm skin around her navel.

'No,' she says in her mother's voice, and pushes him away.

71

After only two hours' sleep, Maddy wakes with a start. She can't remember going to bed. Was Max coming back a dream? It takes another few seconds before she remembers: Max is alive. With a surge of energy she sits upright, holding a hand to her pounding chest. He is lying next to her gently snoring, a line of cushions piled up between them.

Her head falls back on the pillow and she stares at the ceiling which transforms into a blue sky. On their wedding day, he slipped the gold band on her finger, and she was certain they were happy. But had he been? Had he really wanted to be with her? Tears stream down her cheeks until she gives in to sleep once more.

It is 7 a.m. when she wakes again. Sam has slept

through. In the kitchen, she fills the kettle and switches the TV on low.

The baby went missing in the early hours of Saturday morning from the family home.

She turns the TV off and pours boiling water into a bowl ready to warm a bottle of formula milk. He said they could move to the coast, but how can she trust him again? Why has he come back? Mother says he's trying to trick her and take Sam away.

The baby is crying upstairs. She wakes Emily and brings Sam down. His fingers tangle in her hair. She kisses his forehead and touches the two circles of heat on his cheeks then slips two fingers down the back of his top.

'You're a bit warm, darling.' She offers him his bottle and he takes a little while Emily eats her cereal, but then he cries, turning his head from side to side, rejecting any more milk. She lays him in the pram. 'Come and say goodbye to Daddy.'

Maddy takes up a cup of tea. Max is sitting in bed watching the news. She switches it off. Emily runs to him and throws herself on the bed.

'I'll drop Emily at school then take Sam for a walk. You'll stay for a while, will you?'

He nods, his gaze lingering on the blank screen.

After waving Emily off at the school gate, she carries on down Belmont Road, towards the shops, some of which are just opening. A road sweeper trundles along with his cart and grabber in hand; he tries to catch an empty plastic bag cartwheeling down the path. At the kiosk outside Uxbridge station, a small queue of people glance at their newspapers in between flicking their wrists over to check their watches. As she approaches, time seems to slow down and everyone stops and stares at her. A man at the front of the line with two cocker spaniels pulling on their leads holds out his change to the woman sitting behind scores of front-page headlines in large bold letters:

BABY SNATCHED

Maddy blinks at all the faces staring at her. It's in their eyes – questioning if this is her baby. She needs to be careful. Keep him safe, away from all the prying people Mother has warned her about. She turns left away from them, towards the main shopping precinct. Sam is awake but quiet, his cheeks the colour of cherries. Inside the precinct, the metal grille covering H. Samuel clatters open halfway revealing the shiny black shoes of the proprietor. A man in the clothes shop next door is vacuuming as Maddy charges past. It is not until she has walked right through the centre that she comes to an abrupt halt outside an electrical shop.

Three televisions on a glittering podium flicker behind the glass. A woman she recognises is sitting at a table next to a policewoman. Her name is on the table in front of her: 'Detective Inspector Fay Downy'. Cameras flash at them from different angles. Suddenly, the pale face of the woman she knows is filling the screen. Her watery eyes are puffy and shadowed, the blonde hair unwashed, almost mousy. She is looking straight at her. Maddy tries to read the trembling lips. She can make out the word 'please' three times before the woman breaks down. The camera pans back to the inspector. Her fingers lock together and lift off the table when she emphasises a word. The camera pans back to the other woman, holding a blue teddy. Maddy takes in a long, deep breath.

'Terrible, isn't it?' says a voice next to her, giving her a start. An old lady with a shopping trolley bag is watching the televisions alongside her. 'Who'd take a dear little baby?' She looks in at Sam who starts to grizzle. 'There, there, you're safe and sound, sweetheart, your mummy's here.' The woman smiles at Maddy. 'Are you all right, my dear?'

Maddy turns the pram around and hurries back to the high street. It feels colder than earlier, and Sam won't stop crying. It's a shrill sound which sets her nerves on edge. She puts her head down and pushes the pram as fast as she can up Belmont Road, stopping by a bench to catch her breath. Sam's crying so much she feels her own tears welling up. She lifts him out and gasps at how burning hot he is. She digs into his nappy bag for her mobile. Where is it? She can't have left it behind. She tries every pocket but it's not there. Sam's cries become more shrill. What's wrong with him? She lifts him out and her phone clatters to the ground. Shit! Thankfully the leather case has saved it from being damaged. She dials the house number, jogging Sam on her hip.

It seems to ring forever. Max must have gone back to sleep. Worse still, what if he's left? She dials again and is about to give up when he answers.

'It's me,' she gasps.

'What's wrong?'

'It's Sam. He's sick.' A sob escapes her lips.

'Where are you?'

'Belmont Road, near the school.'

'I'll be there in two minutes.'

Maddy bounces Sam up and down on her lap, trying to make him stop crying, but his cries become louder and louder and all she wants to do is make him stop.

72

As soon as Max pulls onto the drive, Maddy eases Sam out of his seat. She holds him tightly and runs indoors. As quickly as she can, she strips the clothes off his hot little body, lays him on a towel in her lap and sponges him down with tepid water.

'We'd better get him to the doctors.' Max looks at his watch. 'The surgery should be open.'

Maddy ignores him. 'Hold him for me,' she says. Max sits on the side of the bath with Sam on his knees, facing him. Maddy wets a sponge under cool water and dabs the pink skin on his back, drawing out the heat. 'He'll be fine as soon as I get this temperature down.' She repeats the process while Max chatters to him in a silly voice. Soon, Sam stops grizzling.

'That was almost a smile,' Max says.

'You see, he's feeling better already.'

'He's still burning up. We ought to get him checked out.'

'He's staying here with me.'

'What about this rash? What if it's...'

Neither of them can say meningitis but she knows they're both thinking it. She wipes her forehead. He's going to be fine. She will not lose another child.

She turns back to the sink and glances in the mirror. Her mother tells her not to give up, that Sam will be fine. Behind her Max has laid Sam across his lap and is taking off his nappy. She spins round. 'Don't do that!' she yells.

'He needs changing and it's keeping in the heat.'

'I'll do it.' She tries to take Sam from him but Max has already undone the tabs and the heavy nappy falls to the floor. There is a tiny crescent-shaped mark the size of a five pence piece on Sam's lower back. Maddy's eyes lock with Max's. Before she can do anything, he's turned Sam around.

'Maddy?'

For a long second she watches him, digesting what he's seen.

Her hand grips the sponge. Barely a drop of water

left in it. 'This is unusual, isn't it?' he asks, swallowing hard.

Maddy blinks.

'I mean it's like the one they showed on the news – on baby Charlie.'

'Is it? You're the father of both of them. There are bound to be similarities.' She opens her hand and the sponge springs back to life.

'I suppose so.' He frowns and lays Sam across his legs and puts a clean nappy on him, but Sam's body becomes floppy.

'What's wrong with him?' Maddy sobs.

'Call the doctor,' Max says in a quiet voice.

'We can't!' she screams.

'Maddy – now!'

She doesn't move, her eyes fixed on Sam.

'Please!' he shouts.

Sam's neck and limbs hang loose.

Max gently passes him to her and he dashes into the bedroom. She catches sight of her mother's flushed face in the mirror. She is crying.

Sam is quiet in Maddy's arms when Max comes back in. 'They said Dr Carey has just finished another call nearby, so he's on his way here now.'

In a matter of minutes there is a loud rap at the door.

Max answers it and races back upstairs, followed by the doctor.

'You were lucky to catch me,' Dr Carey says, taking out his stethoscope.

Max describes what's happened. The doctor shines a light in Sam's eyes. He checks his neck and breathing. The rash has calmed down.

'It's probably a virus,' Dr Carey tells them. His left eye twitches every time he speaks.

'Thank God. I thought it was... worse.' Max wipes his face on his sleeve.

'Give him Calpol and keep sponging him down. These things often go as quickly as they come. Always worth getting it checked out though.'

Maddy nods.

'I didn't know you'd had your baby already, Mrs Saunders. When was he born?'

'Saturday.' She steals a glance at Max. His face has darkened.

'I see. I must be thinking of another patient.'

Her eyes fix in a stare. She nods.

'He's a fine weight, considering. Are you feeling well in yourself? You look exhausted if you don't mind me saying. Do come and see me if you need anything and when you're ready to discuss contraception. Don't leave it too long.' Max shows him out. She can hear them whispering.

When the doctor has gone, Maddy gives Sam some medicine and takes him into their bedroom. Max follows in silence. Once she's rocked Sam to sleep, she lays him in his crib and covers him with a cotton sheet. Max lies next to her on the bed. She tries to hold his hand, but his arms are rigid and he pulls away. He shuts his eyes. Soon her eyes close too.

In her grave of sleep, a worm of sound burrows in her ear. A soft rustling at first. Then, click. She forces one eye open by a hair's breadth. Lying on her side, all she can see through the little crack is the empty space next to her. The rustling starts again and seems to be coming from behind her. The room falls silent once more. Too quiet. She tries to move again, but sleep paralyses her. Another soft click. An unmistakable slam of a car door. At last her eyes flick open, released from a catch. The engine fires up and tyres crunch over thousands of tiny stones to the smoothness of the road. She rolls towards the empty cot and a scream erupts from her throat.

She leaps out of bed and runs downstairs. Max's jacket and the baby's changing bag have gone. She grabs her mobile phone and quickly slips on a pair of trainers. Her mother's voice is loud and clear: *He's be-*

trayed you again. She runs next door to Sarah's house and bangs hard on the buzzer until the door opens.

'Maddy, what's wrong?' Sarah puts her hands out to her, but Maddy can't stand still, turning this way and that.

'He's taken Sam, can you pick Emily up from school today?'

'Slow down a second, what are you talking about? Who's taken Sam?'

'Max has.'

'What, he's alive?'

'He turned up last night and now he's trying to give my baby to someone else, because he's been lying to me about where he's been, and I can't trust him and I need to have Sam back with me in my arms, because I can't lose another child, I can't.' She starts shaking and Sarah comes forward and holds her arms, rubbing them up and down.

'Hey, it'll be all right. Slow down a second. Why would Max give your baby to someone else? Surely, he's just taken him out and he'll bring him back soon?'

'No, he won't, you don't understand. I need to go after him now.' Maddy pulls away from her and opens the car door.

'You're not making any sense. Are you sure you're okay?' Sarah grabs her keys. 'Let me come with you.'

'No, I have to do this, and I need you to be here for Emily.' Maddy climbs in the driver's seat.

'You're sure about this? You don't seem yourself, will you be all right?'

Maddy starts the engine. She bites her lip. 'You'll look after Emily for me, won't you?'

'Of course.'

* * *

Maddy heads straight to Cambridgeshire. There can only be one place Max is taking him. Why doesn't he understand that Sam is her baby? She glances up at the rearview mirror where her mother is smiling her approval.

The voice on the radio says that snow is forecast. The moon's frozen face hangs in the pale blue sky. Silver trees laden with frost line the A1. Everything sparkles in the low sun. It's as though she is entering another land. Her foot presses harder on the accelerator. There is no sign of him up ahead. She needs to get her baby back before he gives him away.

Maddy doesn't remember driving to Lawn End. The last thing she remembers is the light dancing on the trees. When she arrives, it feels as though she was at home only moments ago. The thin moon is high amongst the grey clouds. She stops at the end of the road, more from habit than anything else and it takes her a moment to realise that Max's car isn't there. Her breathing quickens. How has he not arrived yet? A rising dread snakes from her stomach to her throat. She grips her neck. Has she made a mistake, has he taken Sam somewhere else? Where can they have got to? Her mind flashes images of Max's car overturned and on fire, Sam screaming trapped in the back. It quickly morphs into Max's grinning face, driving far away where she'll never find them.

Her pulse won't stop racing. Should she knock on the door? *Wait for the sign*, her mother's voice tells her. She turns the car around, and parks opposite the entrance to Lawn End, by the hairdressers, tucking her car behind another. From here she can see if Max does turn up, but he won't see her.

Fifteen minutes tick by. A Volvo drives slowly past. Her eyes fix on the number plate, CPN 999. Time seems to pause. It's clearly the sign she's been waiting for: *CALL POLICE NOW 999*. She picks up her mobile. Her thumb hits the number nine three times. 'Please help me, my baby has been stolen.'

73

It's not long before Max appears, hurtling around the corner. Without a second thought, Maddy jumps out of her car and runs down the street after him. He's unstrapping Sam from his seat when she reaches them and, as he lifts Sam under his sleep-suited arms, she tries pulling him to her.

'Maddy, no, please.' Max swings Sam away from her and bangs on the door, calling out to Alison.

'But he's my baby.' Maddy's heart pushes into her throat. She reaches for him again. Max dodges her, moving around the side of the car. Sam's almost close enough for her to kiss his sweet-smelling skin.

Alison runs out of the house crying, 'Charlie!' Jamie follows holding a TV remote ready to zap her but smiles when he sees the baby. Max lays Sam in Alison's arms and she sobs into his downy hair as she takes him into the house.

A trickle of lava runs through Maddy's veins. *Sam is your baby, take him back*, her mother's voice instructs her. Where are the police? They need to come and save him. She pushes past Max, into the house. 'I want my baby,' she whimpers but Max holds her arms, keeping her away.

A rumble of thunder cracks open the sky, followed by a sudden deluge of rain. Max shuts the front door and tells Maddy to wait there, but she doesn't want to and she wonders if the storm is inside her, too, because she can feel it building. Jamie is in the living room she has come to know so well. He steals a glance at her over his shoulder then flicks from one channel to the next, the volume rising, louder and louder so it hurts Maddy's ears. She wants to hold Sam so much, kiss his flushed cheeks. When are they going to give him back to her? A flash of lightning illuminates his startled face. Alison sits on the sofa holding him, kissing his cheeks, his hair, his hands, but he wants to be with Maddy, she can sense he wants his mummy. Alison descends into noisy heaving sobs, clutching Sam so tightly that Max gently loosens her grip, whispering to her as he does. When Sam roots around her chest for milk, she lifts her top up and after a few false starts, she breastfeeds him, rocking back and forth.

A crescendo of rain wipes out all other noise. Maddy imagines standing outside soaked to the skin, screaming to be heard, watching Max through the glass, in this other life of his. She relives the moment she first saw inside this house. The shock of seeing the same wallpaper and stair carpet as theirs. Max's face beaming out from photos with his secret family.

Maddy's head clouds over. She steps back and leans against the front door, her eyes half closed. Max is standing near, watching her. Why doesn't he speak? She longs to hold her baby, smell the warmth of his clean skin, hear his snuffling breathing sounds.

Alison looks up as though it's the first time she's noticed anyone else there. She stands, jigging Sam up and down on her hip, her face red and puffy. 'What's she doing here?'

'Come on, Maddy, let's go.' Max touches her shoulder. 'You know her?' Alison is incredulous.

'Look, this is all a horrible mistake,' Max says.

'What do you mean?'

'She's not well.'

'Did she take Charlie?'

Their voices warp in Maddy's head. She sways like a repelling magnet.

'He's my baby!' Maddy screams and lurches forward, but Max grabs her arms.

The rain stops as suddenly as it started. A door slams at the back of the house.

'What the fuck is going on?' A man stomps into the hall, wearing combat trousers, Doc Martens, and a tiger tattoo on his forearm.

'What's he doing here?' Max yells.

'She took my baby!' Alison points at her.

'Did she now.' The man flares his nostrils.

'What have I ever done to deserve this?' Alison yells at Max.

Maddy can't look at the scarlet blotches on Alison's face, the blood pumping through the veins in her neck.

The man muscles towards her.

'Max!' Maddy cries out. Max steps between them so he's face to face with the man.

'What did she call you?' Alison asks.

'Get out of my way,' the man snarls at Max.

'Give my baby back,' Maddy cries out.

Max turns to Maddy and tips up her chin so she has to look in his eyes. If only she could hate him.

'This isn't your baby,' he says gently. 'Alison's baby has a birthmark on his back.'

'He's mine,' Maddy whimpers and reaches out for Sam.

'Get her away from me!' Alison moves backwards clutching the baby to her chest. 'I remember you.' She jigs him up and down, pointing at Maddy. 'It was you in the hospital, wasn't it?'

'Will you shut up for one minute?' Max yells.

'Watch it,' the man says.

'Was it you coming into the house too?' Alison asks.

'I'm sorry.' Maddy's voice is barely audible.

'Don't you think I deserve an explanation?' Alison cries. 'I've been out of my mind and she stands there saying nothing.'

'What is wrong with her?' The man pulls a face.

'Maddy, are you okay?' Max touches her forehead.

'Why doesn't she speak?'

Every sound is muffled, as though her ears are blocked with water. A wave of exhaustion crashes over her, dragging her under. Her eyes want to close but she forces them open.

'So, are you going to tell me how you know her?' Alison asks.

'Shut up!' Max yells.

He turns to Maddy, gripping her arms now, pinching the flesh away from her bones. 'You need to tell me where our baby is, Maddy. Do you hear me?' He shakes her and her head sways back and forth, clicking and crunching, her eyes opening and shutting like a doll.

The baby is crying again. The sound seems to inhabit the whole house, reverberating like a tight violin string. She aches to hold her baby boy. A kaleidoscope of images spins in her head. A telephone ringing and Emily face down in the bath water. Chloe singing to an audience and Maddy finding her dead. The faces of her father, mother and Lisa, the identical wallpaper and the photo of Max with another family. Seeing Alison pregnant and picturing Max falling from a bridge and her baby not kicking, all going around and around and around.

She sinks to her knees, rocking her empty cradling arms. 'He stopped moving and kicking and they said he was dead inside me and I don't know why I was carrying a dead baby; is that what I deserved? They had to scrape my womb to get rid of him and there was so much blood for days and I waited for you to come home to tell you, but you were missing and I needed to tell my husband first, but I thought you died falling from a bridge and I just needed to tell you that I'd called him Sam and that it wasn't our fault; the doctors said it wasn't my fault. But Sam was in the hospital cot waiting for me and it was Chloe who brought him back for us as a gift.'

'I'm so sorry our baby died and I wasn't there.' Max crouches in front of her.

'What the fuck are you telling me here?' Alison pulls at Max's arm.

'Shut up,' Max snarls, yanking away from her.

'Who is this woman?' Alison's accusing blister-red face is more than Maddy can stand.

'I'm his wife!' Maddy yells.

'You fucking bastard!' Alison thumps Max in the back.

Maddy tries to grab Sam, but Alison twists away and elbows her in the face.

'I've got to save my boy.' Maddy lunges again, but Alison is too quick, turning away and kicking out behind her.

'See, he never changed, he's not worth your breath.' The man muscles forward and headbutts Max square on the forehead.

'Fuck off, Ray, if it wasn't for you and your scum of a father lying to me...' Blood drips down Max's face. As Ray turns away, Max surprises him with an uppercut that sends him crashing backwards. Alison screams. The sound of a siren approaching fills the air.

'We were just trying to protect Ali from your lies.' Ray holds his jaw, giving Alison a sideways glance.

Maddy's cold on the floor. Her head is a fug. She cannot keep her eyes open any longer. Max is above her calling her name. The siren grows louder and louder. She is sinking. Noises fade away and she is floating.

Her mum stands before her in a bright halo of light with Chloe. Maddy reaches up and takes Chloe's outstretched hand. Everything blurs at the edges and folds into black.

74

MAX: MAY 2020

There isn't a cloud in the sky and there's little shelter from the heat. Max is wearing flip-flops, shorts and Maddy's white straw hat. He carries a basket on his arm as he shuffles across the lawn. He stops and takes a breath and waits for the pain to pass. His leg's playing him up something rotten today. Doctor says he should use a stick to get about, but he's not ready for that.

Emily is stretched out on the sun lounger reading a book, her skin is already a fair bronze. Max chucks a rolled-up towel on the grass and kneels too heavily making himself wince. He's constructed a Moon Garden next to the black garden. He hopes Maddy will like it. There are a million things he wants to say to her. Every night he lies in bed with imaginary conversations playing out in his mind. Sorry will never be enough.

The garden was in a shocking state after winter. He couldn't face doing a thing except looking after Emily. Soon he is digging into the earth, pressing the new shoots in, patting fresh compost over the top so the plants are solid in their new positions. Emily wanders over and sprinkles water around them from a small can, careful not to wet the leaves in case they burn under the scorching sun.

After Maddy was arrested and sectioned she was taken to a psychiatric hospital. He thought he would fall apart. The doctor upped his medication. But there is no pill that can fix them. He's done too much damage.

From inside the house, the telephone is ringing. Emily scampers off to the kitchen. The back door is open and Max listens to her answer the call. Her voice is breathless with one-word answers, then click. Emily skips towards him, face beaming. 'Mummy will be home in thirty minutes.'

Max hugs her. It's felt like she's lost her mum, she's told him, as well as her sister and the baby. Every night they chat long into the evenings about everything that's happened. Emily is keen to get to know Jamie better. If only Alison would let him see the boys. Charlie must be almost five months old and he misses Jamie's silly laugh and watching him play football.

'Hello, it's only me,' Sarah calls as she lets herself and Sophie in the back gate. The dogs run over to her, and she makes a fuss of them. 'I made lemonade. Thought you might like some.'

'I'll fetch the glasses,' he says and heads for the kitchen. 'Any news?' she calls after him.

'Maddy will be here in half an hour.' They sit at the table in the shade.

'Emily's looking brighter today.' Sarah pours the drinks.

'She perked up as soon as she knew Mummy was coming home.'

'The garden is coming on nicely. Maddy will be so pleased.'

Max nods. He wonders if there will ever be a time when he can talk about everything that's happened and not choke up. He's made it clear he doesn't expect Sarah's forgiveness, or anyone's come to that. Perhaps Sarah hates him underneath it all, but he's grateful they've stayed friendly. The girls come running over. Emily drinks her lemonade down in one go.

Sophie fishes out an ice cube and stuffs it in her mouth.

'Any news on when you'll see Sam, I mean Charlie?'

'Alison's moved in with someone she works with, Rob, I think,' Max says. 'She's not answering my calls.'

'She moved on quick.'

'We've sold the house and split everything.'

'What will you do with the money?' Sarah shakes her head. 'Sorry, it's none of my business.'

'No, no, it's fine, I was going to tell you anyway. I'm going to pay Maddy back every penny she gave me and pay off my debts. If there's any left, I'll treat Emily.' He shrugs and tries to keep the tears in. 'I'm not fit enough to go back to building.' He sighs. 'I want to be around for Emily, for all my kids, if Alison ever lets me.'

'I'm pleased. I really am. And you know I'm here to help you all.'

He attempts a smile. He's seen the way she looks at him, shocked that he's aged so much, but he's grateful for her offer. It's hard to be upbeat about anything until Maddy is back with them, where she belongs. If she can ever forgive him. If she'll let him stay.

A car stops outside the house, engine running. A car door slams. Emily and Sophie run to the gate. Sarah stands behind them; Max stays back. Maddy is full of smiles at seeing Emily. She comes in the gate and hugs and kisses them all. When she spots Max, her smile drops.

Later, when Sarah and Sophie have gone and he is finishing off the gardening, Maddy comes over. He squints at her standing over him, blocking the sun, a halo of sunlight crowning her head. She reaches a hand down to him and he clasps it tight, never wanting to let her go.

* * *

MORE FROM RUBY SPEECHLEY

A Mother Like You, another twisty and engrossing psychological thriller from Ruby Speechley, is available to order now here:

https://mybook.to/AMotherLikeYouBackAd

ACKNOWLEDGEMENTS

Firstly, enormous thanks to my publisher, Boldwood Books, for re-publishing this novel (previously known as *Every Little Secret*). It means so much to me to see it go back into the world with a fresh name and cover. Hopefully it will reach many new readers on its journey.

None of this would have been possible without the love and support of my dear husband, Richard. He has been there from day one, driving across the country to pick me up from my first Arvon Foundation course over twenty years ago, and listening to me wittering on about writing ever since!

This novel was conceived on a writing MA at Sheffield Hallam university, and will be recognised by many friends and fellow writers as *The Black Garden*. There are so many people who have helped me along the way – it's impossible to name them all.

Thank you to my wonderful agent, Jo Bell, for always being there for advice and support and for helping me navigate through my publishing journey. Thanks to the whole team at Bell Lomax Moreton for cheering me on.

My MA tutor, Lesley Glaister gave me encouragement, feedback and support whilst I was writing the first draft. I'm truly indebted to her. Subsequent sections and drafts were read by many fellow writers and tutors, including Susan Elliot Wright, Jude Brown, Caroline Priestly, Philippa Ronan, Jo Berry, Britta Jensen, Fiona Mitchell, Vanessa Fox O'Loughlin, Louise Tondeur and Martyn Bedford. Later drafts were improved by partial and full manuscript reports from Emma Darwin, Shelley Harris, Amanda Saint at Retreat West and Sara Sarre at The Blue Pencil Agency. As *The Black Garden*, this novel won Retreat West's First Chapter competition in 2015, chosen by a literary agent.

Thank you to Graham Bartlett, Police Advisor for your answers to all my questions and for your patience. Thank you for your last-minute advice, Jules Swain, Ambulance Paramedic.

I have used artistic license with a couple of details about Uxbridge, for instance the newspaper kiosk outside Uxbridge station closed several years ago. Any errors in this book are entirely my own.

Thanks also to Richard Skinner at the Faber

Academy for showcasing chapter one of this novel in the Writing a Novel class of 2016 anthology.

Heartfelt thanks to all my family, friends and supporters online and offline, especially Susan Elliot Wright, Rose McGinty, Lucille Grant and Louise Jensen – your support, advice and friendship keeps me smiling.

Finally, all my love to my dearest children, Charlie, Edward and Sophie. I know how lucky I am to have you all.

ABOUT THE AUTHOR

Ruby Speechley is a bestselling psychological thriller writer, whose titles include *Someone Else's Baby*. Previously published by Hera, she has been a journalist and worked in PR and lives in Cheshire.

Download your exclusive bonus content from Ruby Speechley here:

Follow Ruby on social media:

facebook.com/Ruby-Speechley-Author-100063999185095

x.com/rubyspeechley

instagram.com/rubyjtspeechley

tiktok.com/@rubyspeechleyauthor

ALSO BY RUBY SPEECHLEY

Gone

Missing

Guilty

The Uninvited Guest

Someone Else's Baby

Stolen

The Daughter You Left

A Mother Like You

THE *Murder* LIST

THE MURDER LIST IS A NEWSLETTER DEDICATED TO SPINE-CHILLING FICTION AND GRIPPING PAGE-TURNERS!

SIGN UP TO MAKE SURE YOU'RE ON OUR HIT LIST FOR EXCLUSIVE DEALS, AUTHOR CONTENT, AND COMPETITIONS.

SIGN UP TO OUR NEWSLETTER

BIT.LY/THEMURDERLISTNEWS

Boldwood

Boldwood Books is an award-winning fiction publishing company seeking out the best stories from around the world.

Find out more at www.boldwoodbooks.com

Join our reader community for brilliant books, competitions and offers!

Follow us
@BoldwoodBooks
@TheBoldBookClub

Sign up to our weekly deals newsletter

https://bit.ly/BoldwoodBNewsletter